A
SPECIAL
DESTINY

A SPECIAL DESTINY

A NOVEL

Seymour Epstein

DONALD I. FINE, INC.
New York

Library of Congress Catalogue Card Number: 85-82492
ISBN: 0-917657-84-5

Manufactured in the United States of America

10 9 8 7 6 5 4 3 2 1

This book is printed on acid free paper. The paper in this book
meets the guidelines for permanence and durability of the Committee on
Production Guidelines for Book Longevity of the Council on Library Resources.

FOR FRIENDS, PAST AND PRESENT.

"This generation of Americans has a rendezvous with destiny."

—Franklin Delano Roosevelt,
from speech accepting renomination,
June 27, 1936

PART
I

1

I HAD THOUGHT that the technical means of preserving sight and sound would preserve the record of evil, and it has, but only for the victims. The evildoers seem to have been flattened against the curving wall of history. I'm speaking of Hitler, of course. The film footage is there—too much of it—but time has distanced the beast. One suspects that the whole show might have been staged in Hollywood, and the character with the insane histrionics only a bad actor, one chosen by a director with an eye for the surreal. But Hitler was real enough—and that's the difference between then and now. At least for me. For me, it's the nuclear business that's unreal. The Russians sitting on their stockpile, we on ours, both of us programmed into a set of electronic moves that makes us as unreal as our payloads.

But Hitler was real. The vibes of his presence in the world reached me every waking day, every horror-haunted night. Another thing that I believed—still do—was that evil derived its power from unified vision. Hitler's vision was unified. He wanted to destroy as many people as possible to compensate for his own mortality. Not an original theory, I know, but I arrived at it on my own and consequently it has continued in my mind with the force of personal insight. When you are among the many chosen for destruction, you know whether the destroyer was real or not. Hitler was real.

* * *

More real, I think, for the terrifically exciting and deprived life I was experiencing at the time. It was 1938, and while the world was coming out of the famous Depression because of all the war preparations, there were still millions of unemployed, comically low wages, deflated prices (you could buy a pair of shoes for $3.50, a new hardcover novel for $2.00, get a balcony seat at a Broadway show for fifty cents, a plate of spaghetti and meatballs for thirty-five cents), and there was still the sore, cramped soul of a nation that had imagined itself boundless in wealth and opportunity finding itself beggared by the spring-busted, gear-stripped wreck of its beautiful machine.

Roosevelt knew where the center was when he used the word *fear* in his inauguration address—except that he was whistling from the capital grandstand when he said, "We have nothing to fear but fear itself . . ." It sounded wonderful. It lifted up the heart. But everybody knew that we had plenty to fear. We had the next meal to fear. We had the rent to fear. We had emasculation to fear. Millions of men with wives and children finding themselves with nothing to do. The fact that the condition was universal didn't mitigate the awfulness. A man couldn't redesign his ego into a tiny part of the collective misery. The individual ego had been formed when muscle and skill and dreams had exercised it daily. Suddenly that same ego had to dress in rags every day, for years.

Some were lucky. Like me. I had a job. I was a salesman by day and a college student by night. Getting a job in those days often took the combined efforts of friends and family. It did in my case. The odd thing to contemplate now is that while all this mass wretchedness was going on there were young men going to Harvard, Yale and Princeton, and there were young women whose engagements and marriages were announced in the pages of the New York *Times.* These were looked on as some kind of royal residue, leftovers from an ancient kingdom, not really of this world.

This world was twenty dollars every Friday, three nights a week of Accounting 1 and Commercial Law, the subway crush at 7:30 A.M. and 5:30 P.M.—five cents per crush. This world was

the penny-heaven of secondhand book stores on lower Fourth
Avenue, the cheapie movie houses and the voices of Kalten-
born and Heatter telling of Hitler's latest demands. The Czech
crisis was boiling. Hitler swore that he would protect the bullied Germans of the Sudetenland. Eduard Beneš pleaded for
compromise. Women were wearing incredibly wide-shouldered,
boxy outfits at twenty-five dollars. You could get a room at the
Hotel Shelton for ten dollars a night, but I had no one to
whom I could propose a room, would not have dared even if I
had, and was living at the crossroads of so many different
crises that the wonder was I wasn't sucked down my self-
created whirlpool.

I don't know whether I was happy or unhappy. I was one or the
other at such a galloping rate that they blended into a single blur
of fierce consciousness. I see myself rushing to my job every
morning, rushing to my classes every other night, bouncing home
at any hour on the safe, smelly subway, thinking about the weird
world that was opening to me.

Weirdest of all was Hitler, the creature who cursed my existence every day, from a distance of several thousand miles. He
was master of millions, all helmeted and booted, all who would
do his bidding icily, happily, instantly, and his bidding was that
I should die. I was a Jew, therefore I had inherited a list of
spiritual diseases of which I could not purge myself, no matter
what penitence or reform I might practice. It was in my blood. I
was genetically diseased, and therefore I must be eliminated.
When I looked at a pretty girl on the street, it was not because
I was young and horny but because I was Jewish and degenerate.
If I dreamed of owning a car and living in a nice house, it was not
because I was normally desirous but because I was abnormally
avaricious. If I wanted to go to school and increase my store of
knowledge, it was not because I was curious and intelligent but
because I was seeking the means of undermining Western civilization. If I formed an allegiance to the New York Yankees, it was
not because I shared national enthusiasms but because I was
emulating my countrymen in order to subvert and cheat them.
Whatever I thought I was or wanted to be, I was in reality a

13

candidate for the Elders of Zion, whomever or whatever they might be.

I could tell myself that they were liars and madmen, know that they were liars and madmen, know that *they* knew themselves to be at the very least liars, but that didn't affect the living situation in the least. I could tell myself that the race into which I had been born had a great tradition of periodic suffering, but that brought no alleviation. There was the daily business of my ego. What I knew to be true and untrue had nothing to do with that. I needed approval. I needed a world in secret preparation for my coming, and instead I had come to mature consciousness in a world that roared my unworthiness from podium and pulpit. There were Hitler and Goebbels and Streicher and Rosenberg (Rosenberg!) over there, and there were Fritz Kuhn and Father Coughlin and assorted southern bigots over here. Liars all, and they were doing to me exactly what they claimed I was doing to them. They befouled the air I breathed. They denied me my rightful place in the sun. I despised them. I spent far too much time despising them. I had to seize my pleasures, my education, my advancement and my daydreams fitfully and covertly, fearful of exposing my sly, covetous, degenerate desires.

I recall an incident. I was on the Long Island train with Eugene Strauss. It was night. I can't remember exactly what we were doing there. Probably coming back from a day at the shore. It was hot. The incident I have in mind is out of sequence, but that doesn't matter. In my mind, it's a compendium of what I have tried to describe. We were coming back to the city from the shore. There was a well-dressed drunk sitting across the aisle and a few seats forward. He kept muttering, and my nerves, raw and prescient, understood the matter before my ears could make out the words. I believe that Eugene, too, caught the familiar pungency in the stale air of the car. In those days it was as omnipresent as carbon monoxide.

"Goddam fuckin' Jew chimpanzee," grunted the drunk.

Eugene and I exchanged a quick glance. Gene smiled his oblique smile, turning his head slightly and gazing at the dark-

14

ened, dirty window beside him. That smile had a haunted quality, one with which I was familiar. The conductor came down the aisle collecting tickets. He took our tickets, punched them and then came abreast of the hunched *zeitgeist.*

"Ticket, please."

The creature fumbled and said, quite distinctly, "Pay my money to support that goddam Jew ape."

The conductor stood stolidly with his ticket punch dangling from one finger. The *zeitgeist* fumbled in his pockets.

"This your ticket?" the conductor asked, plucking the tab from under the metal flange of the backrest.

"Do you know Fiorello La Guardia?" the mumbler asked.

"Thank you," said the conductor.

"We got an ape for a mayor," the other said. "A Jew ape."

Gene got up and sidled past my knees.

"Where you going?" I whispered apprehensively.

"Not far," he said.

"For chrissake!" I hissed at him.

"It's a matter of accuracy," he said.

Gene walked the few paces to where the man was sitting and said, "Mayor La Guardia is of Italian descent, not Jewish."

"Who the hell are you?" the man asked.

"Eugene Strauss."

"Some kind of kike know-it-all?"

"I know that much."

"How would you like to have your face pushed in?"

By this time, the scattered riders in the car were craning their necks or sinking deeper into their newspapers. Gene didn't flinch or walk away. Nor did the man get up to carry out his threat. He kept sizing up Gene in a sideways, jerky motion, like one of those dolls that go into frantic motion at the pull of a string.

"I would like it if you kept your stupid, drunken mouth shut," Gene said.

The conductor came over at last and said, "All right, let's break it up." To Gene, he said, "Go on back to your seat." To the *zeitgeist,* he said, "If you cause any more trouble, I'm going to call the police at the next stop."

Later, I said, "Suppose he had gotten up, all six-foot-five, two hundred and fifty pounds of him?"

"I will not let that happen to me again," he said.

Gene had learned a lesson I had yet to learn. His experience was different from mine. Much. He had begun to live a life beyond the Hitler experience. I had miles to go.

2

IT WAS ONE of those fine early October days when I met Eugene Strauss. A cold front had passed through the city, sweeping away the end-of-summer muck. Rain for a day, then a gradual clearing, which brought with it the first stimulating touch of fall.

I was going my rounds in the city, trying to prove myself a salesman. I didn't see myself as a salesman, but that was the only job I could get. I needed money if I was to continue college, so I switched to night classes and looked for work. Times were supposed to be improving, a war was coming, but making a buck was still a mean affair.

An aunt of mine took it on herself to help me out in my job quest. I was a favorite nephew, a potential golden boy in her eyes, one who would do the family proud. She contacted Lou Siegal, a relative on her husband's side, and pleaded that this was a nice boy, a bright boy, give him a chance.

Lou Siegal was the owner of a dinky manufacturing company that turned out cheap novelty items such as travel kits, garment bags, sachet pads, things that could be made with a minimum of machinery.

"You ever sell anything?" he asked me.

"Yes, sir."

"What?"

"Magazine subscriptions. Door to door."

"That's a tough way to make a buck," he conceded. "I'll tell you

17

the truth, young man, you don't look to me exactly like a sales-man. Your aunt told me you were going to college at night. So what are you studying?"

"Accounting."

"That's a very practical thing to study. Why don't you look for a job in accounting?"

"I don't know enough yet, Mr. Siegal. I'm not qualified."

"Ah, I see. For an accountant, which you are studying, you are not qualified; but a salesman, for which you are equally un-qualified, you want me to pay you."

Being curious, I asked, "What do you have to know to be a salesman?"

He nodded his heavy, bald head. "Nothing," he said. "The price of your merchandise. How to open your mouth and be pleasant. All right, Saul Klein, I'll give you a chance. I'll give you twenty dollars a week draw against commissions. From this you'll have to pay all expenses—subways, buses, et cetera—and I'll expect you to cover all five boroughs and New Jersey. Maybe even Connecticut. Let me tell you something. I got here a nice line, but it isn't *Evening in Paris*. Frankly, you'll have to go out there and bust your ass. I'll give you a few pointers, but the rest will be up to you. Also, a warning: I'll throw only so much good money after bad. I'll invest in you a couple of hundred bucks, but if I don't get results, out you go. I'm not trying to be tough, I'm trying to be honest. Do you follow me?"

"Yes, sir."

He looked at me inquisitively. "Are you sure you're going to CCNY? You sound like you're going to a military academy. What's with the 'sir'?"

"Yes, Mr. Siegal."

He nodded and, I think, allowed something resembling a smile to touch his turgid features. He said, "Listen, I like a young man should try to improve himself, but while you're on my time I don't want you going into the Forty-second Street library to catch up on homework."

Lou Siegal was a practical man with a shrewd eye and a sense of humor. He knew I wasn't a salesman, but he must have had a hunch that it wouldn't turn out to be a total loss. Time and chance had spiced the air in a favorable way.

He was right about my not looking like a salesman—although God knows what a salesman is supposed to look like. I looked neither handsome nor too disturbingly the opposite. I've been told I look like Paul Muni, a very good actor of the time. There's nothing Anglo-Saxon about me. Brown eyes, brown hair, decent features, I like to think. I don't recall ever being at odds with my own appearance. As far as I can recall, I've always accepted my looks with tolerant recognition.

In my first few weeks with Mr. Siegal—whether inspired by his feckless merchandise or simply lucky, I'm not sure—I hit, quite literally, the jackpot. What I had done was work out a system to deal with my terror at actually going out and trying to persuade strangers to buy this *dreck*. The system was simple. I was selling the line to *myself*. That is, I pretended I was the buyer and I was using on myself whatever cleverness and good humor I could summon up about Mr. Siegal's line of crap. I hit on the ploy of gift desperation. The Siegal line could be featured on the store counters as the perfect little gift when you don't know what to get and you haven't got much to spend.

It worked. Eyes lighted up. I maintain even now that it was a form of self-protection, a way of avoiding the hard job of selling. But whatever it was, I brought back to Mr. Siegal from Bamberger's in Newark an order amounting to more than three hundred dollars, an order from R. H. Macy amounting to over five hundred dollars and to top it off an order from an out-of-town buyer representing a chain of midwestern stores amounting to almost two thousand dollars. All on the simple gambit of that gift counter for puzzled, on-the-cheap customers.

If phlegm can be elated, Mr. Siegal was elated. He felt, in his phlegmatic way, that fate had blown through his battered door on East Fifteenth Street a not-so-handsome genie with a magic touch. I was myself impressed. I allowed myself to think that I had hidden gifts, that I was as protean as Proteus. The Saul Klein pod of potential had burst, and wherever my seed fell fruitful harvests would spring forth.

"Not bad," Mr. Siegal congratulated. "A very good start. Didn't I tell you you had a good line of merchandise here? You already made yourself a couple of hundred bucks. Less your draw, of course. Maybe you should take a little trip up to Boston. Out-of-town expenses, I pay. You'll spend a few days in Boston, believe me, you'll double what you made here."

"Whatever you say, Mr. Siegal."

The Depression was still more in than out, but there was a deadly vibrancy in the air. The long-ticking time bomb was about to explode. The drawn-out dread that had been hounding the world for so many years was about to be replaced by a fiery apocalypse. There would be another world war. To my mind, a certainty. Crazy minds ruled powerful nations, and the dream of death had taken over.

I read the newspapers scrupulously. I read magazines. I listened to the radio analysts. I wondered at this constant search for a *reason*. I wondered at the futile succession of placatory moves. At those who said give the beast this and this and he will be satisfied. I was amazed that it wasn't apparent to all that giving the beast what he asked for only infuriated him. The beast wanted to be opposed, not appeased, because opposition would lead to war, and these conciliatory gestures only delayed the feast.

I knew even then that the Nazi dream was untouchable. To become masters of the world and kill all those they didn't like. A child's savage wish was being loosed upon the world. To become masters of life and death, and in that way to escape mortality. And because these things were true, and because most people, deep down, knew them to be true, it was possible for Saul Klein to sell Mr. Siegal's line of sacheted nonsense. In a world of bloody nonsense, Mr. Siegal's quilted hangers and plastic-lined travel kits had a soothing effect.

There was a special day for out-of-town buyers, I forget which. I handed my card to the receptionist so that she could show it to the buyer I wished to see. I sat down in the waiting room. This was getting to be a familiar routine in my life. I even carried a book in my sample case. Catch up on my schoolwork. Or read the novel that was absorbing me in those days, *The Brothers Karamazov.* I was such a multifarious fellow. Another fellow was sitting to my right, one empty chair between us, his sample case usurping that space. I don't know why, but I took it that he had deliberately staked out that chair to keep some distance between himself and any intrusive other. Something about his appearance. Striking. Striking, of course, is almost always someone who doesn't look like you. This fellow didn't look like me. Not at all. He was so pronouncedly different that I began to look for the particulars of such a contrast.

Begin with his suit: a striped summer fabric, nothing remarkable in itself, the weather having been so balmy, but by the consensus that prevails in such matters no one was wearing summer-weight clothes any longer. Businessmen had switched to fall attire. Even I had switched to fall attire. He also wore a stark, unpatterned, lemon-yellow tie, for which there was no consensus, at any time of year. His blondish hair was combed straight back, no part, and was unusually long for those days. Men were neatly clipped, particularly men who had to make their living through public contact. He had a long, aristocratic face, and he kept his head well back and slightly tilted, as though his contemplations were at an entirely different level from my own. I was so certain that he was sealed into his private atmosphere that it took me several seconds to realize that the words I had heard spoken were addressed to me.

"I beg—"

"I said are you waiting to see Mr. So-and-So?" he said.

"No, I'm waiting to see Mr. Such-and-Such."

"What does he buy?"

"Notions and accessories."

"Does he?" he said, with a slight smile. "What kind of notions are you selling?"

It may not have been intended as a humorous or ironic question, but I took it as such. I said I was selling notions of immortality (I was reading *The Brothers Karamazov*), and my words fetched another, more definite, approving smile. He was so all of a piece

21

—manner, speech, dress—that I wanted to know him better, even if it was for no longer than the time we spent together in this waiting room.

"What are you selling?" I asked him.

Before he could answer, the receptionist called, "Mr. Eugene Strauss," and my neighbor reached for his sample case, brought it to his lap and sat there for one or two contemplative seconds. He would, I assumed, simply get up and disappear. Gone forever. Instead, he said, "Where are you planning to go next?"

"Twenty-third Street. A jobber."

"I'll wait for you," he said.

3

HE DID. I got an order; he didn't. Was I the better salesman? Am I right in thinking I was already matching myself against him? Was I already wanting a little victory? Could there have been that much portent on that day? Why not? Why wouldn't I want to one-up such a dandy?"

He was there in the card-littered reception room waiting for me. We left the building together, my intention still being to take a subway to my next scheduled call. I was conscientious. I wondered if Mr. Eugene Strauss' purpose was to go along with me. Maybe he was newer at this game than I was. Maybe he was hanging onto my coattails for guidance and assurance. I was unctuously prepared to inflate my two cents' worth of experience into a glittering fortune.

But as we stood on the corner, Mr. Strauss' tie aflutter in the breeze, he said to me, "Why don't we check our sample cases and have lunch in the park?"

"Park?"

"Yes. Central Park. It's too nice a day to be going in and out of buildings. I always go to the park in fine weather. That's one of the privileges of being a salesman. No one expects you to be seeing people all the time. I know a little grocery store on Seventh Avenue where we can get some fresh French bread and excellent cheese."

This flamboyant stranger began to walk toward Times Square, where we were to check our sample cases and take the subway to the park. He took it that the matter was settled. As for me, I accompanied him step for step, thinking that at the next step I would bid him so long and go my serious way. Mr. Siegal's warning words were pennants that snapped over my diligent days. What Eugene Strauss was proposing was considerably more derelict than ducking into a library. This was truly stealing time. And yet I went along, step for step, reminding myself that I'd just gotten an order for several hundred dollars, that my commissions more than covered my advance, and that Mr. Strauss with his yellow tie and general strangeness was well worth the transgression.

He asked me where I lived, and I told him I lived in the Bronx. I asked him where he lived, and he told me he lived in Washington Heights. He said that the living room in his apartment had a view of the Hudson River, and at night one could see reflections of the lights on the Palisades. Red and green on black shellac.

"What are you selling?" I asked him again.

"Imports," he said. "Mainly Chinese. Lacquered trays. Mother-of-pearl. Actually quite nice things but far too high in price."

He had an accent. I had been aware throughout of a speech inflection, but by the time we reached Times Square I had pinpointed Germany. My first refugee from that fairyland of evil. Which only increased his exoticism. I looked for some mark of the nightmare on his person, but I found nothing specific, only the general exoticism.

"Are you from Germany?" I asked.

He looked a little troubled. "Can you tell from my speech?"

"Hardly at all," I said, realizing that he had counted on his speech not to give him away. "It's sort of . . . everything."

"You mean my clothes? Yes—well—I expect that it's still in my speech as well. I can't hear it myself. I have an excellent ear for languages. Do you read the newspapers?"

"The newspapers? Of course I read the newspapers. Who doesn't—?"

"Many people," he asserted. "They buy newspapers but they don't read them. They look at the headlines, and then they turn to the sports page or their horoscopes. Haven't you noticed that? Do you think there will be a war?"

"Of course."

He nodded, looking oddly pleased. I was pleased, too. When you are aware of so many differences, an agreement over impending catastrophes can strike a happy note.

So we checked our sample cases, took the subway uptown, stopped at the little Seventh Avenue grocery, and were now strolling toward Central Park. It was about then that it struck me that Eugene Strauss didn't even know my name. Hadn't asked. I asked myself again why I was going along with this peculiar guy. I think I must deal with that now.

I had lived the most important part of my life—the past ten years, almost—in the dank, ill-lit cellar called the Great Depression. We hadn't actually gone hungry in my family, but we had gone spiritually anemic, so grimly anemic that life as a real possibility came to me only in fitful gleams. Those gleams, when they came, produced a condition of near levitation. I could feel the pressure of it against the roof of my head. I would *do* something! I would *be* somebody! What? Who knew? *Something!* But then reality would set in like winter fog and my bones would turn brittle. It was during those fitful gleams that the shadowy figure would appear—almost appear—and its almosthood sang a siren song more seductive than any I have ever heard. Eugene Strauss, with his yellow tie, his long face and his careful English, seemed to have natural connections with shadowy figures and mysterious songs.

"Eugene Strauss," I said. "I heard the receptionist call your name. Do you call yourself Eugene or Gene?"

"I neither. Others call me."

"Which do you prefer?"

"That depends. The preference changes with the person. Some people I prefer to call me Eugene, others Gene. I think I would prefer to have you call me Gene. What does one call you?"

"One calls me Saul. Saul Klein."

We sat on a rise of ground near the zoo. We could see the solid walls of money on either side of the park. The day had gotten

25

warmer. Gene took off his summer-striped jacket and loosened his tie. He sat cross-legged on the ground, the wrapping paper of his sandwich exfoliate, like a stiff flower, and from time to time he would dust bread crumbs from his fingers.

He told me that his family had packed all their belongings after the Reichstag fire in 1933. It took them more than a year to get out of the country. His father's commercial connections made it possible for them to transport to America. The earliness of their departure made it possible for them to bring most of their belongings. It was shortly after that that the Nazis began their national thievery. They couldn't bring much money, of course. His father had continued his legal practice through the worst of the German hardships. His father had an international practice, mostly to do with shipping. Some of his best clients were English. That's why English was the second language in the family, and that's why his father had so often gone to England, and while in England had filled in his wardrobe with Savile Row tailoring.

Clearly, Eugene Strauss took great pride in his father, in his father's English clothes, in his father's international practice and, most of all, in his father's moral compulsion to leave Germany when he did. The pride found its center not in the salvation it must have meant for the family, but in the personal repugnance Strauss *père* felt for the beast. Gene was insistent that I understand that the family had removed itself *voluntarily*, before the decision had become a matter of life and death.

"A friend of my father said the lunacy would pass, that it was only a trick to gain power," Gene went on, "but my father said that to think so was to misconceive the man. This was not a politician's trick but a dreamer's living dream."

He leaned over, dusting the last of the bread crumbs from his fingers. He had such a beautifully precise way of speaking English, with just enough accent and odd word choice to give it style.

"What does that mean?" I asked. " 'A dreamer's living dream.' "

Gene explained what he meant—rather, what his father meant. His father meant that Hitler's dream was a rage against mortality. Hitler wanted to send as many to their deaths as he could before his own came about. The lunatic's revenge for not having been made immortal.

My own theory exactly! I didn't cry aloud the remarkable coincidence, but I could see the outlines of a profound pattern of affinity. I could also see another pattern taking shape in this friendship, if that's what it was to be. Gene did most of the talking; I did the listening. But even so, I was flattered. I took it as a tribute of some kind. I found distinction in the fact that I had been thus selected.

But where were the usual turns of mutuality? You tell me this and I'll tell you that. We were deeply into the secrets of the Strauss heart and he didn't even know my name. Did he? I had spoken the words, but I doubted that he could have repeated them, if asked. Aside from names, how about *my* father, *my* background, *my* inheritance? Not that I was overly eager to get into such things, but it would have been encouraging to have been asked.

Gene said, "My father made a study of Hitler. He calls Hitler the prophet of the death wish. There have been others like him before in history, but never someone so complete, so pure. And never someone with so powerful a country to carry out his wishes. My father says it couldn't have happened anywhere but in Germany."

"Is that so? Why?"

"Because death is the invisible companion of the romantic, and Germany is the most romantic nation in Europe."

"So why don't they all commit suicide, instead of making everybody else miserable?" I asked.

He glanced at me and smiled. He was terrifically self-absorbed, but occasionally he would grant a nod of approval. And I found myself trying to draw such signs from him. That impulse would become the whetstone against which I would hone my mind, my language, my character!

He sat so relaxed in the October air, as if this meeting, this hooky playing in Central Park, was the most natural thing in the world. Here we were eating sandwiches in the city's great park, discussing Hitler's mad mythology, when we should have been going after orders like hungry hounds.

27

"... you see," he was explaining, "in each man there is a wish for all life to end with his own."

"Not in this man," I said.

"Yes, you too."

"How would you know what I—?"

"You just don't realize it yet," he explained. "It's present in all men. Sometimes the wish will collect in one man who has the power to transform it into action. Now that man is Adolf Hitler. He is making arrangements for all life to cease with his own. He won't succeed, of course, but that is his aim. Therefore, if you wish to understand Hitler, you must pay no attention to his *Lebensraum* and *Herrenvolk*, but to his universal death wish."

Yes, yes! I agreed entirely! The theory accorded so well with my own that Gene's father's words were beginning to sound plagiarized, taken whole from the head of Saul Klein.

"What does your father do?" I asked.

"Do?"

"I mean his business, his profession?"

"Didn't I tell you? Yes, I'm sure I did. I told you he was a lawyer."

"That's right, you did. I'm sorry. But is he, you know, practicing in New York now?"

"He isn't practicing anywhere. He's dead."

It occurred to me that part of Gene's exotic charm might be a mild madness.

"Why do you talk about him in the present tense?" I asked.

"Do I do that? I wasn't aware of it."

"When did he die?"

"Three years ago."

"Sick?"

"Cancer," Gene said, very clinically, bringing his hand to his throat in a delicate, two-fingered touch, like a tenor signaling a slight irritation.

That little gesture stirred something powerful in me. I knew as surely as I knew the leaves were changing color that Gene's father's death had been a long and agonizing one.

"I'm sorry," I said.

28

"What is your ambition?" he asked, clearly not wishing to linger on the subject of his father's death.

"Not to starve."

He smiled, for which I was glad. I had begun to look for evidence of a sense of humor. I hadn't been able to detect much of one. I was beginning to fear that a sense of humor was not part of my new friend's baggage. And I was going to make him my friend. He was too much of the world I had been looking for. Eugene Strauss was the guide who would show me where those skull-lifting flights of mine were intending to take me.

"What are you going to do to keep from starving?" he asked. "Are you going to become a very successful salesman?"

"I'm studying accounting."

He made a pained face at that. He shook his head. "Really," he said. "Accounting. Figuring someone else's profit and loss. It's a very good occupation, I know, but I should think you would become covered in dust before you're thirty. I'd get out of that if I were you."

I laughed, not sure whether that judgment was meant to be sincere or capricious. But while sitting there, the capital of commerce all around us, the need for a wage-earning life as deep in me as the marrow of my bones, I suddenly knew that my career as an accountant was over. Just like that! This imported magician had shriveled my career into a pellet and had blown it away!

"And you?" I asked, eager to know how someone like Eugene Strauss imagined his life. "What's your ambition?"

"I'm going to be a playwright," he said, without a wink of hesitation, self-consciousness or vainglory. He sounded as though he'd lived with his calling ever since he was old enough to know its name.

"You are, huh? That's great. Have you ever written one?"

"I've written over twenty."

"No kidding. I mean . . . any produced?"

"Of course not. They aren't good enough yet. I've been teaching myself the craft. I think I'm almost ready. I write every night. And weekends, of course."

Of course! I could see him doing it, blond head bent over desk,

29

looking up occasionally to take in the legendary view from his legendary window. Everything about Eugene Strauss was legendary.

"What kind of plays do you write?" I asked.

Again without self-consciousness, and promptly, "All my plays are about the meaning of life. That means they're partially realistic and partially mystical. I take ordinary situations and complicate them with the mystical element."

"What's the mystical element?"

"Each person trying to fulfill his destiny, that's the mystical element. It's mystical because most people have no idea what their destiny is. Groping toward a destiny is what gives my plays dramatic tension."

I was convinced. Despite his astonishingly impersonal conceit, vanity, ego, whatever, I was convinced. Part of my Bronx self snickered in derision, but I was also spellbound by someone who seemed to know so well what he was doing in a world that boiled with uncertainty and menace. It may have been at that moment that I passed over my own destiny to Eugene Strauss.

"If I'm not going to be an accountant," I half jokingly asked him, "what do you think I should go in for?"

"I think you should write plays, too."

I laughed. "What makes you think I can?"

"Well, of course, I don't know if you have any talent, but I think you ought to give it a try. There's something about the way you talk that suggests you have some natural gift. Besides, it wouldn't hurt. It might be beneficial—for both of us—to have someone with whom to compare, to compete."

4

SINCE EUGENE STRAUSS gave his father so significant a role in his life, I must speak of mine. My father was a silent man. Not gravely silent or wisely silent, just silent. He didn't have much to say. Speech was not one of his pleasures in life, which may have been due to that hopeless Russian accent. He had a midtown Manhattan shop where he did cleaning, pressing and serious tailoring. Actually, he could tailor a man's suit from a bolt of wool to a finished garment. He could cut the pattern and sew it all together with solid craftsmanship. But he didn't talk. He lived in a cocoon of needles, thread, scissors, steam irons, and he had somehow gotten it into his head that communication of the verbal variety was not a necessary function of his life. He left that part of it to his wife, my mother. His function was to take the subway into Manhattan six days a week, open his shop, do his work, come home in the evening, eat his supper, read his newspaper, listen to the radio a little, saying as little as possible throughout. Oddly enough, he would talk in his sleep. Talk or emit the most blood-chilling wails of terror I have ever heard.

My mother, on the other hand, was an intelligent, unschooled woman who loved to talk, who imagined only too well a world of social pleasures and human commingling. People went to shows. People visited other people's homes. Laughter and gossip were exchanged over the dinner table. I was too young to know when it happened, but at some point in my childhood my mother did

31

discover the nature of the man she had married, and then she set about to make him into something other than the dark, isolated man he was. The result was fifty years of domestic madness.

They fought. There was something epic in their years of harsh, hopeless struggle. My mother always suspected that he made more money than he gave out. She was right. When he died, there was the astonishing sum of thirty thousand dollars stashed away in several banks. Enough to see my mother through her old age. I suspect he buried that treasure for the same reasons that would account for his isolation and silence.

Abe Klein was in hiding. He had hidden from the cossacks as a boy, and he had hidden from all the usual form of human intercourse. A man in hiding doesn't speak much. He doesn't want to give away his hiding place. He lives in the imminence of some frightful unknown.

Fights would start over money, over the phone bill, over a piece of fish, and they would go on in bitter acrimony for a day or two, and then all communication would cease. When we were kids, my sisters and I, that long spell of frozen silence was a form of child abuse, justly punishable by flogging for the terror it inflicted. Perhaps that would have given them some sense of what they were doing to their children. But of course they weren't thinking of their children, only their own stubborn selves.

But it was during those dumb contests that we children would become couriers over the ice floes, bringing messages of ready meals, lost socks, needed money and all other such domestic trivia as is exchanged between husbands and wives. This arctic absurdity would go on for weeks, until something, I never knew what, some secret of the bedroom possibly, would signal that the awfulness was coming to a close, that a thaw might be setting in. Then there would be some weeks of awkward peace, during which my mother would resume the pretenses of a normal family, and my father would volunteer a remark on the style of Eleanor Roosevelt's hats, a source of low comedy at the time.

"I wonder who makes her hats," he would say, pointing to a photograph in the paper.

"What's the matter with her hat?" my mother would play along.

"I think she has it on backward," he would say.

My mother would laugh at that poor joke, and that was the sign that what passed for halcyon days among the Kleins were in full season.

I've always thought my father's face a fascinating paradox. He was handsome, handsomer than I, and despite his years and inner darkness his mahogany brown eyes remained as unlined and clear as a child's.

Two weeks after the end of a fight, or three, or four, another argument would start over money, or a torn shirt, or a piece of chicken, and then they would begin again in their limited English, switch over to a more versatile Yiddish, spiking that with Russian invectives that tasted as if they had been boiled in bile and aged with acid. The great freeze would set in again, and my sisters and I would put on our emotional winter gear for our journey over the polar wastes.

I was the youngest. My sisters were out of the house first, and they have both, sometimes bitterly, sometimes in frank relief, admitted that their marriages were as much a prison break as a bond of matrimony. Not that their husbands would have been any better or worse had they come from homes full of light and laughter, but in the case of the Klein girls getting away was easily as much an incentive as getting married.

Which left me alone for some years with the two combatants. Young men didn't strike out on their own at an early age in those days, unless it was to ride the rails, join the army or sign on for the Civilian Conservation Corps. There wasn't the money for the necessary break. Living at home was an economic necessity, even when the home was as bleak as February. Which accounts, I suppose, for the long life of so many abysmal marriages.

My father never spoke to me about his life, nor did he ask me about mine. I don't know whether he was just incurious, or whether he didn't know how to frame the questions, but in any event we never discussed such routine father-son things as my ambitions, my tastes, my friends, my sexual urges, my views on God and the mystery of mortality. There was only one thing that prompted him to conversation. Occasionally, in the midst of one of the great freezes, he might telephone the Bronx apartment when he thought I might be home, calling from his Manhattan shop. If my mother happened to answer, he would ask to speak to me. My mother would then hand me the phone with a look of unspeakable contempt and just a gleam of triumph in her eyes. When I was on the phone, he came quickly to the point.

"Sul"—he could never manage the vowels in my name—"Sul, I want you should tell the mother she should leave me alone."

"Why don't you tell her?"

"It's the place of the children to tell the mother."

"What exactly do you want me to tell her?"

"Tell her if she doesn't leave me alone, I'm going to walk out of the house."

"All right, I'll tell her."

I told her.

Rose rolled her eyes heavenward and clasped her hands. *"Gutt!"* she implored. "If he only would!"

"Do you think he ever will?" I asked.

"And where would he go?" she replied, indicating to me that she had given the question much thought. "Where? Where in this world is there a corner for such a piece of black bitterness?" Her speech was a mixture of English and Yiddish, and what I put down are merely improvised lyrics to match the anguished music I remember.

She was right. He had nowhere to go. Since his marriage—I would stake my life on it—he had never spent a single night in a strange room—hotel or whore's—if for no other reason than to demonstrate the potential of his anger, the depths of his despair. His home was his hiding place and to leave it would expose him to dimensionless terror. The terror he lived with was at least something he could measure.

"You're so unhappy together," I once said to my mother. "How come you married him?"

She performed her routine act of despair, raising her eyes, shaking her head, nodding it, closing her eyes. "How come? How come? I'll ask you. What did I know! I was sixteen. He asked me, so I married him."

"Nobody else ever asked you?"

I clearly recall the curious expression that came over Rose's face. A slight narrowing of the eyes, a hitch of one shoulder. Coquettish? It couldn't be. And yet it was!

"There were others," she admitted.

"There *were?* Then why him? Why Abe Klein?"

Her eyes blurred in the haze of time. She told me what I never would have believed had it come from anyone but Rose herself. She told me there were other fellows who took her to the beach in summer, to the movies, even to dinners at fancy restaurants, but once she met Abe there was no one else for her. She wouldn't let anyone else come near her. Go explain! It was only Abe. She wanted him and him alone.

"I made my bed good," she declared, staring into the past as if it were one of those cosmic black holes that swallowed everything and let nothing escape.

"Were you in love with him?"

She shrugged one shoulder. "Love? I suppose I was in love with him. Believe me, it didn't last for very long. It didn't take him long to show me who he was. Very quickly I stopped loving."

I also remember the look she gave me to round off the telling of that part of her life. During the telling, I thought that this would bring us closer together, enrich our relationship, but what I detected was a flattening out of that momentary high of revelation. An odd compunction. I realized that she was feeling shame, and a little rancor. She was sorry for her confession, and I think she blamed me a little for having led her on to it. It was pointless and hurtful, since it couldn't be changed. Also, it was not something to be discussed between mother and son. Too personal. I believe our relationship did change slightly because of it. Love in its ordinary aspects was not to be discussed between mother and child, and therefore the perfect love of mother for child was distorted because of her confession. It disturbed her in one respect, but in another it freed her to ask me something that had undoubtedly been on her mind for a long time.

"Tell me," she said, "I see you reading books all the time. You're a college man. I never finished public school. With all that learning, maybe you can tell me why it is that you can't know a thing about another person from the outside. Some people look like nothing—*facrimpt, meese*—and yet they have such marvelous brains, such loving hearts. And other people, like your father, look so nice on the outside, but inside is a desert, nothing grows. Why shouldn't there be a way of telling? They got blood tests to see if maybe you got a disease, you shouldn't get married. Why not a blood test to tell you the kind of person you're marrying?"

"I don't know, Ma," I said. "That's what's called the human condition."

"Some condition!"

When my father was in the final phase of his dying, I visited him frequently at a hospital in the Bronx. My mother would be there at his bedside, or on the little patio available to patients when the weather permitted. The tempo of dying is the same in sunlight or shade. They were usually both silent, but it seemed to me that a reconciliation had come about. Two burnt-out cases.

For all the wretchedness of her life, it *was* her life, and she was about to lose the partner who had defined that life. Nostalgia, regret, remorse—those perdurable blue flowers that grow in stone, in ice. And my father, who was about to give up life itself, had become strangely serene. Perhaps having lived so close to the terrible unknown, he was better prepared to let it claim him.

For no particular reason, perhaps to lighten the moment, I said, "Well, don't you look like a loving couple."

My father turned his ravaged face toward me. He nodded, and then put his parchment hand over my mother's hand.

"This is mine switheart," he said, in his incurable accent.

Who knows? Maybe she was.

Nostalgia, regret, remorse—they're not the only things that will grow in ice, now that I think of it. The imagination can, too. My father was silent, my mother busy, my sisters had fled the igloo, and I was much alone in 1938, when you could buy an imported English overcoat for fifty-five dollars, and Eleanor Roosevelt was fifty-five-years-old, and Virginia D. Gildersleeve, dean of Barnard, feared that a dark age was descending, and that colleges would be like the monasteries of old, the only sanctuaries of knowledge, because international gangsterism had entrenched itself in the highest places.

I know the distinguished lady said this, because I was by that time well into my hobby of cutting out such items and pasting them in my scrapbook. The items I chose were supposed to mirror the world, but most often they mirrored my own view of things. I chose those things for preservation that seemed to have the right historical ring, and the comments I made in the same book became a diary of my anxious days, something that would serve to restore this time should I happen to survive the coming Armageddon.

That was a certainty, the coming Armageddon. It astonished me more and more that there were still those who thought it could be avoided. The certainty that it couldn't be avoided became the armature of my life. Everything else shaped itself around that.

What it did was sharpen my curiosity, my appetites. I wanted to read every important book that had ever been written. I wanted to look at every painting that hung in the Met. I wanted to find —at last!—the girl who would clear away for me with the explicitness of her body the oceanic fog of lust in which I lived.

That was the tight, hot, cold, desperate, grubby life I was living. I was alternately miserable and euphoric. I was waiting to be sprung.

5

AND WHO COULD spring me better than Eugene Strauss? Everything about him declared the difference between his world and mine—dress, attitudes, interests, background, experience, ambition.

I, too, had imagination. I knew what life could hold, but so far I had lacked the nerve or the means to go after it. The Klein inhibition. The Klein inheritance of igloo reclusiveness. That's why Gene was much more than just a new friend. He was the potential changer of all things, not because of a show-off need to shine, but simply and splendidly because of who he was.

He was Eugene Strauss, who wore his dead father's clothes (along with an increasing number of his own duds, I observed) because he had so admired his father, and because (I suspect) that quirkiness of dress gave him the cachet he was looking for. He could speak a deliberate, perfect English (with that slight margin of tonal error), and he could for necessary or whimsical reasons assume the accents of the typical German refugee with the valve-leak sibilants and the wobbly diphthongs, and he could (and often did) come on with his version of the typical New Yorker—*"Hey, kinya lenme a buck?"*—but this last was the least successful of his improvisations because it was the most self-conscious.

Perhaps that's why he had decided to make me his friend. I was the real New York article with the right accent and the authentic vulgarities. Not that he enjoyed these qualities, but he felt, I believe, that he needed them if he was to write for American audiences. I warbled the native woodnotes.

Contact with Gene made my unrealized self surface so quickly that I damn near got the bends. I don't think Gene ever came close to guessing what a distance I had to go, or how fast, in order to keep up with him, or not to lag too dismally behind. Theoretically, he allowed the greatest latitude to human differences, but under the real sun and moon he couldn't credit the ignorance abroad in the world.

"Baudelaire," he said.

"What's that?" I asked.

"That," he said, "is a great French symbolist poet. I can't believe you haven't heard of Baudelaire, even in America."

"My ignorance is my own," I said.

"The condition seems to be general."

"How much of the country have you canvassed?" I asked him.

"If it is true in New York, what can it be like in the rest of the country? This is the cultural capital, is it not?"

"There are plenty who would argue with you."

"In any event, *you* have never heard of Baudelaire, and that is most strange. I'll bet you a dollar I can walk in there and find a copy of *Les Fleurs du Mal.*"

There was Macy's, which we were passing at the moment. His French pronunciation was perfect. I repeated *Les Fleurs du Mal* to myself mockingly, gargling the *r* in imitation of my multilingual friend. He did these things—speak French, condescend—with a naturalness that almost dissolved irritation. Almost. Not completely. A new Klein personality was beginning to shape itself around the undissolved portion.

"You're on," I said. "A buck."

"A buck," he said, smiling. "Why is it called a 'buck'?"

"Because the cowboys used to bet a dollar on who could stay on a bucking bronco the longest. The one who won would say he'd won a buck."

We entered Macy's. Gene kept his fair head tilted slightly upward, as if to give his thoughts a purer air to breathe.

"Are you telling me the truth?" he asked.

I was tempted to say I was. The idea of his repeating that with his air of Straussian wisdom tickled me. He would, too. At the earliest opportunity. He was still in the stage of showing off his newly acquired Americanisms. But I said, "No, it's not true," at which he stopped in his tracks and turned to me, his eyes deeply wondering. "Did you just make it up?" he asked.

"Afraid so."

"I mean . . . just now?"

"Just now."

He nodded, shook his head, resumed his walk through Macy's. I guessed it was the on-the-spot inventiveness that intrigued him.

We went to the book department. In those hard-up, penny-conscious days, the books were kept on the main floor. To the rear of the store. Books were a big turnover item then. Millions of remainders. Book club overruns. Gene went to the poetry section, and it was as though his hand was drawn by magnetic force. He plucked out a copy of *Les Fleurs du Mal.*

"Here," he said, offering me the book.

I didn't take it, took out my wallet instead, from which I drew a precious buck. "Here," I said.

He took the dollar and tucked the book under his arm. I assumed that he had decided to buy it for the dollar he had just won. But he kept right on walking, out the revolving doors, into the street. And I followed him, fascinated. Somewhere in the criss-cross of Herald Square, he opened the book, riffled through the pages until he found what he was seeking. "Here it is," he said. He quoted: "*. . . and with my eyes fixed confidently on the heavens, I fall into holes. But the voice comforts me: Guard, fool, thy dreams, the wise have none so beautiful as thou hast. And the voice consoles . . .*" He shut the book and said, "I don't agree entirely with that translation, but the basic idea is right."

Then he told me that Baudelaire had once written to a friend confessing that he was passionately in love with his own mother, and that he could never forgive her for having remarried. He said, "That's something I could easily forgive my mother doing." He handed me the book. "Here," he said, "I make you a present of this superior poet. Read him slowly and voluptuously. You'll thank me for the rest of your life."

"I suppose you realize you didn't pay for it," I said.

"I realize that I stole it, yes."

"You could have been caught."

"If that possibility didn't exist, there would be no particular virtue in the act."

"I'm going to go back and pay for it," I said.

"Don't you dare."

"I'm no thief."

"Neither am I," said Gene. "If I were I would steal it for myself, not for you. I'm not a thief and you know it, therefore in time you will learn how to value this gift."

I did in time learn how to value that gift, but perhaps not in the way that Gene meant. It was not the poetry I came to treasure, but the liberating possibilities in the human gesture. Not to steal —any fool could do that—but the spirit that allowed one to reach down below the surface and toss up into light and air the generous or quixotic impulse. Not to let it swim away. Not to let it always swim away.

We continued to meet at buying offices, at department stores, since we were selling kindred lines, needed to see the same buyers. We continued our practice of lunches in the park while the weather permitted.

When the weather turned cold, we went to inexpensive restau-rants that I never knew existed and that this foreigner seemed to have discovered by some method of European divination. I remember one—the Exchange Something or the Something Exchange—that had swastika designs in the tile floor. The manager had put up a notice to the effect that the floor design was American Indian in origin and had no other political significance. It was so like Gene to have found such a place. They served delicious little pork sausages and mashed potatoes. No checks. You told the cashier what you had on the way out.

"Would you mind telling me how you found out about that place?" I demanded.

"A friend of my mother told us about it."

"Do you like the honor system?"

"No, I like to walk on the swastikas."

I would learn in time that there were growing in the city many

41

such refugee colonies that sought out and passed along information on places and things pleasing to the palate or the pocketbook. Gene was not averse to picking up such tips, but he made
it clear that he was not one of the *Heimat* hand-wringers who wept
over their beautiful losses, finding everything in America so se-
cond-rate. He declared often and forcefully his love for America.
He loved it for its eclecticism.

"Its what?"

"Eclecticism. Don't you know your own language?"

"That's not my language."

"An eclectic," he explained, "is one who selects what suits him
best, whatever the source."

Oh, he was an eclectic, all right, with that ensemble of his
father's suits and coats and his new American fill-ins.

"Were you very rich in Germany?" I asked.

"Comfortable."

"How old were you when you left?"

"Sixteen."

"Are you the only one? No brothers or sisters?"

"I'm the only one."

There was another restaurant he knew in the Village, on Cherry
Street, a section of the city I wasn't familiar with, and that opened
up to me like the heart's Promised Land. This restaurant had
sawdust on the floor, the menu chalked on slate boards, high-
backed booths. The waiter called Gene "Mr. Strauss." How could
he have found such perfect places in the few years he'd been in
the city? There was some magic in Eugene Strauss that drew him,
or the desired thing, together—like Baudelaire's book in Macy's.
A magnetic field of a different kind, drawing like to like.

The remarkable thing was that there was so little swagger in his
sophistication. It made it all the more impressive, that aristocratic, finished sense of self. A royal sense of amplitude informing
him that such a place or such a person must exist, if only for the
sake of his pleasure.

He pointed out to me where another Eugene—O'Neill—had
had his early plays performed. "I've read all his plays," Gene
informed me. "I like *Strange Interlude* and *Mourning Becomes Electra*
best. The others are too narrow."

I had never been that much interested in the stage. Movies, yes. Loved the movies. Who of my generation didn't love the movies, with their vast, dark womb in which to gestate as many selves as the miserable world of light denied? But up until the Strauss epoch, I had found the stage an alien place and form. The few things I had seen I had found strangely intimidating. Being so thoroughly movie-oriented, I was made nervous by the presence of living people moving about, performing their highly charged imitations of life. It gave me a feeling of false duality. I felt that not only did I know they were acting but *they* knew they were acting, and this double consciousness threatened to tear apart the fabric of illusion. Movies escaped the menace by absorbing everything—people, place, story—into their own gray medium.

But Gene changed all that. He was going to be a playwright. He was even going to make me into a playwright (which I took to be a private joke between us), and therefore he/we must know what was being done in theater, and by whom, and how well. We must know how good the competition was, so that we could better judge how much effort would be needed to better it.

Having established professional interest, Gene would buy theater tickets for both of us, assuming that I would naturally want to go, would gladly fork over the cash, and of course I did, although not always gladly. We saw a young Robert Morley in the title role of *Oscar Wilde*. We saw Frank Craven in *Our Town*, which Gene thought was a little too provincial. We saw Dudley Diggs in *On Borrowed Time*, which excited Gene because he found in it echoes of his own mystical themes. We saw Maurice Evans in *Hamlet*, which Gene held in contempt for its mannerisms.

"No freshness," he complained. "No sense of the living play. Just theatrical attitudes. Don't you agree?"

What a joke! *Didn't I agree?* I don't think Gene had the beginnings of an idea how uninformed was his new American friend. Despite his puzzlement at my seeming ignorance, I think he still assumed there was much more than there actually was. I was racing like mad to catch up, but as yet had only a surface glitter of language and a patter of improvisation. But I knew that all of it was as thin as skimmed piss. I had not grown up in the shadow of a big bookcase, to quote Gene's precious Baudelaire. There

43

were very few books in the Klein house, and absolutely no talk of anything but the bare, scorched essentials. I had only recently discovered books in high school. I was a Columbus of ignorance, but I was very good at concealing. That I was. I walked the deck of my adventurous days with a clever, bright-eyed, sardonic air. If I didn't know something (and I didn't know most things), it was only because I knew so much else. I was brimming with knowledge of another kind. Wait one more minute and I would know everything. I would know all of Shakespeare, differential calculus and the relative merits of Maurice Evans.

"How should it have been played?" I asked Gene.

"As if the manuscript had been discovered just yesterday," he said. "With some wonder and fumbling. Not with all that professional polish."

But it was precisely the professional polish that had made the play shine so brilliantly for me! To remember all those lines! To be able to speak with so many modulations of voice, and to gesticulate while doing it! To face a theater full of strangers with such self-possession! It was a miracle! Who the hell was Gene Strauss to knock it? It was laughable!

But I didn't laugh at Gene. I never laughed at Gene.

He phoned me one Sunday to say we were going to the Cloisters.

"The what?"

"No, but this is incredible!" he exclaimed. "How can you possibly not know about the Cloisters?"

Even with all my hasty costuming, my nakedness would occasionally show. But I was beginning to resent his poking his finger at all the bare spots. He didn't have to be so goddam superior. There were some things that I knew that he didn't. The New York Yankees' standing in the league, for instance. The novels of Sinclair Lewis. I didn't collapse in astonishment every time I found him wanting. He was trying to let me know that I should be more advanced in matters of importance, of taste. My instincts should be better refined by this time. After all, how old was I? Twenty-two. That's maturity, for God's sake. Should be. He, of course, was *born* with the right instincts. He, of course, knew where to look to inform himself on matters of importance. Like the Cloisters.

44

"I say it's incredible," he said, "because the papers have been full of it for weeks. There have been articles in several magazines. One would have to blind oneself, deliberately, to avoid seeing it."

"Unless one is interested in different parts of the paper," I said, defensively.

"Tell me what you read," he said.

"I read the headlines, the sports page and my horoscope."

"I'm serious," he said, seriously. "Tell me what you read."

I told him that I read the news from Europe. I told him that I read everything I could get my hands on concerning Germany, Italy and Spain. I told him I had an *eclectic* feeling that those fuckers were going to alter my life in some very important way. "And," I added, "I'm astonished that you don't keep yourself equally well informed in these matters. I should think that your interest would be greater than mine. How come it isn't? I should think, given your background, that you'd be more concerned than me in the shitstorm brewing over there."

I had discovered by this time that Gene had an aversion to the common obscenities. He winced at four-letter words, and naturally I used them when I felt the need to get back at him. Strange, that verbal allergy of his. I wondered why a foreigner should feel so keenly the barb of native obscenity. I would have thought that one must grow up with certain dirty words to appreciate the particular color of their dirt. But Gene was innately fastidious. He had brought from Germany a superstitious regard for the English language. The English language was the language of his special destiny.

"I'll tell you why I don't read that garbage," he said. "I know, as you do not, from where it comes. The American papers quote Herr Goebbels or Herr Hitler as if these little apes were actual sources of information. I know what the outcome will be, so why should I read the daily lies?"

I, too, knew them to be daily lies, and yet I read them avidly, compulsively. Why? Because, like an augur, I kept fingering the mess to see if I could find some truth.

"What will the outcome be?" I asked Gene, in a way that had become almost a catechism.

"War," he said. "Nothing can stop Hitler from acting out his

45

death wish. I would rather spend my time enjoying more important things."

"Like what?"

"Like the Cloisters."

We went to the Cloisters and I looked out one of the west-
facing mullioned windows and saw the George Washington
Bridge, the placid Hudson, the last of the autumn colors daubing
the Palisades. Gene stood beside me, his father's Savile Row coat
draped over his arm, a coat clairvoyantly ordered by the father to
accommodate the son's subsequent style, with its European cut
and its flourish of belts and buckles. That sounds mystical, I
know, but mysticism was half of Gene's stock-in-trade.

"How do you like your new quarters, your majesty?" I asked.

"What?"

"The way you stand there, I get the feeling that the whole thing
was put together just for you," I said.

"Well, you know, in a way it was," he said. "It was put together
for those who would appreciate it, and I appreciate it."

Gene turned and strolled toward some perpendicular wooden
saint or recumbent stone king. There was something funny, perhaps sublime, about this young refugee who could speak of himself in such a way. It was thrilling and ominous. It was brave and
pathetic. I'm sure the difference in our backgrounds accounted—
partially, at least—for his manner, his attitudes. But there did
appear to be something missing—or was it something extra?—in
Gene Strauss. An inner resonating chamber that gave him more
self-determined echoes. Vibrations that in others might have
made for modesty made for Strauss enlargement.

"You know," he said, "we have no time to lose if we're going
to have a career in theater. Everything we see and think and feel
is important. We can't afford to waste time. We both know there's
going to be a war, and there's no assurance we'll survive. Isn't
that so?"

"That is certainly so."

"Well, then . . . Incidentally, my mother asked if you would care
to come to lunch next Sunday, around noon."

46

6

So I met Anna Strauss.

They lived, mother and son, in a house somewhere between Broadway and Riverside Drive. It was an old, gray, turreted stone house that must have been designed and built by some nineteenth-century stockbroker with baronial tastes. It had been divided up into several separate apartments during the terrible 1930s.

The Strauss apartment had four rooms and a kitchen. Three of the rooms served as bedrooms. The living room had an odd triangular shape, as did the building itself, tapering from its wide southern entrance to its narrow northern window. Definitely a room with a view. That single, rounded, plant-laden alcove gave out on a scene very much like the one I had seen from the Cloisters. There was the George Washington Bridge, the Hudson, the Palisades.

Anna Strauss was a small woman, a dainty woman, a woman with a sense of style. She wore thin gold bracelets on both wrists and loops of filigree gold chain around her neck. Her hair was set in a fashion that gave her more height, piled up in a series of waves. Her eyes were sad and brown and pouchy, inquisitive eyes, appealing eyes. Her face, it seemed to me, had been marked by time and terror, but her bearing had a delicate, coiled energy. The only incongruous thing about her was her hands, which were broad and spatulate, like a peasant's. Altogether there was something queenly about Anna Strauss. I gathered that she reigned in this apartment.

"Saul," she said, holding out a hand that, had I been less a Bronx clod, I would have bowed over in the semblance of a kiss. I'll say in my favor that something of the sort did pass through my head. In imitation of the movies. Erich von Stroheim, or somebody like that. But I didn't. There was too much Bronx in me. "Gen," she said, "told me about this meeting in the buying place. I think that is so nice, like a Chekhov story. I even had a title for it—now what was it?—oh, yes!—*Autumn Interlude*—but Gen didn't like that."

She did say "Gen" with a hard *G*. A nickname. I said I was pleased to meet her. I felt a serious deficiency of sensory apparatus. I needed more to take in everything. The table set with shimmering linen in one corner of the room. The window with its many plants. The unfamiliar food set on the table. The northern view of the bridge, the Palisades, the river. Music, too. A radio or phonograph. Everything in the Strauss apartment, I was to learn, had a musical accompaniment. It was so natural a part of the setting that I gave it no separate recognition.

Gene sat on an armchair near the window, much at his ease. I thought he was being a little amused at the spectacle of the north Bronx coping with middle Europe.

The hard *G* in Gen, I was shortly to find out, was a pet name that came out of Gene's childhood. Anna had always given Gene's name its English pronunciation—*Djene*—but the other kids in Hamburg (before all changed to mockery and hatred) called him hard *G* Gen, from the German pronunciation of his name: *Oigen.*

Gene called his mother "Mutti."

Anna said, "Gen tells me that you are also interested in writing plays."

Her speech was more accented than Gene's, by far, but still not in what I thought of as the typical German way. The Strausses were from north Germany—Hamburg—where people were influenced by the British, by the international commingling in that port city. And there was the individual thing, the Anna Strauss thing: an unconscious musicality in every utterance.

"I think he's trying to convince me that I should be interested," I said.

"Gen has a very good—nah!—*wie sagt man doch?*—a very good *intuition* about such things," she said. "Many people don't know they have special gifts. Such a thing is possible. Is there perhaps someone in your family who has special gifts? Perhaps an artistic —nah—" She was again stuck for the right word. She looked at Gene. She always looked at Gene when she was stuck for the right word.

"Tendency," Gene supplied.

"Tendenz?"

Gene nodded.

"Almost the same," she said, looking pleased.

But I didn't want to go into my family. I shook my head, saying there were no special gifts. I wasn't exactly ashamed, just excruciatingly conscious of the withdrawn Klein gloom and this Arcadian opposite.

"Then perhaps you will be the first," said Anna Strauss—and she said it with so easy a grace that I felt it like a gentle swell of beneficence, as if I were a small boat on a sunny sea.

Then Anna asked us to come to the table for lunch. She raised her voice in a two-noted lilt to call out a name—"Air-enst!"— which I was shortly to learn was Ernst, the boarder. Ernst Mueller, artist, who rented one of the Strauss rooms because he couldn't afford his own apartment, whose status as artist gave him privileges in the Strauss household.

Ernst emerged from his room and formally shook hands with each of us. I thought it strange that he should have been absent during the past half hour. After all, it was a Sunday afternoon, he lived in the same apartment, an honored guest, why should he have been excluded? Anna's wish? His own? I reminded myself that there were different customs here.

His handshakes were accompanied by stiff, Germanic bows, even to the Strausses. "This is Saul Klein," Anna introduced. "A friend of Gen's." Ernst gave me a second little bow. He was a slender man with large, clear brown eyes that seemed fixed in a glare of permanent indignation. His hair looked as if it had been polished into place with a buffing wheel. His shirt collar was frayed, his tie a colorless string, his jacket had the greenish shine of endless use, but he looked like an exiled monarch about to reclaim his kingdom.

We all sat down. There were cheeses, cold beef, liverwurst, a cake with lingonberries, a bottle of white wine. Sunday lunch in the Klein house was usually cold chicken or salmon croquettes, which wasn't bad, which was good, but nothing like this, this unreal scene of interesting people coming together to enjoy one of the simple but highly civilized ceremonies of life. One would have had to live under the sulphurous Klein cloud to appreciate the difference. This was sun-bright Olympus. This food was the food of the gods. I felt that this day would have special meaning for me, a turning point. I was engaged in silent celebration. I wasn't free of the Klein curse by a long shot, but I had taken a giant step into an alternative life.

We talked. That is, *they* talked. They talked about a coming Heifetz concert. Apparently they had a lottery going. All chipped in so that one could go to some scheduled concert. Ernst, I learned, earned an occasional few dollars doing fine lettering for some advertising agency. It was rarely enough to pay for room and board, or his share of the musical lottery, but these defaults never lowered his honored status. He was like a Talmudic scholar in an orthodox family.

Last week, Anna had gone to hear Serkin. It was now Gene's turn, but he was deferring to his mother. Anna's adoration of Jascha Heifetz was apparently a family joke.

"She thinks Heifetz sits at the right hand of God," Gene told me.

"If he doesn't now, he will in time," Anna said. "What would be the good of being God if you couldn't have Heifetz sit beside you?"

"Perhaps God is not musical," Ernst suggested, with his own kind of German accent . . . *"Pairhops Got iss not myoosikal."*

"If God was not musical there would be no music," Anna declared.

"Ach!" said Ernst, lifting one shoulder.

His gesture seemed at first a quick capitulation to his landlady's captivating theology, but something else caught my attention. He was a figure of such fierce contrasts, this Ernst. His forehead was perfectly round and smooth and pink, as if the same buffing wheel that had worked on his hair had taken in that part of him as well. His hands, too, carried on their business with scrubbed efficiency. His shirt, however, looked as if it had been questioned by the Gestapo, and his tie looked as if it had died watching. I thought to myself that such tatters were deliberate. For some reason I believed that they weren't necessary.

"Forgive me, but that seems to me a foolish argument," Ernst said loftily, continuing to munch his food slowly and fastidiously, one piece of pumpernickel after the other, each with its modest burden of meat or cheese. "You might as well say that if God did have not a bad smell there would be no skunks."

Anna turned and waved her hand, dismissing the sophistry. "A skunk is only a small animal," she said.

"Music," said Ernst, "is only a sound. Sometimes small, sometimes large, but not always pleasant to the ear."

For me it was a play out of the seventeenth century. An allegory. Anna was Virtue. Ernst was Skeptic. Gene was Hero. I? I was audience. I watched and listened in a haze of fascination, much more interested in the people than in the argument, although I'm sure I imagined it was the argument that was inducing that pearl-gray trance. In retrospect I know that I didn't care what they were saying if only they would go on saying it. Their voices were an octave higher than they need be to override the thundering symphony that was coming from the radio. The whole scene was providing its own ironic counterpoint. Beethoven booming away while Hitler's refugees argued about the nature of God. Apparently it wasn't indicated anywhere in the script that the music should be lowered, or even turned off. Everything was as it should be. The light of the autumn day had painted the color of the scene, and the players were speaking memorized lines.

"Do you really think God makes these distinctions?" Ernst said. "That would be a very curious God. A little too human."

Anna performed her little moue and shrugged. She looked at Gene. Gene looked at me. Was *I* supposed to say something? Then it occurred to me that Gene was inviting me to get in on this costumed action. It was, he seemed to be indicating, a free-for-all, so why not get in my licks? But I didn't. I just wanted to sit and watch and listen.

By a transition I failed to detect, the talk switched to German, and I was completely lost. My catch-as-catch-can Yiddish wasn't up to this high-class German, but I continued to listen with every bit as much interest because another kind of attention had been engaged. German, to me, was a heavy, deadly language, the language of brutality and terror. It wasn't the language my family had pulled out of the Diaspora, and I hadn't been much aware of it until Hitler came along and branded it into my consciousness. Radio and newsreels choked with the hoarse hatred of that language. On this day, for the first time, I was forced to make a separation between the language and the nightmare. Here were these captivating people beguiling their exile in the same tongue.

Finally Ernst turned his gleaming head aside and said in English, "Oh, what matter? I was only joking."

"I know this," said Anna, gently, melodiously, making the gesture I was rapidly coming to know: a little pat in the air with her peasant hand, a blink, her womanly appeal.

Then Anna began to speak of Ernst's painting. Ernst was a cubist. He painted here, in this very room, when the sun had made its way around to the West Side of Manhattan. She was full of praise for Ernst's painting, declaring that he had a technique that made him distinct from Picasso or Braque.

I noticed a change of expression come over Gene's face when his mother launched into her panegyric. He looked across the table at me, again as if to draw me into more personal participation. I somehow got the idea that he was asking me if I thought Ernst's work was all that good, even though he knew that I hadn't seen a stroke of Ernst's work; and even if I had, I wouldn't have an informed word to say about it. But that didn't matter. What I was taking from Gene's eyes was the message that this ritual of Anna's was to be endured with forbearance. As far as Ernst's talent went, it was at best so-so. Comparisons to Picasso and Braque were an exaggerated kindness, the sort of thing that is done by a Lady Bountiful to fierce, tattered artists who had been forced to flee their homeland.

I seemed to have taken the message correctly, but it wasn't a particularly welcome message. I didn't want that much understanding. I didn't want a view so clear that its bright reality would end the enchantment.

There was this one odd realization I took from the day: there had been no talk of Hitler, of Nazi Germany. I wondered why. God knows it was everywhere in the world, such talk, But not in this gray room, not among people who would have something firsthand to say. I thought at first it might be fear and loathing, but time has put together for me a different reason. Anna and Ernst had still not rejected the country that had rejected them. They had only been wounded into silence.

Not Gene. Gene was free. Gene needed no culture or country but the ones he would create for himself.

7

I HAD MET Gene in early October and by the end of November my
life had changed. I'm not sure that my life wouldn't have changed
anyway, being at that age, being the person I was, but the history
of change is identified with the actors involved. Gene was the
principal actor in the autumn of that year.

I had a job, was able to stuff a few dollars in my pocket at the
end of each week. I was still going to school three nights a week,
studying accounting, although I knew I would never be an accountant. I rose and fell to the tidal rhythms of my parents' fights,
no longer affected by them as I once was (I was away too many
hours of the week), but I was still allergic to the pollen of misery
that filled the air of the Bronx apartment. I would know that a new
round of strife had begun without hearing a word, by just testing
the rancid silence that had taken the place of words. I had found
at last another emotional center around which to orient my life.

Latent homosexuality? Forget it. My lusts directed themselves
toward the female mysteries as thickly and needfully as a cocoon
around larva. When I walked through the city, my nerves were
waving tendrils that attached themselves to almost any silk-shod
pair of legs, the globe of a breast, the curve of an ass. I was every
bit as salacious as the Nazis would have me.

Gene was principally responsible for the change in my life, but
not entirely. Something else had happened in November. I have
it in my scrapbook. *Nov. 8, 1938:* REICH EMBASSY AIDE IN PARIS

SHOT TO AVENGE EXPULSION BY THE NAZIS. It was a fairly inconsequential item in a brutal season. A Polish-Jewish kid by the name of Herschel Grynszpan shot and killed a minor diplomat in Paris because his family had been forced to move from Germany to Poland. Dumped on the border. They were doing it to thousands of Jews who had come to Germany. The boy himself had fled to France, but he was in correspondence with his father, knew of the family's doom. In the craziness of his despair, he had somehow got hold of a gun and had made his way in the embassy and had shot a German named vom Rath. Ernst vom Rath. It was reported in the New York *Times* on November 8.

The newspapers carried nothing much that day, or the day after, or the day after that, but on the eleventh, the headlines went up like rockets: NAZIS SMASH, LOOT AND BURN JEWISH SHOPS UNTIL GOEBBELS CALLS HALT . . . JEWS ARE BEATEN, FURNITURE AND GOODS FLUNG FROM HOMES AND SHOPS, 15,000 ARE JAILED DURING DAY . . . 20 ARE SUICIDES . . .

And so on. The famous *Kristallnacht.* The big things are still remembered by most people of a certain age. It was all over the papers and on the newsreels. The shots of old bearded men on their knees in the gutters cleaning up the glass that the bullyboys had smashed. The protests around the world. The pleasure the Nazis took in sneering at the protests. The flagrancy put out by the Minister of Propaganda that the nation was just following its "healthy instincts." The slapstick ploy on the part of the government that held the Jews financially responsible for the damage done by the rioters. The new laws that disallowed all Jews in any trade, that confiscated any insurance a Jew might hold.

After a point, the particulars ceased to matter. The Nazis had announced to the world that they would have their fun and that the variations of that fun would run according to taste. All of it well documented. Cheap cruelty made national policy. It brought on many realizations. One was a dark liberation. The Nazis had pumped out the propaganda that blood was character. If you were a Jew, you were incapable of decency, honor or courage. The Germans had struck out against other nations because they had been wronged in World War I. One Jew had struck back for the viciousness and brutality being heaped on Jews in Germany, but there was no courage or honor in that either. Herschel's action was not to be respected, only avenged.

Everyone knew that the whole show was a colossal lie, but to know something is a lie and to understand the nature of the lie are somewhat different things. Knowing that the Nazis lied hadn't freed me from the suspicion that the lies might have a crumb of truth in them. My mind *was* full of lascivious diddles from morning to night. I had many times skirted around a possible fight for fear of a bony fist in my eye. My behavior and my thoughts were ludicrously short of my ideals.

I was badly flawed, and I knew it, but what I understood now was that the Nazis were much worse. They were without honor. They were without fairness. They were without humor. They should have respected that Paris Jew for striking back, but instead they acted like dogs in a pack, tearing and rending. I wasn't free of the terror they instilled, but I was free of a certain kind of debilitating poison. There was nothing to look for anymore. Whatever I was, the Nazis were worse. Infinitely.

"How much progress have you made in your play?" Gene asked me.

"What play?"

Gene closed his eyes, sighed, shook his head. He was an orchestration of put-upon patience. He didn't seem to understand that this talk about "plays" was a kind of horizon sport—always in sight, always out of reach.

"Are you telling me that you haven't even made a start?" he demanded.

"Did I say I would start?"

"You certainly did. Very distinctly. Not only that you *would* start but that you *had* started. You said, 'I think I've actually written one complete scene.' "

When he said it, I remembered having said it. But it wasn't true, not literally. I had thought that he would understand that it wasn't literally true. I had thought that he would understand that I was being the obliging friend, spinning in the direction of his world, but not crashing into it. A moon not a meteorite.

"In a sense, I have started," I said. "I didn't actually put the words on paper, if you want to know the truth, but it was beginning to sort itself out up here."

I pointed a finger at my temple.

"Why don't we discuss what you've sorted out," he said.

I think it was at that point that it happened. I wanted to say something to him, but it suddenly seemed as ridiculous as discussing water with a drowned man. I wanted to say that the Nazis didn't play by their own rules, that there wasn't a shred of decency in the whole goddam nation, that when a Jew struck back, one pathetic little Jew, seventeen years old, there was no credit for that in their fucking Valhalla, only vicious spite. But who was I to be telling Eugene Strauss this? Strauss *père* had packed up family and goods precisely because of this knowledge. But despite his personal history, I wasn't absolutely sure that Gene saw this truth in the light that I did. But I couldn't say it to him. I don't know why I couldn't, but I couldn't. Friends should be able to confess feelings, no matter how small and obvious, but it was one of the features of our friendship that I couldn't discuss small and obvious things with Gene. I feared his bad opinion. He had seen something in me, and I was contracted to that image, even if I wasn't sure what it was, even if I had to remake myself day by day, clue by clue. So instead of telling him what I really wanted to tell him, about the Nazis being lying, murderous bastards (knowledge he had inherited with his father's suits and overcoats), I told him I had a scene in place and my characters in mind, but that my trouble seemed to be in getting them to say anything . . .

"Five characters," I spontaneously invented. "I've got them lined up like baby birds, beaks open, but I don't know what to put in there, words or worms."

"What's your play about?"

That's the trouble with spontaneity. You never know what it will trigger in someone else. Someone else might be prompted to ask a simple, sensible question. Again I had to be inventive. I decided on playfulness.

"About? I'm not sure what it's about. Does a play have to be about something?"

A certain kind of ambiguous humor delighted Gene, but he turned to ice when he suspected he was being kidded.

"Why did you trouble to open the beaks of your birds if you weren't going to have them say something?" he asked. "And why five, if I may ask?"

"It seemed like a good number. Keep things lively."

"Well, if you'd rather not be serious," he said, turning away.

I was afraid I had gone too far. I feared he would wave a hand and walk away, as he had done before, unwilling to put up with this clownish American. I could tell when he had reached this point. His speech, which normally affected a British accent, became even more inflected under stress . . . *"Well, if you'd rawthuh not be sirius."*

"No, I'm sorry," I quickly apologized, realizing that I had to go deeper into my lie to effect a rescue. "The truth is that I do have something in mind, but my characters seem reluctant to talk about it. I don't know. I just don't have the imagination."

"Shall I tell you something?"

"Yeah, please."

"You do have imagination," he said. "More than you need. The trouble is you have a tendency to dress it in rags."

Now that was true. That was very sharp on the part of my distinguished friend, Eugene Strauss. That's just what I did. Like a Jew in mourning, I went around with a rent in my soul's garments. On the other hand, it must be pointed out that if I sometimes paraded myself in mental rags, *he* always came on in royal ermine. Why was *that?*

I tried to explain my situation. I pointed out to Gene the differences between his background and mine. I had to tiptoe carefully through the lilies of the field because my life hadn't been arrayed in artistic splendor. My family didn't carry on about Heifetz and Picasso, or about the abstract nature of God. My family talked—*when* they talked!—about buttons and shoelaces. But okay, I would be "sirius." I told him I was thinking of writing a play about my own family situation. He drew back in shock.

"That doesn't sound very promising," he said.

"I guess that's why I'm having problems," I said.

(I couldn't say precisely when the theme slipped into my mind, but it was somewhere near that point in our conversation.)

"Then why not drop it?" he said. "You told me that your father

58

and mother scarcely talk to each other. You can't very well build a play on that."

(Another idea came to me.)

"I thought knowing the characters would make it easy," I said, just stalling.

(Another character had just introduced himself.)

"Why not a political play?" Gene suggested. "You're so intensely interested in politics."

"About Hitler and Mussolini?"

"Very topical."

"I don't know the characters."

"Do you suppose that you really know your mother and father?" he asked. "You have to create the characters, in any event."

It went up like a flare, exploding light over the night of my unknowing. I would have said that I knew my mother and father more than was healthy for me, but in the sudden illumination of Gene's words I saw at last the prevailing truth of my life. I didn't know them. Not at all. I only knew what they did and didn't do, did and didn't say, but I knew nothing of their hearts and minds. There was not a blade of grass growing in the interior landscape of either of my parents that was known to me. That was the real revelation.

I went home that evening vibrant with new understanding, and out of that understanding I recognized the new character who had barely moved into view during my conversation with Gene. Me, of course! Saul Klein! *I* would be the centerpiece of my horizon play!

I called him Daniel. Daniel in the Ice Den. Daniel, a volcano of volubility, sitting at the kitchen table and pouring out his agitated heart to parents and sisters. No, *sister.* I decided on only one sister for the play. When I had no idea what to put into the mouths of the characters of my imaginary play, I would people the stage with a multitude of mutes, but now that I had an idea of what I wanted to say, and who would be my sayers, I also knew how many people I would need. So I undid the marriage of the younger of my two sisters, brought her home again, and gave her a part.

I would write a play about my Ice Age family. I would open my play in the midst of one of their polar winters, but instead of the iceberg silence that weighed me down in real life, I would have my character a fountain of volubility. He would talk and talk. He would try to induce, seduce, entice, enrage, cozen or cajole his family into speech. Instead of the plague of muteness that laid waste the Klein household, I would have Daniel talk up a redeeming storm. He would accuse his parents of being Nazis. Oh, yes! My muse had already handed me that club of invention. Hitler's goal was to make the Jews unhappy, and the Kleins were working overtime in his behalf!

I realized I was entering a different world, and I was thrilled and appalled at what I only dimly perceived to be its different laws and liberties. Dull, miserable truths could be alchemized into bright, liberating other truths. I would be the maker of all things! I could have fun and revenge at the same time! I could rearrange the universe!

Wisely—oh, for once in my young life, wisely!—I decided to keep these sunburst revelations to myself. I wanted to share them with Gene, naturally, but why tell them to Gene when he already knew and, even more to the point, assumed that I did, too?

It was at first frustrating, but then fortifying, keeping this cosmic discovery to myself.

8

NEITHER GENE NOR I demanded exclusiveness, but when I told Gene I couldn't meet him on a particular night, or on some weekend afternoon, he would smile his sardonic smile and ask if I was going to play pinochle or baseball with my buddies. Naturally, there were pre-Strauss friends. I continued to meet with these friends and we did what we had always done. Sometimes we would all go to the Van Cortlandt Park playing fields and have a choose-up game of softball. Sometimes we would meet at somebody's apartment (not mine) for a Friday night game of pinochle. Part of the pinochle ritual was for one of us to go to the local deli and bring back a reeking assortment of corned beef and pastrami sandwiches. There would be cardboard containers packed with pickles, cole slaw and potato salad.

I had once described these rituals to Gene, knowing he would find them amusing, and indeed he did find them amusing, but he didn't find it amusing that I should continue to meet with these friends after the inception of the Strauss era. I don't think it was because he was jealous of my time, but rather because he felt I showed a suspect nature in continuing such contacts after he had indicated to me the way and the life.

The pinochle crowd was closest. Three others besides myself. I had known these boys for years. We had gone through high school together. Monk's father owned the old-fashioned dairy store where my mother used to shop. Monk would help his father out several times a week, and whenever I went into the store to pick up some items for Rose, Monk would slip in an extra chunk of fresh farmer cheese or a slab of Muenster. There was Nate and there was Teddy, both perfectly nice, normal guys—that is, they were tolerant, horny and vulgar. No, not really vulgar. Just as good corned beef comes with some fat, good Bronx boys came with some obscenity. If we weren't calling each other names over the pinochle game, or talking about baseball or Hitler, we were talking about sex. Sexual deprivation was rampant in those days, and so was talk.

Of the pinochle crowd, Monk was closest. He was the first to sense that I was drifting away, because, I suspect, he had always been aware of another dimension in my life, or possibly in his own. Monk (Morris) was appealing in manner and in appearance. Sandy hair, brown eyes, easily led to a smile or a laugh. And courageous. Once, when he and I were walking through an empty lot, we were surrounded by four thugs about our own age who wanted everything that could be fished out of our pockets. That or take a beating. I believe we would have taken the beating in any case. But Monk offered to fight all four of them, one at a time, if they had the guts. That's exactly what he said: "I'll fight all four of you, one at a time, if you've got the guts." They all looked at him, at each other, and there passed among them the swift and shameful knowledge that not one of them was willing to be the first. So they settled on grabbing the books I had just borrowed from the library and running off, tearing the pages from the books and tossing them in the air as they fled, yelling, "Sheeny cocks! Sheeny cocks!"—little harbingers of a bigger and bloodier time.

"So what *does* it mean?" Monk once asked me, after a class discussion in poetry. *"What* ignorant armies?"

"Any ignorant army," I said. "How many armies know what they're fighting for?"

"But why by night?" he asked. "Armies don't usually fight at night. They fight during the day, when they can see."

"Night is a metaphor—"

"A what?"

"Not real night. The night in the mind."

I knew that Monk would rather understand than scorn, and that's why he had asked, and that's why I had attempted to explain "Dover Beach" to him, and to myself. And I think that's why, when the time came, Monk said to me, "You're kinda getting away from Friday nights, huh?"

"Between job and school," I alibied.

"I know," he said, knowing more of the truth than I admitted.

"I do have other interests, Monk."

"I figured."

"I'm sort of interested in theater."

"Yeah? You mean an actor?"

"No, plays. Writing them."

"That's great. I'm not surprised. Listen, Saul . . ."

He told me that he knew for a long time that I was leaning away. He said that he knew I was interested in other things, even though he didn't know what those things were. He said that he could spot the look of boredom that came into my eyes after so many hours of pinochle and dirty jokes. He said he could see how much I wanted to be talking about something else . . .

"But listen, we're all changing in one way or another," he said. "If I had a choice, I'd like to go to college and study engineering, or something like that." (Monk scored highest in all math classes.) "But I know I have to go into the business with my father. He needs me, and I need the money. I know I'm going to take over the store one day. That's okay. It makes money. We can't all be what we want to be. But I tell you this, Saul, friends are friends, not always because you got the same interests but because you care."

Those words have come back to haunt and hurt me, in many different ways. I did drop my former friends, including Monk, feeling guilty at the time I did it, carrying that guilt for the rest of my life. But looking back on it, I know it would have taken only a later maturity and latitude to encompass Monk and pinochle and Friday nights and softball *and* Eugene Strauss.

There was a similar falling away from my sisters—although that would probably have been inevitable in any event.

Natalie, my older sister, lived with her own family in Brooklyn.

Her husband, Sam, was the foreman in a factory that made low-end dresses, aprons and smocks. I had been to the factory: a clamor of sewing machines, the pungent smell of dirt, sweat and low wages. Sam rode herd on the piece-workers and cutters. He was a short, thick-muscled man. Not unkind. Natalie told me how many times he took money out of his own pocket when workers were caught short. It was simply a case of conditioning and a hard-nosed credo with Sam. He felt he was destined to "get ahead," and to get ahead you had to be tough—by which he meant you had to have the stomach for the hiring and the firing and the exploitation and the tears.

Natalie had set a minimum of once a week for family visits. Visits to her, that is. One week it was Sam's family; the next week hers. When Natalie and her family visited the Bronx, that would of course obviate the necessity of a Brooklyn visit on the part of the Kleins. She expected me to accompany Rose and Abe on those long subway trips out to Brooklyn. It was almost Byzantine, that schedule of trips. Natalie of the sumptuous spreads and the absolute convictions. There was the right way to do things and the wrong way. Anything in between called for severe patience. Natalie conceded it was a large, diverse world. Not everybody had the same expectations and customs, but within her own family she would measure falls from grace with a micrometer. She had a butcher who knew without asking what cuts of meat were acceptable to Mrs. Wexler. She had a bakery that made breads and cakes like nowhere else. Her sauces were thicker and richer. And her tongue was the sharpest.

"What's the matter, you're too busy to visit your own family once a month?"

"It's more than once a month."

"Excuse me. *Twice* a month. What's happening that's so important?"

"Nothing's happening. It's just that sometimes I've made other plans."

"What plans, Saul?"

"Cut it out, Natalie. Do I ask you how you arrange your days?"

"You don't have to ask. You can see. I have children, I have a husband, I have a home."

64

"I arrange my life differently," I said.

"And that arrangement doesn't include your family?"

"It includes my family, but sometimes I have a prior engagement. Sometimes there's something else I would rather do."

"Ah! Now we're getting down to it! *Rather!*"

With Natalie there was no compromise. She didn't ask what it was that was taking up her brother's time. Whatever it was (unless it was a girl, in which case why not bring her over?) it needn't be so immovable. It could be made to accommodate prior responsibilities. And she was right. It could. But I didn't want it to. Part of the earth-shift caused by the Strauss temblor was an overturning of priorities. It was the old priorities that would have to move.

Eventually Natalie accepted, but she never fully forgave the disloyalty.

My younger sister, Rita, had demands of a different kind. She saw in me her own missed opportunity. She, like Monk, had wanted to go on to college, but the times and the peculiar Klein climate practically plucked her out of that photograph of her graduating high school class and set her beneath the *chuppah* next to Sid Alterman, whose only fecundity was in his sperm count.

Sid had a moist smile and moist, blue, myopic eyes. He worked for a mail-order house. He had something to do with the collating and packaging of the great masses of paper that came flooding off the presses. He was hardworking and well-meaning. He was a loving husband and father. He was a nice *nebbish.* He liked me and wanted very much for us to be friends.

"I'm never going to get ahead in that place," he would confide in me. "What do you think I ought to go in for?"—as if all I had to do was say "law" or "medicine," and he would be magically installed in a new career. Sid wasn't stupid. He was well read. He told me he had read Gibbon's *Decline and Fall,* every volume, from the *Age of the Antonines* to the *Return of the Popes from Avignon,* and there was a secret repletion in his telling, as if he had devoured all by himself a forbidden cache of candy.

Sid's trouble was that he was happy. He was happy with his wife and his children. Books in the library were free. It cost very little to go to the Bronx Zoo or the Botanical Gardens. The worms of high or low ambition had found no breeding ground in Sid's placid soul. Periodically, he would furrow his brow and squint his blue eyes and wonder whether there wasn't something else he should go in for. But no one took that seriously, especially not Rita.

"The funny thing," Rita said to me, "is that I can no more divorce Sid than I can divorce one of the children."

"Do you want to?" I asked.

"I don't want to divorce him exactly, I just don't want him to be my husband. That doesn't make any sense, I know, but it happens to be the truth. If I could leave Sid at home to take care of the children, I would go out and start something new for myself. I thought he was very sweet when I married him, but I didn't know *how* sweet. He's like a stuffed toy. The kids love to play with him. But a grown woman doesn't like to go to bed with a stuffed toy."

"So what can you do?"

"Nothing," she said. "Wait. Make sure I have no more children. Wait until the ones I have are grown, and then get the hell out of the house. Go back to school. Oh, God, you don't know how lucky you are, Saul, that you have a penis instead of a womb. I want to get a degree in psychology. I want to study social work. I want to go out in the world and help idiots like myself. Maybe it can come sooner than I think. Maybe when the kids go to high school, they won't need me in the house all the time. Saul, help me! Make a success! Get rich! When the time comes, help me!"

It wasn't I who ultimately helped Rita, but Sid. Sid with his sweet vacuity and twenty-thousand-dollar life insurance policy. Shortly after the war, he walked in front of a speeding truck on lower Broadway. I don't believe he deliberately walked in front of that truck, but he might have been musing about what else he could get into when he stepped off the curb.

Rita did go back to school, and she did become a social worker —but when she remembers Sid, it is with the pain of a parent who has lost a child.

It's not remarkable that Gene never met anyone in my family. He was as incurious about anyone in my family as I was curious about his. And I was guilty of complicity in the matter. I didn't *want* him to meet my family. Discord, silence and frustration. Where were the glimmers of Elysian light? Where was Heifetz and the right hand of God?

I could have made an exception of my grandfather. I could have advanced my grandfather, as Gene had advanced his father, as a worthy progenitive source. But my grandfather spoke very little English. His language was Yiddish—but he knew all about the right hand of God!

You didn't fiddle your way there: you prayed every inch of the arduous way! I had years ago freed myself from my grandfather's tyranny, and my visits to my grandparents' apartment was partly an atonement for having decided on a somewhat different allegiance.

There was a period in my preteen and teen life when I was indentured to my grandfather's sabbath observances. He would come to pick me up at the Klein apartment every Saturday morning, rain or shine, and he would take me to his synagogue for several hours of boredom so exquisite that it almost reached beyond itself and into the holy submission that my grandfather had been trying to induce in me. My soul literally cramped at the Hebrew text I had never mastered, of the back-and-forth swaying of the *shabbes* pros, at the cabalistic muttering at the podium and most of all at my grandfather's finger, which would regularly and scornfully riffle the pages of my errant prayer book and poke at the place I had failed to follow. This was always accompanied by a rise in his voice as he continued to *daven,* as if he were trying to divert God's attention away from the wretched piece of impiety at his side.

These outrages fix themselves most achingly in the spring and summer months, when I was dragged away from the sanctity of roller-skating and stick-balling streets and forced into a sunless, droning ceremony. At such times, I came close to prayer. I had no choice but to appeal to an authority higher than my grandfather to bring an end to this servitude.

Time accomplished that. If it didn't take, it didn't take, and soon enough I was too old to be made to submit. Instead I would visit my grandparents in their dim apartment on a dim Bronx street. My mother's mother would serve me her incomparable honey cake and ask me why I was still going to school, and my grandfather would raise his eyes from the *Daily Forward,* the Yiddish paper he read, and ask me in Yiddish what I thought of the world I lived in. I told him in English that it was a world in great trouble and badly in need of alteration.

We came to know each other slowly, each speaking a different language, but each understanding the language the other spoke. I discovered from my grandfather that there were distances and angles in human perspective that speech should try to capture. I discovered his dry, sardonic sense of humor. He captured other members of the family in a word. A brother of my grandmother he called "Knubble," because of his fondness for garlic. A sister of my grandmother he called "Shmatte," because she always complained she had nothing to wear. He even had a name for his son-in-law, my father. I wasn't supposed to hear it, but I did. My grandfather thought I had gone, but I was still in the apartment when he referred to my father as "Finster," which could be interpreted as "dark" or "sullen" or "gloomy."

For a time, I hated my grandfather for the bondage he had clamped on my soul. My mother had allowed it, I think, because she felt I was in need of that kind of masculine influence. My father was simply not around on those Saturdays, and even if he were I suspect he wouldn't have had an attitude about it one way or the other. Gradually, I came to revere my grandfather for the liberation he brought to my heritage. I despised accompanying him to *shul,* but I came to love visiting him in that dim, smelly apartment, where we would discuss Hitler and the Nazis, and he would flavor my apprehensions with the salt of his wit.

I could have pointed to my grandfather with some pride, but the language and the culture were wrong. Gene may have been made to suffer for his origin, but he made no late alliance with *Yiddishkeit.* He was a man of the world, and that precluded any narrow identification. The German culture had expelled him, but unlike his mother, or Ernst Mueller, he made the expulsion mutual. He had no interest in becoming an *echt* Jew, either out of conviction or defiance. Just what identification he did make puzzled me.

Once—it was in the late autumn of that same year, a gray, cold day—I saw a familiar-looking woman come out of a French restaurant on the East Side. It was somewhere between Madison and Fifth, or possibly Park and Madison. A fancy, expensive restaurant. Even while I was trying to place the woman, I saw Gene emerge behind her, one hand under her elbow, escorting her out the door. It all fell into place at once. The lady was the buyer for a Fifth Avenue department store. She was a pleasant, middle-aged, rather heavy woman. I had seen her several times in the course of my rounds, and only recently she had rewarded me with a fair-size Christmas order for Siegal merchandise. I remembered it so well because Lou Siegal had so visibly expanded at the name on the order form.

Gene and the lady walked west. I knew that Gene was escorting her back to the department store where she undoubtedly had much work to do. There was nothing in the scene to arouse any suspicion, and yet I found something ineffably strange in it. Obviously Gene had invited the woman to have lunch with him and she had accepted. Nothing remarkable in that—salesmen and buyers did it all the time; and, from the rumors I'd picked up, practiced much greater intimacies than that—but this was a classy lady, a lady with Eleanor Roosevelt inflections of speech, and Gene's ease in her presence seemed prophetically revealing, having as much to do with me as with him.

I would never have asked that buyer-lady to lunch. That was an action beyond my imagining. Had he seen the woman that many more times than I had? I didn't think so. Gene's assumptions were different from mine. He assumed that if he asked Mrs. Quinlan to have lunch with him, she would accept. I wouldn't have dared. I realized it had nothing to do with creativity or good looks, but with *identification.* He identified himself as one who would naturally be accepted by the favored of this world. Even his firsthand Nazi experience hadn't knocked that out of him!

I was right about Mrs. Quinlan. She shook hands with Gene and turned into the side-street entrance of the department store.

Gene continued his way toward Fifth Avenue. I hurried and caught up with him.

"Hello," he said. "That's funny. I was thinking of you. I was going to call you. I wanted to tell you that I've finished my play."

"Congratulations. . . . Wasn't that Mrs. Quinlan I saw you walking with?"

"Yes. We had lunch."

"I didn't know you knew her well enough to ask her to lunch."

"How well do you have to know a person to do that? As a matter of fact, I didn't ask her to lunch, she asked me. She wants to set up a little section in the department store for imports. Let me tell you about the play . . . "

Or did I have it all wrong? Was it the favored of the world who identified with him?

Better than telling me about his play, he said he would give me the manuscript and let me read it for myself . . . *provided* I let him read my play. I told him I wasn't finished, that I'd only completed one act. He said that was fine, that I would have the benefit of his criticism before going on with the second act.

"How do you know it'll need criticism?" I asked.

"All plays need criticism," he said. "I expect you to criticize mine."

Whether he meant that or was just giving his ego a quick coat of camouflage, I couldn't be sure, but given a choice I would rather he hadn't brought things to this sudden crisis. I feared much more what I would say to him than what he would say to me. Mine could be so quickly and easily disposed of. My theme was already known, so realistic, almost autobiographical. Either the dialogue sounded right or it didn't, and if it didn't I could tear up the pages I had written and start over again. Or never start again. But *Gene!* Would I be clever enough to find the mystical thread, and having found it would I be eloquent enough to describe its iridescence?

Since there was less of mine, Gene called first. He told me I had perfect pitch for human speech. All the dialogue rang true. The only trouble—yes, there was a trouble—was that I had written myself into a cul-de-sac. My character talks and talks to and about

70

his untalking parents, and that was quite wonderful, but what will I do in the second act? I confessed that that was the problem that stopped me—but even as I confessed it, I spied my corner of escape. "Give me another day for yours," I said.

"Of course," he said, in a disappointed voice.

I telephoned him the next day and told him he had written a fine play, an exciting play, a significant play. It was important to get the praise out first, to put the seal of approbation on our friendship. But I discovered that having said it, I believed it. Believing it, I was then free to ask a few unimportant questions about *A Special Destiny*. Like what was the relationship between the boy and girl in the first act, when they are both living in New York, he a medical student, she a seamstress of sorts, working on costumes in Broadway productions? Were they friends? Lovers? Are they married? Just an extra word or two could easily resolve that very minor point. And I wondered whether I had missed something between acts two and three that would account for the boy and girl, Carl and Rena, each pursuing his and her special destiny—she a student at the Sorbonne, he in the merchant marine—somehow getting from Paris to New York, where, in the last act, they are married, with children, he a doctor, she a *hausfrau* . . .

"I don't think you missed anything," Gene said. "I deliberately left that unexplained."

I waited. He said nothing more. I knew that I was being challenged. I knew that I was being asked to supply evidence that I was worthy of the friendship he had bestowed on me. A critical point. I reached into myself for critical insight. I came up with this: that it was Rena's destiny to love more deeply than Carl, to sacrifice her own career for Carl's.

The pause at the other end was as brief and vital as the time between two heartbeats. "So you see," he said, "it doesn't need explanation."

I thought it did, but I didn't say so. We were both too enwrapped in the prismatic beauty of *A Special Destiny*.

Give or take a half dozen more heartbeats, and Gene said, "Are you free this Saturday?"

"I think so."

"Good. I'd like you to meet the Rena of my play."

9

SATURDAY BROUGHT DECEMBER and snow. It started the night before, continued through the day, and by late afternoon the hydrant in front of our apartment house was only another white contour on the inundated street.

Ordinarily I was happy with snow. I looked on snow as an ideally white way of leveling life. If I had nowhere to go, no one to see, neither did anyone else. That blanketing omnipresence soothed my irritability.

But not on that day. That day the snow threatened to interfere with my important date. Well, not really a date, since it was *Gene's* friend I was to meet. Girl friend? He hadn't said girl friend, but then I wouldn't expect Strauss to make such a common indication. She was the girl who had served as model for the Rena of his play. Perhaps she was a cousin. Second cousin? Was he by any chance bringing her purposely to meet me? Perhaps she was a lonely girl and she had asked her handsome cousin to introduce her to one of his more presentable friends. And I was presentable. Say whatever else you would about me, I was presentable. Or perhaps this proto-Rena *was* his girl friend, but she was bringing one of *her* girl friends on what was then called in sticky innocence a "double date." On dogsled, of course. How else on this Klondike night?

"You're going *out?*" my mother demanded, when she saw me putting on my galoshes.

"The subways are running," I said.

My father said nothing. This situation wasn't covered in his slim catalogue of father-son relations.

"Are you crazy?" my mother said.

"A little."

"Anything to take my heart out."

I had been more or less waiting for the telephone call that would cancel my date, but since it hadn't come by five I left the house and began my hike to the elevated train. The drifts were high, but the snow depth was only halfway up my galoshes. Of course, *I* could have telephoned and canceled. Most young people today would have. People today are not so ready to use the subway at all hours. We were then. No problem. The subways were safe from almost all inclemencies, human or meteorological. And keeping a date was so much more important then. Consider the sexual frustration. It kept everyone in a high state of tension. There were no TV programs to anesthetize boredom or to bring dramatic precursors of the coming storm into dreary living rooms. One had to discuss current events with one's friends. Parents such as mine didn't understand the terms in which one saw one's futureless future. One had to live quickly and meaningfully. One had to bring every latency to ripeness before it was too late.

And of course I was vibrantly curious to see the girl (or girl friend) who had served as the living prototype of Gene's mystical play. I was curious to see any girl that Gene would acknowledge as friend or girl friend. Such a girl was sure to reveal a Gene I hadn't seen before. Such a girl in her very person would light up dark corners of the Strauss enigma. She would be worldly, of course. She would be clever and ever so informed on things cultural and aesthetic. She would recite Baudelaire by heart, in English or French. She would know all about the Cloisters. She would know all these things with her left hand and with her right she would have gathered all the sexual cunning known to womankind since copulation began. I pictured someone with dark hair, dark eyes and cameo features. I had in mind my own sleek paragon, a leading lady of the time: Kay Francis.

* * *

73

As we all examined each other on the corner of Sixth Avenue and Eighth Street, the designated meeting place, snow whipping around us, scarves muffling our faces, I caught preliminary glimpses of my complete misconception. And when we shook ourselves free of snow and outer garments in one of Gene's subterranean *ristorantes,* I saw that the girl who had been introduced as Ruth Prager bore greater resemblance to a farm girl than a Hollywood siren.

We sat at a table with a checkered tablecloth. Red and white. On the lime-green wall, directly above Ruth's blond head, was a large and remarkably ugly painting of beautiful Venice. The colors on the canvas seemed to have been melted off assorted hard candies. The gondolas looked like Viking warships. Ruth had pale skin and broad features. Her blond hair was braided and that heavy coil was set upon her head like a coronet. Her nose must have been broken at one time—there was a scar on the bridge and a slight flattening at that point.

I think I fell in love with her on the spot.

No, I think I fell in love with her while riding the subway and gazing at the line of familiar ads on the curving panel opposite. I think I fell in love with the *idea* of a Ruth before I fell in love with the living girl. Such a possibility had been incubating in my blood for years. I had been carrying a breeding virus on the trigger-point of wholesale invasion. Or perhaps what was on the point of happening has become so pervasive in memory that I can't reconstruct the parts, only the overwhelming totality.

I do know that the real Ruth was nothing like the imagined one. The male libido proposes a different sex partner for each day of the week, and then fate introduces Ruth Prager, who wasn't even remotely imagined on that month's erotic calendar, and the real complications of love and lust begin.

"Since you two have so much in common," Gene began, "I thought it would be just as well if you met. He"—indicating me —"thinks I don't pay enough attention to detail, to reality, and she"—indicating Ruth—"agrees."

Ruth and I began talking simultaneously, disavowing the charge, which we guessed was more a gambit than a serious accusation. Ruth sat with her hands clasped in front of her. They weren't delicate, alabaster hands. They were big, capable hands, reminding me of Gene's mother's hands, bringing some fleeting notion of unconscious connections.

Ruth said, "Your friend says he welcomes criticism, but I wonder. What do you think?"

With her face as clear as it could be in the anemic lighting of Mama Italy's restaurant, I could see that smiles came easily to Ruth Prager. Also, I could make out an accent. German, of course, but not with the Strauss inflections. How strange it all was! The immigrant flavor in my own family was exclusively Slavic—Poland, Russia, Latvia, a few distant Rumanians—and suddenly my life was fully occupied with another branch of the Diaspora.

"I think—" I began.

"If I didn't welcome it, why would I have brought together my two worst critics?" Gene cut in.

"Two *best* critics," Ruth corrected, glancing at me with a smile that left me slightly dizzy. It seemed to me that she had just announced a plot in which we two were conspiratorially involved. The involvement warmed me like wine. I was delighted and dismayed to have any basis of sharing with Ruth Prager. Dismayed because I could see, clearly, what the situation was between Strauss and Prager.

"Mr. Strauss is an eclectic," I said. "He picks out the best and most useful, even among his critics."

I wasn't sure what I was trying to convey with those words. I think I was trying to signal Ruth, let her know that I was aware of the plot, that she could count on me as a full participant. But it really didn't matter what I was thinking or intending. I was all over the place, floating between a drunken joy and a secret jealousy.

"Oh, yes," Ruth agreed. "Mr. Strauss knows who takes him seriously."

No question about it. Ruth Prager was hotly and heavily in love with Eugene Strauss. This was just a game we were playing. The game was designed to demonstrate Ruth's condition. All the pieces fit, and tightly, and that tightness was a comfort to me. Any looseness in the fittings would have caused a distracting rattle.

But I could relax. My newfound love could be, would be, my own deliriously hopeless affair.

"The thing about our friend," I said, contributing my move to the game, "is that he must avoid the appearance of gratitude at all costs."

That brought a look of surprise to Ruth's brown eyes. I couldn't tell whether Ruth had harbored, secretly, the same thought herself, or whether I had just angled, minutely, the light of her love. She tipped her head to examine it.

"No," she said softly. "I think he knows how to be grateful."

How quickly the pattern arranged itself! Like one of those dotted picture puzzles, popular at the time, in which you connect numbers consecutively until Lincoln or Washington emerges. Ruth and I talking about Gene as if he weren't there. Gene played along by listening in a removed way, as if none of this concerned him, all the time taking it in, most carefully. And, after all, hadn't he been the arranger of this scene? *He* had brought us together. Weren't all the nervous moves arranged by *him?*

You would have to be blind not to see. The glow in Ruth's eyes, the high glow in her cheeks. Perhaps she hadn't had much opportunity to portray her love, and this new, cooperative Saul Klein was giving her the chance to add new colors to her canvas. Oh, she liked me, all right. Why shouldn't she? I was Gene's friend. But I think she would have liked a chimpanzee if it had made the right accompanying noises. How much more satisfying this Saul Klein with his wisecracks and insights. Klein knew, all right, and Ruth knew that he knew, and she counted him an instant friend that he handled his knowing with kindness and grace.

"It isn't a question of gratitude at all," Gene said. "It's a question of understanding . . . "

He paused—a portentous pause—and then he outlined the creative differences between us, something he had obviously given much thought to. I—he put a finger on the sleeve of my jacket—was lucky. I had an ear for the pitch of human speech. I copied the music effortlessly. He, on the other hand, was forced to create his own music because he didn't have that kind of ear, and besides his whole approach to drama was so much different from mine. The characters in his plays would always have to play Straussian music. The people in his plays could never achieve total independence, whereas the people in my plays could. The people in his plays must always serve his theme, while the people in my plays sought their independence and the success of my plays would depend on their achieving it . . .

Did I know what he was talking about? Vaguely. I was a little intimidated by the amount of thought he'd given the whole complex matter. I wasn't sure if it was an analysis or a cover-up, but whichever it was it was done with mesmerizing seriousness. We sat there, Ruth and I, listening with a seriousness that matched his own. There wasn't a modulating cough or smile. Even then I sensed how deeply I was committing myself to the Strauss cause by my silence. Time itself became an accomplice. The more time that went by without some alleviating levity, the more impossible it became to introduce such leavening.

An easy thing for Ruth. She was already totally committed to the Strauss cause. She took Gene every bit as seriously as he took himself. There was something in her look—which took my attention as much as Gene's words—that signaled to my senses as surely as a glance from my mother would signal to my senses when I stepped into the Bronx apartment. A glance from my mother could mean only one thing: a new Ice Age. But I had no clue to the Ruth look until she turned from Gene to me and instantly lowered her gaze in a futile attempt at concealment. Suddenly I knew!

They were lovers! Real lovers! They had fucked! That rumored, wicked, wonderful thing!

I was thrilled and appalled, filled with envy and awe. I had bitten into unearthly fruit. My new knowledge produced a voluptuous shudder of sin. What was I doing here? I didn't belong here. I belonged in my safe, wretched corner of the Bronx, not in this dazzling, Edenic garden. What could I say that wouldn't betray my abysmal ignorance?

"Maybe we should collaborate," I said, meaning something quite other than my words implied. "You write the music and I'll write the words."

* * *

In Mama Italy's restaurant, we talked and talked. In the upper world, it snowed and snowed. Much later, when I trudged my way from subway to home, my legs sank in as deep as to the knees. In the dark, silent foyer of the food-smelling apartment, I heard without seeing clumps of snow fall to the faded, worn rug as I pried off my rubber boots. I could hear the ragged rhythm of my father's tortured snore.

I went into the kitchen and turned on the light. A terrified mouse scooted across the floor. I poured a glass of milk and drank it with parched greed. I pictured a tubular white coldness, such as a surgeon might have inserted to examine the conditions within. What the surgeon would have seen was a Saul Klein dispossessed. Someone else had taken over all the rooms in the Klein castle.

It wasn't the first time. I had been in love before. If the susceptibility is there, the affliction happens early and often. A few summers ago, I had fallen in love with a freckled girl who did cartwheels on the beach. Most recently, I had fallen in love with a melon-breasted girl who could sing in their original language an amazing number of proletarian songs. Being in love was not a new experience.

Nor was I a virgin. That stigma had been removed at the curious insistence of Mr. Siegal's nephew, a cheerful philistine who truly believed that we lived in the best of all possible worlds. There were certain things he considered necessary to man's estate, and when he found them missing he moved with missionary zeal. He counted us relatives, of a sort, and he thought it would reflect poorly on Mr. Siegal's enterprise if its star salesman was so wanting in manly fullness.

He taught me new card games, astonishing permutations of poker. He said, "You go on a business trip, you go to a sales convention, somebody asks you to sit in on a game, you're going to say you don't know how to *play?*" He informed me that the forelady in the factory had a nice, three-room apartment in the Chelsea section. He wasn't saying that Mr. Siegal paid *all* the rent, but the contribution was generous.

"Mr. Siegal!"

"Yeah, Mr. Siegal. Why, what's the matter, you think he hasn't got a complete set?"

And not far from that Chelsea section, also known to Mr. Siegal's unromantic nephew, was another apartment where one could carve one's initials on the incense-thick air, and where the ladies wore one-piece negligees that zippered all the way down the front.

But all that worldly wisdom and rank furtiveness had nothing to do with the Gene-Ruth affair. What I had guessed about them generated an ever-present radiance in my mind. The whores were pathetically real, but Gene and Ruth bestrode my imagination like Greek gods. In that sense, I was still a virgin. When I thought of them together there was never the mechanical business of sex, but an incandescent fusion.

I learned more about Ruth. I learned that her father had been a Berlin labor union official, a pure-blooded Aryan who, like Gene's father, had escaped Hitler just in time. He had lived in double jeopardy, having opposed Hitler politically and having married a Jewish girl.

I learned that Ruth/Rena did indeed work on wardrobes in the theaters of New York, being skilled with a needle, and that she hoped one day to go back to school. She was interested in art, in painting. She worshipped the French impressionists and wished with all her heart to become a serious scholar in the field. She wanted to study art in all of its ramifications—history, techniques, genres, museums, forgeries. She wanted to travel the world and see the places that had inspired the great works. She wanted to cover all the great exhibitions for some leading newspaper or magazine. She aspired to be the editor of the foremost art journal in the world. She wanted to write brilliant essays. And—although she never said so—I knew she would have given it all up, and gladly, for the right words from Eugene Strauss.

And I was in love with her. Each day's dispossession of Saul Klein became more complete as I installed the girl with the golden hair and the once-broken nose in every room. I wandered around so full of her that at times my own voice came to me like a ventriloquist's voice, a made-up voice coaching me through the day's necessary business. When I looked at my face in the bathroom mirror each morning, I wondered how long it would be before I could resume intimacy with that one-time familiar.

That's the way we were—three contenders for glory, mulching the soil for a hothouse full of demons.

10

THE AMERICAN AIR was full of love songs. New movie musicals were laden with love songs. Singers in famous bands introduced new love songs every week. Songs of love unrequited. Songs of love returned. *My baby left me . . . My baby loves me . . .* And I knew all the lyrics. Well, not all, but a surprising number of them. I sang them to myself. Singing them out loud would jeopardize my new status as intellectual, playwright, friend of Eugene Strauss. Also as dream lover of Ruth Prager.

I could conjure Ruth's smile as easily as I could hum the latest love song. I could match the exact brown of her eyes against an infinite spectrum of browns. The line of her body from breast to hip was hooked into my senses like a bit in a horse's mouth, directing me, pulling me this way and that.

But something else was present in the air besides love songs. There I was humming syrupy lyrics, writing a play, suddenly packed full of the potential I had always hoped for, and all of it roared at every day with a hatred so huge and complete that it became a kind of planetary property, like ocean tides or molten magma. More present than love songs were the hate songs from Germany. Love songs would quit after a time, but not the hate songs of the Nazis. They were on the radio and in the newsreels. They were echoed by Father Coughlin in this country, by Sir Oswald Mosley in England, by fascists everywhere. They were

scribbled on the walls of the underground walkways of the city:
KILL THE KIKES . . . BUY GENTILE . . . JEWS EAT SHIT . . .

The effectiveness of it was in the completeness of it. The joy
of it was in the remorselessness of it. To allow it to diminish for
a minute would be to imperil the great blood orgasm toward
which Germany was pumping. The fantasy had to be fed so that
the national erection remained hard and heedless. The terrible
secret (like sex to a boy) was about to be revealed. Civilization was
an evil fairy that had bewitched the true heart of man. The Nazis
were going to restore to the German people the true heart of man
—hatred without reserve, cruelty without remorse.

There was no comfort in knowing it was all a lie. One had
almost too much company in condemnation. The newspapers
that reported the beatings, expropriations, jailings, vilifications
and gleeful lies also filled their columns with cries of horror. By
1938, the terrible secret was out, and the Nazis were no longer
avoiding the truth of it. There were mass protest rallies in Madison Square Garden. Protestant and Catholic prelates came to
synagogues to express their grief and solidarity. There were millions of others besides myself who saw the demented spite of it.
Tormenting a race and then calling them cowardly murderers
when one of them struck back.

That striking back became my other secret obsession. Herschel
Grynszpan. The young Polish Jew who had shot the German
diplomat, vom Rath, who, incidentally (I borrow from later revelations) was a German whose loyalty to the Nazis was under
question at the time, and whose death was probably welcomed by
the Nazis. No matter. Any occasion would do to announce to the
world the return of barbarism.

There was so little to know about Herschel Grynszpan. His
family was among the thousands of Jews who had been deported
back to Poland after having been stripped of all their belongings.
Herschel had fled to Paris. He and his father had exchanged
letters, and in those letters the father described the pitiful plight
of the family. Herschel was seventeen. He was barely five feet tall.
He went to the German embassy with a gun in his pocket and
asked to see the German ambassador on the pretext that he had
an important letter to deliver. He was asked to leave the letter but

he said that it was too important, had to be delivered personally. He was then sent to Ernst vom Rath's office. He was in the office only seconds when shots rang out.

A picture of Grynszpan in the *Times,* profile, out of focus. He looked like one of the kids who hang around on the edges of the school playing field while the heftier boys play basketball or touch football. Spectral eyes, like Kafka's, but (it may have been more subjective than actual) I thought he looked like me. A thinner, smaller, more haunted me.

I tried to imagine a scrawny seventeen-year-old kid, penniless in Paris, somehow finding a gun (bought? stolen?), finding out where the German embassy was located, going there fully prepared to kill, knowing that he might be killed himself, retaining memories of the booted, belted brutes who roved in packs, smashing windowpanes and faces, breaking furniture and bones, contemplating, perhaps, that he might be sent back to Germany, where he would be put at the mercy of the Gestapo. That kind of courage slammed into my belly like a baseball bat. It left me breathless. Could *I* have done that? Of course not. I would have conjured up too vividly deep cellars where unspeakable things would have been done to my eyes, my fingers, my testicles. Did Herschel lack the imagination? Didn't he think of consequences? I have it in my scrapbook, dated November 10, 1938 (Paris): *The young Polish Jew who assaulted the third secretary of the German embassy, examined today by psychiatrists, was reported to have wept when he learned his act had brought new vengeance against Jews in Germany* . . . No, he didn't lack imagination. He had, if anything, too much imagination, responding as he did to what his family was suffering, responding as he did to news of what his action had occasioned.

I was in love with Ruth Prager, but what right did I have to the emotion of love in the midst of a four-alarm fire? What right did I have to the emotion of love when a seventeen-year-old kid, barely five feet tall, sat in a jail somewhere in Paris thinking of nothing but death, his own and the others who would pay for his pathetic, unimaginable courage. I wanted an overcoat—I have it here, the ad I cut out of the paper and tucked between the pages of my scrapbook—and the one advertised by Arnold Constable appealed to me. It said: AN OUTSTANDING COMBINATION OF

WARMTH, LIGHTWEIGHT, WEAR. ALPACUNA OVERCOATS. 26.3%
WARMER. 1½ LBS. LIGHTER. 61% LONGER WEAR. SINGLE- OR
DOUBLE-BREASTED ULSTERS OR SMART RAGLANS. NAVY, OXFORD,
BLUE-GRAY, BROWN, CAMEL OR GREEN. I thought "raglan" was my
style, and blue-gray my color. Forty dollars was high, but I was
earning commissions every month . . . But how did they arrive at
the 26.3 percent warmer? *Warmer than what?*

I sang love songs. I was in love with Ruth Prager. I wanted an
Alpacuna overcoat in a style and color that expressed my personality. I wanted these things and I wanted my personality expressed in love and friendship, in creativity (I was a playwright),
but at the same time I brooded about the seventeen-year-old kid
sitting in a jail cell somewhere in Paris, awaiting his doom. I
wanted to soar in my love and wear my Alpacuna coat with the
same dash as the gentleman in the ad, but I couldn't. There was
a soul-poisoning in this gas of hatred. There are so many ways in
which freedom can be denied and this was only one more way.
Herschel Grynszpan and millions like him were having all freedom and life itself denied. Here I was at liberty to love my friend's
girl friend, write a play, buy an Alpacuna coat, so what the hell
was I kicking about? But that's the beauty part, or hellish part,
about freedom. It has no meaning when it's totally denied. Then
existence itself preempts the ruined stage. But when you walk
around with freedom stuffed in every pocket except for that one
tiny inside flap, then that one tiny inside flap becomes super-
heated with its secret and burns a hole into the otherwise perfect
Alpacuna of each day.

"It's this," I said to Gene. "I'm living a crippled life. I can't take
a complete breath or carry through a single thought without the
Nazis gripping my throat or mangling my mind."

"You're exaggerating," he said.

"Why would I do that?"

He looked at me in that characteristic way of his: tilting slightly
away, angling his eyes to compensate for the tilt, a look of fine
skepticism on his pale, aristocratic face. I wondered then, I still
wonder, whether that immobility of feature was something he had
deliberately cultivated or was a congenital gift. Whatever its ori-

gin, I admired it, envied it, tried to imitate it, very unsuccessfully.

"If you're not exaggerating, then you ought to be ashamed of yourself," he said.

"Why?"

"That you would allow them to occupy even that much"—he looked at the microbe he was holding between thumb and forefinger—"of your day."

"If I were standing in the middle of a raging fire, should I be ashamed of howling like hell and running like mad?"

"But you are not."

"Have you heard of Herschel Grynszpan?"

"Of course."

"Why do you think he shot that fucking Nazi in Paris?"

"Please don't use that language."

"I couldn't think of another adjective," I said. "Why did Herschel put his life on the line?"

"Because he went mad," Gene said.

"Do you think it was madness?"

"Of course."

"Why not a cold-blooded or hot-blooded impulse to take revenge on your tormentors?"

"It was an act of madness," Gene insisted coolly. "Now he will die himself."

"Some call that heroism, or martyrdom, or self-sacrifice," I said. "Nations build statues to honor it. Songs are composed. Why do you call it madness?"

"You see the result," Gene said.

"Then it's the Nazis who are mad, not Herschel."

"To survive madness, in any way, is the highest responsibility of the individual. They want you dead. Then live."

"Gene, are you telling me that you go through your days not thinking of the Nazis at all? Hitler is never on your mind? Not that shitty little cripple, Goebbels? Not that fucking sausage, Goering?"

"There's no need—"

"*Every* need! What's the point of having dirty words if not to use them on dirty people? Dirty words have their use. Can you think of better subjects? Never mind. Tell me how you can avoid thinking of the bastards. I know you've had firsthand experience. What's the trick?"

"I think of other things," he said. "I think of the play I'm writing. I think of my characters. Don't you see that the Nazis *want* you to think of them. *Don't.* That's the best defiance."

Could I believe Gene? I didn't know. It sounded like such a wonderful, desirable liberation, but was it the conscious choice of a superior intellect or the camouflage of an egoist?

Why not some of both?

I didn't know.

Trying Gene's philosophy was like trying not to think of a pink rhino. Or heeding that piece of judicial nonsense: *"The jury will disregard that remark."* It was like holding my mental breath, feeling the threatening collapse of brain cells, and finally sucking in a lifesaving gulp of historical air with all its major and minor gases. Fear and loathing. Hatred and horror. End-of-the-world nightmare and world-saving fantasies.

Herschel Grynszpan remained at the center of my nightmares and fantasies. I invented gruesome peep shows of poor Herschel in the hands of the Gestapo. Pliers and rats and soldering irons, ingeniousness beyond endurance, until I was brought to my knees in vicarious pleas for mercy. I invented escapes engineered by brave French radicals, who, submachine guns blazing, sprang Herschel and whisked him off to a friendly underground that was even now forming against the new barbarians. There Herschel would meet a pretty girl, who looked something like Ruth Prager and . . . etc.

The historical fact was that no one paid any attention to Herschel Grynszpan once the gates closed on him. Individuals don't count. Great armies were massing in Europe. Great populations were being uprooted and expelled. The only individuals who mattered were those who represented the new barbarism and those who stood in the way of it—Roosevelt, Stalin, Churchill. But I decided that Herschel would be my hero and my cause.

What did I sacrifice? Nothing. I bought a forty-dollar, 26.3-percent-warmer Alpacuna overcoat. All the energy of my romantic imagining went toward the Ruth *I* knew, not the one Herschel met in the underground. But I did identify with Herschel. His poignant Kafka eyes became my symbol of resistance. Not Gene's detachment but Herschel's bullets.

I made a vow to honor Herschel each day in my thoughts. Naturally, I was unfaithful, but I tried. I was conscious of my lapses, guilty about them, and always came back to Herschel. That practice established an auxiliary self that has never left me. That auxiliary self made a friend of Herschel Grynszpan, just as my worldly self had made a friend of Eugene Strauss.

11

No ONE OBJECTED to my quitting school. My mother and father were undisturbed by the announcement. Their connection to my schooling had been at best vague and distant. They regarded it as a necessary step toward a money-making career, but since I was already making money what was the point of these nightly exercises? If not an accountant, then a salesman. Salesmen made good money, didn't they?

The only strange and slightly disturbing thing was the unexplained and unexplainable shift from the old Saul to the new. There was no visible reason for it. Saul suddenly full of new activity, writing in the kitchen at night, busy with unknown people, staying out all hours.

"A girl?" my mother asked.

"A harem."

"Don't be such a smart alec. You got a girl?"

"Not exactly. My friend has got a girl."

"Please stop talking in circles."

"Can you keep a secret, Ma?"

"My whole life is a secret."

"I'm fully of proxy powers," I told her. "I'm a proxy playwright and a proxy lover."

"Peroxide? I don't know what you're talking about."

But there was a certain amount of satisfaction in her complaint. She was used to these cryptic episodes with crazy Saul. I tested new words and new ideas on her, and although she had no idea what I was talking about, she did have a sense of being invited into a process that flattered and pleased her. Without knowing what it was, she knew it was the opposite of the dark reiteration that was her everyday life. She felt her own proxy participation in something that had no name.

My father had nothing to say.

Gene took my dropping out of school as an inevitability scarcely needing comment. If the only purpose of my going to school was to subject myself to the dreariness of becoming an accountant, then it was high time that I quit. Better spend my time writing a second act. *He* wasn't going to college. He knew where to go to inform himself on the progressive steps of his chosen career. Since I had decided on the same career, it did seem ridiculous to continue putting on that hair shirt, like a religious penitent.

"Will you go on being a salesman?" Ruth asked me.

"Yes. No. I don't know. Of course not."

"What, then?"

"I'll finish this play, and then I'll move into that apartment on Fifth Avenue, the one between Eightieth and Eighty-first. If the terms are right, I'll go to Hollywood to do the movie version of my play. But, you know"—this said with the world-weary ache of too much success—"my first love is the stage. I'll always come back to that."

"Very amusing," Ruth said.

I did my best to amuse Ruth. It was my substitute for love-play. And she was getting used to this curious specimen of a friend. We did see each other occasionally, alone. She worked around the Times Square section, and I was pretty much free to roam the city. We would sometimes arrange to meet for lunch at a cafeteria near where she worked.

As I said, she liked me, but not for one hallucinatory moment did I imagine that I was the exclusive reason of our occasional meetings. I was just a conduit of information. And neither of us had to worry about the propriety of such meetings. Gene had taken care of that. Gene had, in fact, *promoted* that. He had said,

"Why don't you two have lunch when it's convenient?" His office was in the Canal Street area, and very often his boss wanted him in the showroom for incoming buyers.

But it wasn't really a question of geography. He could have met either one of us, or both, any time he wished. It was the *idea* that appealed to him. He thought, I'm sure, that it was the proper way to be. Very Lubitsch. That was a life attitude. But I suspected a motive as well. I thought he figured to find out more about—well, I wasn't sure what—more about me, more about Ruth, actually more about *himself* through such contacts. Ruth and I would reveal to each other what we would never reveal to him. By having us meet and talk, he could then see each of us separately and learn from the surrogate what he hadn't been able to learn from the source. Does that sound too Machiavellian? Perhaps. Perhaps Gene had guessed how I felt about Ruth and was being the bountiful buddy. Perhaps all of the above. Perhaps none. Perhaps it was just because he was Eugene Strauss, who wore his father's Savile Row suits with filial devotion and personal style. Perhaps because he looked at life in a way that made it necessary for him to arrange his world far differently from the way I arranged mine.

The odd truth was that Ruth and I *could* speak to each other as we could not speak to him. Ruth was in love with him and crippled by that vulnerability. I was in love with Ruth, but secretly, and in some way strengthened by that dissimulation. I could play her confidant while she played variations on her own restless theme. I knew the theme she was playing by heart. I practiced the same fugue tirelessly in my own soundproof chamber.

It may appear as if I were putting myself in the way of a masochistic dose of heartache, but it wasn't so. I didn't hurt when I was with Ruth. I *liked* the game I was playing—and my liking it probably accounted for its success. I was clever and compassionate and only slightly patronizing. I was acting out my love in an antic way, and I found that more relieving than stolidly removing myself from what normally would be looked on as an unprofitable situation. I was getting my kicks out of the love situation. The only things I lacked were her lips and arms and thighs and her et cetera, to quote another poet.

* * *

"I wonder if I could talk to you," Ruth said.

As if there had been any difficulty about that!

We met in her neighborhood, at another of those restaurants that Gene had produced from beneath his magician's cape. We had all three had lunch there the previous week. This one was a hangout for journalists. If you went at the right time you could see Heywood Broun or Westbrook Pegler. The day before we met, an arctic air mass had moved in. The air was brittle. Ruth came in wearing a blue coat, a blue beret and a plaid scarf wrapped around her neck and shoulders. Her nose was red, her eyes teary. I had the curious feeling that if I kissed her she wouldn't feel it, anesthetized as she was by the cold.

We were seated in one of their deep brown enclosures. There was a window high above us that aimed a wintry shaft of light directly at Ruth's head, turning the braided gold of her hair to platinum.

"I would like to ask you something," she said.

Oh, serious!

"Yes," I said, "what can I tell you about Eugene Strauss?"

Ruth had two distinct facial expressions, either of which knocked my heart sideways. She could be angry, in which case her lips would compress, her nostrils dilate and the little scar on the bridge of her nose would blanch. Or she could be happy, in which case she would smile, and her eyes would fasten on me tolerantly as she demanded to know the meaning of my ambiguous words, my frequently ambiguous words. What did I have to keep me steady but the ballast of ambiguity?

"Suppose it's not Eugene Strauss I wish to talk about?" she said, her expression neither angry nor happy: a distant somberness.

"Then I'd be wrong," I said.

We sat there brooding on my wrongness. Ruth considered whether to go on or to make me pay for my smartass attitude by dropping the subject and giving me a very cool companion for lunch. I sneaked a hand behind and checked out my wallet. One of my daymares was finding myself moneyless in such a situation, the girl (Ruth or any other) beginning to rummage in her pocketbook for the money, two waiters and the owner flanking my *schlemiel*hood. But all was in place, including my own jittery self.

Ruth decided to overlook my sarcasm. "I wanted to ask you about his play," she said.

"Oh. His *play*. That *is* different."

"Saul . . ."

"Yes?"

"Do you wish to be my friend?"

"Very much."

"Then I would ask you please not to be so . . . so . . ."

"Wiseguyish?"

"Yes."

"Okay. I agree. I'm sorry."

"Not everything has to be made into a joke," she said.

"You're right. I'm sorry."

"You should be."

"I am. . . . Now what can I tell you about Gene's play?"

And what, I wondered in that ceaselessly conjuring corner of my mind, happened to that golden coil of hair when they made love? Did she undo it? Did it take long to undo? Was it possible for a man to watch her undo it, knowing what was to follow, and keep his sanity as well as his semen? Did she allow a mere man, someone composed more or less like myself, to touch that shining mass, while she yielded softly and sadly, opening her, moving her . . . Dear God, what a stew of fable and aphrodisiac I had concocted for the female role in sex! Women treasured their chastity. Women gave up their virginity to swine like me in tears of remorse. Every sexual encounter was a violation. It was 1938. I had been brought up in the Klein household, where life below the belt didn't exist. All Kleins were like Claude Rains in *The Invisible Man*. If we stripped naked, there would be nothing but air below the navel.

"I would like to know what you really think of Gene's play," Ruth said, her eyes following mine like iron filings in a magnetic field. It was eerie, the way her eyes sought to draw from me this truth she was seeking. "You see," she said, "I'm no judge. I know that you are. I have read this play of his—*A Special Destiny*. Did you know that is what he calls it? I have read this play, and to speak the truth I don't know what to think. Of course I told him I think

92

it's good. If one isn't sure, it's better to be positive than negative, isn't that so?"

I nodded. I said, "Yes, under the circumstances, I would say it was better to be positive than negative."

"But tell me what you think," she said.

"Why do you want to know what I think?" I callously asked.

She looked away. I had given her reasons to trust my discretion, my friendliness. This was disappointing.

"I want to know," she said, "because I want to be helpful. If there is reason to believe he is gifted in this way, then one can be encouraging. If not . . ."

"If not?"

"Then one can take a different attitude."

"A *dis*couraging attitude?"

"Not necessarily discouraging. Saul, why are you pretending to be stupid? You know very well what I mean."

"I don't know very well what you mean. You already told me that you told him that his play was good. Suppose I were to say to you that Gene is only kidding himself about his talent? Would you unsay what you've said?"

"*Are* you saying that?"

"What if I were to say that Gene is a genius, that it's only a question of time before Eugene Strauss' name will blaze as brightly as Eugene O'Neill's?"

"I would believe whichever you say is true," Ruth said.

"I don't know why I'm obliged to give you answers when you feel you don't have to give me any."

"What do you wish to know?"

"What I asked you before—why do you want to know?"

"And I told you already—to know what attitude to take."

We were playing politics—that is, sailing cautiously between a lie and the truth. It was all very simple. Ruth was a girl in love, and she was asking me to guide her in a way that would help her keep her love. She feared blind flattery because she knew it would be seen as such, and would soon lose its effectiveness. She feared ignorance because that would diminish her too. She was pleading for a clue. She was asking to have pointed out to her a fixed star by which to set her course.

And why should I help Ruth Prager in this? Let her suffer the consequences of her ignorance. Why should I lend her my advantage so that she could go on unbraiding her golden hair for Eugene Strauss? What kind of a fool did she take me for? Perhaps if I might filch a few coins from that treasure. Fair is fair. Once in a great while, for favors received, perhaps a little favor given? Little! Only the whole, moist, trembling world!

A basement of moral bargains. Even as I plotted these thief's maneuvers, I was filling up with a noble light. I was an idealist in those days. Despite my lusts and my deceptions, I was an idealist. I truly believed that unrighteous acts stained the soul. Small deceits were okay, even necessary, but the big lie would blight and blast the best part of you. You would be spiritually dead. Look at the Nazis! Hadn't they consigned themselves to hell?

All right, then, what was the truth about Eugene Strauss? Ruth had coerced me into a clarity I might never have sought or achieved on my own. I saw it there in the brown enclosure of the newspaper restaurant, with that shaft of light alchemizing Ruth's hair.

"I think," I said, "that Gene has a vision. If he finds the language to express his vision, he will be a big success. People want to believe what Gene has to say. Even if it's untrue, even if it's sentimental, people want to believe it."

"What is it that they want to believe?" Ruth asked.

"That there is a special destiny intended just for them. If they arrange the circumstances of their lives just right, they will achieve that special destiny. I think that's what Gene believes, and because he believes it it comes across in his play."

"Do you believe it?" she asked.

"No, but that doesn't matter. Gene does."

Ruth didn't have to tell me that she believed what Gene believed. What was this lunch all about if not just that?

But she had found the equivalent of a confession. She reached out and touched me on the hand—a soft, sealing touch.

94

12

CHRISTMAS AT THE Strausses'. Roast goose, *stollen,* and the *Messiah.* Present were old friends and new friends (me). The Zeiglers, the Obersts, the Strausses, Ernst Mueller, Saul Klein.

I had never celebrated Christmas except through a window-pane or a radio program. What did the Kleins have to do with Christmas? I hadn't even celebrated Chanukah. Abe Klein was not a man for any season except the one that prevailed perennially in his underground igloo. Of course I felt deprived observing Christmas from the outside. My whole generation of Jewish kids felt deprived seeing all that ho-ho and tinkling merriment fly into and out of other homes.

What was celebrated in the Strauss triangular living room was a composite holiday, with a little of this and a little of that and a great deal of Anna Strauss and George Friedrich Handel. There was a smallish tree decorated with silver tinsel, candles, and *pfeffernüsse.* And presents. Even presents for me. A necktie and a copy of Shaw's plays. I had brought the Strausses an album containing two Schubert quartets. I had heard Anna say that Mozart and Bach were universal in their genius, but that Schubert was supreme in chamber music. She clasped her hands and murmured beatitudes when she opened my present.

I was told that Elena Oberst's hair had turned white overnight when her husband was nabbed by the Gestapo. A very handsome woman with tragic eyes. Her husband, Rudi Oberst, had somehow managed to escape, and he and Elena had fled to England in a fishing boat. There had been a daughter who had taken ill and died shortly after their arrival in England. That, I thought, would account for the tragic eyes.

Rudi was cast in the role of hero almost on arrival. Being one of the early escapees—and not Jewish—gave him a distinction that many different groups sought to exploit. Jews, of course, were eager to have the growing nightmare confirmed from non-Jewish lips. Every antifascist organization wished to claim him.

He had been a journalist in Hamburg, and, according to Gene, from whom I received all the information, he was something of an opportunist. True, he had opposed Hitler, and true, he had been grabbed by the Gestapo, but once on these shores he had quickly discovered where the peaches were in the great American orchard. He wrote the same story over and over for newspapers and magazines. He was invited to lecture everywhere. In other words, he had made his courageous and laudable escape into a one-man industry.

There may have been some truth in Gene's account, but it seemed to me that there was also some spite. I pointed out to Gene that the man had to live as best he could. Gene agreed, saying that he didn't mind Oberst living, and living well, but that he didn't have to pursue his luck so pompously.

Max Zeigler, the little man with the blotchy skin and rheumy eyes, had been Gene's father's one-time law partner. His wife, Gretta, was a stout little woman with a matronly smile and practically no English.

Ernst Mueller looked his fierce, aloof self.

There was no formal ceremony at the goose-and-Handel Christmas dinner. Everybody talked a little louder than natural to overcome the *Messiah,* which went on scratchily chorus after chorus. This, I made out, was an indispensable part of the Strauss ritual, like the sounding of the *shofar* on Yom Kippur.

Speaking of sanctity, I did notice something special take place at the "Hallelujah" chorus—a holy hush, or a pantomime of holiness. I made out that this reverence had its source in and emanation from Anna Strauss. She was the point person in this

96

curious devotion. All seemed to defer to her. For some reason, I got the impression that the mute maneuvers in this semireligious ceremony had their origin in another time and place, possibly in Hamburg, when Gene's father was alive and having his clothes made by a Savile Row tailor.

Anna's office was performed with sedate piety, and I took it to be the moment of communion between the filigree lady and the God of Art. I saw nothing wrong with it. I was full of admiration. There was a makeshift religion here, and that came close to my own view of things. I, too, believed that the traditional religions were exhausted, but that religious feelings were not. I, too, believed that piecing together a connection to the Infinite was a necessary, but necessarily individual, enterprise.

A little closer attention revealed cracks in the temple wall. I saw Ernst Mueller put a finger to his pursed lips and concentrate on the porcelain boat of gravy. At one point, he raised his eyebrows and gave a faint, despairing shrug. Max Zeigler looked away at the farther wall, on which there might have appeared to his tumid eyes the apparition of a blue-curtained Ark and its scandalized Torah.

And Gene regarded me with what was by now a familiar expression: that bland, challenging look. What was I making of all of this? What would I have to say about all of this? Was it serious or comic? He challenged me at all times to find a proper face to put on these otherworldly mysteries. I did wonder why *I* was the one so challenged—my adaptability, my discretion—and never the other way.

The "Hallelujah" chorus over, the company broke into their own chorus of German-English chatter.

"Do you celebrate Chanukah in your house?" Anna asked me.

"Not really," I said. "We don't do much celebrating of anything. My grandfather sees to it that I have a ticket for temple on the high holidays. He shames me into going."

"You go for his sake?"

"More or less."

"Not for your own?"

"Not for my own. My father—" But I immediately stopped.

Why bring up that dark side of my life? That was a whole other story. But that story, strange as it was, *was* part of me. I think I was trying to offer it by way of explanation. But of what? My merits and faults? My religious indifference? Or perhaps just to contrast my own raw Bronx tundra to this lush, European arboretum.

"Your father is not religious?" she asked.

"Not really."

"And you are not."

"I guess I'd have to say no, not in any conventional sense."

"In some other sense?"

"Maybe. I don't like the answers I've been given, but I'm uneasy about no answers at all."

Anna's bracelets gave off a tiny jingle as she reached out and touched me on the arm. She was a contact person. If possible, meanings were always completed with a touch. "Do you know," she said, "I would have put this arm in fire that this would be your answer."

"What answer?"

"The uneasy part. I could tell this about you. For some people, the whole question can be put aside, but for others, like you, people who—ach!—*wie sagt man?*"

"Sensitive," Gene supplied smilingly from across the table.

"Yah! Sensitive." Anna gave Gene a look of soft complicity, then turned back to me. "Not to be satisfied with the answers, but unsatisfied with no answers. I am that way, too. Do you know what I think? I think it's more important to look for God than to be too certain of His presence. Because a god is needed, a god is there. People who must discover for themselves are the artists."

"Have you made your discovery?" I asked her.

"Oh, I think so."

Handel was through and Schubert took his place. Then there was coffee and wine. The guests left the table and took seats elsewhere in the room. Rudi Oberst sat beside me on the sofa.

"What did you think of a typical German Christmas?" he asked me.

"Was that typical?"

"Oh, yes. Except for the music. That is the Anna touch. Anna tells me that you are much interested in politics. I would like to ask you, if you don't mind, what do you think of the chances for peace?"

I couldn't imagine where Anna had gotten the idea that I was much interested in politics, unless Gene had told her. Certainly I hadn't.

"I don't think there's any chance of peace," I said.

I was sure that Rudi's question was just a lead-in to conversation, so I was a little surprised by the genuinely disappointed look in his eyes. Perhaps he expected Americans to be more optimistic. Perhaps in his lectures he was promulgating the real possibilities of peace. Those eyes, incidentally, were not quite right. They were off the horizontal, one eye lower than the other. It might have been a congenital defect, or an accident, but I naturally wondered whether he'd been messed up by some of Hitler's merry pranksters. I was always seeking clues to the German nightmare. Even in its victims. Something a little perverse in this. I'm ashamed to say now that I examined those refugees for evidence of something, I didn't know what, something that might have triggered the horror.

"I'm very sorry to hear you say so," said the brave journalist who had escaped Hitler's clutches. He had an attractively deep voice. I could understand his popularity as a lecturer. "What makes you so sure?" he asked.

By this time, I could tell the difference between the refugees who tried to capture the American idiom and those who pasted the new language over the old, like posters on a Paris kiosk. Rudi was definitely among the former.

"All those airplanes and tanks," I said. "They must be dying to use them."

"Of that I have no doubt," Rudi said. "Dying to. But they can be persuaded that the cost may be too high."

"The cost can't be too high," I said.

Rudi looked puzzled, as well he might. It was a cryptic remark. He said, "Oh, believe me, my dear young man, the cost can be too high, even for Herr Hitler. Permit me to assure you of this. England and France made him hesitate, but if the United States were to add its voice, make it unmistakably clear that it would move against a warring Germany, you would soon see a change in attitude."

I was flattered that this brave freedom-fighter would take my words so seriously. For some reason, the thought of Gene's father passed through my mind. This man knew Strauss *père*. They were all friends in the old country. I had been thinking of my latest theories about Hitler, and then recalled that they were the theories of Gene's father.

"Logically, you're right," I said, "but what does logic have to do with it? It's the cost that Hitler's after. He wants to send the whole world to its death before his own. The cost is the purpose."

Rudi Oberst reared back and stared at me out of those misaligned eyes. A Picasso look. Two levels of consideration. I had pushed a button and I could almost feel the current.

"Where did you hear such a thing?" he asked, his voice so low that it broke and rattled.

"It seems pretty obvious," I said, coasting on my conceit. "Do you seriously believe that Hitler will stop short of war?"

No, of course he didn't, but being a decent human being he refused to admit it. One mustn't succumb to such a belief. He looked at me as if I were the warmonger sabotaging any chance of peace.

"Do you know what I think?" he said, sadly shaking his head. "I think this war will come because so many believe it will come. This is the one country that can prevent its coming, if it would only speak with one clear voice."

"But this country doesn't speak with one voice," I said, suddenly aware of a thin edge of hostility in myself. It seemed to me that this man was criticizing his sanctuary for not being a little more like the country he had fled. After all, it was *Germany*, the *Germans*, who threw flowers at the beast, yelled themselves hoarse at the sight of his ridiculous face. Why hadn't *they* spoken with one voice? "This country," I said, "has a Congress, a president, and a Supreme Court."

Rudi nodded his head and took my arm in a surprisingly strong grip. His eyes were grieving, as if he were all of despairing Europe shaking all of somnolent America.

Wake up! Wake up! The luxury of your democratic ways will be paid for in oceans of blood!

"Suppose," Gene said later, taking my arm in a much gentler grip, "I were to mention in the first act that Carl is living in a dormitory, that he is only visiting Rena."

I nodded. "That should take care of it," I said. "Incidentally, how did they meet?"

Gene bowed his head, as if in surrender to invincible pettiness. "How did you meet Ruth?" he asked.

"You introduced me."

"That's how Carl and Rena met. Somebody introduced them." He shook his head slowly, resignedly. "You know, Saul, sometimes I think you say these things to irritate me. No matter how much I concede, you find something else that needs further explanation. Tell me honestly, do you believe that such trivial information is necessary to an understanding of my play? Do you believe that every little ingredient must be put in, as if you were baking a cake? So much flour, so much sugar." He spoke calmly, but I could see that his nostrils were tense, his eyes smoky. "You don't seem to understand what I have been saying to you. You say why don't you mention this, why don't you mention that, as if you were totally unaware of the structure of the play."

What I was aware of, for the first time, was the intensity of feeling surrounding this little session. I had thought that his general imperturbability was the result of his profound self-assurance, but I began to doubt that self-assurance. Clearly my niggling demand for details bothered him. It smudged the purity of his mystical dream.

"You're right," I said. "I can see that the Klein recipe is going to ruin your cake. For chrissake, pay no attention to me." That almost satisfied him. But it was no substitute for spontaneous acclaim. That was still missing. Looking for a diversion, I said, "Speaking of Rena-Ruth, why isn't she here?"

"Here? Ruth? Why should she be here?"

"I don't know. I thought that since you're such good friends, you might invite her to your family's high-spirited Christmas feast. There are many friends here. *I'm* here. Ruth is a friend, isn't she?"

A dumb, transparent thing to say. Gene shook his head again. He said, "I guess I will never understand how your mind works."

"Now what is so strange about what I said?" I asked, feeling he was making too much of our different minds.

"I guess it never occurred to me," he said. "Christmas is family. Ruth has her own family."

"But you just said that her parents left for California. That her father got a job out there."

Gene gave me a slow, sidelong look, but what flashed between us was electric-quick and full of meaning. He hadn't said that *Ruth's* parents had gone to California; he had said that he might say that *Rena's* parents had gone to California. But suddenly the construct under both our remarks revealed itself as precisely as a blueprint. The floor plan of his mystical cathedral. Borrowing from the here and now to build the timeless and symbolic.

"You are getting things mixed up," he said.

"I often do that," I said. "Has your mother met Ruth?"

"No."

"Okay."

He circled back. "Why do you feel I should have invited Ruth?"

"This is getting stupid," I said. "Tell you what I really feel— I feel a little paralyzed from that punch. What the hell was in it anyway? My head feels full of smoke."

Gene continued his intense, gray-green stare. He could change any subject in a blink when he felt like it, but let someone else try it and he stared like a cat, not letting his attention stray for a second.

"It would have been misconstrued," he said.

"What would?"

"Inviting Ruth here."

"You know best," I said, then added, "Things are less formal in America. Inviting someone to Christmas dinner doesn't have to have lasting consequences."

Klein, the social expert! What did I know? Nothing. I was fishing.

Gene, still calm and catlike, said, "Her family is having its own Christmas dinner."

"Okay," I said—but we both knew that wasn't true. *Her* family had moved to California.

"She could have invited me, you know," Gene said.

That was true, but just barely. There was a delicate, deadly difference between not inviting out of fear of acceptance and not inviting out of fear of refusal.

"Besides," he said, "you don't know my mother."

13

I DIDN'T KNOW Anna Strauss, but there would be new revelations about the filigree lady that evening. What I witnessed I witnessed piecemeal.

The first fragment took place in a dim corner of the foyer. I was on my way to the john, which was to the right as you walked out of the living room. To the left was more foyer and the front door of the apartment. Dim as it was, I could make out the forms of Anna Strauss and Ernst Mueller standing so postured that they might have been figures in a charade. Anna, fingers interlaced in agitation, in supplication; Ernst standing like a symbol of "Pride" in a silent movie. There was something altogether silent movieish about the man. All his postures were exaggerated in one way or another. At the moment I caught sight of them, Ernst had drawn himself up to a haughty stiffness, his patent leather hair ashine even in that quarter-light. They were in mid-dialogue, whispers of mutual accusation, which I caught in fragmentary German: *"Du bist . . . ich bin . . . quatsch . . . ganz gut . . . "* One paralyzed moment, and then I saw Ernst's eyes dart in my direction. I scurried to the bathroom.

A scene taken in the camera's instantaneous eye, but it was enough and more than enough. A *tableau vivant,* fruitcake rich in meaning. Love and betrayal. Lack of love. Imminent betrayal. Mistaken assumptions. Or could it have been the rent? *Quatsch,* as Ernst said. Not a chance. I could recognize pathos when I saw it. These glimmerings were an Arabian Nights fantasy compared to any dull exactitude. I preferred ambiguities, wanted to play with them. This was Gene's mother, the kind and gracious priestess of the Temple of the Arts. Were there dark, perfumed chambers in the temple's cellar?

They were gone by the time I came out of the bathroom. I returned to the living room. There I saw Anna talking to Mrs. Zeigler, one broad, peasant hand held high on her chest, fingers splayed. She might have been pouring out her mistreated heart to a friend, but I didn't think so. She was probably saying some ordinary thing, but I would have staked my life that her nerves were still vibrating from the foyer scene. Gene was talking to tall, handsome, white-haired Mrs. Oberst. Ernst Mueller was nowhere in sight. Had he retired to his atelier, paid or unpaid-for?

A change of mood. Relaxed nostalgia. More German being spoken. Talk of old times and old places. Even Gene had lapsed into German while speaking to Elena Oberst, something I rarely heard him do. All the German I had heard from Gene were one- or two-word translations. There was no wish to exclude me— these were scrupulously polite people—but they were lost in a spell, lost in their lost world. I looked out the curious Strauss window for some minutes, seeing appropriate Christmas colors reflected on the glassy black surface of the Hudson. I decided it was time to leave.

I made my way to the room where the coats were stacked, and came upon yet another scene. Anna Strauss was sitting in a white wicker chair, her fingers interlaced, as in the foyer. She was crying. Gene was standing by the window, two fingers playing at the window shade, peering outside at the darkness while listening to his mother's tearful words. I hadn't noticed before how white the room was. White walls, white curtains, white bed covers—clearly Anna's room—everything bone-white, except for the motley mound of coats on the bed. I mumbled an apology, turned to leave . . .

"Come in, come in," Gene said, almost impatiently, as if he had been expecting me and I had been overlong in coming. He continued to hold the window shade apart with two fingers. I wondered if he was trying to let some night into this weepy whiteness.

More strange than the scene itself was the Strauss acceptance of my presence in it. Anna didn't appear at all embarrassed. She looked at me with tear-pregnant eyes in which I didn't detect the slightest hint of shame. This was the second time this evening I had inadvertently come upon her distress (I was sure she had seen me in the foyer), but it didn't seem to matter to her. She was crying—well, she had good reason to cry!

I thought of myself as a comparative stranger. I thought that my relationship to the filigree lady hadn't ripened to the point where she could comfortably reveal her sorrows before me. But that, apparently, was my prejudice. She felt differently—and, even more interesting, Gene didn't seem to mind. It was all right for me to see. The meanings here were only half revealed in the time-lapse whiteness. Was something expected of me? If so, what? Perhaps my intrusion was not an unwanted one. Perhaps they had been speaking about me just before my entrance, and now I wasn't being intrusive *enough*. Perhaps everything connected to the Strausses was imbued with magic and tragedy— semimagic, semitragedy—things out of sight, things I could not yet understand but would understand when my education was complete.

"Are you leaving?" Anna asked, quaveringly.

"I thought—yes—I am."

"I'll walk with you," Gene said, coming away from the window.

I thanked Anna for everything, and she raised up slightly in her chair, confusing me, until I realized she was offering her cheek to be kissed. Hesitantly, I did so, taking away with me the poignant fragrance of perfume and tears.

We took a long walk to the Jerome Avenue line. Gene hadn't put on an overcoat, but had wrapped himself in an outsize muffler, round and round, European fashion. He seldom wore an overcoat. We walked past the American Indian Museum, then turned and began walking through an unfamiliar part of the city.

Gene pointed out that we were passing the Audubon cemetery. I'd never even heard of the Audubon cemetery. Was Mr. Audubon buried there? So much I didn't know. I had no other language but English, and that I used so blunderingly, always looking for words, like a kid searching his pockets for the necessary five-cent fare. Gene knew English and German and French. My four years of high school French had left me with a handful of phrases and the uncomfortable memory of irregular verbs. I knew nothing of French symbolist poets, Victorian novelists or what really went on between men and women. My training had been in the primitive simplicities of a miserable marriage. How could I ever manage the subtleties of love and sex? How did this friend of mine manage to acquire so much certainty about everything? I didn't even know where we were in my own city, this section that even in darkness had a look of faded splendor, of abandonment.

"My father," Gene was telling me, "had an affair with Elena Oberst . . . "

The woman leaped brilliantly to mind. I had exchanged some words with Mrs. Oberst that evening. She had asked me about my family, and she had smiled so mournfully when I told her I had two older sisters. She had asked me where I stood in age, and I had told her I was the youngest, which produced another such smile, as if she were drifting through a melancholy mist.

So that was why Rudi Oberst had recoiled so strangely when I spoke of Hitler's death design! It was not the first time he'd heard that Wagnerian theory. He'd heard it before from Albert Strauss, father of Eugene. The cuckolding ghost had come back to kick him in the balls that Christmas evening. What a curious bunch of people! Why were they all together with such a history to share? How little I knew! What variety in human experience I had yet to discover!

"Did your mother know they were having an affair?" I asked.

"Of course."

"What do you mean 'of course'? How would you know? Did someone tell you?"

"I heard them speak of it."

"And yet your mother seems so friendly with Elena."

"Doesn't seem—*is*—and was friendly at the time." He turned to me in the empty, echoing street and (I'm almost sure) smiled his challenging smile. "You find that difficult to believe, don't you?"

"Yeah, I do. You bet I do. I find that very difficult to believe."

"I know you do," he said. "You find difficult to believe anything you haven't seen or experienced yourself. You must get over that. It's too limiting a way to be. It will hurt you as a playwright."

I didn't like his judgment on my mind or character. Our imaginations might work in different ways, but that didn't make his automatically superior. And yet I smarted with the knowledge that no matter which way our imaginations worked, his accusation was true. I did cast out into the darkness of disbelief or damnation anything that didn't fit into the small circle of my experience. The incentive to accept the unfamiliar had to be great. I had an almost blind tendency to reject ways of being too much unlike my own —unless, as in the case of Strauss, there was a potent charm leading me on. Still, I resented. I resented the casualness of his observation.

"Anyway," I said, "who's a playwright?"

"You are," he said. "You have a near perfect ear for the rhythms of speech and a good instinct for the rhythms of feeling. But you must broaden your range of human possibility. You must put your talent to the largest possible use."

"Like what?"

"Like dealing with things that will have meaning for people unlike your own family, for people outside the Bronx."

"*You're* outside the Bronx," I pointed out.

"Exactly," he said, "and that's why I'm able to judge. I have a professional interest. I know that you have the potential to see far beyond what you allow yourself to see. I admire what you do, how cleverly you handle your people, but their lives are so pathetically small."

I could have slugged him! Grabbed him by the arm, jerked him around, and slammed my fist into his cool, pale, arrogant face! How dare this greenhorn speak to me like that! I would teach him a lesson! I would! I must find the right words! Please, God, give me the right words!

"You know something? You take yourself much too goddam seriously! For crying out loud, people are dying by the millions, millions more are going to die and you talk about your professional eye! How can you take yourself so seriously?"

That wasn't at all what I wanted to say!

Gene didn't respond immediately. We continued walking

downhill on a cold, moonlit street. Here and there I saw Christmas wreaths winking electrically in anonymous windows. I saw that we were approaching a bridge, another river. That must be the East River, since I was aware that the Hudson was at our backs throughout this walk. Our footsteps seemed to be the only living sounds in the entranced city. Where was everybody? It wasn't all that late. Not yet midnight. But this was Christmas Eve and Christians everywhere were celebrating the birth of their Savior, and I was walking with my friend Gene Strauss, deeply contemplating a birth of another kind. I was contemplating my own birth. Despite my hostility, my sudden rage against Gene, I knew I was being urged into the world by his casual obstetrics.

"Who, then, shall I take seriously?" Gene asked. "Shall I take Hitler seriously?"

"Hitler can take everything away from you, your property and your life! That's serious!"

"That's not serious," he said. "Hitler will leave nothing behind. He's a mere catastrophe. My own life is the most serious thing I know because it's the only thing whose seriousness I can measure." He waved a hand, dismissing the mere catastrophe of Hitler, turning to the seriousness of his life. "Listen," he said, "Ernst Mueller is moving out."

"What do you mean?"

"Exactly what I say. He's moving out of the apartment. He's going to live elsewhere."

"I saw him and your mother talking in the foyer," I confessed. "Your mother seemed upset."

"She and Ernst were lovers."

Was he telling the truth? Was this a game being played solely to keep me bewitched? I couldn't take in all this royal intrigue. I may be undergoing rebirth, but there were still vestiges of my Bronx self giggling at what I'd been told.

"Why is he leaving?" I asked.

"I think he's found a more generous mistress," Gene said. "Maybe he just wants to get out. The difficulty, you see, is that I must move out too."

"What!"

"I must have a place of my own."

109

"My God, *now!* I mean, *why?*"

He looked at me as if I'd made another of my overrationalized observations. But I wasn't being critical—just shocked. How could he do such a thing at such a time? To his *mother!* For chrissake, *I* worked at home—that is, did my writing at home—and that's what he was talking about, wasn't it? And the atmosphere in the Klein igloo was a hell of a lot less conducive to creative labor than the Strauss keep on the Hudson.

I thought of Anna, High Priestess of the Temple. I restored the image of her in the foyer, her little minaret of hair, her tears. Jesus, what did these guys want!

"It's necessary now that I be on my own," Gene said.

"But the *money!*"

"I have the money. I got a bonus check for five hundred."

Five hundred! Lou Siegal's notion of Christmas largesse was one-tenth of that, exactly!

"But with Mueller gone . . . ?"

"Exactly," he said. "The pressure would be increased."

I shook my head. I didn't understand. I tried to point out the moral kink in his reasoning. He shook *his* head and said, "Why don't *you* move in?"

Now I did laugh. Out loud. He didn't see what was funny about it. I, too, needed the separation from family.

"I don't have the confidence in my talent that you have in yours," I said. "Besides, wouldn't I be taking on the problems you're running away from?"

"Not at all. You could work there free from any family distractions. You would have the best of conditions."

"Yeah, then why are you leaving? Why did Mueller leave?"

"With Mueller it's a simple mercenary thing," Gene said. "As for myself—simply—the involvement is too great."

"What—" I began, wanting to know what kind of "involvement" he was talking about.

"Now listen," Gene interrupted, "surely you must see that the time has come for you to get away from that family of yours."

"No," I said, "I don't see that it's surely necessary."

"You can't begin your real life living there," he warned with quiet emphasis.

We were at last at the Jerome Avenue line. I was still stomach-full and punch-beclouded. There were lurid lights flashing in my head. Intimations of depravity. Intimations of freedom. Such wondrous people, the Strausses! What was behind Gene's suggestion that I take his place in his mother's house? Invitation to maturity? Was he thinking of me? Or of himself?

What did I know? What did I know?

With that familiar refrain, the significance of Gene's words at last penetrated my consciousness. Again he was so right. How had the truth of it escaped me for so long? Of course I couldn't begin my adult life until I had escaped from the Klein wasteland!

14

RANKS OF GERMAN troops parading past elevated stands. Hitler a crazy-eyed impresario, shooting out his arm, orchestrating delirium. Mass delirium. Massive swastikas. Massive precision. The cameras pan away and the long view of mass and precision stretches as far as the eye can see. A sea of marching precision.

In another set, a tall Englishman with a different kind of mustache and a Homburg. In still another set, a squat, plump Frenchman, bald and fussy-looking. The Englishman looks fussy too, but in a British way.

Chamberlain and Deladier boarding and getting off planes, running to Berlin or Berchtesgaden, accompanied by other fussy men in dark suits. Hitler's entourage coruscates with snappy uniforms, medals, braid, batons. What would the democracies use to oppose the beast? The photograph I remember of the French military was a soldier leaning against a pillbox of the Maginot Line, smoking a pipe. The photograph of the British might consist of a squad of pathetic civilians drilling on a country road, spades for rifles. What did Hitler have to be afraid of? England and France would capitulate, Hitler would take over Europe, the anti-Semites of America would form a third party, win election, and Saul Klein would emigrate—where? Canada? Palestine?

And would Saul Klein climb the steps of the White House, gun secreted?

Weekly bouts of schizophrenia. On certain hours of the day, or certain days of the week, I was the young salesman going to buying offices, meeting his dashing friend Eugene Strauss, or his dashing friend's lover, Ruth Prager, and then doing all the exhilarating things that young men do. Dinners in below-street-level Italian restaurants. Discussions about art and life, about his play and my play, while all the time taking in the stores and streets and girls in the city. Being in love with the girl who was in love with my friend. What could be more cosmopolitan, more life enriching? But in other hours of the day, or in other days of the week, I was the spiritual companion of Herschel Grynszpan, imprisoned in the world from birth by the accident of parentage, waiting for my death before having begun to live.

Although the Nazis were liars by nature and by design, I still examined myself for stigmata. Was I a bourgeois capitalist? I was making twenty-five dollars per week draw against commissions. Was I part of the international Jewish banking conspiracy? I had a savings account with less than five hundred dollars in it. Was I a lascivious corrupter of racially pure girls? Given a magical release from my inhibitions, I would have been glad to apply myself; but so far I had two live whores and an overpopulated underworld of phantoms to my credit. Was I a Bolshevik-atheist-apprentice Elder of Zion? I openly professed admiration for the Soviet Union and Karl Marx, but my real hero was Franklin Delano Roosevelt. As far as God was concerned, I had once walked on the beach in the Rockaways on a moonlit night and had it out with God. Either he would show me a sign and save a well-disposed petitioner from the void or we were quits. He showed no sign and we were quits . . . except that I still continued to examine the grotesque world in the light of some divine intention, endlessly playing with possibilities of that intention, even if it was manifestly harmful to man.

When the encroaching horror allowed me to, I enjoyed life. Actual and potential pleasures were opening up like flowers in the sun. I had the necessary bucks. Laughable in the light of my international banker-atheist-capitalist tag, but things were so cheap in those days. Gene and I and sometimes Ruth saw every play that was seriously offered as "drama." I have pages in my scrapbook pasted with the playbills of *Abe Lincoln in Illinois, Danton's Death, Hamlet, Oscar Wilde, Our Town* and *You Can't Take It with You.* There were movies—oh, a forest of movies!—these truly for pennies, if you went to the side-street movie houses that honeycombed the city. *Grand Illusion* and *The Citadel*—I think we saw each of these about three times apiece. Gene thought that the actor Robert Donat had the true cachet of the artist: a slight twist of the mouth, a nasal intonation. Gene said that when he reached the point of influencing producers he would insist that the leading players in his productions have some distinctive quality that set them apart. *Four Daughters* with John Garfield and Claude Raines. Both these actors qualified for Gene's pantheon. The foreign films. *Carnival in Flanders* and *Mayerling.* Charles Boyer, another charismatic star. And *Pygmalion* with Leslie Howard and Wendy Hiller . . .

But when I was by myself, I took a holiday from seriousness, culture, uplift, professional note taking. Then I went to see the *infra dig* movies. The Marx Brothers, Fred Astaire and Ginger Rogers, Gary Cooper, Clark Gable. *Marie Antoinette* with Norma Shearer and Tyrone Power, which Gene had shrugged away with the word *kitsch.*

"What's *kitsch?*"

"Something that pretends to be more than it is."

Was that translation angled to reflect me? Was I pretending to more than I was? Of course I was. I was pretending to talent I wasn't at all sure I had. I was pretending to knowledge I didn't have. I was pretending to courage I didn't have. I was pretending to ambition I didn't have. I was pretending to sophistication I didn't have. The talent of the impromptu playwright who picked it up at the mere suggestion of a friend. The knowledge of the uneducated who frantically gathers a handful of books, stuffs his reading in one pocket, hoping that it will divert attention away from all the empty ones. The ambition of the sycophant, who butters up his buddy by imitating his interests and style. The sophistication of the debonair man in love who becomes the good

114

friend when he can't be the gratified lover. The courage of the dreamer fantasizing the escape of Herschel Grynszpan.

But wasn't there something to be said for a guy who would put himself out on so many limbs? Was that *kitsch* or a true flight of the heart?

15

GENE FOUND AN apartment in the Village, naturally. A top-floor apartment. It had casement windows that opened onto other rooftops, from which one could get a view of the midtown towers. It was as near to Paris as one could get on this side of the Atlantic. The successful salesman of Oriental imports moved into the bohemian life as easily as he'd moved out of his mother's apartment. He was getting on with the vital business of being Eugene Strauss.

And I was getting on with the business of being Saul Klein—which meant counting on Gene's friendship, playing my covert game of love, insulating myself more and more from the cyclic Klein freezes, writing my play and trying to keep my boss tractable with a daily show of energy and enthusiasm.

Mr. Siegal's business tapered off in the postholiday weeks to the point of extinction. As he had predicted: drop dead time. Nobody wanted to see salesmen. It was time for returns, taking inventory, lying low and laying off. I wouldn't have minded that. The commissions I'd earned would easily see me through a couple of months of idleness. I had, literally, hundreds in the bank. I doubt it would be possible to make anyone under the age of fifty appreciate the leviathan look of "almost five hundred." When I think of that ancient bankbook with its grandiose $482 (or whatever) on the last line, I have restored to me a money-proud security that no amount of dollars could buy today.

I suggested to Mr. Siegal that I take a month off. No pay, of course. Live off my fat.

"You want to catch up on your schoolwork?" he asked.

I hesitated, decided to lie. "Yes," I said, not wanting to blow the perfect cover of my other life.

"Listen, I've got nothing against that," he said. "I like a young man should try to improve himself—but—a whole *month?* A week I can understand. Even two weeks. But a *month.*"

Mr. Siegal looked troubled. I wasn't sure whether he approved or disapproved of my continuing pursuit of a profession. It seemed to me there was a touch of disappointment, despite the disclaimers. It came to me for the first time that Lou Siegal had plans of his own concerning me. This short, square man with tufts on either side of his polished crown had become more of an enigma than a platitude. He was equally predictable and unpredictable. I saw him as the latest legatee in a long line of squat survivors, near to the ground because there was less exposure that way. Not without humor, because humor is the yeast in the bread of tears. Absolutely no-nonsense about his business. If art was sacred to Anna Strauss, business was sacred to Lou Siegal, and perhaps in the same way—a needed talisman against the terrors of mortality. A mighty fortress was a man's business.

"Tell me the truth now," he said. "Just what do you want a month off for?"

"Not to be in your way," I said.

"Did you hear me complain you were in my way? I'll tell you the truth, Mr. Klein, I don't completely trust this month off. You're not the kind of boy who takes a month off to do nothing. If you want to take a vacation, why don't you go to Miami Beach and get some sunshine? Frankly, I think you got something else on your mind. You thinking of going back to school full-time? Or maybe looking around for another job? Hah? Did I guess right?"

Altogether too highly charged for the Lou Siegal I knew. It made me cautious. I didn't believe he believed what he was saying. But if it was only a ruse, if he had something else on his mind, then I must tune my registering devices finely. I was aware that there had developed between us this form of mind play, a joust-

117

ing, not unlike the contest that went on between Gene and me. Different content but similar form.

I said, "Mr. Siegal, you can be sure that I'm not looking for another job. Why should I? I like working for you. You took a chance on me, and I'll never be able to tell you how much I appreciate that."

Mr. Siegal nodded, grunted, made a low, deprecating ball of sound. "Gah!"

"As for Miami Beach," I said, "to tell you the truth, Mr. Siegal, I'm a city boy. I'd rather spend my time here than in Miami Beach."

"You read too many books," he said.

"Not too many. Just enough."

He gave his side tufts another little massage, then said, "Do you mind if I talk to you seriously?"

Hadn't he been serious up to now? "Of course not," I said.

"All right, I'll be straight with you and say right out that it makes me a little nervous, this business of wanting to wander around the city doing nothing." *(My God! My own father had never asked me once in my whole life what I did with my time!)* "You're still going to night school studying accounting? Fine. No objections. Accounting is a good thing to know. You've fallen behind in your schoolwork, you want to catch up? This too I can understand. But I have a feeling that isn't the whole story. I have a feeling that this time off is for a look around. Greener pastures. This *too* I can understand. Why not? I looked around for opportunity when I was your age. But I want you to know something, Saul. This business doesn't look like much now, but I happen to know there's a future here. It's growing. I have ideas for the future. And you can have a future here, too, if you want. Not just a seasonal future but a year-round future. It's neither here nor there, but the fact is I have no sons. Like I told you, two daughters. My youngest daughter, Harriet, is nineteen. This is Harriet . . . "

Lou picked up the framed photograph from his desk and pushed a stubby finger at the girl posed to the left of Mrs. Siegal. The one on the right was Sylvia, already married. I had met the still-life, color-tinted Siegals many times in passing, but this was the first formal introduction.

118

I feel much differently about such things now. I find nothing funny in the human dilemma. I did then. Funny or contemptible. And I remember how contemptuous I was of such gross manipulation in the delicate area of love. Arranging things between young people was a coarse and ludicrous practice, smacking on the *shtetl.* Any girl who would lend herself to such a practice was a pathetic creature to begin with, utterly devoid of the shimmer and mystery that generates love.

"Mr. Siegal—"

"I know, you got a girl friend."

"Well—"

"Look, I'm not surprised. I'd be surprised if you didn't. You're a nice-looking young man, you got a good head . . . " He returned to the photograph on the desk, wagged a finger at it. "If this girl had any idea of the conversation we were having, it would be the end of me. A year at least before she would talk to me. A very proud girl." He held a hand on his chest. "Just between us, as men, I tell you that this is a very attractive girl, a talented girl."

Now he held up both hands, his case made. He had nothing more to say about Harriet. His remarks about his daughter had nothing to do with his remarks about the business. "But I'm telling you, Saul, this business is going to grow. I already have my eye out for a bigger place. My bank is ready to lend me—I won't mention a figure, but I think you would be surprised at the figure . . . "

I don't recall that he offered me, or promised me, a piece of the business, but he did color in rose clouds on the horizon. He didn't want me to be idle. If I wasn't out selling, I could busy myself in the place. I could acquaint myself with the books. His nephew would be happy to show me. And, of course, there would be an increase in salary commensurate with a new status in the business. He hadn't settled on a figure yet, but something near fifty a week. What did I think?

I thought it was generous and said so. I said I would certainly want to give such a fine opportunity serious consideration. I thought it was a signal, but I didn't say so. There was something to think about here. A strong indication of how my life could go. I asked Mr. Siegal if he minded my continuing night school for the present, seeing all the more clearly a need to camouflage the important enjoyments of my life. Of course he didn't mind my continuing night school. How a man spent his evenings was his own affair.

"And listen," he concluded, "you got a girl friend, fine. God bless her and God bless you. I don't interfere in private matters. But if you're not engaged—and frankly it would be stupid at this point in your life to be engaged, your future unsettled—if you're not engaged, then it wouldn't hurt to call up Harriet, go to dinner, see a show. If she knew—" Mr. Siegal cut off that dreadful speculation, shaking his head. He shrugged. "All I'm asking," he said, "is that you give some consideration to what I'm saying."

"I'm telling you the threat is immediate and serious," Gene said. "Don't treat it lightly. Don't close your eyes and hope it will go away."

"My eyes are wide open, and I'm not treating it lightly," I said. "So what shall I do about it?"

"Start looking around for another job."

"Oh, Christ!"

"You're an experienced salesman now. Experienced salesmen can always find a job."

"Well, if you don't mind, I'd rather not go through that agony right now. I'm making good money with Lou."

A faint smile touched Gene's lips. "Well, perhaps you'd like to consider being the crown prince of the Siegal dynasty."

"Not funny."

"Or work out a strategy."

"What strategy?"

Gene's strategy was at once simple and skewed. The same thought had crossed my mind, but in a different way. Gene strongly counseled that I not let silence cover the situation. It would be resented. I must take the initiative. Tell Lou Siegal that I was thinking about the opportunity he was offering. Thinking and thinking. I must let Mr. Siegal see that I was a man of scruples. There was this other girl. Known her for five—make it six —years, and as Mr. Siegal would be the first to appreciate, there is a decent way of doing things and there is the way of the swine.

Saul Klein was no swine. Time and consideration were needed. The way of decency . . . "If you are doing the decent thing now," Gene so cleverly rounded out, "think what confidence Mr. Siegal will have concerning his daughter. When the time comes, you can make whatever move seems right. Like finding another job. Like joining the Siegal clan. In any event, you'd have at least a year."

This Machiavellian design was taking shape in Gene's new digs in the Village. I would have been full of the wormholes of conscience living here, but Gene acted like a wealthy orphan rather than what he was: the sole offspring of a distractedly adoring mother in Washington Heights.

And Ruth?

Every time I visited Gene, I looked for evidence of the fabulous rite. I found it. A bottle of nail polish in the medicine cabinet. Food in the refrigerator I knew damn well hadn't been prepared by Gene. A book on one of the end tables I was certain Gene wouldn't have bought on his own. Or borrowed. It wasn't his kind of book. *The Yearling.* Seeing it there had a curiously visceral effect on me. I had read that poignant novel of the season, and I took its presence in Gene's apartment as some kind of appeal, like the curled fawn itself, soft-eyed and vulnerable.

"Maybe you've got a point," I said. "Since there's no one else, maybe I should think of attaching myself to the Siegal dynasty. I'll date Harriet Siegal. I've seen her picture. She looks nice and *zaftig.* In for a penny, in for a pound."

Gene gave me a skeptical look. I assumed he was being skeptical about my intention toward the Siegals, but on second reflection I realized he was commenting on that "no one else." I wondered if confession time was drawing close.

He said, "I wonder if we could get away for a moment from the fascinating subject of Lou Siegal and his marriageable daughter."

"Try."

"I've finished my play," he announced—and after a fearful pause added—"and there's a group that's interested in putting it on."

I didn't doubt it for a second. It had a ring as inevitable as the next day's headlines. I congratulated him. I said with as much grace as envy would allow that I was glad to hear it.

An odd residue left from the emotional boil of his success. That "group." Where did it come from? There was nothing clandestine about Gene's mentioning such a group, but it gave me a sudden glimpse of the hidden side of the Strauss moon. I knew that it was there, of course, but to have it slide into view that way was eerie and arresting. Like any cosmic discovery, it rearranged the universe slightly. It confirmed a busy Gene Strauss, a promoting Gene Strauss, a Gene Strauss who had contacts, who was probably many different things to many different people.

I was reminded of the feeling of that moment some years later when I saw a picture that positioned the insignificant earth in its vast galaxy.

16

ANOTHER ICE AGE had moved into the Bronx. The particulars aren't important. Rose and Abe were in the deep freeze of another fight. They weren't talking. I was the sole courier over the winter wonderland.

"Tell the mother I have no clean socks."

"In the sink, with soap and water, tell him even a monkey could manage for himself!"

Their arctic campaigns were now conducted in near-total isolation. No one around but me, and with my sudden financial independence, my busy other life, there was less and less of me. It may have been for that reason that Rose, in a spasm of despair, invited friends to the apartment. A rare thing at any time, but in the midst of a Klein caper, *unthinkable!*

"An end!" my mother cried. "There has to be an end. He can live like a rat in a hole! I can't!"

So she invited friends, a normal enough thing among normal people, but a dangerous tactic with Abe Klein. Lady friends and their husbands. She would call Abe's bluff. Except that Abe wasn't bluffing. He wouldn't know how to. The friends gathered in the living room, talked, had coffee and cake, looked uneasily around for Abe. (I reconstruct this from subsequent testimony.) So where was Abe? Rose invented a grippy feeling that had come on that Sunday afternoon. He decided to lie down for a while. Maybe he'd fallen asleep. Let him sleep.

123

But in the course of the visit, one of the lady friend's husbands got on the subject of shoes—where to buy the best shoe for the least money, a general subject in those days—and there, like an apparition, was Abe Klein in his socks, one shoe in his hand . . .

"A new kind of heel," he announced. "When it wears out on one side, you turn, and it's like you got a new heel."

Two or three seconds of expanding silence, and then Abe Klein turned on his shoeless heel and left the company for the rest of the evening.

The grotesque incident made Rose rock back and forth in a paroxysm of despair. To have been so humiliated in front of her friends! Only a fiend could have done it! The sight of him framed in the doorway, that recluse, that freak, after refusing to make the commonest gesture of courtesy, standing there like the clown of creation to announce his great discovery! All evening lying in his corner like the friendless rat he was, listening to every word, nothing to draw him into human accord except the subject of a swiveling heel!

"It's all right for you to laugh!" my mother scolded bitterly. "You were not there!"

"I know, I know."

"What is it, Saul?" my mother demanded of my education, my pretense of knowledge. "Please explain it to me."

"I don't know, Ma."

"You must know something about your father. You know so much. I see you writing every night. Tell me."

Anguish that becomes habit is no less anguish. Her cry out of the depths stripped away her daily pretenses and allowed me to see how much violation there was in such incompatibility.

"He can't help himself," I said.

"If he was crossing the street and he saw a car coming, he would help himself," she said. "He would stop. He would run. Why can't he help himself?"

"There's no good reason for it," I tried again, myself groping, myself seeking enlightenment. "I don't think he does these things to torture you. It's himself who's tortured. He's so locked within himself that he can't reach out to another human being. Wife, child, no one. He stops talking to you, to everyone, because he's stopped talking to himself. Everything is frozen."

"And I can go on living with such a person?"

I hadn't realized how close I was to asking the same question. "No," I said.

"So what should I do?"

"You'll never get *him* to leave," I said.

"Don't I know!"

Big Klein conclave. Natalie and Rita were summoned. Abe was confronted with his sins. He must change. The marriage could not go on this way. Even in prison people are allowed relief. They're allowed to see a movie, talk to others. *What is the matter with Abe Klein?*

Abe came charging out of his lair like a polar bear. "You think you'll scare me! Everybody on her side! I got only two hands"— he held them out—"from these two hands she wants I should buy Cadillacs! She tells me what this friend got, what that friend got! I can't make more money than I can make with my two hands!"

"Nobody's talking about money!" Natalie yelled at him.

(I wasn't so sure. It occurred to me that money might be the club Rose used to beat him with for all his other transgressions.)

"You won't make from me a slave!" Abe roared.

"Go to a doctor and find out what's wrong with you!" lashed Rita, frenzied at the prospect of punishment time.

Hopeless, hopeless. He had ceased talking to himself, and therefore could talk to no one else. The roar of his voice was an imitation of the roar of silence in his head. Speech was not a putting together but the jagged pieces of breakage. Seeing it so clearly for the first time, I experienced pity for my father.

"Ma, I want you to pack up some things and come with me," Natalie commanded.

"Go!" Abe thundered. "All! Go!"

And Rose did go. She packed a suitcase and left with Natalie and Rita. I was left alone with my father, my unreachable father, in opposition to whose image I had fashioned my life. I knew it was hopeless, but I felt I must try.

"Pa, would you really be happier living by yourself?"

"I can live by myself! Nobody is going to make from me a slave! Go! You too!"

"I don't want to go anywhere," I said. "I want to talk to you. I'd like to find out what would make life a little easier for you, a little happier. Can you tell me what it is you want?"

He looked at me, mouth open, as if to let in or let out the unspeakable. Nothing came out. Nothing could. There was nothing he could say by way or explanation or mitigation. He was like a man in prison, staring out. Then, in a rush, he stormed to his room and slammed the door.

Two days later, Rose was back. There had been no contact, no reconciliation. She had just come back, and I wonder now whether she had seen something in her freedom more frightening than her life with Abe. Being a burden to her daughters? Or was it that she needed that little separation, that distance, to restore in herself the pity that had tied her to this fugitive?

Abe accepted her return in typical fashion. When he came home that evening and found her in the kitchen, he sat down to his dinner with neither a smile nor a sneer. It was no victory. Dimly he may have understood that he had won in some terribly costly way. The knowledge of this may have moved him in turn to pity.

He didn't change, he wouldn't know how to change; his soul was sealed—a lonely, unapproachable man—but he had been given a new fear to add to all the old ones. Marriage and children may have—*must* have—made him a little susceptible to the possibilities of loss.

Or it may have been *my* moving out, the removal of the last messenger, that revealed to him at last the extent of the wasteland in which he lived.

17

I MOVED OUT because I too could see the absurdity of my life with Rose and Abe. Even Rose had finally fled the ridiculous scene—briefly, true, but she must have known there was no possibility of escape when she had packed her futile suitcase. Her heart must have been withering at the thought of parching others with the drought of her life. But she had taken the step!

And here was Saul Klein still sticking around. What for? What was I? I saw what I was. I was the forlorn, mock-heroic shnook who bangs away at the telegraph key while the Indians are setting fire to the shack. I had been trying to rescue my mother and father from the fate they had made for themselves. I should have known better, even at that age. Rescue was out of the question. You can't talk somebody out of his life condition. Talk is useless. Action—any action—tears off the rotten bandage that conceals a suppurating life.

"Is that room still available at your mother's place?" I asked Gene.

"Mueller's room? Yes, it's still vacant. I told my mother to hold it for you."

"Like hell you did."

"You ask her. No matter. You can move in today."

"How much—?"

127

"You can afford it."

"I don't know what you're being so smug about. It's a question of my needing temporary—"

"I'm not being smug," he said. "You are being absurdly sensitive. I'm glad you're taking this step. Look on it as your true bar mitzvah."

He said "bar mitzvah" like an upper-class Englishman trying out the word just for the exotic feel of it. I understood for the first time the reality of assimilation. I had thought myself pretty much outside the fold, but I was practically a yeshiva *bucher* compared to Gene. His only acquaintance with Jewishness was the savage stigma others had put on him.

I suppose I could have asked my good friend Gene to put me up at his place until I found a permanent place of my own, but I didn't. It had something to do with Ruth. I didn't want to be encroaching on her part-time tenancy. I think it also had to do with that "group" that was going to do his play. I didn't want Gene to think that I was trying to insinuate myself into the new, rich territory of his life. I must never appear to be warming my hands at his fire.

Nevertheless—why *that* room? Simply because it happened to be available? Rooms weren't that hard to find. There's no single answer to it. I might have been wanting to secure the Strauss connection in that way. I might have seen it as a halfway house between the world I was leaving and the world I was entering. Or possibly just the lazy Klein tendency to grab what was available. Or it could have been none of these things. It could have been the build-up of an electrical charge, untraceable as a lightning stroke, cloud to cloud, positive and negative molecules, having to do with parents, substitute parents, filial loyalty, subliminal elements of that perverse human instinct that seeks to go precisely where it shouldn't.

"If you find someone who will be more permanent, then please don't hesitate to rent the room," I said to Anna Strauss. "I can find another place very quickly."

"Yah," she said. "Don't worry. I will give you plenty of notice."

"Eventually, I'll probably move closer to the city," I warned her.

"I understand."

My mother didn't understand at all, or didn't want to. She saw it as heartless abandonment. I who knew what she faced every day of her life was walking out and leaving her to face it alone.

"Natalie and Rita," I said, bringing in my sisters, unfairly, of course, "they don't know?"

"They're married."

That was it. The only acceptable finality, marriage, even if it was lighted by hellfires. I didn't have the heart to point out to my mother that she was married, too. I used another tack.

"I don't know how much time I've got," I said. "There's a war coming. If I was called up, you'd have to accept it. Isn't this better? I want to find out what life is like on my own before it's too late."

"Where? Where are you going?"

"I told you. This friend of mine—Gene Strauss—it's where he lived—there's a room vacant there."

The omission was deliberate. I couldn't tell Rose that I'd be living in a room in Gene's mother's house. I had sketched in the Strausses with the fewest possible lines. My mother daily wished Hitler a Boschian hell for what he was doing to the Jews, but she didn't particularly care for the species of Jew to whom he was doing it. I had no idea where she had conceived her dislike for the German Jews, but she did definitely view them with distaste. They were stuck up, themselves unkind and, despite every evidence to the contrary, had gotten out of Germany with crates of money.

"Where will you eat?" she wanted to know.

"I keep telling you, it's like a boardinghouse. I get breakfast and dinner. Besides, I'll be home, here, at least a couple of nights a week. For all practical purposes, it will be as if I hadn't moved at all."

"Then why move?"

I hesitated, then told her: "Because I'm writing something, Ma. I'm writing a play and I can't write it here."

"Why can't you write it here?"

"Because I have only the evenings to write, and during the evenings you and Pa are either yelling at each other or not talking at all."

"So not talking is good. You won't hear anything."

"No, Ma, it's not good. I hear more when you're not speaking than when you are. Your silence, yours and Pa's, are like an icy conversation at my back. No matter how many doors I close, that icy talk is there. No matter how many sweaters and earmuffs I put on, I can hear that icy talk. It freezes my brain."

How strange that when I finally told off one of the authors of my childhood's bad dream, it should be my mother rather than my father. But we speak to those we can reach, and those we can reach, rightly or wrongly, bear the greater guilt.

For her part, Rose looked at me askance, narrowing her look as she focused on something new in her field of vision. I had brought to her attention something she hadn't allowed herself to see: the possible frostbite of the soul suffered by the Klein children. The fleeting nuances in her eyes were too quick and overlapping for clear definition. Blame into shame into sorrow into helplessness into innocence into defiance.

My father's reaction was typical. "You want to go, go."

Despite all the years of icebound certainty, I still tested the unyielding reality of my father. I asked, "Don't you think it's time for me to be on my own?"

"You earn your own living. You want to move out, I can't stop you."

In hindsight, I see that he was being the realist. In a good Anglo-Saxon family, the father would be encouraging the son's independence. But mine wasn't a good Anglo-Saxon family, and my father's concern was not with the moral problem of my independence but with his own problem of parental responsibility.

"I know you can't stop me, Pa," I said, "but that's not the point. The point is what you think about my getting out on my own."

It was like being on a merry-go-round. We were going nowhere and with a repetitive wobble at the same spot on each circuit. I could try the same question a dozen different ways, and Abe would patiently make his moves away from involvement.

"You earn your own living," he said again, finding nothing in the whole landscape of our years together but that bare branch.

"And you have no opinion one way or the other?" I asked. "Maybe you think it's a good idea, Pa. I mean, if that's the way you feel, I wish you would say so. It would be helpful to me. It might even be helpful to Mom."

"I don't know what you want from me," he complained. "You want to move out, move out. The rent? I'll pay the rent. I paid the rent before and I'll pay it now. You ever went hungry here?"

I was beginning to understand that gesture of his in moments of despair: both hands held out, as if asking to be searched for concealed assets. He had nothing that he hadn't declared, and this applied to moral as well as material goods. But he was never really free of his moments of despair. That's what I understood now. He had only his two hands between himself and the wilderness. If those hands failed him, he would be shoved out and the gates of the city would clang shut.

I said, "Pa, what I'm trying to find out is whether there's anything between you and me other than the rent and food on the table."

He gave me a suspicious, sideways, retreating look. I could see him making for his ice-blue escape hole. In another moment, he would be swimming away in undersea silence. It was a futile inquisition. He would never allow himself to comprehend what I was seeking. My guess was that he was capable of understanding it, but something in the curious economy of his soul cautioned against such investment. And maybe, after all, he knew what he was doing. Maybe things would have been much worse for him, for all of us, if he hadn't been able to maintain that cockeyed emotional balance.

But if he needed a balance, so did I. I had made my final bid, knowing that when I moved out of the Klein apartment I would be saying farewell to my father. Not to my mother. Rose and I

131

would remain bound in the root system that had been allowed to grow, but it was very unlikely that the badly damaged connection to my father would survive the separation.

I was mistaken, however, in thinking the link so tenuous. I would learn that the default of fatherhood could grip the years every bit as tenaciously as its most loving employment.

18

"YOU MUST TELL me exactly what is your schedule," said Anna Strauss, my new landlady. "I will make coffee, but you must help yourself to breakfast. Everything is here. There is bread for toast. There are eggs. There are biscuits. If you wish to have dinner here, you must tell me in the morning. In the evening, you will be undisturbed. You have a nice little desk in your room and no one will disturb you. Yah? I have my radio, which I play very softly. You will not hear."

She was going to be the most discreet of landladies. If she had made mistakes before, she would not make the same mistakes again. There would be no interference, no involvement. The most careful decorum. Everything impersonal.

She kept her implied word. Mornings were solitary. I knew she was up because I could hear muffled morning music coming from her room. That suited me fine. Totally unlike the Klein mornings of kitchen busyness, with Rose bustling over a good breakfast— French toast, *matzo brie,* her own brand of pancakes—but always prepared in the dyspeptic atmosphere of a brewing or continuing battle. Here all was quiet. The kitchen window faced in the same direction as the living room window, and while having breakfast I could enjoy a view of the river, the bridge, the traffic on the West Side Drive, or an occasional steamer riding up or down the river. It confirmed a thrilling reality: I had moved into the *city!* I was at last directly connected to the world I had been seeking.

133

Anna had delivered to her door certain baked goods that I had never heard of, much less tasted. A crumb-topped muffin with blueberries. These were often my breakfast. Or a peasanty dark bread with goose liverwurst or hard yellow cheese. I was sampling other worlds.

Sometimes Anna would appear in her pink peignoir, checking to see if I was managing for myself. On these appearances, she would bring with her a small, fragrant cloud of Mille Fleurs perfume, and after patting things (myself included) either with her eyes or with her hand, she would make a high, trilling noise, a kind of private bird song, wave her hand and return to her room.

The weather had turned miserable, but I felt as if I were experiencing a brand-new, fifth season, one created out of my personal journey rather than the conventional one of the earth around the sun.

Walking to the corner of my new street, I could see the George Washington Bridge and sense how its graceful presence was giving a new dimension to winter, to the city. Imagine seeing the G. W. Bridge the first thing in the morning! My morning view had been, for years, row upon row of apartment houses. Now, if the wind was right, I caught a deep, thrilling, outward-bound river smell.

Everything squeezing together in that winepress of time. Out of the Klein arctic wasteland into the sunny Strauss Arcadia. A play in progress. Ruth of the Golden Diadem. And Mr. Siegal's proposition to consider, to avoid.

Naturally I paid more attention to the family portrait on Mr. Siegal's desk after our friendly chat, particularly to the daughter to the left of Mother Siegal. Mother Siegal herself was a solid chunk of middle-class maternity—impacted neck, thick shoulders, shapeless bosom—as purposeful in appearance as a football player. But not unpleasant. Nor did her marketable daughter, Harriet, appear unpleasant. Quite the contrary. Of course, you couldn't trust photographs, but Harriet seemed to have a generously proportioned mouth, green eyes, bobbed hair. That photograph stays in my mind as a chromatic composition of reds and pinks. Lipstick was a big thing then, and all the Siegal ladies were aflame with it.

I had indicated to Mr. Siegal that I had a girl friend—rather, he had indicated it to me and I hadn't denied it—but the Siegal photograph presented itself each day like a smiling rebuke to my premature attachment. Mr. Siegal said nothing further about it, but neither did he bring me the hoped-for news that Harriet had found herself a bright young intern, please come to the wedding in June . . . you *shmuck!*

Despite my uncertain status, I slipped deeper and deeper into the Siegal business. I was no longer exclusively a salesman. I had become active in other departments. I helped take inventory. I learned how to keep some of the simple machinery in repair. I went over the books with my happy corrupter, Mr. Siegal's nephew, the memory of whose dour face revives in me an inexpungable corned beef and cathouse flavor.

Mr. Siegal marked the progress of my position by asking me in on a conference over the new line he was planning to present in the spring. New packaging, new materials, but essentially the same old junk. What did I think? I thought, of course, that every new number in the line looked like a winner. My immediate plan was to say yes to all of Lou Siegal's plans for the future, knowing it was all a terminal flurry, knowing that the beast was calling all the significant shots in those on-the-edge, not-unhappy, semihallucinated days.

There was yet another snowstorm in March. And buffeting winds. Ice glazed the streets, making it almost impossible to walk. You could attempt a sort of ice-skating glide along the sidewalks, letting the wind take you until you could grab onto a lamppost, a mail box, the side of a building. Then you might propel yourself by a combination arm and leg locomotion.

I was standing on the Thirty-fourth Street corner of Macy's preparing to risk a crossing when a gust took me, led me a crazy-legged foxtrot into the street and sprawled me on my ass, Alpacuna coat and all. An oncoming cab jammed on its brakes, went into a skid, and the left rear wheel passed so close to my head that

I could feel the side of the tire against my hair. Another inch or so and my head would have resembled a mashed melon.

I had been carrying the Remington portable typewriter that Macy's had advertised for $39.50. Perhaps if I hadn't been carrying that eager purchase, I would have been better able to navigate. Were the gods trying to warn me?

By a convolution of thought not too difficult to imagine, my accidental brush with death led me to Herschel Grynszpan, to whom I typed a letter several days later, on my new, undamaged, Remington portable typewriter. I addressed it:

> Herschel Grynszpan
> Prisoner
> Somewhere in Paris
> Paris, France

I suppose I could have gone to the French consulate, or embassy, and asked for more precise information, but I doubted they would have given it to me even if they had it to give. Besides, I liked the message-in-the-bottle approach. If my letter reached him (which I didn't expect), I fancied he would feel that his brave action had gone out to the world on oceanic tides, touching everywhere. I wrote:

Dear Herschel Grynszpan,

I am an American Jew who wishes to express admiration for your courage and comradeship for your cause. I read that you wept when you learned what had happened in Germany as a result of your action. I'm sure you know this, but I will say anyway that the beasts would have found another excuse, and soon, to behave as they did. Words are small comfort, but they are all that I, and millions like me, can give you. I understand what you have done, understand what you lived with before you did it, understand and sympathize with what you are living now. You are in my thoughts. I have a feeling that the shots you fired were only the first of the many that will one day destroy the beast.

I hope this reaches you. I hope someone will translate it for you. I hope you will find some comfort in the knowledge that you are a hero in my eyes and in the eyes of decent people everywhere, Jew or Christian.

> Yours in sympathy and comradeship,
> Saul Klein

I used a carbon to make a duplicate. Read now, it sounds stiff and hortatory. Well—can't be helped. It was probably as effective a thing as could be said to a seventeen-year-old kid in a French prison awaiting trial for murder, contemplating the possible prospect of falling into the hands of the Gestapo. I didn't know how extradition worked, but knowing the Nazis I was sure they would pull every diplomatic string to get their eager hands on Herschel Grynszpan.

I did write the truth, however. There wasn't a day in that end-of-winter season in which I didn't devote some small portion to frail Herschel. I lived with two obsessions. One was Ruth—rather Ruth and Gene, since what I felt for Ruth was linked to what she felt for Gene. My other obsession was the impending war, which was now sealed in the action of German troops marching into dismembered Czechoslovakia. Herschel Grynszpan, because of his act and my response to his act, became the allegory of the impending war. God alone knew how many had been lingeringly tortured or quickly dispatched by this time, or how many were yet to be destroyed, but Herschel personified them all for me.

When possible, I listened to every hourly broadcast of the news. When Hitler marched into Prague, I waited for the joint ultimatum from England and France. When it didn't come, I knew that the war was only waiting for its declaration. The radio reported that Madrid was now calm, that the Spanish Civil War was all but over. Fascism was gloatingly triumphant everywhere. Sooner or later, unless the French guillotined him first, the Nazis would get their hands on Herschel. Sooner or later, the Nazis would get their hands on everything.

Not too many years earlier, I had read pulp magazines like *War Aces* or hardcover serials like *The Boy Allies in Europe*. "The Great War" was of course World War I. The myth of my boyhood. Tales of Allied troops going "over the top" in a hail of machine gun and shellfire, bullets and shrapnel tearing their bodies to pieces. I had arrived at a theory that because of the photographic evidence another war of such dimensions could never happen again. People may be stupid, people may be brave, but the great majority were not insane. War had become insanity. Having experienced the horror once, they would never do it again.

Unfortunately, I had evolved another theory, already mentioned, the one I shared with the Strausses, father and son. Hitler *wanted* war. He wouldn't rest until he had his war, until he had set into motion the necessary business of sending the rest of the world to its death as compensation for his own. And *I* would be in it. The inconceivable would happen, and I would be part of it. That looming reality would be like turning a Sixth Avenue corner and instead of the usual row of buildings seeing a glittering mountain of ice with a knight charging up its slope on his panoplied horse. It was fairy tale in headlines and broadcasts. God, after all, had no special plans for me. He wouldn't alter the way of the world to accommodate my presence—this God in whom I didn't believe.

"I wrote a letter to Herschel Grynszpan," I told Gene.

"To whom?"

"Even you have forgotten the name! The kid who shot that German in Paris."

"I didn't forget his name," Gene said. "You used it in such a peculiar way. As if he were a friend of yours. What do you mean you wrote him a letter? Where did you send it?"

I told him how I had addressed the letter.

"What did you say in the letter?"

I told him what I had written in the letter. We were walking in the Village on a freezing Sunday morning toward the end of March. I don't know why the sound of "March" persists so gently in my mind when all the experience I have of March is as nasty as a heavy chest cold, full of phlegm, mounds of filthy snow heaped against the curbs. It was that sort of day. Gene was dressed in his father's overcoat, the one with the large lapels and the belt in the back. Hatless, of course. Gene never wore a hat.

He thought men's hats looked ridiculous, with their wide, rakish brims. Made everyone look like a gangster.

"Whatever made you do a thing like that?" he asked quietly.

"Nothing *made* me do it. I did it because that poor slob is so much in my mind. I think of the guts it took to do a thing like that."

Gene continued his quiet thoughtfulness for several more seconds, then he said, "It's very unlikely that your letter will ever reach him."

"I know that," I said, "but miracles happen."

"Did you write a return address?"

"Of course."

"Which one?"

"Which one? *The* one. Where I'm living. Your former address."

Gene nodded absently. We continued our walk across Washington Park, came out on Fifth Avenue, continued north. We were going to meet Ruth later. We had arranged a rendezvous on Fourteenth Street. From there we were all going to go to another of Gene's mystery restaurants, this one Greek. Then we were going to see a French movie.

"I wish you hadn't done that," Gene said.

"Why not?"

"Given that return address, I mean."

"For chrissake, why not?"

Gene shook his head slowly. He said, "I hope you never learn the reason why not."

"Come on! What possible difference could it make?"

He gave a slight shrug. He said he couldn't be specific, there was nothing to be specific about, however . . . however, if it had somehow slipped my mind, the Strausses were not citizens of this great, good country. I didn't know that? Well, if I had stopped to consider some of the information I had been given, I would realize that they hadn't been here long enough. But again—so what? Well, what was one to say? Being an insulated American and a stubborn realist, I failed to see what any European would pick up in a second. And what was that? Why, simply, that such a letter would get in the wrong hands. Someone might wish to investigate connections between the sender of that letter and

Herschel Grynszpan. To some eyes, that letter might seem to have a coded message. Did it all sound preposterous? Perhaps—but was there anything more preposterous than what was actually happening in the world? Was there anything more preposterous than the Nazis?

"But you said yourself that the letter was not likely to reach him," I pointed out.

"That's what I'm afraid of," Gene said.

I couldn't—or wouldn't allow myself—to credit Gene's sinister romanticism. Nor did I ever see any reality in his fears. What I did come to see—through the persistently haunting memory of Gene's pale smile—was the kind of scar left on those who had been clawed by the beast.

19

SOMEWHERE JUST WEST of Sixth Avenue, in the Forties, was one of those grimy little buildings that still line the side streets of Manhattan. The top floor was occupied by a theater group calling itself the Forty-Something Street Players. It was a combination acting school and theater. Plays by unknowns were performed by other unknowns. Here was where Gene's play was being bullied together by Leo Shulkin, a six-foot-four, bass-voiced, thumping, tyrannical, generous, unknown impresario.

Everybody was just getting started. Everybody was a Marxist. Everybody was collective in principle and bloodthirsty for individual fame.

Leo Shulkin's ego was easily a match for Gene's. He swallowed people whole and gave them back to themselves a piece at a time. Not Gene. Leo was deferential to Gene. Great respect, or envy, or possibly both. There was something about Gene that Leo couldn't quite define or control. Gene was a kind of royalty, and not knowing how to handle someone that aloof and self-contained, Leo turned to intermediaries. I was one of them. His regard for Gene as a playwright seemed genuine enough. He trumpeted *A Special Destiny* as a fine play, an original play, a play that announced a new, important talent.

"Don't *you* think so?" he demanded of me, his voice sounding like the downhill beginning of an avalanche.

I said I thought so.

141

"Gene tells me that you're writing a play, too," he said.

He had a way of looming up like a tree, standing close, fists on hips. There was nothing casual or oblique about Leo Shulkin. He power-played his height and his voice and his masculinity exactly as a sexy woman would power-play her charms. He even had a scraggly mustache when face hair in America was still somewhat suspect. Villains or the overly suave had mustaches.

"It's not finished yet," I said.

"I know it's not," he said. "I was wondering whether you let people look at things in progress."

"Well . . . "

"I don't blame you," he said. "I'll give you my theory on that. I call it my coffee-can theory. Once opened—pfsss!—you get that special whiff only once, then it's gone. Kept unopened, it keeps its flavor. I'm not urging, just asking. Come here a minute, Saul. Sit down . . . "

Leo commanded in a way that made compliance easy. Pride or individuality seemed not to be involved. An irresistible, impersonal force compelled his own behavior, and if tremendous Leo Shulkin was forced to submit to the Shulkin imperatives, who the hell were puny you to resist?

He wanted to talk to me, frankly, man to man. It was evening and we had just witnessed the rehearsal of the first act of Gene's play. Gene and Ruth were off in another corner of that large, messy, smelly room, talking to a bunch of aspiring, perspiring actors and actresses. Folding chairs strewn every cockeyed way. The windows were the wire-reinforced kind, opaque with a century of filth, probably unopened since the McKinley inauguration, sealed by successive paintings. There was a stage. Air entered through the opened doorway and other crevices common to such firetraps. The predominating smell came from the skillet grease used by the short-order coffee shop on the street level.

Leo surprised me by saying that he'd been trying to get me apart all evening to have these few words with me. He said he knew I was a close friend of Gene's, and being a playwright as well . . . well, I was the ideal person to talk to about . . . well, about certain questions that had come up in his mind about the . . . well, the play . . .

I knew, didn't I, that he, Leo, had nothing but the greatest respect for that guy, Gene, but there was something about Gene that made even the colossal Leo a little wary about a direct approach. Maybe it was Gene's European background. Maybe it was something in the manner of the man. Did I know what he was talking about? Uncertainty in the area of communication. Never knew for sure whether one's words were being received in the way they were intended. Had I ever experienced that with Gene? Had! Well, that was good to know. One didn't want to feel alone in these things. Made one feel a little on the stupid side. All right, then, this is what he wanted to talk about. . . . Did I remember the last act?

One leg crossed over the other, a tree limb of an arm stretched along the back of my chair, his massive head tilted toward mine, his breath incendiary with coffee and onions, Leo Shulkin sought from me the assurance that I too felt that the last scene in the last act was a bit obscure. I agreed that it was a bit obscure, but said, "Why ask me when the man himself is standing right over there?"

Leo didn't even glance in the direction I was indicating. He nodded, squinting at something far beyond the scaling walls. He said, "I did ask the man standing right over there, and do you know what he told me? He told me that the form of his play was circular. The end curved back to the beginning, leaving the audience something to think about when they walked out of the theater. He said a good play never ended in the theater but long after, in the hearts and minds of the theatergoers. What do you think of that?"

"It sounds like something that should be true," I said.

"Right! Agreed! It sounds great. And I believe it, in a way. But it doesn't clear up the fucking mystery for me. I'll tell you something, Saul, just between you and me. I feel that we on the messy side of the curtain owe the audience a sure sense of what we're doing. I'm all for mystification, but the mystifiers have to have some purchase on the mystery, otherwise"—here he rubbed his fingers together in a texture-feeling way—"the whole thing begins to smell of carelessness, and, Jesus, I hate carelessness! Do you know what I'm saying?"

143

Yes, I knew what he was saying, but I also felt I owed Gene my principal loyalty. I was feeling guilty in the pleasure I took in all this talk of "obscurity." I told Leo I had read Gene's play several times (a lie; I had read it only once) and that it seemed to me that an understanding of Gene's play had to take in the understanding of who loved whom, and how much. That, after all, is what shaped the destinies of the characters. It was Rena's destiny to have loved Carl more than he loved her. It was Carl's destiny to have accepted that discrepancy for his own benefit.

As I said it, I knew it to be true, but I wondered whether I had derived my insight from Gene's play or from Gene's life.

Leo's reaction first puzzled, then alarmed me. He relaxed his grizzly bear encirclement, for which I was grateful. Instead of nodding, as I was expecting him to do, he shook his head, saying nothing. In the silence that followed, the feeling grew in me that I had made a dreadful mistake. Leo was about to strangle me. I had offended his stupendous pride, pride of perception, pride of sensitivity. I had dumped shit in his creative well. Worst of all, I had destroyed his confidence in the play. It was all over. He was calling off rehearsals.

"Listen," he said. "I would appreciate it very much if someone —*you*—would slip in a few lines—no, *me*—you write the lines and I'll slip them in. Just a few lines that will get that idea across. Just as you said it to me then. Her destiny, his destiny. Would you do that, Saul? I swear on my father's life insurance policy that it will remain just between us. I realize that you two guys are friends, that it would be a touchy situation. I'll take all the credit and all the blame."

"Why not ask Gene to do it? It's his play."

"I would, I would . . . but to put it bluntly, I don't think Gene *can* do it. What he does, he does beautifully, but he doesn't do everything. Who does? Gene seems to have trouble with simple explication. You know, the few necessary, unglamorous lines that keep the goddam train running on track. Oh, believe me, it'll make a lot of difference. You'll be doing your friend a big favor."

"But Gene is not to know," I said.

"The *last* thing! Good Christ! What do you take me for?"

"I'll try."

Leo squeezed my shoulder. "Listen, Saul," he said, "when you've finished that play you're working on, I hope you'll let me get a look at it."

I had already developed a strong sense of paradox. Being a noble sneak didn't tax my moral muscles. In one way, I would be helping Gene advance toward his special destiny; in another way, I was playing around with a dangerous conceit—that he couldn't arrive without my help.

There was something about it I didn't like, so I did what I often did in those days—I put it out of my mind.

20

A SPECIAL DESTINY was performed in a hotel, in one of those expandable conference rooms. The theater was formed by folding back partitions to the desired open area, the cost increasing with the area. There were about a hundred people in the audience, mostly relatives and friends of the performers. Certainly the author's connections were there. Anna Strauss was there. The Obersts were there. The Zeiglers. Ruth was there. I was there.

The girl who played Rena—Hannah Jacoby—had a husky voice, deep-set eyes, busy hands. Naturally, I had Ruth in mind —Ruth with her blond hair, large eyes, quiet hands—and consequently Hannah seemed all wrong for the part. But either Leo had a different view of the part or the Forty-Something Street Players had to make do with what they had.

Hannah played a tense, nervous Rena. A young man with bright blue eyes played Carl. Each had his highly charged, highly individual thing going. I feared a fiasco. Which showed how much I knew. It all worked beautifully.

There had been no serious objection from Gene about the condensation to two acts. However romantic he might be in his creative mode, he had (I was beginning to discover) another side for the practical world. There were lines in the second act that Gene had never written. They didn't make the play, but they did draw a better defining line around Gene's mystical fuzziness. It was Rena's fate to love Carl more than Carl loved Rena, and the

Hannah-Rena handling of the role gave a wholly believable edge to that interpretation.

I was right about Gene and his vision. All he had needed was the suitable language. But I hadn't imagined that it would happen so soon. I still wasn't absolutely sure that Gene had found the voice of his vision, but that didn't seem to matter. The shadow of it was recognizable enough to pass for substance.

That first performance was so fraught with the future that I find myself poking around for auguries. In a very real way, my life did depend upon the outcome. I suppose things would have gone quite differently had the play failed, but things do begin and they continue and it matters not at all whether an alternative was ever really possible.

My alternative, I suppose, was to have severed ties with Eugene Strauss that very evening. I could have given way to my feelings, admitted to myself that I couldn't take his success, his play, his Ruth. I could have run back to the Bronx, those ice-covered, infertile fields I knew. But who in his early twenties is so practical? You have to live many more years before you're willing to accept the practical expedience of sparing yourself pain.

The small cluster of people in the hotel auditorium became a microcosm of the world. They believed in Gene's vision. Since there was no curtain, there were no curtain bows. The cast gathered together on the stage, held hands and accepted the enthusiastic applause. One wag by the name of Saul Klein yelled, "Author! Author!" in a fit of ecstatic envy. There was no way out of according Gene his due, and it seemed to me that the least painful way to do it was with total abandon, in a sense-drugging dervish dance.

The cry of "Author!" was taken up by the partisan crowd from Washington Heights. Gene got up and turned around, looking at me with his pale smile. I noticed that puffy blue vein that branched from the corner of his left eye to the corner of his temple in moments of stress. I wondered where he had magicked that outfit he was wearing. Part of his sartorial inheritance? It had vertical gussets in front and a belt in the back that came around and buckled in the front. He wore the same stark yellow tie he had worn that day in the buying office. He wore a marigold in his buttonhole. He wore a faint smile of victory.

A little later he said to me, "What do you really think?"

I didn't hesitate. I had been preparing for the moment. I said, "I think you've written a damn good play. Everything worked. It was believable. Despite the fantasy, despite the unexplained parts, it was believable."

These words were overheard by Ruth and Anna and Anna's friends. I guess I wanted them to be overheard. That was part of my role. I would not be found wanting in the right sportsmanlike attitude. Even with a mouthful of ashes, I would smile and speak my praise clearly and ringingly. The obligation of a formal accolade had fallen to me. I was Gene's "best" friend—or perhaps I was trying to secure that distinction by my little speech. I sensed that when he asked me about my "real" thoughts, he was asking not only about this play but about my view of his special destiny. He was asking me to confirm the vision in his play and the vision he had of himself. He was asking me whether I didn't agree that he had taken the first sure step toward the grandness he expected from his life.

Things became quickly and increasingly fevered that evening. Gene and Ruth and I and the Washington Heights contingent went to the hotel lounge for a congratulatory drink. The rest of the cast and its company scattered around the same lounge. Gene went over to the various tables to express his gratitude. He shook all hands, but it seemed to me he held Hannah Jacoby's hand a little longer. I was still sitting at the table Gene had just left, but the table at which Hannah was sitting was close by, close enough to see and even to hear. I shifted my gaze enough to notice that Ruth was looking at what I was looking at. There was really nothing to see, only Gene standing and smiling at Hannah as if to say that she'd given his lines their true, inner meaning. He was in her debt.

Hannah was herself aglow. One wouldn't have to be all that close to make it out. The dark-haired, dark-eyed girl sat within a self-generated circle of joy. She caught her underlip between her teeth and shook her head in the sheer helplessness of it. I heard her say, "It was such a *good* play!"—and there was a contagiousness in her radiance. One wanted to put both hands into it and scoop up a mouthful. This was my first exposure to theater rapture.

Hannah wore her hair distinctly even then: long and tightly drawn to the back, giving her brow a full, smooth convexity. Her nose was soft and undefined, her lips almost plump, but those deep-set, coal-black eyes suggested a lively, aggressive mind.

I realized that I was looking at this other girl with Ruth's eyes. I was making comparisons, picking out things to fault, fearfully finding things to admire, or distrust. I was considering Hannah's attractiveness from Ruth's point of view. I was seeing Gene, seeing Ruth see Gene, seeing Ruth see me seeing her and Gene, and what passed between us in a few quick glances was voluminous enough to have occupied a long, spaghetti-and-wine-filled evening at Mama Italy's fateful restaurant.

Gene returned to our table, and shortly after that Leo Shulkin approached with someone he introduced as Ben Something. Ben, Leo informed Gene, was starting up a new theater journal, one that would be much aware and responsive to new things and new people, particularly the small groups breaking their hearts in obscure corners of the city. Ben wore a double-breasted, dark-blue suit, spoke with a Boston accent. He congratulated Gene on the play, said it was a serious piece of work, hoped that it would run for several more weeks because he intended to inform friends and critics about it.

I exchanged smiles with Anna, with Ruth, over this. I thought I would burst into a spontaneous blaze at any moment. My own disgustingly envious nature, of course, but Gene was partially to blame. He had opened me up to these possibilities. I had been living my dark, igloo life in normal discontent and he had reached in and dragged me out into the terrible world of ambition and competitiveness. If I hadn't been brought so close to the sun, I wouldn't be sitting now in smiling dissimulation, waiting to go up in flames.

Ben Something went away. Gene leaned toward me and informed me that he expected me at his apartment in about an hour. A little party. He had asked the cast over. I wondered when he had managed to do that. I hadn't seen him do it. But Gene was obviously managing many things that I didn't see.

Anna Strauss put out her hand and touched mine. She said, "Gene told me how much you helped him."

"Me!" I laughed. "I didn't do anything except give him a lot of cranky comments. I'm glad he didn't take me seriously."

"No, no," Anna insisted softly. "Gene told me how you gave him such very helpful—nah!—"

"Criticism," Ruth supplied—and I immediately wondered if Ruth had moved into the word-filling role. "You were very helpful," Ruth confirmed. "Gene told me so, too. Particularly with the end of the play. He told me about that."

"Did he?"

It was the first time I'd heard from someone other than Leo Shulkin that there'd been a contribution to the play's final form. Gene hadn't deigned to tell *me* about these credits. He'd told others, however. Ruth, his mother . . . why not me?

I looked at Gene and he returned my look with his usual bland smile. He seemed to be saying that I had my own well-known inattentiveness to blame. He seemed to be saying that he had acknowledged my contribution, but I was just not remembering. Was that possible? Had he spoken to me directly about the condensation of the play? I know damn well that he had said nothing to me about those extra lines of dialogue that had sutured up the few open incisions he had left with his careless, romantic knife. I know I had said nothing about having done so, and Leo Shulkin wouldn't have dared. He was too smart to incite conflict at that time and put the whole thing at risk. Or did Gene remember having heard those lines before, the ones Leo was supposed to have written in? Did he remember them and decide to cover the whole uncomfortable complication with an enigmatic smile? From my increasing knowledge of Strauss ways, that struck me as being the likeliest of all.

Nor had Gene told me of the occasion when Ruth had been introduced to his mother. Obviously, they had been introduced.

Perhaps this very night. It seemed so to me, judging from the looks Anna gave Ruth. Guarded, summarizing looks, as if she didn't know quite where to place this young woman with the golden braids.

21

WE TOOK TAXIS to Gene's apartment in the Village. I was in the same taxi with the glowing Hannah Jacoby and three others from the cast. They spoke of muffed lines and gross ineptitudes, but beneath the self-criticism bubbled the purest joy I had ever beheld. I sat in my corner and nursed the knowledge that I had an ear for dialogue. I was not completely an outsider. I was writing a play. I had helped Gene write his, was instrumental in pumping out of *A Special Destiny* some of the miasmal gas.

Gene, always a step ahead of fate, had nested bottles of champagne in his refrigerator. (They could be had very cheaply in those days.) But how did he know that he would have this triumph to toast? He didn't. Nevertheless, he was prepared for it. That's the important thing. That's the vital, all-differentiating thing. That's the way Strauss played his cards. He was never afraid of jinxing his luck with too much confidence. If circumstances had forced a retreat, he would have retreated. He would have had a much smaller party, a consolation party, with two or three good friends (myself included?) and we/they would have discussed revisions.

This was a happy Eugene Strauss, as happy as I'd ever seen him. Which didn't mean that he'd changed from the pale, cool, aristocratic prince into a jolly good fellow with slaps on the back and uproarious belly laughter. Not at all. He was still pale and

152

cool and aristocratic, but somehow less *aloof.* He seemed suddenly to be able to distribute himself everywhere. I had thought that the Straussian charm was a one-on-one phenomenon, selective, confined, but I made out that evening that it could be as ecumenical as the Catholic church. At last I understood that puzzling immobility of feature. He didn't (as I did) have to invent different expressions for different people. He let others accommodate themselves to him. It was so much less tiring.

I was beginning to perceive the special relationship between Eugene Strauss and his special destiny. His special destiny would be of his own making. He would never let it direct him. He would never allow it to take him where he had no wish to go. That calm face and those equable eyes were evidence of the inner controls that assured direction.

Leo Shulkin was also a man in charge of his fate, but his direction was like that of a taxi driver going crosstown in midday traffic. Leo was still being very deferential to Gene, but he had become a bit more pushy in his deference. That booming bass was now proclaiming Leo Shulkin as well as Eugene Strauss. The source of that change was apparent. The glass of champagne in Leo's hand looked like a throttled bird in a bear's paw. I didn't notice who kept filling that glass—himself or another—but I did notice that it was never empty. Leo was a slow drunk but a progressive one.

I don't think anyone could have predicted it, but when it happened it did seem to have the force of inevitability. Two such personalities.

"You amaze me," Leo said to Gene, and said it with the attention-getting reverberations of a brass gong. "I wish you would tell me your secret."

Gene smiled. "What secret?"

Naturally, everyone in the room was paying attention. Saul Klein, for reasons of his own, was paying attention to Ruth Prager. Ruth, who sat on the floor, her back against the side of the sofa, was paying her own attention. She was looking at Hannah Jacoby look at Gene Strauss. Oh, yes, she did. Ruth, that is.

Look. Nerves were wired that night to a queer circuit, the current darting eccentrically here and there.

"The secret of your *English,*" Leo said—and there was the least little shove in his smiling flattery. "I mean, goddammit, how does a foreigner write such a fine play in *English? Dialogue,* for chrissake! I mean, for chrissake, the *idiom!*"

"But you are mistaken," Gene said, in his calmest, most self-possessed voice. "You insist that English is not my language, but I tell you that it is. I've been talking and thinking English most of my life. Not only British English but American English as well."

Leo shook his head and smiled and leaned toward Gene in a way that might have been tipsiness, but looked to me like a tilt of truculence. "Prove it," he said.

I didn't think it possible for Gene to pull a complete surprise on me any longer. I thought I had heard the complete Strauss repertoire. Variations could go on endlessly, of course, but I assumed the major compositions were known to me. This, however, was new. Gene changed his normal British accent into a creditable Missouri flatland and recited: "You don't know about me without you read a book by the name of *The Adventures of Tom Sawyer,* but that ain't no matter. The book was made by Mister Mark Twain and he told the truth, mainly. There was things that he stretched, but mainly he told the truth. That is nothing. I never seen anybody but lied one time or another . . . "

A bravura performance. Gene's second triumph of the evening. There was a spontaneous burst of applause when he had finished. Why (I asked myself) had he kept that little act to himself in all the time that I'd known him? It was unimportant, a conceit, but nevertheless it was always there, something he could have fanned out like a card trick whenever he felt the need to dazzle. Obviously he never felt the need to dazzle me—in that way. Was that a compliment or a put-down? I didn't know.

I looked at Ruth. I was beginning to understand her fears. She must have seen more—or other facets—of the Strauss personality. He was different things to different people.

"Did you have any idea what you were memorizing?" Leo asked.

"Not completely," Gene said. "I used a lot of the language

154

before understanding it. I just went on taking it in. I knew understanding would eventually catch up."

Leo shook his enormous head, shrugged his enormous shoulders. "Fabulous," he said, and finished his champagne in a gulp.
Knew that understanding would eventually catch up!
Well, what was wrong with that? Wasn't that a man's reach
exceeding his grasp? Half smashed myself, I tried to bring a
burning-glass focus on Gene's words, hoping that a proper understanding would illuminate in a single flash the hidden mysteries of Gene's world. I wanted to burn a hole through the pale,
aristocratic skin of my friend's personality and discover what
there was to discover.

But I was looking at too many things at once. I misdirected my
burning glass. I burned a hole, all right, and what I saw was a truth
I had already learned but hadn't admitted: people will stumble,
run, *fly* to anyone who acts in the sublime confidence that understanding will eventually catch up!

Then Leo Shulkin was sincerely drunk. Drunk, he became qui-
eter, but despite that, or because of it, even more overwhelming.
He decided to overwhelm Hannah Jacoby. Hannah didn't look
like the kind of girl who needed assistance in handling men. She,
too, was sitting on the floor, diagonally across the room from
where Ruth and I were sitting. Her legs were stretched and
crossed. They were good legs, solidly rounded calves. Hannah
was wearing a black pleated skirt and a white blouse, the outfit she
had worn in the play.

Leo had positioned himself beside Hannah, but facing her. He
wrapped his big arms around his legs while giving Hannah his
immense, undivided attention. I saw nothing strange or threatening in this male maneuvering. But then I saw Leo uncoil himself
so that his torso now arched across Hannah's legs, hip on one
side, elbow on the other. Hannah shifted uneasily. The pincer
movement was at last getting to her. She said something to Leo
—and then, suddenly, there was Gene saying something to Hannah, and whatever Gene had said provided Hannah with the
opportunity of slipping out of Leo's encirclement. Whatever
Gene had said or requested involved the kitchen, for that was

155

where the two of them went, leaving Leo with arms once again wrapped around his own legs, and with a dreamy, Tartar chief's smile on his face.

In all this fascinating byplay, Ruth had quietly slipped away from my side. Then she was there, her coat over her arm, saying to me, "Saul, are you planning to stay much longer? I must leave now. I have to be to work early tomorrow."

I sat for a few uncertain moments, caught in a silly web of semidrunkenness, amusement and alarm. I thought of telling Ruth to sit down and behave, but the look on her face warned me against any such flippancy. I wanted to explain things, tell her that she had it all wrong, that Gene was merely rescuing a girl in distress, as was only natural to his super, cavalier self. But then it dawned on me that *I* might have it all wrong.

"Wait," I said. "I'll go with you."

I went to the kitchen and found Gene there, his butt propped against the sink, talking earnestly to Hannah. Hannah stood with her arms folded beneath her splendid breasts, swaying a little from side to side, as if giving a metronomic beat to Gene's words. They both looked at me.

"Ruth has to be to work early tomorrow, and I'm taking her home," I announced, a little too ringingly. "Is that all right with you?"

Gene regarded me expressionlessly for the space of two or three heartbeats, then said, "Of course it's all right with me."

I turned and walked out of the kitchen, out (with Ruth) of the apartment.

I didn't know where Ruth lived. I had never taken her home. I had a vague notion that it was somewhere around Columbia University, a notion taken from Gene's play. Something said in the play gave me the idea that Rena lived around there—and if Rena lived there could Ruth be far away?

We walked the empty Village streets for an aimless while, looking more or less for some means of transportation—a subway, bus, taxi—but I had no idea which means of transportation would be appropriate under the circumstances.

"Where do you live?" I asked Ruth.

"A hundred and twelfth. Just west of Broadway."

"We'll take a cab," I said.

"Too expensive."

"I'm rich."

"I didn't know."

"Oh, yes. Big advance on my play. Money no object."

"How nice for you."

"Yes, it is nice to be rich."

We propelled ourselves along with that kind of banter, just turning over the great, heated engine of crisis. Somehow or other, we found ourselves on Seventh Avenue, and I was able to flag a cab. We got in and started our trip north. Was Seventh Avenue a one-way street in that paleolithic period when our futures were being hand-fashioned stone by stone? And where was the famous Manhattan dazzle? It wasn't all that late—not yet one o'clock—but the streets were as deserted and glum as in the Bronx.

"I remembered what you said," Ruth said, from her corner of the cab. "You said he would succeed if he found the right language for his vision. Would you say he had found it?"

"I would say," I said, trying to spoon-feed the situation, aware of countless things, both real and imagined, "I would say that you can't tell from one play. You can read whatever you want into it. A first play, eager players, eager audience, it had only to avoid being a flop to be a smashing success. I think it did succeed in expressing—in projecting a vision—"

I improvised in jig-time. Very loose, very glib. I had no trouble finding the words to keep the nervous seconds as light and bouncy as Ping-Pong balls. Was I being so glib for Ruth's sake or for my own? Both, I imagine. I was aware of her state and of my own. Impossible to know where hers ended and mine began. Mine depended on hers from second to second. Was it possible, for example, that I was about to be handed the divine jackpot? No, of course not. That's not the way life worked. The way life worked was the way things happened. Ruth leaning away, deep into her corner, one hand covering her face, sobbing her furious sorrow from Fourteenth Street to Forty-second Street, while I sat with one awkward, careful, *consoling* hand on her shoulder.

Dumbly I sat, feeling somehow rebuked for all the fun I had managed to derive from my surrogate love affair. *This* was not funny. This was pain.

"You *saw!*" she wept.

"What did I see? Nothing. Some clowning around at a party. A kind of hysteria. Everybody was hysterical."

"He was jealous."

"Gene? Of whom?"

"Of that *girl.* That *Hannah!* Of Leo crawling all over her! He couldn't stand it!"

"You're being ridiculous. Leo was drunk. You saw that. He was making Hannah uncomfortable. He was becoming a giant nuisance. Gene saw what the situation was. If you ask me, he was being very courageous. I have a feeling Leo can get—"

"You weren't watching," Ruth cut me off, accusingly.

"Was I not!"

"I wasn't talking about the last five minutes. I was talking about the whole *evening!*"

"What did you see the whole evening?"

She had stopped crying and was now staring miserably out the taxi window, having (it seemed to me) switched to another language to find the right words to express her feelings. I couldn't be sure of this, of course, but it seemed so to me. Denouncing in German. Gene, Hannah Jacoby . . . me?

"That girl," she said, more calm now, more biting because of it, "was looking at Gene all evening. Her eyes didn't leave him for a moment."

That wasn't true. I know it because I know when Hannah looked at *me!* And she did, quite a few times!

"Well, Gene can't be blamed for that," I said. "You don't get a ticket in this country for unlicensed looking."

"Please don't try to be funny," she said. "Things like that don't happen by themselves. One must be encouraged."

"Well, I can see that you've made up your mind about something, true or not," I said. I wasn't sure whether the resentment I was feeling had been borrowed from Ruth, or whether I was just getting tired of fronting for Gene, or whether, finally, I had just grown tired of her damn, stubborn *preference.*

158

Then she surprised me, saying, "And you were looking at her, too. Was I imagining *that?*"

"No, you weren't imagining that," I said, gladly. "Why the hell shouldn't I look? Just tell me that—why the hell shouldn't I look?"

"You want to know why?" Ruth said, scornfully. "I will tell you why. Because she is not an attractive girl, *that* is why! I don't know why anybody should look at her, with her *Berliner* face!"

Uh-oh! What was that? I knew what that was. A Berlin face? A *Jewish* face?

The taxi sped on. Ruth sat stiffly averted. The single drop of poison hung pendant between us. Bile-green. Strangely, I wasn't horrified. That kind of corrosive was in the air, and it didn't shock me that Ruth would mix a dab of it with her own unhappiness. Everybody's nature was a little subdued to what the world was working in, like the dyer's hand.

Now there was a second collapse, this time against me, Ruth sobbing at everything: her fury, her jealousy, her fall from grace. She was herself half Jewish. Her father had earned his anti-Nazi credentials. She was crying now because intemperance and heartbreak had driven her into such a dirty corner. She lifted her head, and as she did so the taxi jerked ahead. She gave a little, tear-sprayed laugh.

"So much for that," she said.

"So much for what?"

"I wanted you to kiss me."

"I can still do that."

"Then do."

She smelled of tears and perfume: Anna Strauss' signature. I felt the faintest sexual stir, but it was almost an abstraction in this crisis of the heart. It was as distant as the Palisades, which winked at me sporadically from street to street as the taxi sped along Broadway. This, then, was the great moment, the imagined moment, and it was about as thrilling as a damp bathing suit. Ruth's lips felt inert and rubbery—but then at the end of the kiss, she slid her lips along my cheek and applied that same moist softness somewhere just below my ear. It spread electrically to every nerve in my body.

"I'm living alone," she said. "My father and mother have moved to California."

I said I thought she had been living alone all this time—the time, that is, that I knew her—but she said no, she'd been living with her family until recently. (How then, I wondered, had she managed those overnight occasions at Gene's apartment? More continental liberality on the part of parents?) After her parents had gone to California, she explained, she had stayed on in the same apartment. Rents were going up, and she would have had to pay just as much in a smaller place.

I knew that Ruth was inviting me to spend the night with her, and my heart bulged like a frog's throat . . . *Run, Saul, grab! Don't think! Don't moralize! Don't hesitate! Grab this sad, golden moment or you'll regret it to the last, dimming, ninety-year-old sigh of decrepitude!*

The taxi finally arrived at Ruth's place. I got out and opened the door on Ruth's side. She walked to the front of her apartment house. I paid the driver, gave him an oversize tip. "You want me to wait?" he asked. I'm not sure why I said yes, but I did. I was inexperienced. I was in love. Most of all, I was nervous, so nervous that I feared messy consequences.

The unripeness of the moment reached perfection in the second or two it took me to walk from the taxi's side to Ruth's. She smiled in a sad, weary way, gave her head a little shake, put her hand to my cheek and said, "Good night, Saul. Thank you for being such a good friend." Then she turned and walked into her apartment house.

I let myself into the Strauss apartment, tiptoeing stealthily to my room, undressing, getting into bed. I no longer had any idea of the time. I was in the unmeasurable zone that belongs to sleep. Lurid lights played over the inner landscape of hours that had just passed. I moved up for a closer inspection of the objects that had been placed in that landscape of hours. There were meanings only half revealed. I didn't expect to penetrate to meanings in my stuporous state, but I did expect that the effort would rock me to sleep.

Five minutes? Ten? No longer than ten, and I heard, or thought I heard, the door of my room open. Even as I turned my head, I identified the presence I couldn't see. I recognized the mingled fragrance of *Mille Fleurs* and sweet vermouth, Anna's nighttime drink.

A whisper: "Saul?"

I didn't know quite where to find my voice. This darkness and the dislocations of the evening had left my normal reflexes in a jumble. I made a throaty noise, which, if nothing else, centered me in the room. But I wondered at this hushed approach. There was no one in the house except the two of us.

I heard Anna move, and the next thing I knew she was sitting on the edge of my bed. "Now," she said, still whispering, "I wanted to tell you that there will be this nice old lady living here tomorrow. Her son will bring her in the morning. She will be no bother."

"Oh," I whispered back, my vocal chords as thick as *shlag*. "Okay."

But still, in the morning. Why this whispering?

For some reason, my heart had set up a steady violence of its own, as if aware of something my mind hadn't as yet perceived.

"I didn't want you to be too surprised when you came from work tomorrow," she whispered.

"Okay," I whispered back, thinking she could have told me all of this in one of her bird passages in the morning.

"You see," she explained needlessly, "I have the extra room, and I must have the money."

"I understand."

All whispers. Not a movement on her part or mine. By this time, my eyes were thoroughly accustomed to the darkness, which was not complete darkness, there being a faint filtering of light from the street lamp outside. I could make out Anna's silhouette. She was wearing that familiar peignoir.

"So," she whispered, "what do you think?"

"About the old woman? It's—"

"About Gene. His play."

So. That's what this spooky night visit was all about.

161

"It's only the beginning," I said. "He'll write another play, of course. He'll be what he wants to be."

"Do you think so? I think so, too. Yes. He will be what he wants to be. Are you glad for that?"

"What do you mean? Of course. Sure."

"It is not always so 'sure.' Sometimes one is not happy for another's success. You have a good nature."

"Not me."

"Oh, yes, you,"—and I felt her hand touch the blanket—and then in a maneuver I couldn't follow, she slipped into my bed, putting a warm, gentling hand on my chest, as if she had guessed the tumultuous condition within. I remained motionless. Even my breathing had been reduced to quick, surreptitious intakes of breath. The air in the room had been distilled to a dangerous volatility. The least jar would set off a devastating explosion.

What? Was there some sexual custom or courtesy I'd never heard of? Had there been steps in this incredible passage I had failed to recognize?

"Yes," she went on whispering, "you have a good nature." Startlingly, she brushed against what I had been trying to conceal. Then she added, mysteriously, "That is why."

Smoothly, weightlessly, she raised up and arranged the rest.

PART
II

1

My scrapbook wasn't given over entirely to Armageddon. There were odd items in there that tell me more about myself than daily entries in a conventional diary would have done. For example, this ad run by Browning King, men's haberdashers. A natty-looking gentleman attired in what would appear to be B.K.'s best spring outfit. A baffled snake is looking at the man, a question mark over its head—the snake's head, that is. The slogan reads: "Oh, debt, where is thy sting?"—and then it goes on to explain that an extended charge account awaits you at Browning King. Buy now, take months to pay.

It was April 1939.

Looking at it, I recall the chagrin I felt at not understanding a pun obvious enough to run as an ad in a newspaper. The assumption, of course, was that everybody would get it. Merchants don't throw away money on overrefined subtleties. But Saul Klein didn't get the reference, and so he looked up *sting* in his recently acquired *Bartlett's:* "O, death, where is they sting, O grave, where is thy victory?" (1 Corinthians, 15:54–55).

I thought that clever, so I cut it out and pasted it in my scrapbook. A year earlier, I would have passed by that line as just another of those arcane items I needn't trouble to track down. But now, well into the Age of Strauss, I was taking a good deal of trouble to understand things. I wouldn't let an unfamiliar word go by without reference to the dictionary. Reading had reached the fissionable stage: one book exploded into ten, ten into a hundred.

I was paying strict attention to the immediate world as well as it thundered downhill. I read that Adolf Hitler's fiftieth birthday was celebrated in Berlin with a monster rally and a parade of frightful weapons. More newsreel pictures of the beast on a podium as thousands flowed by with precision pounding and stiff banners. Like Gene's father, I was making a study of Adolf Hitler.

Sometimes I would sneak into the little movie houses that showed nothing but newsreels and selected movie shorts. That was the TV of the day, and if you were a news nut, as I was, you could get your bellyful of premonitory pictures. Pictures of Hitler stooping to receive a bouquet from a fat-cheeked, golden-haired, German girl-child, all curtsies and fainting ecstasy. (Was I blaming children as well? Yes, yes, all! Just as they blamed the blameless! Their blond blood was as inexpungeably tainted with barbarism as my Jew blood was tainted with capitalist-Bolshevik-race corrupting world conspiracy.) Pictures of Hitler turning to fat Goering—who clutched his field marshal's baton as if it were a penis-icon modeled after some pagan German god—and saying something that produced a jiggle of assent from that happy paunch. Hitler with one thumb hooked into his Sam Brown belt, the other hand saluting the flags and the faceless crowds that flowed by.

I saw nothing but that face. I zeroed in on that face, watching the nostrils widen perceptibly when those stiff banners with the swastika emblem passed beneath. So would one breathe in the rarest perfume. Another confirmation of the Strauss/Klein theory, Hitler was smelling death and it delighted his soul. This deranged child had been given the supreme birthday gift of all time: the greatest military machine on earth to play with.

No clippings of Herschel Grynszpan, however. There was nothing to clip. Herschel had disappeared into history. I looked carefully through newspapers and magazines but could find nothing about Herschel. My letter had probably been worn into extinction through bureaucratic shuffling. And Gene had thrown a scare into me with his hint of the worldwide reach of Nazi tentacles. I wasn't scared for myself; I was an American—one could still say that with some confidence—but the Strausses were not. I didn't write to Herschel again, nor did I visit the French consulate, but I did continue my secret, one-sided relationship with the seventeen-year-old waif.

He would be my next play. Indeed, I was already writing a play about Herschel even while completing my first play. My first play no longer occupied my thoughts. It was by this point writing itself. My first play still had no title, but my second play did. It would be called *The Liberation of Herschel Grynszpan,* even though I hadn't the vaguest idea how he would be liberated.

I went on living the life of an alarmed American. I scoured the newspapers, and I sang to myself the lyrics of the latest love songs. I read that Dr. Eduard Beneš, former Czech president, would visit the New York World's Fair, which was scheduled to open at the end of that month. I read that David Sarnoff had dedicated the new RCA building at the World's Fair to television, a new industry for the "world of tomorrow." Television? What was television? I'd never heard the word before. I read that Paul Muni (I'm supposed to look like him) was appearing with Bette Davis in *Juarez.* I read that Robert Donat (he of the charismatic way of speaking) was appearing in two movies.

In four months, the Nazis would invade Poland, so they must have known by that time that they would invade Poland. They must have been very busy with plans. Which divisions would lead the assault and which would be back-up troops. How many divisions they would deploy along the western front and what sort of deal they would make with the Russians.

If Rudi Oberst was right, one firm statement from Franklin Delano Roosevelt would have altered those plans. But Rudi Oberst didn't understand that the leader of his former country was breathing in the perfume of death. Logic has no power over that.

I wanted to understand things, therefore I couldn't, like

Herschel Grynszpan, cancel my life. To want to understand is to want to live.

I wanted to understand Gene's look when I told him I was taking Ruth home.

I wanted to understand Ruth's palm against my cheek when she said good night at the door of her apartment house.

I wanted to understand Anna Strauss' hand against my cheek when she said, "Now you go to sleep."

2

I TRIED TO sneak out of the apartment on the ordinary spring morning following the extraordinary night. I didn't have the necessary faculties to deal with the nameless thing that had happened. It was a confrontation with which I would have to live, but as yet I didn't know how. I would be at the dead center of helplessness, without word or gesture to help me.

Did it really happen? I would have been so happy to consign it to the sticky underworld of dreams, but the nerves retaining last night's episode were all waking nerves—sentient, tactile nerves. My dreams have always retained their dream integrity, never to be confused with the conscious Klein.

Whose fault? Mine, of course. With my Klein conditioning, I was certain that it was my fault. The very biological arrangement of things made it my fault. I was the possessor of that constant, throbbing object, therefore I was at fault. And therefore it was impossible for me to see Anna Strauss in the ordinary light of day. I didn't have the beginnings of an attitude. She was the Gorgon Medusa. I would be turned to stone!

But I didn't know Anna Strauss very well. If the truth be told, I didn't know anything very well.

She blocked me in the foyer, told me there was coffee in the kitchen, come. Taking me by the sleeve of my jacket and leading me away from my desired escape. She was wearing the same pink peignoir. I was as will-less in this as I had been will-less in the

other—and as in the other intensely conscious of every hal-
lucinated word and movement. It was a continuation of the most
stupefying occasion of my life, and I was powerless to do anything
but go along with it. But even while yielding, I thought to myself
that this was a form of coping, that I was coping.

She indicated my usual chair in the kitchen, sat opposite me,
her hair arranged in its usual way, her eyes tender and pouchy—
and amused? Yes, I think so, a little. Then she had the audacity
to ask, "Did you sleep well?"

The question seemed as shockingly intimate as the act we had
performed. So this was the way it was done! Just let *manner* take
the burden of what can't be expressed, can't be explained. The
Strauss way. I was reminded of Gene standing in the kitchen of
his own apartment, propped against the sink, talking to Hannah
Jacoby, looking at me as I explained that I was taking Ruth home,
letting *manner* take the burden of it all.

But this was Anna's usual morning greeting: *"Did you sleep
well?"* Had last night made no difference? Would we continue in
the same way, morning greeting, evening chat, she the friendly
landlady, I the bumptious boarder who closeted himself most
evenings and pecked out words on paper? I couldn't believe it.
There must be some consequence from last night's unreality.
Inwardly, I squirmed to escape, but at the same time a part of me
had separated itself to stand as witness to another of life's remarkable scenes. I was looking for the human quality that would account for these sorcerous actions.

Anna had set the kitchen table as though for an occasion. There
was the cornflower-blue bowl filled with dusty yellow mimosa.
Anna loved mimosa. She loved wisteria. There was orange juice,
coffee, those crumb-topped buns.

"Was it a nice party?" she asked.

I nodded, not exactly avoiding her eyes, but touching them like
a runner rounding first on a line drive.

"The old lady," she said. "Mrs. Zimmerman. She will be no
trouble." I nodded again, recalling the ostensible reason for
Anna's invasion. Those nocturnal whispers came back to me, and
with them the precise mix of *Mille Fleurs* and vermouth. I was
relieved that there *was* an old lady, that I hadn't merely imagined

she had said that. "Even dinner," she said. "She must have certain foods. I will prepare them and bring them to her room on a tray." Another nod from me, and Anna continued with her list of particulars. "She has very little English. Hello, goodbye, a polite word, that's all."

This, too, was how it was done. You take up whatever routine business the next day brings, and with a few casual brush strokes a massacre or a debauch is concealed.

Without a break in her tone, as if it too was part of the next day's business, she said, "Now you must listen to me." She reached out, took me by the wrist, gave it a slight shake, as if to arrest my fugitive attention. "You must not feel too bad about last night," she said. "I see that you are feeling bad. I know what you are thinking. What will happen, eh? What kind of terrible affair? Now I tell you this and you must believe me. Nothing! Nothing will happen. Important for the moment, and then not important. It will happen again or it will not happen again, as both wish. The important thing is that everything remain as before. Yes?"

A very serious, assenting nod from me. I understood. Important and not important. As both wish. In short—what? Was I about to take the place of Ernst Mueller? Secret, sacrilegious couplings at the Strausses'? I felt—I don't know what I felt—a wing rustle in the dark, a dim red light of warning at the far end of this bizarre and gentle wantonness. I still longed for release. I was feeling an increase of confidence about managing the crisis (actually, Anna was managing it for me), but it was stretching me out too fine. I wanted to be out into the day, alone, so that I could recurl into my own shocked center. I wanted to deal with this unreality in my own way. I wanted to adjust my moral machinery in my own way.

"So," Anna concluded, "and now you must tell me about this girl."

"Which girl?"

"The girl with the hair like a *bauersfrau*. This Ruth. This Ruth Prager."

Ruth! My God! How would I ever explain this to Ruth? But I didn't have to explain this to Ruth. I didn't have to explain anything to Ruth. She was Gene's girl friend, not mine. Yes, but I was in love with Ruth.

Where had that love gone in those sinful hours? Maybe I wasn't in love with Ruth at all. Maybe what I thought was love was only a backed-up drain of lust. Maybe I was cured.

No, I wasn't cured. At the mere mention of Ruth's name, the sickness was back. Another lesson learned. The two things could exist side by side, like two buttons, each activating a different circuit. Press "Ruth" and all the rooms in the Klein interior castle were emptied out and Ruth Prager installed in each of them. Press "Anna Strauss" and I would blind-touch my way to the unlighted, subterranean rooms, until I found the one where a blood-warm statute would mount me in the whispering, fragrant darkness.

"What about her?" I asked.

"Is she living with Gen?" Anna asked.

"Living with? No, not that I know of. Not living with. They see each other."

"Just an affair, then?"

"I'm not sure what's going on. Gene doesn't say anything about it to me. I know they see each other often, but I know that Gene sees other people as well."

"Other girls?" Anna asked, holding her hand against the side of the blue bowl. She pinched off a tiny, dead ball of mimosa with the fingers of her other hand.

"I don't know," I said. "I think so."

Anna tilted her head and gave me her scolding moue. We were by now well over last night's Dionysian celebration. This was another day. This was how it would be. I would service the High Priestess, and the next day's ordinary business would shrive us both of our sins.

"I will tell you what I think," she said. "I think this is not the girl for Gene. There is something—ach!—*wie sagt man doch*—too—"

"Unrefined?" I suggested.

"Yah! So! Unrefined."

"Like a peasant?"

"So! Like a peasant!"

I ate my crumb-topped bun and sipped my coffee, still aching for the morning air, the bridge, the touchstones of my new life. I wanted out, but it was no longer a case of airing my guilt. I wanted to turn over in my mind the extraordinary behavior of others.

3

. . . CRUDE, AMATEUR, GAPING with holes, but appealing for all its faults. There is something significant being said here, significant in its implications if not in its theme. In a world where the individual is being thrust aside by brutal forces bellowing mindless slogans, it is good to be reminded that what passes between a single man and woman can touch the heart more deeply than a stadium full of flags. It is interesting to note that the author of A Special Destiny, *Eugene Strauss, is himself a recent refugee from the country where flags have become a major industry and where mindless slogans substitute for the heart. Some of Broadway's majordomos would do well to spend an evening in the company of these fresh-faced youngsters. In the eyes of this viewer, Hannah Jacoby calls for special mention. She brought to the role of Rena a vibrancy that galvanized every scene. . . .*

From a major newspaper. The play ran for two months, which was considered excellent for the Off-Broadway of that time. There was even some talk of Broadway interest, but that died away. The small audience dwindled, the weekly rent could no longer be paid and the folding chairs were stacked away.

Gene wasn't crushed. Why should he be? For all his love of the "mystical element" in his plays, he was a thorough realist in the world. He hadn't even hoped for two months. One would have satisfied him. He understood (he explained to me) that without the right theater, the right budget and the right performers you were necessarily limited to a short life.

Now there was Mr. Sussman. Shortly after the show closed, a Mr. Sussman got in touch with Gene. He had been informed that Gene had written a good play. Unfortunately, he had been on the West Coast during the time of its run, but he'd heard from Ben Something that it was a damn good little play, and he, Arnold Sussman, was a man in search of damn good little plays. Say, rather, people who were writing damn good little plays. Could they get together for a chat?

"Ben gave me your play to read," Mr. Sussman said to Gene (all this detailed later), "and I like what I've read. It's a good play but it's a starved play. I could see the bones. They're nice bones, but people buy theater tickets for meat. I got a hunch you could write a play with meat, given a chance . . . "

What did Mr. Sussman mean by "meat"? He meant another full act. He meant more fully developed characters. He meant, most of all, a denouement everyone could understand. He wanted explained, chapter and verse, just how the young couple end up as they do. Instead of "leaving it to the imagination of the audience," he wanted it written into the play. Instead of the "fine sheen of possibility" praised by Leo Shulkin, he wanted one scene, two scenes, where the sea change takes place before the eyes of the audience.

"So you see," Gene said to me, "you were right. I should have listened to you sooner. People do want things nicely explained. I hope you will continue to set me straight on these things."

"What do you mean by that?"

He meant that Mr. Sussman had offered him a proposition. Mr. Sussman had asked Gene if he was working, doing what, making how much. Gene had told him, and Mr. Sussman had proposed to match his present income if Gene would quit his job and rewrite *A Special Destiny* according to lines set forth by that hard-nosed, adventurous benefactor. It would mean a reworking of the whole play, not just the insertion of a couple of scenes. Since the basic play was there, Mr. Sussman thought that three months should do the trick. Four at the outside. He asked to be shown week-by-week progress. No guarantees, of course. Risks on both sides. But that's the way life was. If he liked what he was seeing, he might extend another month. If he didn't, he would terminate at the end of three months. No hard feelings. Money well spent.

"I would like you to go over what I've done before showing it to Mr. Sussman," Gene said to me. "Would you do that?"

"Sure."

"Because you have the eye for explicitness, know where it's needed."

"Explicitness is my meat."

"I hope you know what I mean," he said. "I don't mean it disparagingly. I mean the best sense of the explicit."

"The very best," I said—and then, just to end the slightly seasick swaying, I asked, "Suppose you quit your job and the golden Mr. Sussman gets cold feet?"

"That is a point," Gene said. "I've thought of it. I had a lawyer draw up an agreement."

"What kind of agreement?"

"One in which I'm guaranteed the three months' pay whatever happens."

"And Mr. Sussman agreed to sign it?"

"Of course. He's a businessman."

Counting the feathers in an angel's wing? Does one do that? One does if one is Eugene Strauss.

So Gene sauntered into the shining anteroom of his special destiny. He became very busy. He had three months to produce a play with enough meat to take to the Broadway market. No more daytime lunches. Daylight was a candle in the sun of that three-month contract. Now our meetings took place mainly in the evening. Gene had quit his job and worked in his Village apartment during the day, and we met, when we met, in the Village, after his day's work was done. Sometimes Ruth joined us, sometimes not. In one way or another, the subject of all our discussions was Gene's augmented play. Sometimes he would read a scene aloud, turning to me after such a reading, using me as a litmus test to see if the chemistry of his revised text was carrying the proper balance of mysticism and explicitness.

The Gene-Ruth mystery remained, although I was seeing it almost exclusively from Ruth's side now. I was more in her company than in his. Ruth and I formed an ad hoc committee to deal with the emotional crisis of Gene's preoccupation. Ruth was sure I saw Gene more than she did, and she tried to get me to admit that it was so. I told her it wasn't, and it wasn't, but it was clear that certain understandings were beginning to change.

I began to look for signs: eagerness turned to mere patience; the ballast of love becoming the sag of burden. There was nothing to see. When I finally asked Gene, he said that nothing had changed, nothing. He was very busy, as I well knew. Ruth? Well, he and Ruth were friends, just as they'd always been.

"But I thought you were more than friends," I said.

"I think of friendship as a very important thing," he said. "What does Ruth say?"

"She doesn't say much, but she does think that you see me more than you do her."

"That just isn't so."

"So I tell her."

"I have a deadline," he said, his fine brow furrowing in annoyance. "I thought she understood that. I thought you both did."

"We both do."

"Then why are you bringing me messages?"

"I'm not bringing you messages. No one asked me to give you a message. *I'm* doing the asking."

"What exactly are you asking?"

"I'm not sure—*exactly*—what I'm asking. I guess it's this: I guess you take for granted that I'm doing my own work most evenings, but Ruth doesn't work most evenings. I guess she's wondering why she isn't with you more often."

I saw a covert, reminiscent look appear in his eyes. "That again," I heard him whisper softly.

"*What* again?"

He shook his head. He said, "When I'm not satisfied with my day's work, I don't care to be distracted or consoled. I want to be by myself. I've said that before, but it doesn't seem to register on Ruth. You do understand, don't you?"

"Yeah."

"I wish you would explain it to her."
"All right, I will.

Oh, yes, something had changed. We all knew that. We seemed to be in some kind of holding pattern, waiting for the *explicit* signal that would announce the change of state.

And now there was something else. There was the constant awareness of an invisible presence hovering in daylight and in dark, between the interstices of thought and the hesitations of speech, between the lines of anything I read or wrote. I had no name for it. If I could have given it a name, perhaps I could have brewed an antidote. It was like one of those optical illusions one found in magazines. Looked at one way, it was two silhouetted profiles facing each other; looked at another way, it was a vase.

I kept remembering that Christmas-night walk through an unfamiliar part of the city with Gene, when he had told me about the affair between his father and Elena Oberst, when he had accused me of living in too limited a world. My moral view of the world was surely changing, but I could still find no place to fit that nameless night, and the nights that followed that nameless night. There weren't that many—only two other occasions—but it was already clear to me that repetition wouldn't dissipate the effects. The mixture of hallucination remained. The mixture of pleasure and sacrilege remained.

My problem was with Gene. A new caution had set into my behavior, and I think he detected the change. I can't be sure. It might have been the change in me that made him seem different. *Did he know?*

That was the figured bass I had to pencil in for all our daily improvisations.

I continued burrowing into my own play with animal tenacity. It was my escape and my shelter. I was urged on by the need to prove myself to myself, to Gene, to Ruth, to the world. I had caught Gene's luminous disease. I wanted to prove that my qualities of character and mind could create a destiny every bit as special as Gene's. I suspected that Gene had wrung his creativity out of his fierce need of a special destiny. I determined that I would wring a special destiny out of my creativity. That was my arrogance. Something to match his.

I, too, worked every evening. I still had my job. I was still performing my balancing act between being Mr. Siegal's protégé and my own secret life as something special—artist, creator, some nameless, glowing thing in my head.

Anna brought coffee to my room in the evening. She opened the door noiselessly (she had demonstrated that deft trick before), set a noiseless tray on the table, whispered, "I will look in later" and slipped out.

She knew she must leave me alone, and she did, but she always "looked in later." Did I want anything? No. Had I made progress that evening? Some. Oh, some was very good! Worthwhile things yielded so slowly. She knew, she knew. She had said the same thing to Gene so many times. But wasn't it time to relax? She knew she had little to offer in the way of good advice, but she had learned a few things in her years, and she would like to give me the benefit. One of the things she had learned was the recognition of natural limits. Yes. Each person has natural limits. It was like a wall. Once you begin to feel yourself crowding up against that wall, you must stop. Everything will be pressed out of shape if you insist on going on. She thought she had detected my natural limits. It was not a mechanical thing, but she could sense it in the air when it had come about. Then it was time to relax.

We went into the triangular living room, where Anna sipped vermouth and told me how it was in Hamburg before the sickness set in. She told me of the small but select circle of friends, professional people, artists. Each week they would meet in someone else's house, and poets would read their latest poems, a novelist would read from a work in progress, or they would have a musical evening. Trios and quartets. Her husband played the cello. It gave to each week a center. Something to look forward to. Not to fall into the terrible boredom of small talk, professional talk, doctor and lawyer talk. She had been to such evenings. Terrible. A slow crippling of the spirit. No, that was not the way they had lived in Hamburg . . .

We sat in the dark mostly, because darkness enhanced the view from the living room window—the bridge, the river, the lights on the Jersey side, the reflected lights on the black lacquered surface of the Hudson. Mrs. Zimmerman, the new, ancient, obscure boarder, was by that time folded into her past as into a blanket. Anna told me that she had a brother, an uncle of Gene's, who had emigrated to Canada long ago, who had made a tidy fortune in canning fruits. She didn't quite understand his business. He owned neither the canning factory nor the orchards. Everything was done by paper, but he made lots of money, so much money, and he cared very little for the plight of a sister. People—even those very close—had disappointed her greatly.

"Now you must tell me," she said at last. "What is your play about?"

"I'm writing it to find out," I said.

"Did you know that this is what Gen says?"

"I know."

"Is it the same with you?"

"Not really. I know what my play is about. It's about what I'm familiar with. It's about my family."

"You don't wish to speak about it?"

"It's not that . . . it's just that I don't know *how* to speak about it. That's why I'm writing this damn, endless play. I speak about it in the only way I can—indirectly, by giving everyone a mask."

"Then what is your play about even with the masks?"

I gave it some thought. I wanted to stay away from Straussian mysticism, but at the same time, and for the first time, I understood the difficulty of putting my ideas *in other words*.

"I guess I'd have to say that my play is about escape," I said.

"From your family?"

"From the person I am when I'm with my family."

"Who is that person?"

I felt a twitch of annoyance, feeling that I would break off at any moment this unwanted interrogation. I was under no obligation —and yet I did feel an obligation, not toward Anna Strauss but toward somebody or something else.

"I don't know who that person is," I said. "I don't exist when I'm with my family. No, that's not true. I do exist, but in a special way. I'm like a court stenographer when I'm with my family. I listen and I record. I suspend my real life and just take down evidence of this other life I was born into. I understand my mother a little. I don't understand my father at all. My sisters are my sisters. That is, we share a common past, but we're pretty much strangers in out present lives. It seems to me now that I've always been witnessing my family, never really part of it . . ."

For all the strangeness that had passed between us—something I still couldn't define or fully acknowledge—I found that I could speak to Anna. I could speak to her more freely than I could to Gene or Ruth. I don't know why this was so. Perhaps it was a displacement to ease the confession I could never make.

I felt a falling off of the constraints that always held me when I thought or spoke of my family. I told Anna of the cycle of arguments, and of the great, futile quest to wring from my father some acknowledgment of my life. I told her how sorry I was for my mother, whose life was draining away like a sinkful of dishwater. I told her I had always lived in the spaces left by my family, my schooling, my jobs. I told her about the euphoric lifts that always left me a little dizzy and spent. Did she understand what I was saying? Oh, yes, she understood! My goodness, so much of her life had been the same, living in the spaces allowed between the lives of others. And yet other people had come to mean so much . . . too much . . . "I think that other people come to mean too much to people like us," she said.

"What do you mean 'like us'?" I demanded, ready to step out of that inclusion.

"I mean," said Anna, "we are not selfish enough. We give to other people too much power, the power to hurt us."

Of course she meant Gene—her "Gen"—and I rejected the inclusion. Count me out! Gene might have the power to hurt her —and I was sorry for that—but I wasn't in that ball park of vulnerability. Was she trying to get me to share her maternal griefs? Was that the kind of union she had in mind when she glided into my room in an aura of *Mille Fleurs* and vermouth, reading me those passages in erotic braille? I was about to say something on that score, but she spoke first, asking, "What does Gen say of me?"

"Say? What do you mean? He doesn't say anything."

"Tell me, Saul."

"I don't know what you want me to tell."

"Does he not like me?"

"Don't be ridiculous. Of course he likes you. You're his mother."

What the hell did that mean? My father was my father. Did I like him? Neither like nor dislike, but the abysmal gulf between.

I could make out only a silhouette in the semidarkness, but the lines of that silhouette were drawn with desperate precision. *This* was the center of her life. Not Jascha Heifetz, or the god she had created out of her special need, or even her memories, but Gen, Gene, Eugene. She had invested too heavily.

"You're the most important person in his life," I said, beginning to be a little afraid of where I found myself. It was only a momentary spasm. I quickly shook it off, but something domestic, parental, seemed to be shaping itself out of that talk. Mother and father discussing son.

"I may be the most important person in his life," she said, "but not for the reasons I would wish."

I could understand that.

I could tell that Gene was changing. I could see how he was altering his vision to further his ambition. Not crassly, but in a way that would allow him to become what he must become. There had to be meat for the public to eat. The bones mustn't show. Gene was willing to put meat on his mystical bones, to vary the amount and kind according to the season.

And Saul Klein—idealist, pragmatist, friend—was willing to help. Not as Gene's mother sought to help. More independently. More acceptably.

Was this, then, the man? Eugene Strauss, the ambitious young man with a special destiny aglow in his eyes, accepting eclectic help where he could find it, rejecting tenders he couldn't use. I didn't know. What I did know was that Gene was controlled and controlling. It was like knowing someone who had been born without the reflex of blinking. There was always the steady gaze, the measured response, the regard and balance and politeness.

4

SUMMER.

The World's Fair in Flushing Meadows was playing like an animated showcase of a world about to be destroyed. The Trylon and Perisphere became symbols of doom.

But the crowds came. It was a tremendous show, everything from GM's "Futurama" to Coney Island rides. One of those rides was the so-called Parachute Jump, a tower and a gondola that pulled you up a hundred or so feet, then released the chair on which you were riding. You slid down with a fake parachute billowing above.

We went there, Gene and Ruth and I. It must have been the end of June. There were banner headlines in the papers every day. The Danzig crisis was being drummed up in the Nazi press. Hitler tore the air in demoniacal frenzies. The coming war was rooted in everyone's mind, and that may have been partially the reason Gene decided to play "chicken" with me on that damn parachute thing. I think all men our age were wondering about their courage.

I hate heights. Gene probably guessed that by the way I looked up at that tower. "Come on," he challenged. "Not me," I swore. "It's perfectly safe," he scoffed. "I'm sure it is," I said. "Oh, well," Gene shrugged. "Let's go," I capitulated, with a sinking heart.

I have one other thing to propose about that episode. I have no way of proving this, of course, and yet I believe there was a reason for this challenge, something that registered on me as changes in air pressure register on a barometer. *Did Gene know?* I wasn't sure. I was looking for signs. Anything might be a clue. The way a question was framed. A shift from a minor to a major key, or the reverse. A dare to go up in something as ridiculous as a parachute jump.

It was just barely possible that he knew, given the Strausses, their aristocratic decadence. And it was just as possible that he didn't know. This was the new thing between us, hovering, unspeakable, tragic, comic—I didn't know what; a combination of all —but something in the way he goaded me over the Parachute Jump suggested a changed attitude, a different awareness.

So we went up. I quickly discovered that if I looked straight ahead I could control the awfulness. Gene, naturally, looked straight down, taking in the dizzying fullness of the thing, waving to Ruth. I would get through it all right. I would prove that I wasn't all that wanting in the qualities that Gene had in such abundance. The trouble was that he did it with such ease, while I had mountains of fear and inhibition to overcome. It cost him so little, these contests. Why had I contracted myself into this mismatch with Eugene Strauss? It *was* a mismatch. His play, Ruth, this stupid toy—and yet I maintain that the price of it was not too high. Matching myself against him stretched me out as nothing else could. I was made into someone I might never have been.

Later, we decided we would go from one foreign pavilion to another, putting together an international lunch. Antipasto at the Italian pavilion. A bowl of onion soup at the French. Some baklava at the Turkish.

I don't recall which pavilion we were leaving when Ruth took my arm and said, "Isn't that the actor you're supposed to look like?" She pointed to a man in a summer suit and Panama hat, and indeed it was Paul Muni, or his double. "I don't think you look like him at all," she said.

Gene, too, turned to look, and when he turned back he slammed into someone coming from the opposite direction. The contact needn't have been that violent, but the other man, who was with a woman, was clearly not going to make any allowances. I mean that the other sonofabitch *saw*. He saw that they might collide and Gene did not. I, too, saw. I saw that when the other man saw that collision was unavoidable, he didn't try to minimize the contact but deliberately rammed into Gene, putting his shoulder into it like a football player. He almost knocked Gene down.

"Why the hell don't you look where you're going!" barked this sweetheart, giving Gene another straight-arm shove, insolently, nastily, all muscles and macho, just looking for an opportunity to cream somebody and show his tootsie the kind of man she was with.

I don't know about my courage. That's why I went up on the damn parachute thing. Certain occasions or people make me afraid, so afraid that I can't act. Then there are other occasions, other people, who also make me afraid, but I'm able to overcome my fear, and I can act. I suppose it depends on the grounds of the challenge, on what it is I value more than I fear. This bastard I recognized immediately as my mortal and eternal enemy. I recognized him on sight. I had seen him on school grounds and in subways. I had encountered him in swimming pools and on dance floors. He was the universal thug. He lived for the opportunity to threaten and hurt.

He was shorter than me, but he had a dark, wiry, tough look. He could have been a welterweight champ looking for a bit of mild exercise. My mind works that way. All my potential adversaries spend every free moment in a gym. His eyes were the eyes of a man who lives for the moment of slaughter. Such a man normally paralyzes me. But here was a difference—he wasn't picking on me, he was picking on my friend Gene.

For his part, Gene stared at the man in amazement. He wasn't afraid, I could see that, but he was caught in a spell of incredulity. He simply couldn't believe in the man's attack. He was staggered by the physical assault, but even more by the verbal assault.

"Well, what the hell are you looking at, you jerk! I'm going to give you about one more second to apologize!"

I'll never know what I would have done if I were the one under attack. Weaseled out, no doubt. Perhaps apologized, used words

185

to extricate myself from that nose-breaking craziness. But it wasn't me being threatened. It was Gene. And because it was Gene, I had the time and the perspective to savor fully the ugliness of the man. Because it was Gene and not me, I had the room to weigh my fear against my hatred. Because thousands were fleeing the thugs of this world, because Herschel Grynszpan had shot a German official in Paris, *this* thug became all of Nazidom rolled into one package. Because of the Parachute Jump (which I had just conquered), because of Ruth, because of Anna, because of all that Gene was and I was not, because, finally, I couldn't bear to see so perfect a specimen of special destiny battered and bloodied, I stopped thinking and piled into the shit.

Rushed him, arms flailing, and discovered in a few dreadful seconds how right I was. He was laced with steel cables. He was already ducking and fencing like a pro. I was a frantic machine, hoping that one of my thousand fists would land somewhere discouraging. I could see his eyes alight with anticipatory joy. He was going to take me apart. He shoved an iron bar into my belly, and I wondered how one asked for time to puke when there was no breath for asking. I never saw it come. It fell against the side of my face like a monstrous weight, pressing me into darkness.

In what seemed like another second, it was light again. There were all sorts of people surrounding the strange arrangement of Gene standing above me, Ruth kneeling beside me, and myself looking up into a perfectly blue, cloudless summer sky. I saw two men in blue surrounding the killer. Plenty of witnesses, plenty of accusations. He had started it all; that criminal, that fascist, ought to be locked up. I was feeling no pain, yet; just a slight tearing sensation along the side of my face, as if I'd had a rough shave. But even the pain that was to come was part of the joy I was already feeling.

It was over, that was the beautiful thing. I had done. I had won. That is, lost, but won through losing. I had acted for Gene. I had struck off a commemorative medal. Something warm and moral trickled through my revived consciousness. There was no exoneration in it, but there was something less to exonerate. Then I became aware of another trickle, this one over my lips and chin.

* * *

Later, with a plug of cotton in one nostril, inserted by a nurse in the first-aid station, we made our way to the subway.

Gene said, "I had no idea you were such a brawler."

"Neither did I," I said.

Ruth, who had been quiet, asked, "Why?"

I, full of heroic disclaimer, said, "I didn't know what was happening until it was all over."

A lie. I knew damn well what was happening, and *why* it was happening. But as long as I kept the reasons to myself, I thought, I could keep that commemorative medal.

"Well, that was brave of you, Saul," Gene said. "You saved me a beating. How can I repay?"

"I'll try to think of something," I said.

5

AT THE END of my play, my hero, Daniel, leaves his home in the Bronx. The last scene has Daniel standing by the door, suitcase by his side, father and mother each in his and her way accusing him of betrayal and ingratitude. He has tricked them all. Silent for weeks, he has frightened them into unaccustomed speech. Withdrawing from his family, he has drawn his family together. Now that he has accomplished that, he is leaving. Why?

DANIEL: Because I had to create a family to leave before I could leave, otherwise I would be dragging all of you wherever I went.

MOTHER: So now that you have a family, why do you leave?

DANIEL: Because I have to find out what to do with my freedom. I have to find out what the rest of the world is like.

FATHER: It's like here.

DANIEL: Then I'll have to play some tricks out there, too.

SISTER: And us? Where do we figure in your freedom?

DANIEL: You're my family. Now that I'm free to leave, I'm also free to come back!"

(All remain in that brightening circle of realization as Daniel picks up his suitcase and walks out the door. Curtain falls.)

* * *

188

Declamatory, even cloying, but that's the way things were. Everything polarized. Communism-fascism. Freedom-slavery. War-peace. Civilization-barbarism. The only people left with any hope of peace were those who believed in the power of prayer.

But a play is not life, not even a mirror held up to life. The starts and stops within a play are controlled by the author's purpose and sense of design.

The *real* mother didn't stand in any brightening circle of realization. The real mother was aware of a darkening and enlarging circle of fear.

"What will you do, Saul, if there's a war?"

"I don't know, Ma. What do men generally do when there's a war?"

"Are you trying to kill me? Every night I lay awake thinking. What if there's a war? What will you do? Where will you go? Saul, a neighbor told me maybe you can get a job in some kind of factory where they build things for the government. If you're doing something they need, maybe they won't take you in the army."

"Ma . . . *Hitler* . . . you've heard of him? He wants to wipe out all the Jews in the world. Who should be in the American army if not a Jew?"

My mother rolled up her eyes and clapped her hands together in wordless horror. She knew all about Hitler, may he be buried head down like an onion. But that was an old story, a recurrent nightmare for Jews. Nothing new in Hitler. But armies were armies, war was war, the business of the ferocious *goyim.*

Ancient survival instincts were too ingrained in Rose, so I said, "What are you worrying about? Roosevelt said this is not our war. It's not America's war. England and France will take care of Hitler."

But she was not to be put off with such stuff. She listened to the radio. Her fearful heart knew the score. She knew that what was about to happen would eventually suck in the *goldeneh Medina.*

"At a time like this, he lives in a stranger's house," she said.

"If I see something is going to happen, I'll come home," I assured her.

* * *

189

I gave Gene my finished manuscript to read. He kept it over-night, and we met the following evening at his apartment. The strange thing was that the time between my giving him the manu-script and our meeting was not spent on the cross. It wasn't that I didn't care what he would say—I did—but I just couldn't imag-ine him saying anything devastating. I guess the play itself had given me that confidence. Either that or I was beginning to see that the realities of my life might be just as nebulous to him as his were to me. The only difference—the beginning and continu-ing difference—was that his life fascinated me while mine had been no more to him than a quick glimpse from the window of a speeding train.

"I like it," he said.

"No 'buts'?"

"No 'buts.' I think your lines could use some polishing, but that's more a matter of taste."

"Not too realistic?" I asked.

"It's a realistic play. You handled it very well. That was very clever, having Daniel turn the tables that way, using silence against his silent parents. Creates just the right tension."

"Thank you."

"I'm really delighted that it worked out so well," he said. "Would you like me to show it to Mr. Sussman? He's interested in new material."

"Well, thanks, but . . . the fact is, Leo Shulkin is interested in doing it, and I sort of promised . . . "

"Leo has no money," Gene pointed out, with cold, gratuitous logic.

"But I promised."

I saw a faint, familiar grimace pass over Gene's face. I had seen that grimace before, many times. I had seen it when I had con-fronted him about Ruth. It was something that appeared—uncon-sciously, I'm sure—in the face of what Gene regarded as mistaken thought or action.

But there was another scruple this time. I didn't want the same person considering both our plays. There was danger in it. I think Gene, too, saw the danger. If Mr. Sussman preferred Gene's play, wanted to produce Gene's play and not mine, then I would have another mouthful of sour lees to grind my teeth on. But if by some miracle he preferred my play, handed Gene's play back to him, I would have been party to the greatest double-cross since Jacob tried to pass himself off as Esau. Our balance was delicate enough.

"Maybe you're right," Gene said—and then, in an aside that may have been more connected than it appeared, he said, "So you're seeing Ruth this Sunday."

"Do you mind?" I asked.

"No, I don't mind," he said. "I've said before that I don't mind, many times, but you still seem uneasy about it."

"Why did you bring it up, if you don't mind?"

"Because Ruth made a special point of telling me that she was seeing you. I told her there was no reason to keep me informed."

And I was shocked at the possibility that these were the actual words he had spoken to her. I didn't believe they were. They were too unfeeling, too unlike the Gene I knew. Or thought I knew. The gracious Gene. The courtly Gene.

"I don't believe you," I said.

"Why don't you believe me?"

"Because you talk as if there's nothing more involved here than the switching of Sunday companions. People *mind* about things like that. Don't you mind at all about Ruth?"

Gene was silent for several moments. It occurred to me that this might be the point where he would tell me to mind my own business. Or perhaps just move on to another subject. He said, "I'm not in love with Ruth, if that's what you're asking."

"That's what I'm asking."

"Well, now you know. I would have thought that was clear long before this."

"Did you think that it was always clear?"

"What do you mean?"

"I mean was it always clear to you that you weren't in love with Ruth? Was it always clear to Ruth? You must have known how much in love with you she was. Everybody else seemed to know. *I* knew."

"I don't believe these things are always as clear as you think they are," he said. "There was probably a time when I felt differ-

191

ently, but the fact is that I have told her, on many occasions, that it wouldn't be the wisest thing . . ."

We were in his apartment in the Village. He was sitting on the settee, I opposite. The open casement window behind him was alight with the leveling sun. A pulsing aureole around his head. Saint Eugene. I couldn't see his face all that clearly, couldn't make out an expression that might guide me. I wondered if it was wise for me to pursue this any further. I was pushing into new Strauss territory, territory I couldn't have known existed before because I had never been able to make out its shoreline before. But it must have been there. Shrouded in mist, perhaps, only intermittently glimpsed, but always there.

"Wise," I said, picking up his word. "What does wisdom have to do with it?"

"You know what I mean," he said. "I was trying to indicate there wasn't enough of a—a—"

"Mutuality?" I suggested, inserting the word into that one chink in his armor. Language. My better ear. My native advantage. Why this hostility? I asked myself. Why? He was stepping out of the way. He was giving his buddy a clear shot at his heart's desire. Maybe that's why. Maybe I was being too unequivocally reminded that I owed my possible happiness to his indifference.

"Yes . . . mutuality," he said. "There wasn't the mutuality."

"Okay," I said. "There wasn't the mutuality. Which surprises me, in fact, because it sure as hell looked as if there was. It did to me. I think it did to others as well. I think it looked to all the world as if there was mutuality."

"There was feeling," he said, his expression tightening. "There was a good deal of feeling. Of course there was. But there does come a point where one has to decide whether one is in love or not."

"Yeah, I'd say so." I was about to say more. I was about to ask him approximately when it was that he decided he was not in love with Ruth. I would have liked to mark that point on my own topographical map of feeling. But he spoke first.

"I will tell you something, Saul. I'm not sure I'm capable of falling in love. That's possible, you know. Not everybody falls in love, just as some children never get the usual childhood dis-

eases. I don't think I've ever been in love. I've felt very affection-
ate toward others, very warm, but I'm not sure it was love. How
do you know when you're in love?"

I had a ready answer. Experienced Saul. Vulnerable Saul. Saul
had had all the childhood diseases. "You know you're in love
when you're kicked out of all the interior rooms and the other
person takes over. That's how you know. When you feel dispossessed."

"Well, then, I've never been in love," Gene said. "I've never
felt dispossessed. But I have felt very grateful. Particularly to
Ruth. I know I don't have to tell you this, but Ruth is a very
generous—"

"But not exactly helpful," I put in.

"What do you mean?"

"I mean someone who can be of help—to you—now—at this
point in your career."

Gene gave me one of his sidelong glances. He wasn't sure of
the drift of my words. He wasn't sure how much irony was intended. Nor was I. It had slipped out. I think I saw distrust in his
eyes for the first time. He had always depended on me to know
where the borders were, instinctively, and to avoid incursion.

"I don't know that anybody can help me," he said, "although
Ruth has a great deal to give."

"Not exactly what you need," I said.

"What do I need?"

"Oh, I don't know . . . maybe someone with a little more
imagination, someone with a little more of the right imagination.
Maybe someone who can be of more material help. Ruth can
hardly provide for herself."

Now that I'd said it, Gene gave me the strangest look. He
smiled, faintly. He wasn't absolutely sure that I was being realisti-
cally straight, but there was something there he would like to
acknowledge. I was near the mark. Yes, it was true, Ruth was not
exactly helpful. It was not her fault, it was no one's fault, but there
you were . . .

"Why are you saying these things, Saul?" he asked me, not
antagonistically, just curious.

"Because they're true."

"Why wouldn't they be equally true for you?"

"Because I'm not you," I said. "I'm not sure about my career. Not like you."

"And you *are* in love with Ruth," he said.

"That is true," I said.

We went down for dinner later. We went to the restaurant I've always referred to in my mind as "Gene's place," the one with sawdust on the floor and the menu chalked on a slate board. Gene ordered by saying, "I'll have the . . . " as if he knew which were the good days for beef, which the best for fish. He probably did. Then I saw him raise his hand, as if some final illumination about love or expedience had just occurred to him, but he was only acknowledging a salutation from across the room.

"Would you excuse me a minute?" he said, sliding out of his side of the booth.

The whole thing was played in pantomime: the man with whom he shook hands (gray, aquiline, a resemblance to Conrad Veidt), the older woman to whom he was introduced, and over whose hand he bowed, as I had once imagined myself bowing over Anna's hand. There were smiles all around. Gene even *looked* different. No, that's not true, he didn't look different, he looked suddenly like the Gene Strauss the world knew rather than the Gene Strauss I knew. I don't know how to make this distinction except to compare it to other simple revelations that come when they come, making you wonder how you could have missed their meanings before.

I knew what significance there was in Gene standing so much at his ease before those two strangers, his hair styled somewhat like the older man's, his youth and handsomeness shining in that Village restaurant. He was an embodiment, a metamorphosis of sorts, even a phoenix. He was an affirming presence. I could see what I thought those people were seeing and thinking, and I thought they were right.

In the subway going to Washington Heights, I took my play out of the manila envelope and read it through again. My characters once again became living creatures carrying on within the enclosure of my head. I grinned at some of the things they said. An old gentleman sitting across the aisle, both hands resting on the handle of his cane, with a neatly trimmed, white mustache, smiled at me. It seemed to me that two interstellar lines of experience had crossed somewhere in space.

I was happy. I was happy with the play I had written. That play was my line of experience and it felt authentic to me—as authentic, perhaps, as that of the old gentleman sitting across the aisle. I was happy that Gene approved of my play, and I was happy that I was going to see Ruth, and I was happy that I had at last admitted to someone that I was in love . . .

At that point, my happiness faded. I recalled my conversation with Gene. I realized again how far I had pushed into new Strauss territory, and the realization was a sobering one. He might never forgive me for having done so. I had named certain things, and he had not pretended ignorance.

My friend Gene was naturally charming, and he didn't hesitate to use his charm. He drew to himself and he removed from himself, charmingly, according to his need. He hoped everybody would gain from their Strauss experience, but it was for his own gain that he set the compass of his charming world.

But in that respect was he different from most clever, ambitious people? Was he different from me?

No, he wasn't different . . . except of course he was.

6

IT WAS HOT. By noon, the city was a glaring kiln. Buildings and pavement absorbed heat they would exhale later in the evening.

"I don't know why, but I love to do this," I said to Ruth.

"Do what?"

"Spend a scorcher like this in the city. Everybody grabs bathing suits and runs like mad to the beaches, leaving this big, beautiful city to anyone willing to take the heat. I'm willing. You can do anything. The whole city is yours. You can wander into an air-conditioned restaurant or an air-conditioned movie. You can sit down in a cool corner of Schrafft's and enjoy a double-scoop ice cream soda while reading how Jay Gatsby loved his faithless Daisy."

"You make it sound like *Fantasia,* your hot day in the city."

"Exactly! It is *Fantasia.* A whole city all to yourself. *This* city!"

I was being entertaining. Trying to be. But cautious as well. I was feeling my way toward *her* state of heart and mind. She wore an embroidered peasant blouse with little red tassels, off the shoulder. I took that as evidence of some kind. I wasn't sure of what. I asked myself if she would have worn such a blouse if she were truly heartbroken. It seemed too lighthearted a thing to wear in heartbreak. A denial of desolation. An attempt, perhaps, to entice me. Such round, smooth shoulders. What was the matter with Eugene Strauss anyway? I glanced at her frequently, trying to pick up signals. Each time I looked at her, I noticed the

196

fine wisps of hair left by the upsweep at the nape. Ignited to whiteness by the sun. I imagined their gossamer touch against my lips if I should kiss her there.

She wore a light cotton skirt, flat walking shoes. Her responses to my words indicated that she was listening carefully, but there was a weighted quality to her attention. She was like a ship low in the water because of the heavy cargo it carried. I had made it my day's dedication to lighten that cargo, make her buoyant.

We had met as planned, in front of the Forty-second Street library, and we were now walking along the side street that flanked the library to the south. We were going to lunch. We had planned lunch as the first stop in our day's odyssey. Bryant Park looked darkly green amid all the white stone. The marble side of the library was in shadow, but the building across the street loomed like a cliff of heated brass. Passing through that street made me feel as if we were passing through rollers that would leave a permanent imprint on memory.

I told Ruth that I had completed my play and that Gene had read it.

"What did he say?" she asked.

"With a reservation here and there, he liked it. He thought it was quite successful."

She nodded, her gaze steadfastly on the griddle-hot sidewalk. She said nothing, but what was there to say? I had shown my play to Gene and Gene had liked it. Should I offer to show it to her? No, I didn't think so. I had a hunch she'd had enough of other people's plays. And she looked so sad, and all the more beautiful and sexy because of it. I could by now tell what an impossible thing I had undertaken, trying to cheer her up, trying to turn her mauled emotions toward me. What a thrilling thing it must be to have all that sexual wealth offered to you! What the hell was the matter with Eugene Strauss? It was his. This girl could hardly walk for the grief of having her sumptuous gift refused.

How strange and stupid of Gene not to pretend whatever had to be pretended to keep Ruth Prager amiable and available. What difference love? *Say* love! Say *anything!* But then I came upon a more mature insight, realizing in that moment how oppressive unwanted love must be. This in turn revived another vivid scene:

197

the foyer in the Strauss apartment—Anna Strauss and Ernst Mueller whispering away the last of their affair. A pocket of darkness invaded the brilliant day. A chill of sacrilege. I thought that Ruth was too honest and healthy for the Strauss decadence. She was well out of it.

And how long this day would be, each moment of it steeped in this mixture of melancholy and maneuver! I had isolated my love —and it was not yet noon! I felt like the proverbial miser plunging greedy fingers into his glittering hoard of minutes.

Ruth cheered up considerably in the cool, cavernous restaurant I had chosen. It was a dairy restaurant, somewhere near Seventh Avenue. Open on Sunday. A Jewish restaurant, naturally. What else around Seventh Avenue? The waiter was so typically what he was supposed to be that I suspected he was making fun of both himself and us: a little mirrored mimesis on a boring Sunday afternoon. The Jewish waiter playing the Jewish waiter.

Ruth was puzzled by his antics. She was only half Jewish, and that half German bred. She was still not completely familiar with the New York style. I undertook to explain. The comedy routine of the Jewish waiter with the wry face and the rye bread. A small serving of catastrophe between the borscht and the blintzes.

She smiled. I tasted victory. I had ruffled the flat nap of her sorrow. She was reachable.

"Do you know that your friend has no sense of humor?" she said.

My friend! No longer *hers?*

"Oh, I think he has a sense of humor," I said, "but just not about himself. He finds other people funny."

We sat in the dim restaurant feeling sorry for Gene Strauss, so wanting in one of life's more pleasant attributes. A drop of condescension that quickly evaporated. It was no good. Neither of us could keep up for very long the pretense that Gene was seriously wanting in any department.

"That is true," Ruth said. "He has no sense of humor about himself, but he does find others funny. He finds you funny. Not ridiculously funny but cleverly funny. He has told me so many times. He would repeat to me things that you had said. You *are* funny, Saul. Tell me, is it something that comes naturally, or do you have to think about it?"

"I haven't analyzed it."

"I think you have. Saul, why is Gene the way he is?"

"All roads lead to Rome," I said.

"What do you mean?"

"Nothing."

"I know what you mean," she said. "I promise you that all roads will not lead to Rome. But don't you wonder the same thing about him?"

"How should I know why Gene is the way he is?"

"You seem to know so much."

"Do I?"

"Gene says so. He says you are a person whose mind selects only what is right for it, and then it builds on what it selects."

"Gene has never told me that."

"Well, he has told it to me. Those were his very words. And he meant it. And he envies you for it. I know I do. My mind is a garbage pail full of useless junk. Gene says that your only trouble is that you don't take yourself seriously enough."

"And Gene takes himself too seriously," I said.

"Yes," said Ruth. "He takes himself much too seriously. Why does he take himself so seriously?"

She couldn't let it alone. I said, "Gene has a special destiny to achieve and only one lifetime in which to achieve it."

She gazed at me for long seconds, ending the gaze by lowering her eyes to her plate. Evidently she didn't care for the blueberry blintzes and sour cream I had recommended to her. Most of it remained uneaten. Or she just wasn't hungry.

"Doesn't everybody?" she asked.

"Maybe, but Gene's special gift is that he makes other people believe in his special destiny. Why shouldn't he take himself seriously? Everybody else does."

We left the restaurant and reentered the blazing street. It was like being clamped in one of those machines that my father used in his shop—the press that steams out wrinkles. Only our wrinkles remained as we walked. We walked in the direction of the movie we had planned to see in our hot excursion of the city. See again, rather. We had both seen it before. It was a rerun. *Pygmalion,* with Leslie Howard and Wendy Hiller.

A mistake. An awful mistake. Even Shaw gave love a chance. His own creation could awaken Professor Higgins to love, and seeing that must have hurt Ruth. I was becoming aware that everything hurt Ruth. When you are suffering the particular hurt she was suffering, there's scarcely a thing seen, heard or remembered that doesn't bump your bruises.

I said something about Leslie Howard being an ideal actor, not seeming to work at the business at all. I said that it seemed to me that Leslie Howard must have taken up acting as a hobby, something to do in his spare time.

She looked at me curiously, and finally asked, "Wasn't there something else you noticed about him?"

"What?"

"The resemblance."

She didn't have to say the resemblance to whom. All the world had only one reference. Nevertheless, she was right. There *was* a resemblance. How odd to have had such a steady exposure and not to have noticed. The same longish face. The same aloof, aristocratic manner. Was it with this in mind that she had suggested that movie? What a question! Of course. And it *was* she who had suggested it. And did that make me the cat's-paw again?

It was by now late afternoon, nearly four, the molten part of a hot day. For all my attempts at diversion and lightness, we were still into the punishments of miscued love. It was everywhere, like the day's heat. I could see it better on Ruth than in myself, naturally. She displayed it in three dimensions and in full color. My own condition was internal.

But all this acquiescence to what must be was beginning to fade —fade and be supplanted by a snarling opposition. Against Ruth. Against myself. Against Gene. Fuck this plaintive noise! Why was I putting up with it? Why didn't I just complain of the heat and take Ruth home? Why didn't I say I was bored stiff with this perpetual clinic of the whys and wherefores of Eugene Strauss? We were now walking in separate atmospheres. I had given up trying to invade hers.

But despite my resentment, there remained a little corner of commiseration for Ruth. She seemed so utterly scorched by what she was feeling. I had a perverse desire to kiss her, just to see if the taste of it would be in my mouth.

"I'd like to know just what the hell went on between you and Gene." I finally demanded, goaded by her silence and her scorching. "Just what the hell went on?"

"What do you mean, Saul?" she asked, taken aback by my sudden attack. "Nothing went on. What goes on between two people? I can't explain."

"Sure you can explain!" I snarled contemptuously. "It couldn't have been all that mysterious. I don't believe in all that mystery crap. That's Gene's line, not mine. Things *can* be explained. If I hadn't done some explaining, if Leo Shulkin hadn't done some explaining, Gene's play would have got no further than that loose-leaf binder. It would never have seen the light of day. Things can be explained. Einstein explained, Karl Marx explained, even Christ explained. All that pink cotton candy of his. The unexplainable. Meaning by omissions. That's not the way it works. Meaning is in what is *said,* not left unsaid. Shakespeare's plays are full of said things. Did you ever hear anybody going around quoting what Shakespeare didn't say? I mean—Jesus!— were the two of you floating around in space when you were together? Something must have been said . . . *done!* That's what I'm asking—*what?*"

Ruth took my tirade with bowed head. I was ranting for both of us, and I believe she found some relief in it. Not the words themselves—I could have shouted the Koran aloud, for all the sense of it—but the heart's release in volume and passion.

"What did we do?" she repeated. "Nothing unusual. We talked. We talked about his play. We went to movies. We would go to little coffee shops and have coffee and talk more about his play . . ."

"Was he ever nasty?"

"Never."

"Did he want . . . odd things?"

"What odd things?"

"I don't know. You would be the one to know. I've heard, read,

201

that people do have strange inclinations. It wouldn't surprise me that Gene did. Strange sexual inclinations. How about that?"

"Oh, Saul."

"Oh, Saul! I'm sorry! If I'm asking strange things, it's because the whole thing is so damn strange. I only know how he is with me. I can't imagine how he is with other people. Have you ever wondered how he is with other people?"

"All the time."

"Then it shouldn't surprise you that I wonder too," I said.

"Tell me how he is with you," she said.

"Very polite. Very considerate. Very sincere."

"Sincere? About what is he sincere?"

"About everything. When he advised me to drop accounting, he was being sincere. And right, too. I never would have made a good accountant. I don't know, maybe I would have, but never a happy one. I'm glad I followed his advice about that. When he encouraged me to write a play on my own, he was being sincere. When he told me I would never grow up until I got away from my family, he was being sincere. I mean, he had nothing to gain by telling me that, did he? He really was telling me that for my good. All right, maybe it fit into his plans as well, but that doesn't mean he wasn't right. He's always been considerate and always sincere . . . but, goddammit, it has somehow always worked in his favor!"

Even while I theorized on Strauss, I was aware that I was theorizing on Strauss. It came to me that we had done nothing all that boiling day except theorize on Strauss. Even when we were not talking about him directly, we were talking about him in some collateral way. Even the movie we had gone to see was an extension of our inexhaustible consideration of Strauss.

"It's true," Ruth agreed. "He is always considerate and sincere. Like Professor Higgins."

"Is that why we went to see that movie again? Is Gene a Pygmalion?"

She shrugged.

"Real people are not like the movies," I said. "For one thing, people never make love in the movies. It's something that might happen, or has already happened, never happening."

"Yes? And so?"

"Yes, and so did *that* make a difference?"

"Now you are talking like a little boy."

We walked on. I *stalked* on. Half a block later, Ruth tugged at my sleeve. "Please, Saul," she said wearily. "Please don't be mad. Be nice."

Her appeal hit me like a surprise blow to the stomach, emptying me of my puffed-up wrath. Why, indeed, had I asked such a silly, stupid, *boyish* question? Only because I wanted to *know,* know for sure, despite the fact that every human evidence was there in abundance, in sorrow. Someday I would have to get over my little-boy prurience, why not now? The time was overripe. Here was Ruth Prager of the golden diadem who had made love with my friend Gene, and nothing had been altered by that fundamental fact. Her hair was immaculately in place, the little scar on her nose hadn't disappeared and her unhappy hazel eyes dwelt on other losses.

"I'm sorry," I said.

We had dinner in an Italian restaurant, not the one in the Village, the one with the velour painting of Venice. Somehow we had wandered to the West Side, in the Thirties, and there we had found an Italian restaurant. After dinner, we walked to Fifth Avenue, over to the East Side, and then back to Fifth Avenue. Exhausted, we took an open-air, double-decker bus to where Ruth lived. The night air rushed at us like a huge blow-dryer, evaporating the sweat on our bodies.

"Come," Ruth said, when we were at the front door of her apartment house.

A small, brown, food-smelling elevator took us up to the third floor. We were alone in the elevator, but we both stood in silent constraint, as if a third party were present, someone before whom it would be embarrassing to speak.

We entered her apartment and embraced in the darkness as soon as the door was shut. She took me by the hand and guided me in the darkness, whispering, "Wait." In a few seconds, she was back in my arms. It hadn't taken her long to shed the few summer things she was wearing. My body couldn't quite take in the fullness of hers. I unbuttoned my shirt and pressed against her for better comprehension. I still had my clothes on and could still partially conceal my stiff ache of comprehension. But I was having difficulty with my breathing again. I didn't seem able to draw in a complete lungful of air. I had to be satisfied with slow, surreptitious intakes. And yet I would have been content if we had stayed that way until the sun came up. It would have been enough for me.

Frankly, I had no idea how the thing would be done, despite my Anna experience. There was too much darkness and too much Ruth—and so Ruth took me by the hand again and led me in the darkness to her bed.

I finished undressing and lay down beside her, big and helpless. My eyes were beginning to make out things in the darkness. A glint from her hair, her legendary hair, coronet of my lust. A ghostly curve of flesh. Lines that led to that unimaginable convergence. I put my hand there, and she covered my hand with her own, and then made accessible to me what had been as chambered as dreams.

I was shocked at the sight of myself in the bathroom mirror. Loins, thighs, penis—all caked in blood.

It scared me—then moved me in a solemn, tender way.

7

ORDINARILY WHEN I wake up things come at me in a rush. Who I am, where I am, what dismal or joyous event had taken place or was impending.

That morning I awoke from a dream that had incorporated into itself the roughness on which I slept. I dreamt that I was back in the Bronx, and that I had made my bed on the worn carpet in the living room. My mother sat on one end of the sofa, weeping. My father sat at the other end with the evening paper folded on his lap, his face turned away from the spectacle of his son's attempt to bring peace to the Klein household through this silly maneuver. In the dream, I moved against the coarseness of the carpet to demonstrate to myself and to my parents that this was my new bed of sorrow. The movement nudged me toward consciousness . . .

I was in my shorts, lying on my back against a large towel. Opposite me was a dresser made of dark wood. It was surmounted by an oval mirror. Next to the bed on which I was lying was a chair heaped with my clothing. I knew where I was. I turned and saw something even more remarkable than Ruth's body beneath the sheet. I saw Ruth's *hair!* Undone, voluminous, its mass lying along the pillow, shaped by a turn she had taken in her sleep. Then, as in a finished game of cards, memory threw down the rest of its hand: the ride home on the bus, the blind embrace, the long, sleepless industry of sex—three times? more?—and then the large towel Ruth had fetched to cover the sticky moistness of her menstrual blood.

I tried to levitate out of bed so as not to awaken Ruth, but as I padded toward the bathroom, she spoke: "You had better take a shower now, because I shall need the bathtub to wash out the sheets."

So the new reality began. I gathered my clothes from the chair, went to the bathroom, took my shower, washed the bloodstains out of my shorts, put on trousers and shirt, came out of the bathroom feeling like a Hemingway hero. Ruth was standing in the room wrapped in one of the bedsheets, holding another bundled bedsheet in her hand. We stood there in the morning light like two figures in a Greek tragedy, each carrying some bloody evidence of our crime. Ruth walked past me with a smile, taking my shorts from me in passing. "I'll hang these up," she said, and in saying so revealed to me how much of the practical, stitched, everyday world she was familiar with.

She was in the bathroom a long time, showering, washing, preparing her woman's body for the rest of the day. By this time, it was fully light, and I could make out the details of her apartment. The bedroom in which we had made love. Another bedroom. The living room. Tables and chairs that had the look of Germany. A bookcase, which I examined, seeing many titles in German, but some in English. *The Importance of Living* by Lin Yutang. *All This and Heaven Too* by Rachel Field. A book about Leonardo da Vinci. Several volumes of collected plays. I could make an informed guess as to who recommended those. Bought them? A gift?

It was almost eight o'clock. It was Monday. I had to go to work that morning. Didn't Ruth? I was feeling a novel kind of fatigue, something more light than heavy, a hollowing in my head and chest. It produced a faint, pervasive ringing that made me want to close my eyes in a half-sleep and listen.

Ruth came out of the bathroom, and I stood transfixed at the sight of her, not knowing how to deal with this latest revelation. I looked, then looked away. I was a sneaky, slightly berserk photographer, not wanting to be seen taking these contraband pictures, knowing I would be selling these prints to my amazed heart for the next hundred years. Ruth with bare breasts and wet blond hair hanging straight down her back. Ruth wearing pink panties, beneath which I could see the sanitary pad and the belt holding it. Ruth with solid thighs and finely postured shoulders. Ruth undismayed by all that I was seeing, all that she was permitting me to see.

She smiled and said, "Yes, I have a body. Does that surprise you?"

I shook my head dumbly.

"Something does surprise *me*," she said.

"What?"

"A Saul Klein without words."

I acted instinctively, did the best thing I could do, went to her and embraced her, smelling the soapy wetness of her hair, and a faint something else: the sheer otherness of her body. I realized how exclusively I had lived with my own, and how surprising a part of that longed-for union is the physical reality of one's partner. The infrequent whore had been only an uneasy incarnation of my solitude. Ruth standing seminaked with wet hair and pink panties brought me the tangible intrusiveness of love and lover.

She put on a bra, her robe. She combed her hair, opened a drawer and took out another towel, enclosing her hair in two deft movements. She said, "Did I tell you that my vacation begins today?"

"No, you did not tell me."

"They have given me a week off with half-pay. Isn't that generous?"

"Have you made any plans?"

"On half-pay? Oh, yes. I'm on the point of packing for a trip to the Riviera."

"Better not. A war is about to start."

"Do you think so?"

"Can there be any doubt?"

"I still think they will stop at the last moment. They must. It will be the end of the world."

It was unbelievable! Sitting at Ruth's kitchen table, watching her slice oranges, put up coffee, see her fantastic turban, her robe, my nerves still carrying the soft, moist message of her body.

"Seriously," I said, "haven't you made any plans to go to the mountains, the shore . . . someplace?"

"I have made no plans."

"Then what will you do?"

"Oh . . . I thought I would go to the beach during the day. Sleep late. Take a bunch of new books out of the library. Go to the museums. There's so much to do that costs practically nothing in this *Fantasia* city of yours. You said so yourself."

"I agree," I agreed, trying to keep under control a different kind of swelling excitement. "There is. It sounds like a perfect vacation to me. Were you planning to do anything today?"

"I think today I shall go to the Museum of Art. There's a special exhibition—"

"What time?"

"I don't know. No special time. In the afternoon."

"I mean, when will you be coming back? Here, I mean. When will I be able to reach you later? *Will* I be able to reach you later?"

"Of course."

"Four?"

"Yes, four, if you wish."

"I wish!"

I wished! Very much! I was pregnant with plans. I ate an orange, drank coffee, went into the bathroom again to examine my eyes for signs of the metamorphosis. Nothing to see except the muddy look I take on after too little sleep—and, I newly assumed, too much sex.

I embraced Ruth once more before I left, feeling under my hands and next to my body the living complex of parts that had arranged themselves in that ultimate for me, and my throat clogged again, and I kissed her coffee-smelling lips, and fled, eager to put into action my stupendous plan.

I went first to the Siegal loft. Lou was already there. I asked if I could speak to him. He said he had never observed any difficulty on that score before. I reminded him of my long-delayed vacation. He had said I could count on a vacation week, with pay, any time during the summer. I said I knew that I should have given more notice that this would be the week, but truthfully I hadn't known myself that this would be the week. Okay, okay, but why the rush? Why now? Now, I explained to Mr. Siegal, with, I think, convincing urgency, because this friend of mine had let me know only this past weekend that he was taking an automobile trip to Canada, and it was the sort of thing I had hoped might happen, I've always wanted to go to Canada, and it was indeed short notice, but this was a dead time anyway, as he'd said himself, and if it wasn't too much of an inconvenience—

"Are you eloping?" Lou asked.

"What? Eloping . . .?"

"I thought maybe you were running away with your girl friend to get married."

I braked hard, realizing that I had been racing on slick ground, climbing sidewalks, skidding dangerously here and there. If I was going to further my career in deception, I had better concentrate. Lou Siegal was no fool. Even in my panic, I knew that life wouldn't end with this week. I was snowblind in August, but I knew September would come.

I put on a solemn, troubled face. I said, "No, Mr. Siegal, I'm not running away with my girl friend to get married." (The odd thing—it didn't occur to me until that moment—was that I might be doing just that; that I would encourage such an outcome if it were at all possible.) "In fact, one of the reasons I'm going to—" I broke off. I shrugged. I was being my most devious self, trying to convey the part of a young man embarked on an expeditious move. I didn't invent particulars. I just gave Mr. Siegal a sidelong, uncomfortable look, as one might who understood the nature of Mr. Siegal's suspicion and was answering as best he could, answering without totally compromising honor. I finally met Mr. Siegal's poached, conjecturing eyes, and I didn't flinch. Life might not end in this transforming week, but it would surely change, and I wasn't that much concerned about the changes between Klein and Siegal. I had more important changes to think about. I just wanted the world nailed down for a week. I'd take care of everything later . . . later.

"So go," Mr. Siegal said, rubbing his nose, glancing at the family portrait on his desk, getting into his voice the mild surprise of a man who has been approached with a perfectly reasonable request, and from whom a perfectly reasonable response could have been anticipated. "You got it coming."

I took the Broadway IRT to the Bronx. I had a location on the western edge of the borough in mind. Only a week ago, when that Sunday date with Ruth had been made, thinking how nice it would be to drive to the shore, perhaps presciently alive to other possibilities, I had scouted out some auto lots dealing in second-hand cars. I had found them in the newspaper easily enough. This one was not all that far from the old Klein neighborhood. I had seen there a convertible green Chevy I liked.

I bought it. Just like that. My first car. Drove it around the block and bought it. I did have a driver's license. I had taken driving lessons at the insistence of Mr. Siegal's pragmatic nephew: *"What! In this day and age, a man almost twenty-four doesn't know how to drive a car? Go take a few lessons. Get a driver's license. Any day Lou's liable to ask you to take a trip, take samples, maybe ask you to rent a car, you'll tell him no, you don't know how to drive? Don't be a shmuck."* I took the driving lessons, rented a car from the agency to take my test, received a license. I had also, in my inspired cunning, thought to stop at my bank and get a certified check for the price I had seen on the car. I became a car owner in a flurry of papers.

I followed directions and went to the Motor Vehicle Bureau to register. I signed all the necessary things, inquired if there was anything I had left undone, fearing that some long, hairy, punitive arm would reach out from nowhere and keep me, flailing and desperate, from ever reaching four o'clock.

But I did reach four o'clock, drove to Ruth's apartment house, went upstairs, rang her bell, and there she was, like the Rena of Gene's play!

The beach, of course. Every day of that hot, conspiratorial week, we went to one of the city's beaches. Jones Beach or Long Beach or the Rockaways. We came to prefer Jones Beach, which had only recently been opened, a project of the peerless Robert Moses. Banks of flowers instead of the usual beach scrub, stretches of clean sand. I had bought a thermos bottle (among the other innovations of my life), and we made iced coffee, sandwiches. We took blankets, left early in the morning, arrived a couple of hours later, spread-eagled under a brassy sun—front, back—then into the water, our fried flesh practically sizzling on contact.

"I thought you preferred the city to the beaches," Ruth reminded me.

"Only on Sunday," I reminded her.

"I think it was a matter of transportation," she said.

"I think you're right," I said.

We had dinner wherever, some fish place at the shore, or back in the city at some Greek, Hungarian or Armenian restaurant on the East Side. I could always find a parking spot for my little green Chevy. *I* bought the theater tickets this time for the plays I thought Ruth and I would like. *Knickerbocker Holiday* with Walter Huston. *The Philadelphia Story* with Katharine Hepburn. And movies. *The Wizard of Oz* and *Goodbye, Mr. Chips* with Gene's charismatic Robert Donat. *Algiers* with Charles Boyer and Hedy Lamarr. A mixed bag of approved theater and downright kitsch.

We spent the nights at Ruth's place, making love in a delicately gymnastic way to minimize the friction to our sun-abused flesh.

"Is it all right when you're that way?" I asked.

"Do you mind?" she asked.

"No, it's just that . . . "

"What?"

"I thought it might be uncomfortable."

"A little, but I don't mind. It's safe."

Safe? Safe? Oh, that kind of safe!

I couldn't simply disappear. I told Anna I would be spending a week at the shore. My vacation.

"Do I bother you?" she asked.

"Bother? Not at all. It's not a question of bother. It's a— vacation."

"I understand."

Well, Jesus! Anna Strauss wasn't my *mother!* She was my . . . my what? I didn't know. Whatever she was, I owed her no explanations. This weird part of my life would dissolve in the chemistry of time. Surely Anna Strauss didn't look to me for salvation. I was neither son nor lover nor husband. I was her boarder. We were, together, a nameless, nocturnal accident, something that happened spontaneously out of loneliness, lust, a complexity impossible to sort out. But I was not responsible for Anna Strauss. I owed her nothing but decency, regard, perhaps a helpful mutuality.

And Gene.

"I've taken a room at the shore," I said. "I want to go over the whole play once more. I had some ideas since we last spoke, and I want to see if I can incorporate them without tearing the whole thing apart."

"Do you have a title for it yet?" Gene asked.

"War and Peace in the Bronx."

He thought for a moment, a smile hovering on his lips. I could see that he was wondering whether I was serious or not. He said, "That's a wonderful title."

Preoccupied with dissimulation, I was still elated at his praise. "Do you really think so?" I asked.

"I do . . . I wish you had let me know."

"About the title. What dif——?"

"About taking a room at the shore."

"Oh? Why?"

"It sounds like a good idea. I think I would have liked to go with you. Would you mind?"

Oh, think! . . . "You know," I said, "I didn't even think of asking. I just assumed you were hammering out your weekly quota of words and didn't want to be interrupted. I thought you had to hang around for consultations with Mr. Sussman."

"Well, I am hammering out my quota, but I won't be missed if I'm gone for a few days."

Think! Think! . . . "Is Mr. Sussman finding enough meat for his investment?" I asked.

A stall. What wizard words? What maneuver? I would have to say no to him in one way or another. Somewhere in the magnificent ocean of the English language swam a tiny school of perfect fish that I must net in the next few seconds.

212

"He seems to be pleased so far," Gene said. "I've given him an idea for another script. He's very interested. He's certain war is a matter of weeks away. Incidentally, he has movie connections. He's very interested in this other idea for a movie."

"That's great!"

"When are you going?" he asked.

"Well—truthfully—I'm on my way now."

"I see."

"I've bought a car. Secondhand."

"Really. It sounds as if you were making a getaway instead of taking a vacation."

"In a sense."

"What sense is that?"

"In the sense of wavelengths. Receiving only my own. You once said something about that. You once said there are helpful and harmful wavelengths."

Gene nodded. It was a checkmating move. He couldn't insist on tagging along in the face of my stated need to be alone. The reason I'd given was inarguable. But something in his eyes told me he wasn't entirely persuaded. There was some busy conjecturing in those eyes. I didn't even want to think about their possible causes.

"Well, I hope you have a productive week," he said, handing me back my passport and waving me across the precious border.

"Thanks."

I had simply telephoned my mother to tell her I was going away for a week.

"Where are you going?"

"I took a room at the shore. You know, sun, bathing . . . "

"Do you know you have a family, Saul?"

"What's that supposed to mean?"

"You come and go like a wanderer, a person without a home. What's happened to you?"

"Nothing's happened to me. The years happened to me. I got older, Ma. You were sixteen when you left your home. I'm almost twenty-four."

"I got married."

"I know," I said, dropping the words like stones in a pond.

"How do you feel about all of this?" I asked Ruth, as our week drew to a close.

"Unreal."

"Enjoyable?"

"How can it not be enjoyable? A royal fête. At the court of the Sun King. Something different every day. Saul, you must stop spending money this way. It's insane. It doesn't have to be a nonstop entertainment."

"Is that what I am, an entertainment?"

"Don't pick my words apart."

"Right. No apart picking of words."

We were sitting in a restaurant that was built on wooden pilings over inland water. We had driven north and then east. "Fitzgerald country," I called it. I had no idea where we were. The windows of the restaurant faced west, and there were sun-bleached, tar-smeared poles slanting up from the water. We saw a garish sun touching its bottom on the horizon; 865,400 miles of orange diameter glaring within the compass of a single windowpane. It turned the water a violet hue. I saw a gull alight on one of the poles, twitch its feathers fussily and then make an announcement of stunning symmetry to the soft, brilliant air.

I had been waiting for the question all week: "Does Gene know?"

"Know what?" I asked, determined that she would have to be as explicit as she made me be.

"Know that we're together."

"I don't think so. I didn't tell him. Did you?"

She closed her eyes and turned her head. "Why do you say you don't *think* so?" she asked.

"Because I'm not absolutely sure. Gene is good at putting things together. I told him I was going off for a week to work on my play. He said he was sorry I hadn't let him in on my plans. He said he would have liked to join me at the shore. Mr. Sussman, incidentally, is interested in having Gene do a movie script. I

214

don't know—certain things have a way of getting through—by osmosis."

"It must have been embarrassing, having to make excuses," she said. "I think you would have been pleased to have him join you. What did you tell him?"

"Just what I said. I said I wanted to be alone to put some finishing touches on my play."

"Did he believe you?"

"I'm not sure. Do you think I should have told him the truth?"

"I thought your play was finished."

"It is."

Ruth looked out the window. The sun was halfway down the horizon. The scene was like one of those cosmic illustrations of the birth and death of planets. Without turning to me, she spoke: "Gene was never finished with his play. He talked about it all the time. Even when it was in rehearsal he talked about it, asking me did I think he was saying too much or not enough, did I think it was believable or not believable."

"And did you tell him?"

"I told him what I thought he wanted to hear."

"That was the right thing to do, but do you think he guessed you were doing that?"

She turned back to me, her eyes taking on their oblique cast. Slightly Oriental. Maybe one of those Mongolian invasions had reached where her ancestors had lived.

"I never knew what to tell him," she said. I noticed her eyes thicken with tears. "I never knew what to say to him. He is so considerate of other people, it is true, but he demanded from me what I couldn't give."

"What was that?"

"To be *him*. To give him some part that was missing. To be a bridge, and then to remove the bridge when it wasn't needed." She regarded me with accusing eyes, as if I had failed her in the way she had failed Gene. "I felt so sorry for him," she went on. "I don't think you know how much he tortures himself. He wants to be more than he is. Do you know what I'm saying? He is not satisfied with his play. He thinks it did not succeed, much less than he intended. He knows how much you and Leo helped to make it better, and he is bitter about that. Always, always, this pressure. Do this for me. Make a miracle. He wanted that from me. He wanted me to tell him what was missing, and I didn't know, I just didn't know. I didn't have the gift for it. He didn't forgive me for this. He would not admit to such a thing, but it's true . . ."

So there was my answer. I had insisted on knowing what went on between them, and now Ruth had told me. Translucent shadows on a screen, but the shapes were clear enough. Pride wouldn't allow Gene to demand from me what he had demanded from Ruth—and poor Ruth had so much less to give.

Well, what it was, simply, was that he wanted a return. Never expressed in those crass terms, but there was the other side of the coin of consideration and politeness. The argument of frustration. What was the good of love if when he withdrew and time returned, the line still remained unfinished, the vision remained unattained?

The week would end and life would resume for all of us. I would go on being Gene's friend, and he and I would talk as we had done before. About what? Why not this purloined week? Men talk about such things, boast about such things. He had—*explicitly* —freed us both to have this week of frenetic sex, and Ruth's eyes had taken on their pensive look, and I felt more apprehensive than buoyed, more empty than replete.

8

Fifth Avenue tree Limb Kills Man on Bus.

I had cut out that item because just a few days before I had plucked a perfect leaf from an overhanging limb while riding on the Fifth Avenue bus with Ruth. That unlucky man had also been riding one of those double-decker, open-air buses. I had cut out another item, this one a bold, banner headline: GERMANY AND RUSSIA SIGN 10-YEAR NON-AGGRESSION PACT. Also this: *Sidney Coe Howard Killed by Tractor on Estate. Playwright Is Crushed in Berkshire Garage.*

Gene said, "I read his play *The Silver Cord.* It's about possessive mothers. Did you ever read it?"

"No."

"You should. It's good."

Leo Shulkin loved my play *War and Peace in the Bronx.* He said it had the kind of power generated by Odets' *Awake and Sing,* but without the propaganda. He said it was cheerful Chekhov, catching the doom and details of domestic paralysis, but offering a credible way out. I recalled that he had come on with similar hosannas about Gene's play, but I chose to find more genuine enthusiasm about mine. Naturally.

He had left several messages for me with Anna during my week's absence, and we met the day after my return. He directed me to meet him in the coffee shop at the foot of the building where the Forty-Something Street Players rehearsed. The same deep-fat smell and the fat, bald proprietor with the soiled apron.

"I want to get started right away," Leo boomed.

"Good," I said.

"I let Hannah Jacoby read it," he informed me. "She thinks it's great. I want her to do the part of the mother."

"Wonderful!"

"And I've got someone to play the part of Daniel. He's only a kid—about twenty-one—but he's a fucking genius. I swear. They do come along every once in a while. I'm only praying we can get started before someone grabs him. He says he'll do Daniel. He likes the part. Is that all right with you?"

"I haven't even met the guy," I said. "Besides, you're doing the casting. . . . Leo, do you mind my asking a personal question?"

"I don't mind anything."

"Where's the money coming from?"

"From me."

"You?"

Leo gave me his Tartar look: mustache-concealed smile, inscrutable eyes. He corrected the "me" to include the originating source—his father. His father was a painting contractor who had branched out into the paint manufacturing business. He had a factory near Atlantic Avenue in Brooklyn. He sold paint to the contractors at half the price of the national brands. He was going to be a rich man, and he wanted Leo to be whatever Leo wanted to be. He gave him three years. He'd finance Leo's theater ventures for three years. If Leo made it, well and good, he wouldn't owe his father a dime. If he didn't make it, he would go into the painting business with his father.

My father was not, never would be, on his way toward wealth, but the Shulkin father-son relationship seemed fashioned beyond the luck of money.

August 30. HITLER NOTE KEEPS NEGOTIATIONS OPEN: BERLIN HOPEFUL FOR PEACE. SLOWS WAR MOVES.

They would invade in two days, so there must have been division after division of the *wehrmacht* deployed along the Polish border. There must have been squadrons of Stuka bombers keeping their engines tuned along the eastern frontier. In two days the world would know how much Berlin hoped for peace.

September 1.

I abandoned my Herschel play. Perhaps I would go back when the tidal wave receded. That is, if I survived.

I had no hope for Herschel.

Lou Siegal was full of plans. New, heavy equipment arrived at the shop.

"In lieu of the situation," he said, "I think you'll be needed more inside than outside." Somewhere he had heard the expression "in lieu of," which he took to be a fancier was of saying "in view of." He aimed a thick finger at me. "The problem," he decreed, with heavy portentousness, "will be production. Do you follow me?"

I nodded. I followed him, but I was considering with sinking heart only the fact that my freedom would be curtailed. As outside salesman, I had the time and freedom to finagle lunches with Ruth, with Gene, or to meet with Leo Shulkin and consult on the fabulous furnishings for the dream castle we were constructing.

"We're also going to need more space," Mr. Siegal confided to me. "Half the seventh floor in this building is available. They're asking an arm and a leg, the bastards, but I'm going to take it. What do you think?"

"Oh, yes."

He regarded me in his heavy-lidded way, trying to take a reading on my state of commitment. Was I showing the proper spirit, or just sloughing off these questions? He wasn't sure. I was. What the hell did I care about smart executive moves? I was a man in love. I was a man whose finished play was in the early, intoxicating stages of production. I was a man of draft age in a world at war. Not this country yet, but there was as little doubt about that eventuality as about Hitler's ultimate aim.

Mr. Siegal told me he had bought heavy-duty sewing machines and a heavy-duty stamping press. Not new. A fortune new, but in excellent secondhand condition. And you just don't walk in and buy such machines. You have to bid for them. "Maybe," he mused, "I should have taken you with me. You're going to have to learn how to swim with the sharks."

He was right. Lou Siegal was always right in his hard-nosed, bald-pated, practical way. But it was as clear as his shining scalp that an unheard music was leading this clumsy waltz. I was strenuously trying to stay in step, but my heart wasn't in it.

Finally, disappointed that I wasn't picking up as quickly and brightly as usual, he asked, rather sullenly, "Why do you think I spent thousands of dollars buying machines like that?"

"Are you thinking of bringing out a new line?"

He sighed and raised one heavy shoulder. "A new line," he grunted.

Then it came to me. A war in Europe had started. Heavy-duty sewing machines. A heavy-duty stamping press. Of course! He probably had no contract yet, but he was anticipating. A tidal wave of contracts and subcontracts. I felt a recoil against such opportunism. A shadow of it must have passed across my face.

"What do you think General Motors is doing right now?" he asked. "How do you think a country wins a war? They outproduce the other side, that's how."

And speaking of production, I had made no progress in that other campaign General Siegal had laid out. He didn't say anything specific, but I could see that this series of smart moves included more than just machinery. He had allowed time and room for wisdom to ripen, but as yet I had given no unequivocal sign of ripening. I had been hoping that the campaign would be dropped, that Harriet would have made the happy connection by this time, but it evidently hadn't happened. I resorted to my usual diversionary tactic.

"How did you know these were the machines you would need?" I asked.

He nodded his ponderous head. "I didn't know," he said, "but sometimes you have to take a chance. That's where experience and judgment come in. Being a smart businessman, a smart anything, sometimes means acting on what you're not totally sure of. You can't always be absolutely right. Sometimes you have to close your eyes and jump."

I nodded at his general shrewdness. I nodded, latterly and reflectively, at what I was beginning to perceive as his gift of analogy. I considered for the first time how much he had managed to convey to me without ever once having made a direct statement.

The outbreak of war freed Anna Strauss to speak of Germany at last. I sensed something superstitious in this. To have openly invoked the gods before this might have been taxing divine will, but now that the gods had allies she was more confident. She even felt confident enough to invoke her own Delphic powers.

"They will win battles," she said, "but they will lose the war."

"Is that a fact?" I said. "What makes you think so?"

I was inwardly quailing before the brutal fact that the Nazi forces had all but demolished Poland in a few weeks.

"I know this," Anna said, decisively. "They will make it so, to lose."

"Are you saying they want to lose?"

"Yah! They want to lose. They do not believe in victory, only defeat, and so they will arrange to lose."

Whistling in the dark, but in the Straussian mode, much in keeping with the filigree lady's other theories. I couldn't take it seriously. My own oracle told me that the Nazis wanted to win, and that they had arranged everything with diabolical efficiency, and that they would know all too well what to do with their victory.

"I hope you're right," I said.

We were sitting in the kitchen. It was morning. I was having breakfast. Late summer hung over the river and the bridge, seen from the kitchen window in a soft haze. Anna had been right about Mrs. Zimmerman. That little wraith had remained almost invisible, hiding in her room, making mewling noises when she did appear. Poor Mrs. Zimmerman, a human dustball blown to this alien place by a violent gust of wind.

As Anna had predicted, Mrs. Zimmerman didn't bother me, but something else did, had, and I had ended those nighttime passages, not by pronouncement, but by withdrawal. Since returning from my week at the shore with Ruth, I had taken to staying out most evenings. I saw Ruth frequently. I went to movies. There were more and more frequent meetings with Leo Shulkin as he progressed toward actual rehearsals. *My play! Rehearsals!* And, of course, Gene, who was nearing completion of the rewrite of his subsidized play.

That perfumed, secretive thing. Like a lighted street lamp, it was unseen in daylight, had no daylight reality, but it glowed phosphorescently and continually in the dark of my mind. Some things are meant only for the dark. To speak of it at all, to anyone, would be to give it daylight existence, and I couldn't allow that to be. To give it daylight existence would be to sanction it, and it was not to be sanctioned. Anna had given me that one admonition to regard it as nothing at all, a noctural happenstance, but her saying so hadn't assuaged my sense of sacrilege.

She had continued to come to my room at irregular intervals, touching her finger to my lips, slipping in beside me. But there was a key in the door of that room. I had never used it. After my week with Ruth, I turned the key each evening before going to sleep. I don't recall ever hearing the doorknob turn. I think Anna was aware that it had ended about the same time that I did.

Why didn't I go away? That would have been even more definite, and it would have spared me the discomfort of daily confrontation. I didn't want to be there any longer, but I hadn't come upon the word or the gesture that would be my signal of release. A vague responsibility held me. A vague incompletion held me. I would eventually leave on my own, and not too distantly, but there was that indefinable interim during which I waited for a signal. Something was needed that would balance the part I had played in my own ensnarement.

Gene had wanted to break away from his mother, and he had casually suggested that I move in. Gene had wanted his pleasure with Ruth, but at a distance, and when that distance was threatened he had brought it to an end. In critical moments, Saul Klein would step in as Gene stepped out. That may not have been exactly how he conceived it or perceived it, but that's the way it had worked out.

Was he passing his unwanted women along to me? Did he know

what had happened between mother and friend? Had that happening been more or less prefigured? Was it part of a plan? What refinement of decadence would account for such a thing? Would a little turn of the lens bring an entirely different morality into view? Was I some sort of way station for the superfluities of Gene Strauss' life?

No answers to these questions, because these questions couldn't be asked. Not while some semblance of sanity or moral equilibrium remained. Maybe, in some thunderous moment of reckoning, there would be questions and answers.

Or would all of this be absorbed in the normal metabolism of time?

Anna sensed something else, my quickened impermanence, and wondered what it might mean in terms of Gene. Another contact broken?

"Will you be seeing Gene tonight?" she asked, in her offhand way.

"Not tonight."

"Do you not see each other as before?"

"Oh, yes," I answered hastily, untruthfully. "The same as always."

"He has promised to come here tomorrow for dinner," she said. "Will you do me a favor, please, and remind him of this."

That was odd. Gene had a telephone in his apartment, could easily be reached. Why ask me to tell him? Because, I figured to myself, she wanted *me* to tell him. For some reason, she wanted that gambit.

"Mrs. Strauss—"

"Still Mrs. Strauss!"

She was right! What idiocy!

"Anna, my parents have been asking me—"

"Yah! Your parents. I know. They do not want you living here. Now listen to me, Saul . . ."

Suddenly, surprisingly, she was weeping. She had on her pink morning robe. She stretched out her arms along the tabletop of chipped enamel, doing nothing to conceal or control the flow of tears, rubbing it in good that she was a woman well acquainted with tears, letting them flow as naturally as she would water her plants.

" . . . This has not always been my life," she recited, in cadence with her tears. "I had my own house. Servants. Friends. Evenings with people, not always alone. Evenings with educated and interesting people—*bedutender Musiker*—and I will not—*will not!*—be treated like a dishrag! While my Albert lived, I was never unfaithful. Him to me, yes! Oh, yes! Many times! Never I to him! But what am I to do? What life do I have here, day after day? Taking care of this old woman for a few dollars. This is not your business, yah? I do not make it your business. You are not responsible for me. I have a son. I only tell you so that you can know what happens in a life. Perhaps you can use it in one of your plays. And you can tell my son this, too. You can tell him that I know, I know —*ich weiss genau*—what it means, this new apartment, this new life. Now I tell you, if you want to find another place, I cannot stop you. I understand. My goodness! You are a free person. But give me some time to find somebody for the room. Stay until the end of the month—"

"I had no intention—"

"—and you must tell Gene this. You are his friend. You must tell him to be careful, not to go too far . . ."

"Your mother thinks the Germans will arrange to lose the war," I said to Gene.

He thought about that for a few seconds, then said, "I think she is right."

I shook my head. "There's something in the Strauss logic that escapes me," I said. "To me, they give the appearance of wanting to win—of *winning*—hands down, and in the most efficient, murderous way possible."

"Oh, I'm sure they think they want to win, right now," Gene said. I noticed that he was wearing a new suit, at least new to me. It was a blue-gray tweed, a material so soft in appearance that it was all I could do to keep from testing it with my fingers. I imagined a magical loom somewhere in misty Scotland that spun

224

out yard goods only for those who had proved their warrant to a special destiny. He said, "Does it make any sense for a nation that is engaged in a world war and truly wants to win to behave as Germany does? Why should they mobilize world opinion against themselves, unless in some deep way they are already preparing, taking revenge for, their ultimate defeat?"

I had never thought of it in that way. America was not in the war yet, but a nation that would blind itself to the consequences of bringing the United States into a war against it must surely have a kink in its survival instincts. Now the Strauss reasoning did make a kind of romantically perverted sense—and because it did, I could make out a parallel between the German paradox and Eugene Strauss. Perhaps Gene could see the German error so well because he knew so well how to avoid such an error. The charm. The civility. The fair-haired, calm-eyed charisma. And yet, with all that magnetism going for him, he managed to create a considerable amount of fear and suspicion. Perhaps his understanding of Germany derived from certain affinities as well. The truth was that he had hurt others. Perhaps not meaning to, perhaps not even aware that he had—ah, but that was impossible! He must know. Ruth. His mother. Me. Whatever our friendship had been, it was no longer the same. We were drawing apart, and it seemed to me that the fact was a matter of no great moment to Gene. Which could only mean that he had never been aware of, or had not valued as I had, that friendship.

"You were in Washington Heights the other night, weren't you?" I asked, remembering for some remotely relevant reason Anna's strange request, and my having acted on it. I had phoned him, discussed a possible dinner in the Village, casually mentioned that he was expected in Washington Heights.

He nodded. "Speaking of arranging things," he said, "do you arrange not to be at the apartment when you know I'm coming?"

"I wouldn't say I arrange it. I figure it's time you and your mother want to yourselves."

He gave me a bland, skeptical look. "You're very occupied these days," he said.

"Well, yes . . . rehearsals . . . *War and Peace.*"

"Is Leo enthusiastic?"

"He seems to be. . . . Apparently he does have money of his own. Or money as good as his own."

"I know," Gene said.

I wondered how he knew. I wondered if he had been in touch with Leo, with Hannah Jacoby. No reason why he shouldn't be. He was on good terms with everyone. If people felt neglected or betrayed, it wasn't his fault. He had made no promises, asked for no greater involvement than he himself was willing to undertake. And wasn't he right? I could think of no promise he had made that he had left unfulfilled. Involvement with Strauss was in the eye of the beholder.

But wasn't there something wrong with someone who read so little between the lines? Was that deliberate indifference or emotional myopia?

"I expect I'll be moving," I announced. "Maybe by the middle of next month."

He became silent and reflective. "That isn't necessary at all," he said.

"What isn't?"

"I hope you believe that it makes no difference to me that you are seeing Ruth," he said. "I hope that isn't the reason."

"I don't see what the two things have to do with each other," I said.

"I thought you might be blaming me for the guilt you mistakenly feel," he said.

He was right, but not in the way that he thought.

"Listen," I said, "there's something I've been meaning to tell you. I was with Ruth that week at the shore, when I was supposed to be putting the finishing touches on my play. We weren't at the shore, really. We just went there during the day."

"I figured something of the sort. You might have told me."

"But that has nothing to do with my moving," I told him. "I'm not sure what I'm going to do. My mother is convinced the world is coming to an end, and she'd like to have the family together for the occasion. She may be right, you know. In any event, I may move back to the Bronx for a while, just to calm her nerves. You might think of doing the same. For Anna's sake, I mean."

If nothing else, I had performed the duty Anna had imposed on me. I wasn't sure what Anna was trying to tell Gene, but whatever it was I had performed my part.

But Gene was suddenly and icily the Gene I knew, drawing back, saying. "That's out of the question."

"Okay," I said. "You know best."

9

It was still a foreign war, but many of us were already in it. We had begun to live our war lives. We went about our jobs, read the newspapers, listened to the news broadcasts, watched the newsreels, continued our private entanglements, but the war was as much with us as though a bomb had been dropped on Broadway. Everything was revved up, intensified.

The interior atmosphere in which I lived was as full of elements as the one surrounding the earth. There was Ruth. There was my play. There was Anna. There was Gene. There was Herschel Grynszpan, caught in a stop-action frame in a prison somewhere in Paris. There was my job. There was the war. Exciting and terrifying. All of it coming together as the elements in the outer atmosphere came together, building up into an omnipresent cloud, an eerie glow at the center, implicit with change. I woke each morning thinking of the war or Ruth, went to sleep each night thinking of Ruth or the war. Sometimes, I connected the two in dreams.

Once I dreamt that Ruth and I were walking up one of those boardwalk ramps in Coney Island or the Rockaways. Off to our right was a vacated, ghostly still amusement park. The boardwalk was similarly vacated. An overcast day. The oppressive isolation surrounded the dream like a gas. We stopped at a boardwalk stand—the only one open—and the bare-armed hot dog vendor there was wearing a swastika armband. He also wore the fatigue hat of a German infantryman. He handed us hot dogs on a metal tray, nodding his head in the direction we were supposed to look. We turned and saw a German tank with its Maltese cross parked on the other side of the boardwalk. As if on order, we crossed the boardwalk and stood obediently at the side of the tank. I examined the mud-encrusted, massive, intricately machined tread. Hopeless, hopeless! Nothing could match the brutal superiority of German machinery. On the beach, near the breakers, German soldiers were lined up in military formation. They marched up the steps to the boardwalk on soundless boots. In dread, I waited for someone to approach us and ask the fatal question. The dream found its center in the suffocating uncertainty of Ruth's answer. She was the one who had to decide whether to answer in English or German. Our salvation depended on the choice. One or the other would save us from being blown to bits by the tank's penile cannon. No one approached us, but I could see off in the distance a small, haunted figure standing near the entrance of the amusement park. The dream informed me that it was Herschel Grynszpan. Terror accumulated like the ancient execution of stones—until I woke myself with a cry that began in the dream and ended in consciousness. It was a replica of the cry I had heard so often coiling out of my father's nightmare-ridden nights.

"Do you have nightmares?" Anna asked me the next morning.

"I'm afraid so."

"Yah. I too."

"Leo Shulkin is planning to open my play by the middle of October," I told Ruth.

"Oh, how wonderful!"

"Yes."

"You don't seem terribly excited."

"I am. It's just . . ."

"What?"

"I just wonder whether my play isn't something Leo is doing in a slack season. Nothing else around."

"You know that isn't so. You told me he is putting his own money in it. Why should he do that? No one wants to throw money away. Do you think he was more enthusiastic about Gene's play?"

"I get that feeling."

"But you told me yourself—"

Yes, yes! I had told her myself. I admitted that I had told her myself. I admitted that Leo had made comparisons to Chekhov and Odets, but I wanted her to walk with me along the primrose path to paranoia. Gene's play was serious business; mine was a slapdash piece of foolery. I had done it on a dare, like the Parachute Jump.

"I suppose," I said, "I should consider myself lucky that anyone is willing to do it at all, no matter how."

"Yes," she quickly agreed. "You should consider yourself lucky. If there's anything one wants to do in this life, one had better do it quickly."

We were in perfect agreement about that. Doomsday was in the air, along with a terrifically pungent excitement, the smell of ozone, the smell of burnt cordite. Ruth talked about it, as did I, as did everybody, but only I could measure the hidden displacement in Ruth. Every newsreel bomb burst was a replica of her own interior devastation.

"How long do you think this war will go on?" she asked me.

"Years."

"How will it end?"

"Hitler will be destroyed. Not because of anything I can see, but because any other outcome is unthinkable."

"Isn't it funny to be alive?" she said. "Alive right now."

"Why funny?"

"Because it may all end with us. Have you ever thought of that? All those thousands of years of history, all that evolution, and we may be the final actors. I suppose we should be grateful that we were let in before the door closed."

"I know what you mean," I said. "I have thought of it. It's like the ocean's edge. I thought of it when we were at the beach. All those thousands of miles of water ending there, right there. Why there? It seemed so arbitrary. And yet everything ends somewhere, even the universe. But I don't think that we're the final actors. Something tells me that the world will survive. You and

I will survive."

She nodded, was silent. I think she too thought we would survive, but at that ragged moment of her life she wasn't too pleased with the prospect. The war was her private metaphor. It offered her an acceptable alternative.

We made love, not every time we were together, but often. And Gene was always there. He combined us in the only way we could be combined: he renewed my love each day with the constant threat of its dispossession.

10

WAR AND PEACE IN THE BRONX had its first performance in another hotel, an older hotel than the one in which Gene's was performed, but conveniently located and accommodating a larger audience. Hannah Jacoby played the part of the mother, and that clear-eyed, soft-voiced young man, Josh Green, played Daniel. His real name wasn't Josh Green, of course. Every Jew in theater changed his name in those days. His real name was Jacob Greenblatt.

It's hard for me to imagine a competence of which I am totally devoid—Jascha Heifetz, Joe DiMaggio—the kind of competence that can be perfected but never learned. Acting talent seems to me such a congenital trait. One may study and study, practice and practice, but unless there's the inherent thing it will only go so far. Straining only reveals the seams. The naturals absorb their art or skill through their skin, and everything they do enhances the gift with which they were born.

Josh was such a talent. He had the singular thing Gene had praised—the individual mark, the cachet. Josh's was a soft, marvelously flexible way of speaking. He was the vocal opposite of Leo. Leo's voice gave the impression of rocks grinding in the earth. Josh's words came in a frictionless flow, the rhythms and inflections informed by an instinct that seemed to operate independently of its possessor.

Josh, too, was a Bronx boy, the South Bronx. He told me that

232

he was brought up by an aunt, his father having been gunned down by the mob (another father fixation?) and his mother having run off with a *tummler* who toured the borscht circuit in summer and played cheap Miami night spots in winter. All honeytoned and seraphic, as if this were the ideal background for a boy, fun and games.

Josh lied as easily as he drew breath, and there was no consistency in his lying. Others told me stories about Josh's beginnings that were totally at variance with the stories Josh had told me. He would interject the truth whenever the mood moved him, not in remorse or to prevent detection, but simply to add the flavor of truth to the general conceit.

That was all right with me. I didn't lie as a matter of course, but neither did I find the truth that sacrosanct. I too manipulated facts. But I did keep the truth as one of the finer intimacies to be shared. Gene knew the truth about me. So did Ruth.

Leo Shulkin believed there was an aunt in Josh's background, and a mother, and also a home for boys. No legitimate father.

I got to know Hannah Jacoby better because of Josh. Hannah hated Josh, hated and feared him. She pleaded with me to get Leo to replace him. She acknowledged his talent, but she was terrified of him, and she tried passionately to make out a case. Her claim was that Josh might turn in a virtuoso performance, but the play as a whole would be damaged by his presence. He was a little monster. He had a diabolical way of making others look bad in a scene. She didn't know how he did it, but he did, just for the mean hell of it. She couldn't work with him.

"Then why don't you tell Leo?" I asked.

"I did. He says I've got to learn to work with anyone who comes along. That's the actor's occupational hazard. I *know* that, but there can be exceptions even to that rule. Josh is the exception. He isn't anyone. He's special. He's evil."

"He's also very good," I said.

Hannah narrowed her eyes and dilated her nostrils and gave me a bitter look. "Thanks," she said, and turned abruptly away.

My previous experience with Hannah had been that night of the Strauss-Shulkin confrontation, at the celebration of Gene's play. Leo's Tartar chief smile and the kitchen scene. The night of that dark, unmentionable culmination. I wondered if Hannah's complaint wasn't motivated by something other than Josh's malevolent influence. I wondered if that "something other" wasn't behind Leo's lofty advice. Josh making Hannah look bad might be a petty revenge under the guise of a tough professionalism.

Everything about the rehearsal of my play was a mixture of Black Art and Revelation. I had written the lines, but I had difficulty recognizing them on hearing their transformation. The voices I had heard in my head were not the voices I heard in the bare loft where the play was rehearsed. My voices shared my experience, my personality, my meaning. *These* voices were the voices of strangers. Different personalities giving different meanings to every line. I didn't think them all wrong, inferior, but so astonishingly different.

I had no idea what could be done with a line. It had always been other people's lines I had listened to in the movies or on the stage. Josh, for a fabulous instance. He imbued my lines with his own personality—not his offstage personality, which was altogether different, but with that other self that took over in the alchemy of acting.

He would improvise small changes in every line while speaking the line, so that the meaning that would emerge conformed to the new Daniel being created through Josh's mutable genius. This street urchin who couldn't get through a single sentence without its quota of *fucks* and *shits* could modulate someone else's words with the skill of a Heifetz.

Often, Hannah would take me aside and hiss her fury. "Is that what you wanted?" she would demand. "Is that what you had in mind? He's *using* your lines! Not for the play, for himself! He's making the whole thing into a one-man show. Nothing he does is in the spirit of the play! Don't you see that, Saul? Tell the truth! Is this the play you wrote, or is this something Josh Green is using for his own glory?"

I admitted that it wasn't exactly what I had in mind, but I also had to admit that it was better than what I had in mind. I realized she was right in her accusations, but I also realized Josh was right in his improvisations. He was so dramatically, spine-tinglingly right that he might just lift the play out of its amateur, hole-in-a-corner status and make it something larger, better, dazzling, reputation-making. Wouldn't she want that?

No, she wouldn't. She had her own pride. She didn't want to be lifted by a Josh Green, thank you. She'd do her own lifting.

But she stayed with the play, bringing more and more to her own role, ferociously inspired to surpass herself, to surpass Josh, which of course she couldn't do. The play was predominantly his in the first act, and so rigged that his silence in the second act, his central silence, left all the other voices hopelessly secondary. One waited for the return of his voice even while listening to the others.

Josh was not unaware of the spleen he pumped up. He said to me, "What the fuck is she bitching about? That big-titted *yenta* can be a real pain in the ass. You know what she wants, Saul? I'm tellin' ya. What she wants is a good hosing. Ya know? I think you oughta give her a good hosing. It'll quiet her down. We'll all have some peace. Look, am I taking anything away from her? Am I? She's good. I tell her she's good. But you know what her fuckin' trouble is? She's got too much fuckin' *character*. You tell her—don't say I said so—but you tell her not to be so fuckin' fine. Tell her to be more of a selfish shit. She'll go much further that way."

Naturally I didn't tell Hannah anything of the sort. Why should I peddle Josh Green's corrupt philosophy? As for the other, the "hosing"—I was in love with someone else. I didn't want any part of that intramural dogfight. That was Leo's job.

War and Peace in the Bronx succeeded as a play—even more so than Gene's play. It was a good play remarkably well acted. The reality of a trapped, unhappy, self-destructive family was brought to life by mere words.

Leo began a bulldozing campaign. His theater entrepreneur, Ben Something, was present on opening night, and my play received a front-page review in his theater journal. It received that attention mainly because of Josh, and it probably suffered its final fate for the same reason. Word-of-mouth had it that there was an exciting talent to be seen in a little play Off-Broadway. "Off-

Broadway" hadn't been given official status yet. It was still a geographical identification rather than a numerical one.

The play was praised. I thought I saw Leo's large, commanding hand in this: "In the tradition of Chekhov and Odets, Saul Klein, the author of *War and Peace in the Bronx,* has brought to the stage a slice-of-life realism that is undercut by comedy at its most tragic and haunted by tragedy at its funniest . . ."

The hotel auditorium was filled every night for almost two months. Leo made back his investment, and it began to look as if the author of the play might come in for a cut of the pie. Gene came to see it, of course, and he was generous in his praise of the performance, the direction and especially of the play itself.

"Of course, you're lucky to have Josh," he said, "but the play would have attracted attention even without him."

My parents came to see the play, naturally. I wasn't sure which Rose wouldn't forgive me for, seeing it or not seeing it. In any event, I told them about it, and they came, and Rose didn't have much to say. My father's credo being silence, his silence didn't surprise.

"A lot of people are coming to see," Rose observed.

"That's supposed to be good," I said.

"Anybody you know? Aunts? Uncles? Cousins?"

"No, I haven't seen any of those. Natalie and Rita are coming."

My mother nodded. "Well," she said, "I'm an uneducated woman. I don't understand. It looks like it's your own family up there, and then it doesn't. I don't know. I don't know what I think. Maybe I'll know later."

Natalie slowly shook her head. She said, "Tell me, you wrote the play or you just took notes?"

"You should know," I said. "Have you heard any of it before?"

"Yes and no. Word for word, no . . . but all of it has a very familiar ring."

"It should. I didn't make up the story. That I experienced."

"I see. I didn't know that writers used their own experience. I thought they made everything up. I thought that's what writing meant."

"Now you know."

"Now I know."

Rita said, "I'm the sister, right?"

"Not exactly."

"I am. Oh, my God, Saul, I don't know how you could have written something like that! I don't mean you shouldn't have, just that I don't know how you *could* have. I was scarcely able to breathe. I couldn't believe what was going on before my eyes. I felt that somebody had left a door open, and all through the play I wanted to get up and close the door."

"Your play is so much more natural," Ruth said, the significant omission being *than whose.* She said, "If I didn't know who had written that play, I would still know that each of those characters was related to Saul Klein. I can see you in them, them in you. That fellow who plays the main character—what's his name? Josh Green?—he's an exceptional one, isn't he? I think you're going to have a very big success."

Bigger than Gene's? I think the implication was there. We had reached the stage where Gene could be mentioned only in a certain way. I could speak of meetings with Gene, even tell Ruth what we talked about, but it had to be kept in some timeless, motionless medium. It was as if we were talking about a defunct pagan god, one allowed room in the pantheon but no voting rights. I experimented with keeping Gene entirely out of our conversations, but sooner or later she would give a tug on the reins.

"Aren't you seeing your friend anymore?"

"Sure."

"I thought maybe you weren't seeing him anymore. You hardly ever mention him."

I mentioned him.

No big producer appeared to glorify the name of Saul Klein. God knows it wasn't for want of trying. Leo, who had sniffed his own possible elevation, tried mightily. He put back in advertising most of his recouped money. He spent hours on the phone pleading and cajoling. He gave out blocks of tickets to labor groups, political organizations, women's groups. He roared and roamed through the canyons of the city, arm twisting, Pied Pipering. But eyes had turned elsewhere. It was only a two-acter. It was too confined in scope. The world had passed into a new, all-consuming history. A war was on. Producers were looking for something big and relevant.

Then Josh Green announced that he was leaving the cast. He had been surreptitiously negotiating for a much larger part in a much larger production. Anyone in the cast would have done the same, I imagine, but Josh did it with a smile and two days' notice. I think he rather liked the consternation he left behind him.

Saul Klein and Hannah Jacoby made common cause over a shared fate. We suffered the same slow hemorrhage of desire and disappointment. We founded a new religion, sending up prayers regularly for a sign of beneficent concern.

"You know," Hannah declared, ringingly, "I simply do not believe that this play will be allowed to die. That's not just special pleading. It's not just because I'm in it. It's because of the theme. I mean, it's a theme that says something about the generations, about all immigrant families in America. Not just Jewish families. All! It says something about the crippling inability of people to communicate with each other!"

I learned something about Hannah's own background during that time. She told me that her father was a rabbi, and that her own life had become a daily contest, different from the one going on in the play, but one every bit as bitter. Her father didn't approve. It was as simple and total as that. He thought actresses were little better than whores. The play's closing would mean having to find a new job, but continuing her career might mean her having to find a new family.

I told her that I owed her an apology. "You were right about Josh," I said. "I regret now that I wasn't able to see the truth of what you were saying. Too much dependence on one person. It was just as you said—a one-man glory train. The play would have been better off without him. Sure, he's terrific, but so are you.

Josh may be a gutter genius, but I can see now that his tricky, egotistical performance sucked the integrity out of the play."

The futility of frustration.

"Saul, you remember what I say," Hannah said, more an incantation than a statement. *"War and Peace* will be picked up. Somebody is going to invest money in this play. It's too good to be left to die. If I can't believe that, there's nothing I can believe!"

Tweedledee and Tweedledum trying to puff life into a corpse.

Ruth came back to the subject of the characters in my play. She wanted to know if their prototypes existed in life. I could well imagine why she wanted to know.

"The people in my play are made-up people," I told her. "They would have to be. I don't know my parents well enough to exploit their characters. For God's sake, my father doesn't even talk! I mean, *really,* not at all! I couldn't very well have a nontalking character, could I? It's only the situation that's similar."

She looked at me with a faint, skeptical smile. Maybe she was right. Maybe I knew more than I—or Gene—thought I knew. Maybe the truth about people can only be discovered by invention. I may have changed the outlines, but the heart of the matter had been taken from the real hearts of real people.

Nevertheless, I felt hostility toward Ruth for forcing me to examine my own truths in this way. I took quick revenge. "Do you think that the Rena of Gene's play was actually you?" I asked.

She didn't answer, and I immediately felt remorse. She looked away and remembered things that I couldn't begin to imagine. She took a tangent, saying, "I don't think you and Gene are as friendly as you once were. Am I wrong to say that?"

I considered some seconds before answering. Of course it was true, but I hadn't found a way yet of dealing with it. Ruth's observation gave me the opportunity.

"I don't know how I feel about Gene, to tell you the truth," I said. "I'm very mixed up in my feelings. Which shouldn't surprise you. I think you've been mixed up a hell of a lot longer than I have. You know, if it was just a case of Gene Strauss succeeding, going on, finding his special destiny, then one could say goodbye, good luck and so forth. But it isn't just that. It's what he takes with him, or leaves behind. I got a hunch I'll be following the career of Mr. Strauss for the next hundred years, and I'll be damned if I want to spend my time that way! Even *some* of my time! The thing is . . . the thing is that I don't think we've affected his life very much. That also bothers me. We haven't affected his life very much one way or the other. I don't think he'll spend much time thinking about us. Maybe he will about you, I don't know. I shouldn't speak for you . . . but my own feeling is that his only real companion is his special destiny. We can't get rid of him as easily as he gets rid of us, *that's* what I'm saying! He's taken up room—important room!"

Ruth listened to my surprisingly long speech—a speech that violated all the taboos between us—and at the end of my speech, after a few seconds of considered silence, she said, simply, flatly, "Yes."

11

BECAUSE THE WAR had begun and all things would henceforth be changed, I wrote a letter to the French consulate in New York, using the Bronx as my return address, asking about the fate of Herschel Grynszpan. This time I received a reply. It said that Herschel Grynszpan had been found mentally unstable at the time of his crime and had been removed to a hospital where he would receive treatment.

In a way, my fantasies about springing Herschel had come true. A different cast of actors and a different (but not unimagined) set of circumstances, but his rescue had been effected by French resistance. Would Herschel now join the French army and meet his death bravely fighting the *wehrmacht?* The *wehrmacht* . . . the *luftwaffe* . . . *panzers* . . . *blitzkrieg* . . . the daily vocabulary of the newspapers and the radio now that the German armies were rolling across Europe. By September 10, the *wehrmacht* was sweeping around the Warsaw defenses. By September 18, the Russians were driving into Poland from the other direction, and by October the *Times* was no longer making banner headlines out of the daily carnage. Poland was finished. There was a full-scale European war on. Ships were being torpedoed. And now certain things were being revealed that had been known before but had been buried for the sake of a diplomacy that had failed.

There was a British White Paper: "Vivid accounts of the tortures practiced at Buchenwald given in memoranda included in reports by F. M. Shepherd, consulate, Dresden, on the basis of statements made to him by former prisoners at that camp . . ." There followed an account of the practices that were already known to some. Beatings with barbed-wire birches. (Did that mean they took a birch rod and wrapped barbed wire around it, and *then* whipped bare flesh with it?) There was the sweat box. Many inmates, it was reported, fell out dead after a treatment. The report wasn't detailed about this device. There was the tree-binding and the merry-go-round, where the victims' arms were bound tightly around a tree behind him so that his feet barely touched the ground, and if he didn't move fast enough to please his tormentors they kicked him in the ankles. There was a place called Dachau, its practices already known but hitherto concealed, again for the sake of diplomacy. Here prisoners had their heads shaved upon arrival. Three hundred were jammed into huts designed for sixty. The camp was surrounded by an electrified fence of barbed wire, and it was strictly forbidden for inmates to go near the fence. Guards were posted in towers with orders to shoot anyone approaching the fence. Newly arrived prisoners hadn't been apprised of the camp rules, and they were beckoned by the guards to come closer, and when they did the guards opened fire with machine guns. If prisoners were to be released, they were lined up in the morning at 5:00 A.M., made to stand for four or five hours before a camp doctor got around to examining them for any incriminating marks on their bodies. Then they were doused with water from a hose in temperatures below freezing . . .

These reports were released in the *Times* on October 31. They were known long before. They must have been. I cut out the pages containing the report. It began on page 1 and continued on page 5. Also on page 5 was an advertisement of a "Russek's Coat with Blended Mink" at one hundred dollars. Hurok was presenting the Ballet Russe de Monte Carlo. *Abe Lincoln in Illinois,* with Raymond Massey as Lincoln, was still playing on Broadway. Also *The Time of Your Life, The Little Foxes, The Man Who Came to Dinner,* and *The Philadelphia Story.* The movie houses were featuring *Mr. Smith Goes to Washington* with James Stewart and Jean Arthur. *Mutiny on the Bounty* with Clark Gable and Charles Laughton. *Of Human Bondage* with Leslie Howard (whom Gene resembled) and Bette Davis. *Babes in Arms* with Mickey Rooney and Judy Garland. Also *Goodbye, Mr. Chips* with Robert Donat, *Knights without Armor* with Robert Donat, and in the second-run houses, *The Citadel* with Robert Donat and *The Lady Vanishes* with Robert Donat . . .

It seems to me that these movies have gone on and on, playing endlessly as reruns, into the era of television, that era that David Sarnoff foretold in the ill-fated World's Fair of 1939. It's as though the world that was passing had intuited its demise and had left this museum record, as the ancient Greeks had left their record on the bellied, circular sides of their amphoras.

I wonder what Robert Donat was really like, as a man, not an actor. An idealist, as in *The Citadel?* The gentle, lovable type as in *Goodbye, Mr. Chips?* Or maybe a sour crank, jealous of his fame, ungenerous. Curious how a name will insinuate itself in personal history simply because of coincidence. Robert Donat was around at the time of the Strauss episode. He appeared in many movies. He possessed a charismatic something in Gene's eyes, a way of speaking, and therefore he became eponymous. The Donat era. A very personal appellation, just before the outbreak of war, when everything was beginning, everything was ending.

I had my own ideas about the Nazis. It would seem that all the psychopaths had been weeded out in Germany and put in charge of the concentration camps, but I didn't believe it. Once embarked on their adventure, ordinary Germans became cruel as a matter of principle. To allow even a trace of compassion into the new air of Germany would begin the decomposition of their national dream. Once the horror started, it had to be continued in a total way. To begin once again to make fine distinctions of conscience would drain the world-conquering energy Hitler had instilled in the nation. The only way to prove their world-conquering worth was to prove their civilization-shattering inhumanity. Innocent blood became the highest badge of honor. The highest heroism was not the conquest of all fear but the conquest of all scruples.

Everything crowding into that juncture of time. I thought of other times in history, times I would like to have witnessed—the

Palestine of Christ, the United States of Lincoln—and I realized that my historical preferences marked me as one whose curiosity always inclined in the same way. I was more interested in person than in epoch. I would like to have seen how the person affected his time rather than the other way around. To have been allowed access to another time—a week—and to have actually breathed the air and listened to the talk (my miraculous passage would of course provide me with an understanding of all the necessary languages) in that remote Roman colony while a Jewish preacher made his preachments, or in a few northern and southern cities while the Civil War raged, would be to satisfy my deepest hunger for undiscovered countries. To have a firsthand, historical account of how those who have profoundly affected posterity affected their own time.

Was I a Miniver Cheevy? I don't think so. I can't imagine a time in which the curiosity about another time wouldn't exist. Perhaps it was this inclination that made it impossible for me to wholly accept the times in which I lived. I did accept them in the sense of living through each day and waking up to the next, but it was somewhere around the war's beginning, around my dissolving friendship with Eugene Strauss, that I realized I was living through one of the most sensational of historical times, one that would have been the hands-down, number-one choice for revisitation of some future Saul Klein.

I lived it day by day, getting colds, riding the subways, feeling the daily ache of imminent loss, and yet each of those ordinary days was edged in an eerie glow. I knew I was living through the supreme historical fantasy. I knew that a few hundred years from now there would be someone wishing with all his curious heart to know what it might have been like to be alive in the time of Hitler. That's why I could never wholly accept the times in which I lived: I was living it in fantasy as well as in reality: I was witnessing each of my days in the backward-looking wonder of futurity.

And what had my present self to report to my future self?

That Armageddon had to be sandwiched in between running noses, running subways and the pain of personal loss.

That Perfect Evil remains outside the imagination while small betrayals occupy the mind and heart.

12

AFTER POLAND, THERE commenced the hopeful-dreadful lull. The world, because it wanted it so desperately, allowed itself to think that the next terrible step wouldn't be taken. My mother was certain of it.

"You will see," she said. "You will see that they will make some kind of agreement. What, are they all crazy? They'll stop it."

"Do you think so, Pa?" I asked my father.

"Do I think so?" he said. "Why, they ask my advice? I know what goes on in their heads?"

We were sitting in the kitchen. One of my weekly visits. There had been an observable change in the Klein craziness. Now they were both talking in my presence, even though the aroma of roast chicken was undercut by something I could never mistake: that frigid staleness. It had taken a world war and my decampment to bring it about, but even so I counted it a small miracle. I knew there had been a fight. I could smell it as surely as a dog smells dog piss—and, smelling it, I offered up a silent prayer of thanksgiving that I was no longer tied to that dragline of dreadful days. I'd cut myself free. Not entirely, but enough to give my life a different direction. The peculiar, ugly knowledge of my own family no longer dominated my life.

I knew there had been a fight, but I didn't know when it had begun, I wouldn't be forced to follow its tiresome course, and I wouldn't know when it had ended. For this I was more grateful than I ever thought I could be. I made some pretense of a continuing concern, I even paid lip service to my past involvement, but in reality what I did was celebrate my liberation. To be rid of that curse was a large blessing even in that cursed time.

"Nobody knows what goes on in their heads," I said to my father, "but everybody guesses."

"I don't guess," was his response. "What will be will be."

My mother slipped me a mute, eloquent look. She was indicating to me that the fact that they spoke in my presence hadn't changed the basic rules of their warfare. I had set myself up as a neutral country, and my ambassadorial role made it necessary for them to communicate with me in each other's presence.

"What makes you think they'll come to an agreement?" I asked my mother—and then I added an irony that my new status allowed me: "People don't come to agreements so easily."

Rose nodded, understanding my reference. A new unsureness had set in between my mother and me. Part of it was due to my having moved out, a treachery she still hadn't pardoned, perhaps would never pardon, but there was something else in the air besides that treachery and the arctic staleness and the roast chicken. Ever since seeing *War and Peace,* Rose had adopted a new attitude toward her always problematical, now suspect son. Rather, an absence of attitude, a judicial distance.

She was unimpressed by my talk about the "imitation of life" that theater represented. She relegated my explanations of the "method and function of drama" to the kind of verbal clowning around I had employed in the past to keep us both amused. Only this time she wasn't amused. She was silent and withdrawn. When I probed, asked questions, she would shrug and shake her head. When she did speak, it was to let me know that she didn't find her life a fit subject for comedy, or tragedy, or any form of dramatic study. Tragedy it was, yes, but *private* tragedy, something to be kept from the eyes of others at all costs. Exposed to the world that way, it became a mockery. Besides, there was a *happy ending* in my play. Was there any happy ending, *here, in this house?*

Why had I written such a play? Is that the way I saw her, saw all our lives? A joke? All that unhappiness only a subject for comedy?

"Ma! For cryin' out loud! You saw for yourself. You saw what went on on the stage. Is that what goes on in this house?"

"No! That's exactly what I'm saying! It has nothing to do with this house! It's not even true!"

"You would have liked it better if I told the truth?"

"I'd like it better if you didn't tell anything. If you wanted to write a play, why didn't you write about something else?"

"Because something else didn't interest me."

"Then you *were* writing about your own family."

"About my family *situation,* not my family."

"Please don't talk in circles."

In circles was exactly the way we talked every time we talked, each pursuing a different truth. Rose was right, of course. I had used my family. Who the hell doesn't, in one way or another? And what family doesn't resent being used in that way?

"Everybody was laughing," Rose said, bitterly. "People not talking to each other is funny?"

"Not ha-ha funny. Sometimes people laugh to keep from crying. People laughed in the audience because they recognized themselves in what they were seeing. There was sympathy in their laughter."

"There are times in this house when we talk, you know," my mother said.

"More silence than talk," I said.

"This I know," she said. "But when there's silence in this house, you too are silent. Hah? Why didn't you have your actor keep quiet in the first act? Like you are quiet."

"Because you can't make a play out of silence. Somebody's got to talk, or else everybody will walk out of the theater."

After some seconds of thoughtfulness, Rose said, "I'd like to ask you something—if you had such feelings about your family, if you had to tell the whole world about such things, why didn't you put the blame where it belonged?"

"I didn't want to put the blame anywhere," I said.

She nodded, shrugged again, raised her hands and let them fall. "Well," she said, "I hope you have lots of luck with your play —but I'll tell you one thing, my Saul, you didn't make your mother's life any easier. I just don't understand."

Nor did I, at the time. I understood the mortification, all right. Like a fool, I had thought that the different treatment, the happy ending, would redeem everything, but that was a stupid mistake. Rose saw no happy ending to her life, and therefore the play became a bitter travesty.

I understand better now the particular grief it caused her. It's the awful knowledge that comes to most parents, educated or uneducated, loving or indifferent, that the image projected was not the image received. The parent lives with the myth of his or her life, while the child is in the process of self-creation. The two processes don't go well together.

My father had nothing to say about my play. Nothing. Except this. When I was getting ready to leave that evening, I walked into the foyer to get my coat from the hall closet. From there I could see my father sitting on the sofa in the living room. I was reminded of the dream figure that had appeared to me that night in Ruth's apartment. He turned and looked at me, a curious smile on his lips. I didn't understand the smile at first—and then it seemed to me that I was at last receiving a message from this uncommunicative man!

He was congratulating me on the play! He was thanking me for seeing that it was not he alone who had created the Klein wasteland. He was informing me that he knew only too well how he had been viewed by his children, these moral products of "the mother," and that he had been powerless to change that image, because it was partly true, even preponderantly true, but not *entirely* true!

When I left that evening, I took with me the bizarre applause of my father for having seen the truth and for having presented it in that way. It didn't change the relationship—we were too fixed in our attitudes for that—but it did set up a tiny shelter in the vast ice fields of memory.

13

"So you're definitely going to move?" Gene said.

"Yes, I've found a place."

"Where?"

I told him I had found an apartment in the Forties, not far from the rancid, airless place where both our plays had been rehearsed. It was a fourth-floor apartment, walk-up, overlooking a street that was traffic-snarled during the day and empty at night. Across the street was a blackened church whose statuary was covered in wire mesh to protect it from the catholic depredations of the pigeons. In no way as pleasant as the Strauss Belvedere-on-the-Hudson, with its view of the river, the bridge, the Palisades. But it was my new point of independence, far enough away from all who had with too much or too little care invaded my life.

"Did Anna bother you?" he asked.

"No."

"Then why?"

"Personal reasons."

"Ruth?"

"Ruth has her own place."

"Then what personal reasons?"

"I need to be by myself," I said. "Like you."

"I thought you were by yourself," he said.

"It didn't work out that way. I was having to explain things."

"What things?"

249

"Oh, you know . . ."

He looked at me, unsure of the ground between us. What did I mean by "explain"? What "things"? Explain "Gen" Strauss to his own mother? But wasn't that what he had set me up to be, a conduit of information? And what else had I to do but explain mysterious, ambitious, unfilial Gene Strauss to the filigree lady, his mother? My play? Well, hell, I had written my play, hadn't I? And wasn't it a lucky accident anyway? An accident, by the way, that would never have come about but for the spellbinding wizardry of the Strausses, son and mother. Where was my gratitude?

We were again in Mama Italy's restaurant. Gene had phoned me at work to make the arrangement. I had met him at his apartment, and we had walked the several blocks to the restaurant. It was the middle of November and the weather had turned to an ideal, pre-Thanksgiving briskness. It was time for overcoats and gloves, leaf-turning and a seasonal chemistry that stung my nerves with tart expectancy.

I had seated myself on the side of the table that faced the painting of velour Venice with its Viking gondola and garish colors. I recalled the first time we had all met here, myself prefixed by the knowledge that I was in love with whatever girl I would find in Gene's company. Looking at the painting now, I felt a dizzying rush of nostalgia. I wished for a replay, but then I weighed the two—the Saul of a year ago with his simmering eagerness, the present Saul with his touchy awareness—and I knew I was irrevocably attached to the present Saul.

I gazed at my candy-colored Venice, understanding that it wasn't a question of happiness—I was far happier now—but that I had lost a fondness for the younger Saul. A very disillusioning thing, to find one of your past identities so wanting, but better to find it than to bury it. I had been too simple, too accepting, too condemning. I couldn't help being what I was a year ago, and in recognizing this I recognized that my parents couldn't help being what they had been all their lives. I had the advantage. Rose and Abe had played out their unhappiness before me, teaching me to run as fast and as far as I could in the opposite direction. That's what this past year had been—a rush toward opposites. I wouldn't want to give up any of the ground I had gained.

"I can understand your wanting to be on your own," Gene was saying, "but I just wanted to make sure that it wasn't because of any mistaken . . ." He hesitated, and I felt sure that the final secret would at last be revealed, and I would be free of that burden. But he took a different tack, saying, "I want you to know that Ruth's going to California is purely coincidental. I had no idea she was going. I knew nothing about it until yesterday. She's going to San Francisco, to be with her parents . . ."

I half listened in a haze of wretchedness, thinking only that Ruth was going to California, that this is how it would end, that she hadn't said a word to me. She had told Gene, but not me. She was going to California. To be with Gene? No, that wasn't the pattern likely to emerge from this weave of heartsickness. It was indeed coincidence. Gene was going to Los Angeles, Ruth to San Francisco. That's where her parents were, in San Francisco, and that's where she would be going, that's where she wanted to be. There was no dream conspiracy here. Gene wanted nothing more from Ruth, and Ruth was in flight, in flight from Gene, from me, from the far too many places that bore the taint of her unhappiness . . .

Mr. Sussman? . . . Gene was telling me something about Mr. Sussman. . . . He was telling me why *he* was going to California to work on the script, to work on the idea he had told me about . . . about the father who goes back to Europe to work in the underground. . . . Mr. Sussman, that enterprising man, saw topicality in this idea. The instant theme. High potential. Mr. Sussman had written to his Hollywood connection that a really first-class movie idea had fallen into his hands, and that he had the right man to do the script. The Hollywood connection wished to know if Gene Strauss had ever worked on a shooting script. No? Well, then, tell him to get his ass out here and learn. They weren't offering a contract until they saw a completed script, but their week-to-week "pay" was an unbelievable amount of money in Depression terms.

Was it my imagination, or was I already looking at a changed Eugene Strauss? It's hard to say because apparent changes in Strauss may have been due to real changes in Klein perception. Sometimes I saw what wasn't there, and sometimes I didn't see what was. But I do believe Gene contributed his share to the changing image. If I was not mistaken, he had put on a little weight. But then he had almost verged on the skinny in the year I had known him. If I was not mistaken, he was having his fair hair cut in a different way, a way that preserved the symmetry and the undulation, but with a little more American grooming. If my perceptions were not deceiving me, the patina of romantic mysticism had been rubbed, and what I was seeing now was the emerging face of a somewhat different man, not a stranger, but not an intimate. Handsome in a different way. A young man whose inner stratagems had become more visible around the eyes and mouth.

"When are you going?" I asked him.

"Fairly soon. It seems to be a case of doing it quickly, if at all."

"That makes sense. Will you be going for good?"

"I doubt it. They'll soon discover who they've got, and I expect they'll send me packing."

"You must be terrifically excited."

"I don't know. Should I be?"

"Sure you should be. First crack out of the box, and you're off to Hollywood. What about your mother?"

"What about her?"

"I don't know—I thought—well, I thought maybe you'd—"

"What?"

"Take her with you."

A queer look. He'd always found a different expression when I'd been guilty of one of my Bronx absurdities. This was an oblique, uneasy look, almost as if he had anticipated the challenge.

"You're not serious," he said—but not with absolute conviction.

"Probably not," I said. "Just a thought."

"Did Anna say anything to you to make you have such a thought?"

"Nothing in particular. I mean . . . well, I mean, anything she might have to say would depend on what she knew. Does she know?"

"That I'm going to California? Yes, she knows that."

"When did you tell her?"

"Last night."

"And when did you tell Ruth?"

He gave me another sidelong look. "I didn't tell her," he said. "She told me. That she was going to California. To be with her parents. She just called to say goodbye, you see. I'm sure she told you that."

"No, she didn't."

"Well, then, she was probably . . . I suppose it was easier for her to say goodbye to me first . . . "

It was quite an effort on Gene's part. There was embarrassment and pain here, and he was doing his best to be discreet, merciful. Making the best of a prickly situation. But neither of us believed what he was saying. Ruth had said goodbye to Gene first because everything after that would be easy. I had always been the easier one to deal with because she never had, never could, love me.

Gene repeated that there had been no knowledge on his part, no collusion. He was absolutely sure that Ruth would be in touch with me. I could see that he was already planning another telephone call to make sure that Ruth *did* get in touch with me before leaving. I could easily imagine (so could he) Ruth spiriting herself out to California without facing the discordant music I represented. Was it really possible that she would do such a thing? Of course it was possible. Who doesn't run away from unpleasantness when one is already carrying such a load of it?

No, I didn't think that Gene and Ruth were going to California together, not because either or both would scruple against it, but because I knew that Gene wasn't interested. He was interested in something else. I could see that he was interested in something else by the way he kept glancing at me in that tentative, testing way, as if the very surface pressure of my being would give him the clue he was seeking.

"Why don't you just say it?" I tried, encouragingly. "Or ask it."

"I wanted to ask if you would—will you be going back to Washington Heights?"

"Your mother's place? My clothes are there."

"I wonder if I might ask a favor of you?" he said. "I wonder if you would try to find out for me—if you could get some kind of insight into Anna's frame of mind. You do have a great sensitivity to what people are feeling, and, frankly, Anna has a tendency to get upset at changes."

"You mean like your going to California?"

"Yes."

"What do you suspect?"

"I don't suspect anything. I'm just asking you to see—"

"But what should I look for?" I asked.

"Oh, I don't know. Nothing in particular. Just her general manner, I guess."

"Should I report to you immediately?"

He looked down at his plate. "I won't be leaving for at least a week," he said.

"Well, in that case you'll have a chance to see for yourself whether anything unusual is going on, won't you?"

He nodded, accepting my sarcasm as the price of the favor he was asking. What he said next was probably true. "She would conceal it from me," he said.

I didn't have the heart to go on goading him. I wanted to get away. There were investigations of my own I had to make, other objects for my sensitivity and concern.

"If I see anything unusual, I'll let you know," I said.

14

I GOT IN touch with Ruth and she agreed to meet me. I couldn't
bear the thought of her leaving without a word to me. Or if she
did phone, lying about Gene, telling me something that wouldn't
agree with what I already knew. Walking in the park, she told me
she would have called me had I not called her first. She wanted
to tell me she would be joining her parents for Thanksgiving.

"Why, are they separated?" I asked.

"What?"

"Nothing. Just a little undistinguished Bronx humor."

"What are you saying, Saul?"

"That the world is in a bad way."

"With that I agree," she said. "That's why I want to see my
parents. Perhaps it's time for families to be together."

"Some families."

"Not yours?"

"My family has been having its own war for as long as I can
remember," I said.

"That strange family of yours," said my golden-haired, vanish-
ing love.

"That strange family of mine," I echoed.

"Are they really as unhappy as you say?" she asked.

"No. I made the whole thing up. I felt I needed something to
stimulate my creative juices, so I made it all up. Actually, my

mother and father are ideally mated. They never have a cross word."

"I don't believe you."

"I don't believe you either," I said.

"What?"

"I heard you were leaving."

"I know you heard," she said. "You heard it from me, just now."

"Oh, Jesus, Ruth!"

She closed her eyes, trusting me to guide us along the path we were walking. She gave up the charade. Still with closed eyes, she spoke in a low, strained voice: "I don't know, Saul. I want so much to be rid of this part of my life. Please don't misunderstand. Not because of you. I enjoy being with you. Much more so than with Gene. There was always trouble with Gene. Always hurt. Even when he was being as nice as he could be, there was hurt, because I knew . . ."

Her eyes were open and she was studying the path on which we walked, as if she expected some God-inscribed sign to appear there, something that would make these heavy, inadequate words unnecessary.

"I know what you knew," I said. "First hand."

"What is it?" she asked, like a tired child. "It can't be that this sickness I've been carrying is what people call love. It's so unpleasant. I thought love was supposed to be pleasant. Everything about it is so unpleasant. I don't think it would make any difference if Gene were to die. I don't need him any longer to go on being sick. My body has learned how to manufacture the poison all on its own. It goes on manufacturing the poison whether he is there or not. And it tires me so. It makes sleep so welcome. Did you know that? I look forward to sleep. I'm so grateful when it's at last time to go to sleep . . ."

She fell silent for a short, unhappy spell, and then she resumed: "Yes, I called Gene to say goodbye. I see that he has told you. Please don't . . . please, let's walk . . . please don't be hurt. I had to say goodbye. I'm the one to talk about being hurt, yes? The blind leading the blind. Saul, if I could help you, I would, gladly. You are the one who has been kindest. You are the one I will remember after I've forgotten Gene. No, that's not true. I will not forget Gene, I'm afraid. But neither will I forget you. I do want to go away and be with my parents. Isn't it funny to be walking and talking about this unimportant sickness of mine when the world is on fire? . . ."

I listened and listened as she went on in that tired, rambling way. It was truly as if she were sick, feverish, and these were the babblings of her fever. We walked past a boathouse. There were no boats on the pond at this time of year. The green rowboats had been hauled into the shed, turned upside down, left to ruminate and flake until next spring.

I had asked for a change of venue for this meeting, this possible finality. I asked if she minded taking a drive to Van Cortlandt Park. It was Sunday. It was cold. Van Cortlandt Park was one of the early repositories of my daydreams. In my teens, I would go ice-skating on the frozen pond, and for reasons I could no longer recall anticipations like a string of firecrackers would pop all over the place when I visited this park in cold weather.

I fell in love here, not for the first time, but in memory a time set in fixed colors. The event was accompanied by the wooden thunder of ice skates clumping around on the scarred floors of the boathouse. There was a girl sitting on a bench on the opposite side. I watched her lace up her pretty white shoes, and I fell in love. I added my own clumping to the boat house racket, and then slid down the ramp to the frozen pond. I skated around in my pseudo-racing style, watching for those white shoes all day. Some years later, in one of those dependable repetitions time offers, I read how Konstantin Levin came tumbling out of a similar place in Russia, showing off for Kitty. Tolstoy had invested his character with feelings too much like my own for mere coincidence. We became kin.

"It isn't going to be just for a visit, is it?" I said to Ruth.

"I'll probably stay for a while," she admitted.

"Give up everything? Your job? Your apartment?"

"What does it matter?"

"We could get married," I was amazed to hear myself say. I had no premonition of such a proposal. "Why go out to California when you know Gene is going to be out there? Haven't you had enough of that? All right, you won't forget him. Neither will I. Who forgets? But I can guarantee you that he won't be thinking much of us, if at all. Look, I've got a good job. I'm writing another play." (I wasn't. I'd given up the Herschel play. But it was only a temporal lie. I *would* write another play.)"My reputation is as good as Gene's, you know. I made some money on *War and Peace,* and I expect I'll make much more on my next play. You'll be able to quit your job and go back to school. Study art. Become what you want . . ."

I was begging. Recalling my feelings, I use the word without shame. I couldn't imagine my life the day after these departures. No one seemed to give a damn about my future. Despite what I knew, I saw complicity in this double desertion. I knew that each was going in a different way, but I felt I had to stop this emptying of my life or I would die of it. So the truth is I begged, offered bribes, shed tears, courted shame. Well, there it is. I did, and I know now that it's possible to do much more shameful things for much more shameful reasons.

Ruth took my arm and leaned her tired, doleful head against my shoulder. She was wearing the same plaid scarf over her head that she had worn in the journalists' restaurant. The rough wool scratched my cheek.

"I must go, Saul," she said.

"To be with Gene?"

"I'll never see Gene again."

"Or me?"

"I don't know."

There were many more hours to that day, but they were only variations on the same tortured theme. I begged her not to go, to marry me, and Ruth could only repeat that she must go now, that it was imperative that she go now, that if she didn't go she would become sick. I gave up trying to dissuade her and switched to alternatives. We had dinner—a kind of chewing reprise of all the previous hours—and we worked out a tentative plan in which I would come out to California after some months. Or she would come back east if she found the schools out there were not offering the courses she wanted.

But she would go back to school, that was definite. In my

semisomnambulistic state, I felt we were doing a rewrite on Gene's play, changing the action to fit more credibly into the patterns of reality. Without either of us mentioning the false theatricality of Gene's arrangement, we both agreed that once she began her studies she would pursue them as zealously as others had pursued their special destinies. She said she planned to go on to graduate school. I seconded that, broadly hinting that I was no Carl, that I would aid in her destiny as I had aided in another. I was good at that.

Naturally, I returned to the center of my futility, urging her to stay, assuring her that I would absent myself for weeks, months if she wished. In fact, she would have to get in touch with me. I would be moving to my new address in a day or two. I would have a telephone installed. I would loan her the money to begin school here, a long-term loan, repayable in a thousand years, no interest.

The day did finally end, and I left Ruth at her apartment house. I was worn to a hallucinatory clarity, knowing at last that the only mistake was Ruth's physical presence here when the rest of her had fled so completely to the other side of the country.

I took the subway uptown, spending the sick minutes devising new plans to check the inevitable. I couldn't endure the thought of tomorrow, and the day after that, and all the days of my unimaginable future.

15

"How IS IT that you do not go with your friend?" Anna asked me.

"Nobody invited me to go. Nobody is paying me to go."

"But they are paying Gen," she said. "He said they will pay him, but he didn't say how much. Did he tell you how much?"

"Why would he tell me if he didn't tell you?" I asked, half angry, half shocked that Gene hadn't made specific plans about caring for Anna. Why would he keep such information from her? Was he planning simply to walk out on this burdensome part of his life? Leave Anna destitute? No. Out of the question. "Listen—" I began, but she was already speaking.

"Do you know," she said, "I'm surprised that Gen would go under such conditions. He told me he had no written contract. Did he tell you that? Yes? Well, that is what surprises me. His father would never have permitted it. His father was a lawyer. Did you know that? A very brilliant and successful lawyer. His firm represented many English, in shipping, those that had shipping interests in Germany. I asked Gen if there was a contract and he said no, it was just an understanding. He is to go to California and write this movie thing, and they would pay him each week—"

I interrupted, thrusting the necessary question between her words: "Is he going to send you money?"

"—and do you know what I am thinking?" she went on. "I am

thinking this: what if they do not like what he has written? What then?"

"They'll pay him anyway," I said. "They may not make the movie, but they'll pay him. I understand that's the way it's done."

"Do you think so?"

"I know so," I said, and then diverted the theme of Gene and Hollywood. "It's amazing how much money there is when it's needed for killing people instead of caring for them. We're building a new air force, a two-ocean navy. Contracts going out like crazy. Where did it all come from? Yesterday there was money for nothing, and suddenly it's like an oil well. Dollars gushing up out of the ground. We ought to declare war every twenty years. Stand on either shore and blast billions into the oceans."

Anna glanced at me from the other side of the kitchen table. That's where we had placed ourselves on this last night of our strange, disintegrating union. It had occurred to me that the antidote to one kind of madness was the activation of another. I was being just as compulsive as she, opposing my obsession to hers. She wasn't used to that, didn't care for it. She watched me suspiciously, rebukingly, warning me with her eyes that I had no right to play with her greater sorrow. But there was something in my playing that puzzled her. My notes were not compatible with her own heavy-hearted music.

But she hadn't answered me on the money question. Was she trying to get from me some assurance that Gene would continue making his contribution to her support? Was she actually afraid she would be cut off entirely? But that wasn't my affair. I absolutely refused to make that my affair. I would be leaving tomorrow. Not back to the Bronx, as I had hinted to Gene (that would only add more desolation to what I was already feeling), but to my new midtown apartment. Had Anna found another boarder? Was she making efforts to replace me? I had seen no sign of it, although I had given her more than a month's notice.

All right, then, here's what I would do: I would get in touch with Gene tomorrow (he hadn't left yet; he would be around until the end of the week, he had said—flying, he had said—so looking forward to his first plane trip), and I would confront him with the situation. I would demand to know what the hell he intended to do about his mother, about *his* responsibility. And what business was it of mine? Perhaps none, but his own manipulations had made it my business . . .

None of my business, you say? Right, you decadent bastard! But you damn well made it my business, didn't you? You with your nice little game of blindman's buff! Into the pagan catacombs where all sorts of unspeakable things are allowed to happen! All kinds of nighttime things that must never be exposed to daylight! Right? But I'm exposing it right now! I'm asking what you intend to do about your mother! How much money will you be sending, big shot?

It was laughable, my stepping in like some Victorian pillar of virtue, demanding decency and duty, when the real story would have curled Dickens' whiskers. But even as I wobbled on that moral tightrope, I was beginning to make out things I hadn't been able to make out before. Some things, I could see, were not as important as I thought they were. I had slipped into certain attitudes as I had slipped into my Alpacuna coat, because they looked nice on me, because they kept my self-esteem warm, but I was beginning to see that Anna may have been right about what was important only for the moment, and then was not important. The fiercest pleasure can't begin to compete in time against the slightest offense.

But fuck it! I was leaving tomorrow. I would sort all this out at some other time. Right now, the important thing was for me to get away, just as Gene was getting away. It was his responsibility, not mine. But had he taken *care* of his responsibility? Was he going to play the complete shit where his mother was concerned? I couldn't believe it. Was he miserly? I had never seen him in a spendthrift mood, but that didn't mean anything. It mightn't be money at all that Anna was talking about. She kept looking at me accusingly, conspiratorially, as if only we two knew the real truth about Gene's going.

Well, I had no truth other than the one I had been punishingly given. I wasn't particularly curious about any other truth. I just wanted out. I had my own bleeding secrets.

Anna glanced out the window. "Did Gen tell you when he plans to come back?" she asked.

"No, he didn't. Didn't he tell you?"

"No-o-o," she said, drawing out the word in her melodic way.

"He must have said something."

"He said he will see. He wasn't sure. It depended. He will be in touch. Did he promise to be in touch with you?"

I mumbled something.

"I have special privileges, you see," she said, giving herself a mock flourish of distinction. "My son told me very definitely that he would be in touch, he would keep me informed. He will telephone. He will write. He will continue to send money. Am I not a lucky woman?"

"Anna—"

She turned away from the window, her eyes thick with unshed tears. There was something in her manner that made me aware of the enormous resolve containing those tears. She placed her arms with their tinkly bracelets along the chipped enamel of the kitchen table. She clasped her hands together. Something had broken in her, causing her voice to rattle. "I am an old, interfering woman," she said. "It is a very unlucky thing to have only one child, and to have this one child so—nah!—so not loving—"

I shook my head, made a vigorous dumb show of denial. *Loving* or *not loving* were the wrong words. She was talking about the most cross-grained relationship there was—parents and children. *Christ, I should know!* It hit me with a slapstick whack that I had made such a complicated and esoteric business of the Strauss family when my own was every bit as complicated and, except for the accent, esoteric.

". . . there was a sister," Anna was telling me. "Did you know that? Gen had a sister, but she only lived for five months. The doctors never knew what to tell me. An infection. Perhaps if she had lived things would have been different. I would not have been so—"

She didn't finish the sentence. She didn't have to.

"Gene does care for you, very much," I said flatly, feeling obliged to make the statement, true or not true.

Anna smiled and shook her head. She said, "I was not the wife my husband wanted, and I was not the mother my son wanted . . . *Schön oder distinquiert* . . . This I heard my husband say to a friend. I was standing right there when he said it. That a woman should be either pretty or distinguished. Yah? And I was neither." She waved her hand airily. "As if I were not there, he said it. He did not mean me, of course. I was Anna, *süsse* Anna, I had no need of such things. It was not necessary for me to be pretty or distinguished. I was Anna." She closed her eyes briefly and dilated her nostrils, as if to take in fully the bitter fragrance of her memories. "So," she said briskly, "Gen is going and I am to stay here. That is how it ends."

"What ends?" I asked

"And you will leave tomorrow, yah?"

"Yes."

"You will have breakfast?"

"Okay."

"Good."

I slept badly that night. I guess I must have slept some because there were definite breaks in the linked chain of thoughts that dragged through the hours. I composed scenes—mainly with Ruth, some with Gene—scenes of accusation, supplication, making my heart race, making my mind burn away sleep.

At some exhausted hour, I awoke from another blank interlude, having to go to the john. I got out of bed and walked into the foyer. I saw a crack of light beneath the bathroom door. I returned to my room, waited, listening, and when things became urgent I peeked out again. The light was still showing. I thought it too long a time, and so laden with silence and dolor, I went to the bathroom door and knocked. No answer. Cautiously, I tried the door. It opened.

Anna was wearing her pink peignoir. She had rigged up a crazy cat's-cradle of rope around the shower curtain bar. I remember distinctly how inept it looked. But it was sufficient to its purpose. Anna hung there quite dead. I touched her lifeless hand as a death-frightened animal would sniff a corpse, sensing by instinct the quiet, ultimate difference. The coldness of death was in Anna's hand.

Methodically—I could get through the next few moments only by the most methodical, step-by-step application—I opened the medicine cabinet. I took out one of my razor blades and cut the strands of that sloppy cat's-cradle, and Anna's body slid with terrible solidity into my arms.

I carried her body into the living room and laid it on the worn carpet. Ruby and emerald lights from across the river provided stage lighting for the scene. I knelt beside the body, folded my arms into my own body, and then rocked back and forth, keening my guilt, my final, nightmare bequest.

16

SOMEWHERE ON THE West Side, in the Sixties, there was one of those decaffeinated organizations that offered the flavor of religion without the narcotic of God. Gene informed me that the funeral service would be held there.

I wondered if he had informed Ruth, whether she would attend. She was still in the city, I knew. Would be for at least another week. After all, Ruth had known Anna. I dreaded the possibility of seeing Ruth there. I'm not sure why. Perhaps I thought it would be another unstable element in a situation quivering with instability. I feared a breakdown. I might just shut my eyes and start running again.

But why should Gene invite Ruth? That was ended. Gene didn't believe in having people around for sentimental reasons. Remember that Christmas party several eons ago, when the world was full of fresh surprises instead of dive-bombers? Gene couldn't get over my asking why Ruth hadn't been invited to the Strauss goose-and-Handelfest. But you never could tell about the Strausses. He might just summon Ruth, and she might just come. It might just accommodate Gene's strange view of proprieties and Ruth's inextinguishable hope.

She was not there, thank God. Other people were. Who had gotten them all together? Who had made the necessary arrangements? The mourners, the place, the officiating whatever-he-was, not rabbi or minister. I knew I hadn't. I had fled the Strauss rooms as if burned by black fire. I had nothing to take but clothes, and I threw them into my suitcase and fled as I would have fled from the burning cities of the plain.

Not immediately, of course. There were some arrangements I was forced to make. I had to arrange for the police, for the ambulance. There was a whole night of questions and official movements and lurid unreality. By lurid dawn unreal Gene stood in the same triangular room that had so enchanted me a little over a year ago.

He stood over the dead body of his mother, not crying, but breathing in the tragic air as if it had been drained of oxygen. His pale face was chalk-white. The telltale vein that branched from the corner of his eyes to his temple looked puffed and painful. I watched him take in quick, shallow breaths, hoping even in my sick delirium that I would at last see a breakdown. How I would have welcomed it! It might have been the solvent for both of us. I might have forgiven him. It might have restored friendship between us. It might have defined his sin, and then I could have forgiven him. But he didn't break down. Instead he looked at *me* —looked at me as if demanding an explanation—and all I could do was stare back at him, blankly, not knowing what it would be but beginning to seek within myself for the form of a great refusal.

A nightmare is a private thing, or should be. One shouldn't find oneself plunged into someone else's, as I found myself plunged into Gene's. My protesting reaction was that this was *not* my nightmare. This was Gene's, and I would not let him make it mine. My involvement was ended. It was a bad involvement, a wicked involvement, but one I had neither sought nor advanced. At worst, I had been a stupid, supine accessory, but not an instigator, not an exploiter. I held Gene responsible, and how I behaved depended on how he behaved. Things could never be the same between us because of what happened, but then things had been in an accelerating process of change anyway.

I didn't dare go back to my parents' apartment, although I was parched for the kind of bustling, furious consolation my mother could and would offer for such a lunatic occasion. I could almost hear her whiplash I-told-you-so's. Taking up with such profoundly unkosher people. What did I expect? These people were wrong, wrong from the start, wrong in their deepest instincts. Perhaps she wouldn't have the words for it, but she would somehow manage to have the message writ large and eloquently on her face. The message was simple, however mistaken, however unjust: these people had lost the trick of survival; these people were half in love with death.

I went instead to my own new-old, mildewed, fourth-story apartment, the one across the street from the time-blackened, Catholic church. I had only a few sticks of furniture there—a cot, two chairs, a table. I despaired of sleep, but fell asleep immediately, and indeed did have a nightmare: a harried, suitably sick one.

I dreamt we were in the studio where my play had been rehearsed, the folding chairs lined up in rows as if for a performance. The players in the dream were seated on the folding chairs. Gene and I in one row, Ruth one row ahead, head half turned, listening to our dream words. Gene shook his head in typical fashion, coolly advising me that I must rid myself of my crippling fears, that I must surmount the smallness of my views and take on a new openness and courage. All of this contained and conveyed within the soundless enclosure of dreams. Gene motioned with his head to Ruth, and in response she floated across the room to where Leo Shulkin awaited her. Leo, too, sat in one of the folding chairs. He turned his head toward me, deliberately signaling my attention, that dreamy Tartar chief's smile on his face. At that point, the dream became infused with menace. Without actually seeing it, I knew that Leo was opening his fly, still keeping his head turned toward me. He reached out with his other hand and directed Ruth onto his lap in an unmistakable way. Ruth adjusted herself to these manipulations, straddling Leo, glancing at me with a sad smile, mutely pleading for understanding, mutely imploring me not to be angry. She wouldn't have done this except for the special circumstances. I did understand that, didn't I? It was part of the script, the script that Gene had written. I turned in protest to Gene, but it was no longer Gene, it was Anna. She too was smiling in her wistful way, pointing to where in the script these actions were indicated. I cried out in hoarse distortion of nightmare sorrow. Anna shook her head, admonishing me, telling me that it was not important, that everything would remain as it was. She indicated to me that I should turn away. It was not polite to watch. But I watched helplessly and saw Ruth sink down on Leo, saw her tilt her head back in terrible ecstasy . . . escaping at last from the dream's imprisonment through my own awakening cry . . .

Normally I forget my dreams—unless I awake in time and commit their details to memory.

It was a chapel of sorts. A room with chairs, a platform, a lectern. Only the first two rows were occupied. Anna Strauss, who had a large circle of friends in Hamburg, summoned only this handful at her death. The Obersts, the Zeiglers, even Ernst Mueller. There were some others unknown to me. My gaze kept returning to Ernst Mueller, whose clothes looked as shabby as ever, but whose hair and pride gleamed fiercely. Something stiff and recalcitrant, as if this occasion were the latest gesture in the lady's amorous argument.

No coffin. Nothing. I learned that Anna—who had made her wishes known long before—had already been disposed of in a crematorium. Another shock to my Bronxite sensibilities. I'd heard of it, of course, but as the practice of faraway places and people. India. Real people, however disaffiliated, would never ask to be reduced to ashes. Not barbarous, perhaps, but surely pagan.

The pastor, officiator, whatever he was, was a tall man with a long, solemn face. He had been in conversation with Gene when I arrived. His luminous eyes shot azure darts around the room as he surveyed the pitifully small congregation. He reminded me of the young actor who had replaced Josh in my play, zealously earnest in an off-putting way.

"Dear friends . . ." he began, and his voice surprised me with its chesty resonance. Its timbre reminded me of Leo Shulkin and my recent dream. ". . . we are here to commemorate the life of Anna Thérèse Strauss"—Thérèse!—"and to mourn that life for the evil done to it by savage men in a savage time . . ."

269

I knew what Gene had been telling the blue-eyed officiator. Well, he was right. Damage *had* been done by tearing up by the roots the filigree lady. Anna Thérèse Strauss would not have taken well to transplanting even if a much friendlier soil had been provided. She was European to her peasant fingertips. I wondered whether Gene had told Blue Eyes that he, Eugene Strauss, only son of Anna, might have been kinder, more patient, more understanding. More forgiving? Yes, that. Perhaps that most of all. But why should he have to tell Blue Eyes that? It goes without saying that all sons might have been all those things. I could have assisted my own mother out of her wretched marriage, insisted on it, given her a decent alternative to go to . . . except that I was too busy with my own alternatives.

" . . . there are those who have set down certain rules concerning the manner of life's passing," the officiator went on. "There are those who define human behavior in terms of sin or virtue, according to ancient precepts, ancient moralities. I say if there is to be condemnation let it be against those who crush life, not against those whose lives have been crushed.

"Anna Thérèse Strauss loved music, art, gentleness, all that was civilized and civilizing. She made her home into a haven for a few of the many who have been cast out by humanity's latest scourge . . ."

Warmed to his theme, Blue Eyes left Anna Strauss in her little refugee corner and mounted higher and higher on rhetorical wings. I had the feeling that he might have been waiting for just such an occasion to test-fly this sermon. He said that the break in civilization we were witnessing came as no surprise to him. He had been expecting it. The unholy alliance between the vested interests in religion and the vested interests in government were bound to produce this most bloodthirsty of devils . . .

I agreed with everything he was saying. I listened with internal jumps of yea-saying, conscious of the very same evil, flooded with righteous light. But in the back of my mind scurried a little gray mouse, like the mouse that would scurry across the kitchen floor when I switched on the light in the Bronx apartment. Small, swift, surprising, living its own crumb-gathering life. Unwanted, a thing to be eliminated with traps and poison, and yet as true as anything else in the kitchen.

Anna Strauss was a symbol of civilization, but she was also the dilettante, the parasite, the hysteric, the self-dramatizing and, finally, the vengeful woman. Gene was the talented, charming aristocrat, but he was also the cruel and opportunistic oppressor . . . No, not cruel, since cruel implies the kind of deliberation that was absent in Gene. He was both generous and hurtful. He was exhilarating to know and deadly in his quest for a special destiny.

And I? I was stuck with a conscience that didn't know how to define or expunge its sin. I even had taken away from me the release of confession, because confession would defame the dead, and one must speak nothing but good of the dead. This was Anna's bequest to me, and as I sat there among the meager mourners that same small scurrying mouse darted across my mind. I thought: what does it all matter? I thought: what a joke this humanness was, made as we were, needing such a multitude of things, and creating so many punitive attitudes toward satisfying those needs.

I felt something lift away from me. I saw the possibility of forgiving both myself and Anna.

Hand shakings and *aufwiedersehns* in the side street. The building we had just left was encircled by a low, fat railing with bulbous brass couplings. The architectural ornamentation of another era. Anna Strauss had been caught between eras, and she was no longer in place. Reduced to ashes.

I shook hands with the Obersts, the Zeiglers, Ernst Mueller. I felt I was having conferred on me a special status, not a relative, not really a friend, but a surrogate of some kind who had sadly failed in his function. It could have been the fever of my imagination, given the occasion and the iciness of the day, but it did seem to me that I was being vaguely absolved of some vague sin.

Perhaps there was one among them who did know—did know and did not condemn. Perhaps it was tall, mournful Elena Oberst, she who had looked at me so mournfully last Christmas when I told her of my younger brother status. She looked at me even more mournfully now and kissed me on the cheek. The touch of her feathery lips immediately brought to stark, glaring life the bone-white room where Anna had offered her own tearful cheek to be kissed.

I came at last to Gene, shook hands with him, not certain what gesture would be appropriate in this hopeless tangle of nerves.

"Wait," he said.

I waited, and when we were free of the others he took me by the arm and we headed toward the park, which was only one block east. He didn't speak as we walked side by side. He was wearing his father's double-breasted overcoat with the large lapels and the belt in the back. He was bareheaded, pale, drawn, that blue, branching vein marking his brow like an emblem.

"Do you mind walking a bit?" he asked.

"No."

We continued east on the park path. The path was clear, but the snow of several days ago lay in dirty patches along the sod lining the path. Clouds covered the sun at frequent intervals, which made the brightness, when it came, even more brittle. The heatless sun stressed the cold. When we spoke, our breaths were like the circular symbols of speech cartooned in Aztec drawings.

"I have something to ask you," he said. "Please don't misunderstand. I'm not accusing you of anything, but I know that under the circumstances you might think it best to conceal things from me. As a matter of consideration, kindness . . ."

Had it come at last? Was this the time, the awful, inappropriate time of confession? The ghoulish specter rising up before me would have to be blotted out. This was not the time for it!

"Concealing what?" I asked.

"Was there no message?"

"Message?"

"A note of some kind. Something written. Something spoken."

I realized I wasn't accurately taking in what he was asking. Was he accusing me of concealing something out of fear of self-incrimination? He had already said that I might be concealing something out of consideration for him, but then I could "consider" him in so many ways. Or was he intimating something else?

272

Was he intimating that Anna had signaled her intended suicide and I had failed to understand, failed to act in time?

"There was no note that I was aware of," I said. "I mean, nothing written. Gene, if I had found a note, do you seriously believe I would have kept it from you? Or am I just not understanding what you're saying?"

"There's nothing special to understand," he said. "All I'm asking is whether you have any information to give me. You were there. You were the last one to speak to her."

I glanced at Gene, who squinted at the bony, leafless trees. That blue bruise of a vein looked edematous in the gray light. I had never seen Gene as victim before, and it gave me a depleted satisfaction, as if we had both been running for miles, and he had been the one to quit. I had never been more curious about him. Every detail was a clue.

"She did say some things," I said.

"What things?"

"She said she was surprised you would go to California under such conditions. She said your father would have disapproved of your going out there without a contract. I think she wished there was more security."

"For her or for me?"

I said nothing. Gene closed his eyes and pressed two fingers against the lids. He shook his head. "Security," he whispered to the freezing city. "I should think that would be the last of her concerns. If it had been up to her, we would all have been in concentration camps. She didn't want to leave Germany, you know. It was my father."

"Why didn't she want to leave?"

"She said if people like the Strausses left, Germany would be given over entirely to the apes. She said the good people must stay and oppose Hitler. Can you imagine? Hitler was already chancellor. One of the local party chiefs lived on the same block where we lived. Swastikas from every window. She wanted to hold her head up and defy them. She made it a point to walk past that house with her head held high. She was going to fight Hitler with such weapons."

"It's a good thing your father didn't listen to her," I said, myself seeing Anna every bit as foolish as her son saw—but at the same moment linking her to Herschel Grynszpan. The desperate, necessary gesture, altering nothing, affecting everything.

Gene said nothing. I wondered if he had heard me. I sensed the terrific remove of his thoughts. He was in another time, another world. Slowly he came back to this one.

"Did she saying anything—specifically—about my going?" he asked.

"Not directly."

I saw more fear now than self-justification. In his eyes, in the angle of his head. I couldn't be sure of this, but I think he was trying to signal to me: be cautious! He was asking me to be careful in what I remembered, in what truth I chose to tell. He was asking me to be the good friend he had trained me to be, and I felt a growing hostility to that request.

"Not directly," he said. "Then how?"

"She didn't say directly that she wished you wouldn't go and leave her here by herself," I said.

"Did she want me not to go? To throw away this opportunity?"

"No, she didn't say that."

"Did she want me to take her with me?"

"She didn't say that either. I was the one who brought it up."

"Yes, you did," he said, "and I wondered at the time whether it was your own idea or hers. You must have seen how impossible that was. If I didn't take this opportunity now, it might never come again."

"What opportunity?"

"To write this script, of course."

"Oh."

"What are you trying to say, Saul?"

"I'm not trying to say anything. I'm just trying to answer your questions."

"Then tell me what *she* said."

"She mentioned a sister. She said things might have been different if your sister had lived."

Gene shook his head incredulously. "My sister!" he whispered. "An infant death! What did that have to do with anything?"

"You asked me to tell you what she said."

Gene nodded, consulting again with the distant scenario in his head. "I will tell you something," he said, in a tired, defaulting way. "We had a beautiful house in Hamburg. There was one particular room . . ."

Whether Gene had suddenly become endowed with powers beyond any I had ever seen in him before, or whether I had been keyed to clairvoyance by all that had happened, I don't know, but as he spoke images leaped into my head as vivid and detailed and enlarged as color slides in a dark room.

The one particular room in Hamburg was a room of translucent light. One wall of the room was constructed of glass brick. A solarium of sorts. A room to Anna's specifications. A miniature botanical garden. It had a local reputation. It became known as the famous "Strauss" room. In it Anna had arranged a jungle of potted plants and hanging plants. Here and there cages of canaries and parakeets. And here Gene played solitary games of hunter. Stalking tigers. Here is where the chairs would be set out for evenings of chamber music. Among their friends were fine amateur and even professional musicians. Gene's father played the cello. He could have been a professional had he wished. Gene never slept when there was an evening of chamber music. He would listen from his room on the second floor. One evening, when the guests were gone, he slipped out of his room and walked halfway down the staircase, to the point where he could see into the jungle room. He didn't know why he felt compelled to do that. Perhaps it was something in the voices of his parents. He saw his mother and father sitting side by side, each in one of the folding chairs that were set out for such evenings. While he watched, he saw his mother draw to herself the large handbag that had been deposited on the chair beside her. She reached into it and took out a length of rope for his father to see. What she said was quite distinct. Gene remembered it word for word. "You do not think I will use this, but let me assure you, Albert, I will. I have no fear of death. None whatever. Don't go too far with me. I warn you. I'm not a woman who will go on, no matter what, for a mouthful of food. Remember this well. When the time comes, I will not hesitate." And Gene had heard his father reply, "Yes,

Anna, I know this courage of yours. You're a much braver person than I am. I believe you."

Gene stopped talking and we continued our walk in silence. The path we had taken curved toward the south end of the park. Soon we would be at Fifty-ninth Street, and there I knew we would part, possibly forever. He was leaving tomorrow, or the day after. He had delayed his flight to California, but men with a special destiny must not be diverted too long.

Nothing could check the next step in Gene's career, but this part of the history was not yet complete. This was a valedictory scene, and it was taking place almost at the very same spot where my part in the history had begun a little over a year ago. I said nothing of this to Gene. I had learned what useless sentimentality there was in such an observation. I was much more interested in the story he had just told me, knowing there was surely a reason for the telling, figuring out even as we took these last steps the reason for his telling.

He wanted me to know that this day had been foretold long ago. He wanted me to know that it wasn't an accident that he had been drawn out of his room, halfway down the stairs, so that he could witness the scene in the jungle room. He had inherited more than his father's clothes. He had inherited that grisly legacy as well. He had been compelled to witness the scene by a mystical power, because he had been meant to live with the threat of it as his father had done, and he had been meant to escape that threat by a greater imperative.

Now did I understand?

Yes, I did. I understood that sophisticated, *mittel Europa* Gene had lived with a legacy similar to my own. A different kind of war, but a war all the same. A war in a green and musical setting, but a war all the same. And, like me, had lived for long with the need to escape.

"Listen," he said to me, "why don't you move into my apartment? The rent is paid for the rest of the month, and it's so much nicer than the place you've got. I'd feel better, knowing you were there."

There was a time—and not so long ago—when I would have

welcomed that offer as the looked-for gesture of friendship. I didn't welcome it now.

"I don't think so," I said. "I'd rather stay where I am."

He nodded, having anticipated my reply.

The truth was that I didn't hold him responsible for Anna's death, but knowing more didn't make me more forgiving. It was no longer a question of understanding. I understood as much as I wanted to understand. Understanding stopped at the point where our separate natures began.

We were at last at the subway. Gene had one hand on the banister. He was leaving my life, and I wanted nothing so much as to see him go. He had changed my life, but I wanted to be free of him. He had already taken the first step down. He held out his hand, and I took it.

"In any event, I'll write," he said. "Will you answer?"

"Of course," I said.

He nodded and went down the steps, holding one hand aloft as he descended.

PART
III

1

THE WISH TO live in multiple time zones must have always been there. Perhaps that's why I began my scrapbook, guessing that past, present and future would be involved with each reference. Surely I had the future in mind. I see it now as an early bid for survival, like an insurance company gambling on my longevity. The past is a full symphony orchestra tuning up before the concert. Practice bars and trills, hinting at the masterwork to come, but never the work itself. Memory—everyday, working memory —deals in bars and trills.

And chills. Like the advance of the German armies across Europe. I read the headlines of May—NAZIS AT CHANNEL, TRAP ALLIES IN BELGIUM; CROSS AISNE RIVER 60 MILES FROM PARIS: FRANCE CAN'T DIE, REYNAUD TELLS PEOPLE—and I'm living in another time zone. I find restored in myself the belief that France couldn't die. I find myself reconstructing the taxicab army of the First World War and a different outcome from GERMANS OCCUPY PARIS. Even though I know the score of the finished symphony, memory works on the practice bars and trills, and I have restored to myself sensations that all subsequent history has left intact. I know what the outcome was, but my lungs feel emptied of air as I read the headlines. I recall my growing disbelief in the reports from London and Paris. I'm convinced that nothing can stop the Nazis. They are invincible. They will storm into the hospital or house where Hershel Grynszpan is living, drag him into the street, put out his Kafka eyes.

Goodbye, Herschel Grynszpan. I couldn't figure out how to spring you from that Paris jail. If I were a different man perhaps I could have. Perhaps I would have had someone sneak in a submachine gun, overpower the guards, have a van waiting around the corner . . . but my realistic heart sinks at the weight of implausibility and the reel snaps off in mid-escape.

I didn't know what happened to Herschel Gynszpan, but I do know what happened to Hitler and the great *wehrmacht.* That's the symphony. They won and they won, as Anna predicted they would, and then they lost. And it may very well be that they contrived their own defeat. It may very well be that Gene and his mother were right. Would a nation intent on victory have taken on Russia and the United States? Hitler's behavior proved Gene's father's thesis—*my* thesis. Hitler involved the world because his appetite for death was limitless. The idea of whole populations escaping his death plan enraged him. And in the end, of course, he wanted to murder the German nation too.

But that's the finished work, the whole symphony. Memory works on bars and trills. Herschel Grynszpan. The revival of *War and Peace in the Bronx,* which came about at the time the Germans were crushing France, the summer following Gene's departure.

"Write a third act," Leo Shulkin commanded.

"No. You're nuts. You know how the play is structured." *(Christ! Gene had once said the very same thing to me!)* "Daniel talks and talks, and then Daniel is silent and the family talks and talks. Where is there room for a third act?"

"Make room," he implored.

"Why?"

"Two-acters are losers. They smell of the armpit. Three-acters are at least dressed for success even if they never make it."

"That's a bunch of crap."

"I know it and you know it, but *money* doesn't know it."

"Where's money?"

"I'm talking to it."

"That's good," I said. "When you get some let me know."

"No," he said. "I can't. I've got to get the three-acter before I can get the money. I can't get it from my father. I won't ask my father. He financed this play once."

"I'll let you in on a little secret, Leo," I said. "I don't want to work for nothing either. I don't want to invest myself in the same thing twice for nothing."

What Leo did was raise money for the author, Saul Klein, through a deception. He told his father he was buying an option on a new play. A thousand dollars. *A thousand dollars!* For a third act! Coming from a world that bought life's sustenance and pleasures with coins and single dollar bills, the word *thousand* blared like a flourish of heavenly trumpets. A thousand dollars—and not even as Gene had received his sugar tit, in weekly allotments, but all at once, one check, with that grand sum stippled in red.

He would seek the rest of the money from other sources once he had the third act in his hands.

I wanted to tell Gene this. I waited for his letter so that I could tell him that I had gotten one thousand dollars to write a third act for *War and Peace*. But no letter arrived—which was what I had expected. Why should he write to me, evoking what had best be forgotten?

I did get a letter from Ruth, however. She wrote how glad she was to be with her parents. Her father, who was a tool-and-die maker in Germany before he became a union leader, was now the foreman in a factory making parts for the aircraft industry. They were living south of San Francisco. She would be going back to school starting with the spring semester. She would be taking language courses—French, Italian—and courses in art history. Had I heard anything from my friend? She had heard about Gene's mother from Elena Oberst, with whom she had become friendly while still living in New York. It must have been awful for me, being there when it happened. What a terrible experience. She had been thinking much of this past year, and she felt most sorry for the pain given to me. That was selfish and unnecessary, involving me in that way . . . *"Dear Saul, I apologize for that, and I hope someday you may forgive me. . . . Your friend, Ruth Prager."*

My first reading of the letter was a chromatic blur of excitement. The fact that she had written at all overwhelmed what she had written. I began planning a trip to California. I would tell her that I forgave her in person. I would use part of my thousand-dollar windfall for travel expenses and for a room somewhere south of San Francisco.

I carried the letter with me the next day on my way to work, reading it over on the subway, reading it over during lunch, and some specifics began coming through. I thought how curious it was that Ruth should have become friendly with Elena Oberst, that the silver-haired, tragic lady should have informed Ruth of Anna's suicide. It was like opening the wrong door and being stared at by several familiar, startled faces. Why should Ruth have become friendly with Elena Oberst? Reasons suggested themselves. Simple reasons. Devious reasons. People enlist support when striving toward difficult and desired goals.

And why all the belated sympathy for *my* pain? What had happened to her own? Was she trying to tell me that now that she had gotten over her own, she was able to appreciate mine? And if she had gotten over her own, was this all she could summon up for me? An apology? Sorrow for my involvement? A hope that someday I might forgive her? And, capping it all, or rather underlining it all, that official, sealing signature: *Prager!*

Christ! Prager! As if she were writing a department store to cancel her account! As if she wanted to be sure that I was certain which of the many Ruths I knew was writing! As if we hadn't served each other exquisite pleasure in the delicate sheaths of our sunburned flesh!

Or was I misunderstanding everything again? God knows I had misunderstood things in the past. Maybe these formalities were just another instance of language and culture disparities. I wrote to Ruth, telling her how glad I was to receive her letter, telling her I was writing a third act to my play, that Leo Shulkin was planning a new and bigger production, that I had even received a very nice advance, that I should very much like to visit the West Coast . . .

Three weeks, four . . . no reply.

There were indeed language difficulties and language disparities—with Ruth, with Anna, even with Gene—and my greatest mistake was to think that different meant better, higher, finer. I've gotten over that—but that's no guarantee against other mistakes.

I'm not sure whether I quit Lou Siegal for honest or phony reasons. Both, I think. My employment there was no longer an honest contract. Head and heart were elsewhere. Of course, if I hadn't received that thousand from Leo, I would have stayed on. The honest and the phony parts were inextricable. I had a superstitious fear that if I didn't quit I would never write a third act, that the play, whatever I did with it, would never succeed.

"So what are you going to do?" Lou asked, looking at me from his disbelieving, suspicious angle.

"I'm going to finish a play."

"What?"

I told him then. I told him I had written a play while in his employ—on my time, not his—although I confessed that there were times when my head was full of this other enterprise. I told him that the play had been produced once, with some little success, that now the play was going to be revived, that I had been asked to write a third act and that I had been paid to do so.

"Paid how much?" Lou asked.

It was a natural enough question. Writing a play was a piece of juvenile nonsense he could tolerate, argue against, even argue for; but money was competition, and he wanted to know what he was competing against.

"It isn't a question of money," I said.

"Yeah, I know, I know, but tell me how much anyway."

"A thousand dollars."

He was taken aback. He had expected a few hundred, at most. A thousand dollars was serious.

"So you're going to throw away a good job, a future, for a thousand bucks? What happens after the thousand dollars? Where do you go from there?"

"Probably into the army."

He nodded. "Listen," he said, "it's your life. But if you don't mind the advice of an older and more experienced man, you're making a big mistake."

"You're probably right—"

He leaned forward, the buttons of his vest clicking along the edge of the desk. "Don't be a *putz*, Saul," he shot at me, with sudden, heavy ardor. He pointed a finger at me out of his bunched fist. "I'm not supposed to tell you this, but since you're about to make a damn fool of yourself, I have to. I already got contracts. They're shipping me thousands of yards of canvas and webbing. I can't tell you what it's for, except to say that it's for the army. It's not a question of being a draft-dodger. It's a question of where you're needed."

"If we got into the war, I'd enlist anyway," I said.

I said it to sidle away from Mr. Siegal's argument, but in saying it I established a quick, new truth in my life. We would be in the war, and I would be in the army. Both inevitabilities, and for the first time in my life I had no doubt as to the appropriateness of my future. I never really saw myself in Mr. Siegal's business. Writing a play had been spindrift blown off a tumultuous year of my life. It was not, when it happened, a natural cry of the heart.

These speculations were mirrored in Lou Siegal's eyes as he sat there looking at me, truly concerned about the future and the future's possible harm.

"Tell me something," he said. "Why did it never occur to you that I might be interested in seeing the play you wrote? I would have enjoyed seeing the play you wrote. It was produced, you say. I would have taken my family."

Harriet?

"You're right, Mr. Siegal," I said. "I should have told you."

He rubbed the top of his hairy ear, and then he said a peculiar and poignant thing: "You didn't do me justice, Saul."

He was right. I didn't. He was a hard-nosed, small business-man, and he had made damn sure that he got his money's worth out of me, but I didn't do him justice. I had figured much more significantly in his plans than he had in mine. I didn't have to accept those plans—I couldn't—but I should have recognized the sincere interest he took in my life and have honored it in some way.

I didn't tell my parents about quitting my job or about the revival of my play. Rose had enough to contend with—the war, her husband. Learning that I had quit my job would only be taken as a sign that I was further severing the ties of safety. She was—as I was—a quick and accurate interpreter of signs.

So I said nothing. I paid my visits and pretended the world was going on as before—my job, the arctic wasteland. On one of my weekly visits, I could smell the stale freeze as soon as I walked in.

"How are you, Ma?"

"Fine."

"How are you, Pa?"

"All right."

We sat down in the kitchen and began on the roast chicken, or the meat loaf, or whatever. Passing of plates. Comments from me on the war. And, then, surprising both them and myself, I sighed in weariness, "Oh, Jesus!"

"What?" from my mother.

"Will it ever end?" I said. "What will it take? The end of the world? It's very near to that, and the two of you just go on."

"What are you talking about?" Rose asked.

"You know what I'm talking about."

"Why don't you ask the right person?"

"Will it ever end, Pa?"

"What are you talking about?"

"Forget it."

We all sat in silence. We ate. I had joined their miserable club. I would be silent, too. I don't know how long we sat there—five minutes, ten—and it was like an invisible plate passed from hand to hand, another course to the meal . . . *my play!* We were acting out *War and Peace in the Bronx!* I had become as silent as Daniel. Life imitating art—*and they both knew it!* The existence and meaning of my play became as real to them as the food on our plates.

"It's the place of the children," my father said.

"Pick up your head, Pa," I said.

"What?"

"Pick your head up. Don't talk to the chicken. Talk to me. Talk to your wife."

He didn't. He kept his head down, but he shot me a furtive look. "What's the matter with you?" he asked.

"Nothing's the matter with me!" I yelled. "I'm fine! I just don't want to hear about your troubles anymore! Both of you! People are dying by the thousands, but nothing is more important than Rose and Abe Klein having their own war, not giving in, not talking first! Okay! I know! I'm not going to change things around here, but neither do I have to sit here and be a part of it any longer! If you want me to come here in the future, then you invite me when you're not having a fight, when there's no evidence of it around! I'm not interested in your fights any longer! Your fights are too unimportant! There's a much bigger one going on!"

Did they reform? Of course not. They went on having their fights, had them until my father took sick, many years later. Life does imitate art, but only sometimes. Finally it had to be me who reformed. I no longer felt the obligation to subject myself to their lifelong misery. I returned my cold heritage. It was their private affair, not mine. That the world in flames couldn't divert my mother and father from their own icebound vendetta was a bitter truth and, perhaps, the excuse I needed for my departure.

I had invented a better outcome for Daniel.

2

THE BRITISH RESCUED what they could from the shambles at Dunkirk, the French capitulated, Hitler performed his delirious jig at Compiègne and I found a way of extending *War and Peace* to three acts.

I could control the world of my play; I had no control over the world I lived in. The world I lived in had allowed the beast to prepare his feast. It hadn't understood that the beast's dream was a dream of death. I had hoped that a world war and a Jewish calamity of biblical proportions would at last put an end to the Klein cycle. I didn't understand (but soon did) that mass murder was simplicity itself compared to the dark, twisting tunnel we dig in ourselves.

The play got some of the backing Leo hoped for, not all. There was a small theater he knew of that was still too expensive but available. Leo closed his eyes, gambled and won. *War and Peace in the Bronx* received good reviews for a second time, but this time in more important journals. It ran for eight months. The month after that was Pearl Harbor.

Mr. Siegal and his family came to see the play. I met Harriet at last. She came with her fiancé, who was (my prophetic soul!) in the last year of his internship. The fiancé was a nice-looking guy with dark eyes and a crop of black curly hair. If anything, Mr. Siegal had understated his younger daughter. She had copper-colored hair and greenish eyes and was as comely as the comeliest daughter of Zion. Lou gave me a sly, sidelong look, directing me wordlessly to gaze well upon what I had forfeited. But there was also regret in his eyes. He had adopted me, and I had abandoned him. Even if I hadn't stayed with the Siegal business, I could have joined the Siegal clan, and I know he would have liked that.

My family came, too—which surprised me. I thought Rose would have nothing more to do with my stage doings after that first exposure, but some word must have gotten to her—and to my sisters and their husbands. In a way, it was comic. Rose had backed away suspiciously from that first exposure of Klein history, seeing herself ill-used by her son. But now that the play had attained a certain notoriety, was being written about in the papers, advertised in the papers, was *the* subject among her friends, she was finding herself a little less ill-used. Yes, she had always known that Saul's head was elsewhere, not school, not his job. She never could figure out Saul, with his books and his reading and his writing, but she always had a feeling that something would come of it. As for the the play itself—well, it was like taking a little incident and making a whole *megillah* out of it. That's what playwrights do, no?

My father was silent, of course, but approvingly silent. He wasn't quite sure what I was trying to say in the play, but he did know, knew it for a certainty, and held on to it with grim satisfaction, that he had somehow modeled for the father in the play. I never really discussed it with him—I doubt I would have gained any great insight if I had—but I knew he regarded the play as the great exoneration of his life. All that he had maintained internally had been summarized before his eyes. All that he had been unable to say had been said. He didn't shake my hand or hug me or even try an experiment with words (that surprising medium), but he did look at me differently. No accolades. Not a smile. A covert, scolding look, as if I had waited too long to write his vindication.

Natalie, who had been very unhappy with the shorter version, still shook her head. She said, "You should call it *Fairy Tales in the Bronx.* Tell me, Saul, are you looking forward to a real happy ending?"

"Are you kidding?"

"So what is a play—wishful thinking?"

"You might say."

"Look, whatever it is, it works! God bless it! I hope you make a pile!"

Rita, on the other hand trembled on the verge of tears. She said, "This time I identified with *you*, with *Daniel.* I felt I was walking out the door with him! Now I *know* my life is going to change! And Mom and Dad's, too! You wait and see!"

I thought her second idea even more quixotic than her first. Of course my parents didn't change. The only difference was that they ceased carrying on their peculiar warfare in front of their children. I could still tell when a siege had started, but neither one tried to use me as a courier over the ice floes.

Some years later, when I asked Rose, she said that things were more or less the same. "Why," she asked, "did you think that your father could change?" She didn't say that she couldn't change either, but I think it was implied. I asked if they still fought over the same old things, and she astonished me by saying that they didn't fight at all. Occasionally, they would just stop talking. Just like that? Just like that. But for what reason? What was the signal? Rose shrugged. She couldn't say. It was like a telepathic thing. They both knew it was time, and they stopped talking for a week or so.

Gradually, I came to an understanding. I figured out that the only way they could continue their life together was to continue its loveless ritual. To end it would introduce them to strangers, and they were too old to cope with that. They would rather live with the terrible familiarity they knew.

The cycles finally ended when my father took sick. I've often wondered whether his terminal illness produced that otherness they had both carefully avoided, and whether the last year of their life together had been an awkward love affair.

Hannah Jacoby, who again played the role of the mother in the three-act version, let me know that she now had total affinity for the part. It had to do with her own home situation. Her father was threatening to sit *shivah* for her, to read her out of the family. She had argued and argued, pointed to the Yiddish theater and its respected place in the Jewish community, but her father was unmoving. She had told her father about the early morality plays in the Christian religion. She had told him about Greece, where the most serious human concerns were acted out on the stage. And wasn't religion itself, the Jewish religion, with its Torah and *talaysim* and *tfillin*, a kind of theater?

"Ouch!" I said, thinking of my own grandfather.

"What?"

"My guess is that you shouldn't have said that."

"You're right, I shouldn't have. How did you know?"

"In your father's eyes, that makes God a performer."

"Isn't He? Even in the Bible He performs."

"*Man* performs. God *ordains.*"

It was night, after one of the evening performances of *War and Peace.* We were walking away from the theater. I had taken to meeting Hannah after evening performances. It was summer. I had made an additional thousand dollars in royalties. Saul Klein and a possible career were beginning to merge into a single image. It had rained earlier that evening, and in walking past Bryant Park I breathed in a sweetness all the more piercing for its being in the middle of the city, at night.

"What *do* you believe?" Hannah asked.

"I believe that God is a fabulous playwright, better than Shakespeare," I said. "The only trouble is that He won't let us see the script."

"*We're* the script," Hannah said.

We turned at Forty-second Street and headed toward the BMT, Hannah's transportation home. I decided I would accompany her home. Time didn't matter. I had all the time in the world—or very little.

"Have you heard from your friend Gene?" she asked.

Why the "your friend" from everybody? First Ruth, now Hannah. Others, too. Even Leo Shulkin had referred to Gene as "your friend." Was it a distinction of some kind? Or a stigma?

"No," I said. "Have you?"

"Me? No . . ." She hesitated, then decided to say what was on her mind. "What did he tell you?" she asked.

"About what?"

292

"About us."

"Nothing. Was there something to tell?"

We walked past the movie houses. I could see the latest news circling the *Times* building: BRITISH BEAT OFF MASS RAIDS . . . NAZIS WARN BRITONS TO GIVE UP . . . It was so palpably clear that something had happened between Gene and Hannah that I felt like an intruder.

"I could never figure you two out," she said, and in saying so made a confession. She had had an affair with Gene. She was telling me this by pointing to the puzzling Strauss-Klein relationship. There might not seem to be a connection there, but I could easily make one out from the angle of incidence Hannah's words presented.

"What was there to figure out?" I asked.

"Were you friends or not?"

"I thought we were. What did Gene say?"

"He said you were a great help to him, that you could be very clever, but that you were too possessive and demanding. Is that true?"

"Maybe . . . What else did he tell you?"

"He said he was the one who gave you the idea for *War and Peace.*"

"In a way, that's true."

"He said you had a natural ear for dialogue and that you could have a career as a playwright, but that you would probably marry your boss's daughter. Do you have a boss, Saul?"

"Not now."

"Were you thinking of marrying his daughter when you did have one?"

"No."

"Then why did Gene say that? Was he lying?"

"I'm not sure that he was lying. He may have thought he was telling the truth. If Gene thinks something, then of course he thinks it's the truth. What else did he say?"

"Why should I be telling you all this?" she asked.

"Because we're both finding out things about Gene," I said. "It's good to find out things about Gene, isn't it? He revealed so little about himself."

293

"Then why don't you tell me what he said to you about me?" Hannah demanded.

"I would—so help me God—if I had anything at all to say. But, Hannah, he never told me anything about you. Not a word."

"Then how come he told me so much about you?"

"I don't know. I'm surprised that he did. On second thought, I'm not so surprised. We did have a special relationship. I did help him. He did help me. He also hurt me. Maybe I hurt him, too. I don't know. I guess I'll never know."

Hannah nodded. Apparently she was well acquainted with how such things happened. She said, "I found out a lot about you, but very little about him. He told me how unhappy you were at home, but he didn't tell me how unhappy he was at home. He must have been if his mother was the kind of woman who would commit suicide. He told me he had asked his mother to rent his room to you, that you would never have gotten away from your family except for that. Was that true?"

"Yes."

We were almost at the subway. I told Hannah that I would accompany her home if she would let me. She said it would take far too long, but I said I didn't mind. I didn't. I couldn't imagine spending my time in any more enjoyable or interesting way than this—this! We descended the subway stairs and I sniffed the not unpleasant odor of dirt and steel and high voltage. It had the friendliness of familiarity, that smell. It was my reading room, my think tank.

Hannah's Brooklyn train thundered into the station a moment after we arrived on the platform. A sign? It was a night of signs. Only a tissue-thin wall separated me from revelation. I would learn something tonight, something that would be as important to me as my meeting with Gene. There was a constriction in my chest because of it. I was reminded of the night when Anna Strauss sat on the edge of my bed and asked me for my opinion of Gene's future. Then, too, I had to get by on short, insufficient intakes of air. So, too, that night with Ruth. I wanted to end this inquisition, but I felt obligated to continue. I felt obligated to the Saul Klein who, if lucky, would be alive five years, or twenty, or an eternity from now.

"Hannah?"

"What?"—a little twist of annoyance in her voice.

"Was there anything else he said about me?"

The train rocked, Hannah shrugged. The game had reached an unprofitable stage for her. She wasn't sure she wanted to know any more than she already knew, or to divulge any more. She said, "I didn't take notes, you know. I can't remember everything he said. He may have said more, but I just don't remember. It may come back to me on another occasion. Why is it so important to you?"

I was learning something else that night. I was learning that Hannah curdled very quickly when a subject had been stirred once too often.

"It's important to me," I said, "because I'm afraid Gene Strauss is going to have a very lasting effect on my life."

That rekindled interest. She wanted to know why Gene would have such a lasting effect on my life.

"What, exactly, do you want to know?" she asked.

"About that room I rented at his mother's place. That's where we stopped."

"Gene told me it became a very awkward situation," she said. "According to what he said, his mother wanted you to move out, and that it was up to him to tell you. That's what was so embarrassing, because he was the one who had urged you to move in."

"Did he say why his mother wanted me to move out?"

"No . . . Why *did* she want you to move out, Saul? Did you try to rape her?"

I smiled—if that grimace could be called a smile. It was clear to me that I would learn nothing reliable from Hannah. Gene had evidently brewed for her one of his mythic potions of half-truths, lies and conceits. For the first time, I wondered how much of what he had told me was made of a similar mixture. His father, Anna, Rudi and Elena Oberst, Ernst Mueller, the jungle room, Ruth, everything—a shimmering displacement—and I swayed between illusion and reality to the point of seasickness.

To restore myself, I said, "I think Gene's mother wanted someone more compatible in the house. Someone nearer her own age, her own culture. Someone who could speak German, who understood the values, the music. I think that was the trouble from the very start. I didn't think that background mattered, but I see that it does, very much. You may speak the same language, but too often you're not referring to the same things."

We ended our talk of Gene there. I realize now that I had done again what I had done so often in the past. I had explained away what Gene could not, or would not, explain for himself.

The hall in the Brooklyn apartment house had its own richly mingled odor of the day's trapped heat and the evening's trapped meals.

"I'd ask you to come in but everybody's asleep," Hannah whispered.

"I understand," I whispered back.

I kissed her, tentatively. She stood perfectly still, having expected me to kiss her, but not having decided on a response. Then, slowly, she slipped her arms around me and came in close. I kissed her again.

"Do you like me, Saul?"

"You know the answer to that."

"Hold me."

We stayed that way, locked together in a hallway in Brooklyn, a little afraid of the incursions we had already made, already knowing the consequences. It may have been the closeness that muffled her words. I drew apart.

"What?" I asked.

"Tell me the truth," she said.

Strangely—or not so strangely—I knew what she meant. "You're very good," I said. "What is best, you'll go on getting better."

3

I SEE NOW that there were two special destinies to consider: the one Gene gave to the characters in his play, and the one he assigned to himself. The characters in his play were not supposed to know their special destinies. They groped. Gene may have groped, too, but he groped under a fixed star. It was not the star he indicated to others, but the one that shone brightly within his enclosed firmament.

Anything might have fouled up his fine navigation. He could have made bad connections, involvements that would have detoured his journey a damagingly, perhaps fatally, long time. He could have been killed in the war . . .

My outfit supplied weather information to the Field Evacuation Hospitals set up behind the front lines in France and Germany. The C-47's would fly in, load up the wounded that needed more extensive surgery or medical treatment than the field hospitals could provide and then they would take off for England. Actually, our function had become more complementary than essential. The wounded couldn't wait, and the weather had very low priority on flight clearances. The C-47's seemed to blind-touch their way back and forth across the Channel.

At some point the front began moving faster than we could pack up our equipment and chase after it. Patton (we were mainly following him) was not a general to worry about keeping all his ducks in a row. He just wanted them moving. In that way, we scurried through France and Germany.

I remember driving into the city of Kassel in a jeep. We had to find an airfield on the outskirts of the city. My commanding officer had a map, but the terrain had been greatly altered. "Let's go up that street, Sergeant," he said. "That" street was a broad, inclined, cobblestone avenue with streetcar tracks running up the middle. Since it continued in a gradual rise toward a distant crest, it was impossible to know what was beyond. The city had been taken only a few days before by American forces.

The city had also been bombed. No one had to tell us that. It was no longer a city. It was something the language never had need to describe before. It looked as though an enraged giant bent on terrible revenge had banged both fists on every standing thing, seizing what was left with both hands and crushing it to crumbs, to dust. But even before we rode into the visible evidence, we had been assailed by the smell. It hit us outside the city and grew thicker as we drove through. Fifty thousand people, we later learned, had been asphyxiated in air-raid shelters because the surrounding fires had consumed all the oxygen. The dead remained where they had died. There wasn't the equipment to excavate the bodies.

Miraculously, the broad street on which I drove had been left untouched. I continued to drive, insanely obeying some kind of traffic pattern when there was nothing on the street but us, nothing on either side of us but those compost heaps of brick and concrete. It was like being on another planet—a silent, sinister, awful-smelling planet. For all we knew there might be a German machine-gun emplacement at the top of the street along which I nervously drove, a nervous captain beside me.

Something warned me to slow up as we came to the top of the long street. I did slow up, rolled forward a few more feet, then almost pushed the brake through the floor of the jeep. The street had ended abruptly. Directly below us, some thirty feet, was a river. In the river was a bridge, a huge steel bridge, its beams still intact, its middle broken, its superstructure fallen from either bank into the river. The Fulda River seethed through the steel beams. We knew it must be the Fulda because that was the river indicated on our map. But no one had told us that a vast bridge would be lying in the river, the bridge we were supposed to cross.

Massive man-made things seem right only when they are standing as they were designed to stand. The *Normandie* lying on its side in a New York harbor was a terrifying sight. So was this fallen bridge. It overwhelmed my senses, and so it was not until later that I could piece together vague, elliptical thoughts that had formed at that extraordinary sight . . . *Germany!* That fairyland of evil that had haunted my days and nights, that had cursed my existence. I had been brought these many miles to see the broken-back beast lying helpless in a brown river. That I should have been allowed to see this seemed to me a deep, personal vindication, something I would carry with me for the rest of my life. I drew the spirit of Herschel Grynszpan to my side so that he could witness it with me . . .

I wrote to Hannah from Blackpool, London, Orléans, Paris, Valenciennes, Cologne and Kassel. I worked on a play all through the war. It was a wonderful way to keep terror at bay. I finished it in Kassel while sitting around in idleness, waiting to be returned to the States. I had written the play with Hannah in mind, but unfortunately (I mean, *fortunately!*) she was appearing in a Broadway play at the time of my return home. Her first Broadway play—although she'd had quite an active time of it during the war. She had been busy with repertory groups in the city, and then had joined a group that toured the camps along the eastern seaboard. They were even sent to the Caribbean. Hannah had learned to dance so that she could take part in the musicals. After the war had ended in Europe, she had tried out for a part in a new play on Broadway, and got it.

Hannah was as good as she had hoped to be. At least I thought so. She did not. Or said she didn't. Or if she did, her belief in herself was so hedged with superstition and guilt that it amounted to a chronic pathology—like a millionaire who lives in constant dread of poverty. Throughout the war, my letters to her always contained some litany of assurance. This obligatory service hadn't been included in the marriage ceremony performed by her father in his Brooklyn synagogue (the groom in uniform), but I think I knew even before the ceremony that I was taking on the function of part-time exorcist.

The war had softened Rabbi Jacoby's view of things. News of the fate of Europe's Jews was beginning to leak out, and that was changing all human attitudes. Past moralities shrank into insignificance in the face of the supreme evil. If Hannah wanted to be an actress—well, let her, there were worse things . . .

Suicide, heartbreak, the rebirth of my play, marriage to Hannah. There was enough and more than enough to carry me into the army and the years that followed. I didn't think about the future. There was no future. There was only the removal of that which made the future impossible. It was astonishing, however, how quickly the everyday, nagging considerations of the future were restored once the future was restored.

There was the GI Bill. I would go back to school and get a degree. What kind of degree? Well, hell, I don't know, you know, a *degree.* I mean, even if I decided to continue writing plays, a degree in English wouldn't hurt, would it?

Here is where the strange alliance came about. Hannah and Rose. That Hannah should have encouraged a quick return to my interrupted career was understandable, but that my *mother* should have added her voice to that encouragement was staggering, when it wasn't funny. It was both, staggering and funny. My own guess would have been that Rose would opt for the solid, the steady, business, salesman, even a teacher, if that's what I wanted.

Instead she said, "But you know you can write plays, so why don't you do it?"

"It takes a long time to write a play," I said, "and there's never a guarantee that anyone will put up the money to produce it."

"Money?" she said. "You saved up a lot of money during the war."

I smiled to myself. I wondered what figures she imagined. Nevertheless, it was true, I had saved a respectable amount of money over the war years. Hannah had put away the money I sent home, lived on the money she made. And there was the money I made on *War and Peace.* I couldn't start producing plays, but I could surely invest in myself for the next two or three years. That

I finally did so I attribute more to Rose than to Hannah. Not that I valued Rose's judgment more than Hannah's, but that Rose bore a closer relationship to the corner of my conscience that needed assurance. It was okay for me to go on doing what I seemed to do best, even though the world I had known before cried out against such dangerous frivolity. Rose had given it sanction.

I didn't actually sit down and ponder the question but let it kick around in my unconscious, where most of my mental aches and ambiguities get resolved or lost. I believe Rose worked out something in her own life by backing Hannah. A vicariousness of some sort. A warning to follow my instincts early in life rather than late. Not to waste years. She summed it up best herself, I believe, when she once said to me, "Everybody—the whole world!—had to go to war because of one lunatic, so why shouldn't you do what you want?" There may seem to be a little bend in the logic, but I understood.

My father, of course, had nothing to say. The prewar episode of my play had thrown interesting lights along the walls of his underground dwelling, but that didn't mean that he had any conclusions to draw. War, the death of millions, the incineration of cities hadn't changed the boundaries of his existence. He could function only within those limits. That's the way he was.

I've never been able to define exactly the connection between Rose and Hannah. I don't believe my mother ever mentally made Hannah another daughter—blood was blood—but she did make her a diverting, prideful part of her life. She took pleasure in Hannah's successes. If the theater in which Hannah was appearing was within subway distance, Rose would be in the audience at least once, sometimes more than once.

And in her way Hannah reciprocated. She liked Rose. Naturally, I had told Hannah about the Klein ice fields, the inexorable rhythm of freeze and thaw, just as she had told me about her father's unyielding rejection of her career and her mother's sorrowful inability to oppose her father. "But he finally did change," I said. "Not really," she said. "He doesn't accept it; he just tolerates it. He has yet to see me in a single performance."

Perhaps it was the way Rose had handled the intractabilities of

301

her life that aroused Hannah's admiration. Divorce was still far from being an acceptable remedy. Hannah understood why my mother continued to endure that life, but she applauded the spunky fight Rose waged. Hannah's own mother had succumbed so early, so completely. Rose didn't leave the marriage, but she did leave the arrangement. She ceased to consult my father's wishes entirely. She would go to the plays in which her daughter-in-law appeared. Her daughter-in-law's own mother never did. When the time came, Rose babysat for us, sleeping over quite often at the apartment on Eighteenth Street, and then at the house in Hastings.

"Doesn't he object?" I asked her.

"Sure he objects," she said. "To what doesn't he object?"

"Do you have fights because of it?"

Rose smiled, shook her head, closed her eyes and raised one shoulder. The perfect pantomime: *Do we have fights because of it? Of course we have fights—because of that, because of anything—but I do what I want. Maybe someday he'll move out.*

But Abe never moved out. He got sick—and Rose took care of him until he died. At some point, there must have been an internal announcement of that impending death, and it brought about a metamorphosis in Abe Klein. He faced death with the serenity of one who had lived a life of light, laughter and forgiveness. It was as if he believed in an afterlife and was certain of his own place in paradise. Rose shook her head over it. "I don't understand," she said. "He acts like a man who has had a very pleasant life, nothing to regret."

If you turned that idea inside out, it might look more like the truth. Living underground all of his life, Abe might have looked on any other condition as deliverance.

When Rose was close to her own death in that seaside Home where she spent the last few years of her life, she said something to me that set up a small but persistent reverberation—then, now. We were sitting on the patio of the Home. There was a splendid view of the bay and the Verrazano Narrows Bridge. Hannah was not with me, and so Rose could ask the question: "Is Hannah happy?"

"Why not?" I said. "She's doing what she wants."

302

Some seconds of sunshine silence, and then she said, "I get the feeling sometimes that your Hannah is not a happy person."

"Who's happy all the time?" I said.

Rose nodded. Her mind made its own dimming journey, then she said, "I had no idea when I married him . . ."

Maybe that was also part of the affinity. Rose was right. Happiness didn't come easily to Hannah, although there are plenty who would envy her. But we measure success by those we envy, not by those who envy us. Hannah is a fine actress—much better, I believe, than some who have gone on to, as they say, stardom. She played mostly in repertory groups, which were very active then. Her summers were always occupied. The kids (two) often wondered why we never went on a real summer vacation. The fact is we did go to the mountains or to the shore, but mainly because Hannah was appearing in summer stock in the Catskills or out on the Island. I guess it didn't seem like a vacation to the kids because so often there was the same tension and irregularity that marked their year-round lives.

And at times the same kind of euphoria. There was that, too. When things were going well. When there were good reviews, responsive audiences—most important of all, perhaps, when Hannah could look forward to an engagement in the fall. It was an active, professional life, the kind of life she wanted, but not quite as resplendent as she wished. I knew that she wanted to be asked to come to Hollywood, but it never happened. Strange, that. She knew that the thing she valued most in herself, in the art itself, militated against a big, gaudy success; yet she still went on cultivating her seriousness, making no compromises, never yielding to the meretricious—and *still* wishing for her share of the glamorous and the splashy.

When I pointed out the contradiction, she said she knew, she knew, but it had happened to others, hadn't it? She would compile an impressive list of the names to whom it had happened. I don't think I ever told her about Gene's theory of the charismatic emblem. She would have scorned the theory. One shouldn't need tricks, like that terrible Josh—who, incidentally, did become a "big name" in Hollywood. I agree that one shouldn't need tricks, but there does come a point when one must yield to the force of things as they are—stupidly, obviously, meretriciously *are!* It made her bitter, that limited success. It reinforced her lifelong fear of impoverishment.

It's possible that having to deal with Hannah's frustration was therapy for my own. Not that my fate paralleled Hannah's; fate isn't that symmetrical. I did have one fairly big success. It was not the play I had written with Hannah in mind while waiting out the end of the war in Germany. That one was never produced, which may have been a good thing. The successful play was the one I had once called *The Liberation of Herschel Grynszpan,* only now I had changed both the title and the name of the hero, on the outside chance that the prototype might still be alive.

It didn't make me rich, but it did make me free of any future Mr. Siegals. One of the odd perquisites (there were many) of the play was the teaching career it opened for me. I've never regretted that arrangement. I had begun to hear a rattle in my freelance life.

Naturally, I avoided talking about Ruth to Hannah. Hannah knew I had been in love with "that girl," but she took it to be another of the residues left over from the strange Strauss-Klein period. I think there was an assumption that Gene and I shared girls—which was not altogether wrong, but not essentially right. I didn't think of myself as having *shared* Ruth. I scarcely even consoled her. But I had fallen in love with her—and at a time when it was likely to inflict the worst ravages. I also remember the sex, but only as certain photographs remind one of having seen those photographs before. Flat, one-dimensional. I can reconstruct the heart-stopping rite if I try, but it takes a deliberate act of will.

But I don't have to reconstruct the pain. That will come on its own, causing me the ache of a wound that is healed but subject to the weather of the mind. Then I will pay attention in the streets and buses and subways, not knowing what I would do if I actually saw her, not certain that I would have the nerve to greet her, but acknowledging in that way her real, continued presence in the world.

Not that I *know* there is a continued presence. I've never tried to contact her. She has never contacted me. I have never caught sight of her—in New York, in San Francisco, or in some predestined corner of the Uffizi or the Tate.

But sometimes I will look.

4

GENE WASN'T KILLED in the war. I learned this from Leo Shulkin, who had seen Gene when he was on the West Coast. I learned that Gene had gone from his script-writing job into Special Services. After the war, Gene had returned to Hollywood (which was when Leo met him), joined one of the major movie companies and continued his career—only this time, according to Leo, not as a writer but as a producer.

We rarely mentioned Gene, Hannah and I. Once, however, when we were walking in Greenwich Village, a section of the city that evoked memories for both of us, she said, "I could never do it myself—I think you can understand why—but I've always considered it a miracle of some kind that in all these years *you* have never contacted your dear chum Gene to see if once—just once! —the right word in the right place might work in my favor. He did think me a fairly good actress at one time, you know."

"He's not my dear chum," I said.

"No? I thought he was."

"You know better."

I just barely refrained from pointing out that there was a time when she was pretty chummy with Gene herself. I said, "There's nothing to stop *you* from reminding Gene of the girl who so beautifully played the female lead in his first play—his only play. If memory serves me, I believe he kissed your hand in thankfulness."

"You know very well I can't do that," Hannah said.

"I don't know that very well. Why can't you?"

"Because it would be too humiliating."

"I was under the impression that people in theater did it all the time."

"Well, this person doesn't!"

We were having one of our bad periods, when Hannah would say things—wild, hurtful, untrue things—and then would sink into the deepest remorse, rocking back and forth, as I have seen her father do in his deepest devotions. She had gone without work for six months. She was convinced she was through in theater, would never again appear on stage. I learned in time that when she permitted herself to be sucked into one of those moods life could, and often would, become unbearable, for herself, for me, often for the children. She lost interest in everything—food, sex, the state of the world—everything except that one bleak fact.

I admitted then—I admit now—the legitimacy of her complaint. It was perversely unfair that fate hadn't handed her one of those simple gratuities that come to people when they persevere. Hannah had persevered. She had persevered with courage and with integrity and ever-increasing artistry. But that's the way the cards fell. She was never in a long-run play, even in a minor role.

I wrote another play with Hannah in mind, but that lived ingloriously for less than a month. Hannah had the lead, and she was again singled out by reviewers for her fine performance. It didn't save the play, but it did lead to the role of Madame Treplev in *The Sea Gull,* in which (we both believed) she gave the best performance of her career. Then began one of the happiest times of our marriage.

We had dinners out very often. We had sex binges with rekindled hope for aphrodisiac. We walked through streets where every familiarity was touched with grace.

Inevitably came the turn in fortune, and then another slide into self-doubt and despair. Hannah and I never stopped talking completely, but we did repeat the Klein cycle in our fashion. Good periods and bad periods, turning and turning. The old adage inside out: be careful what you pray against, you may have to repeat it.

Hannah's success in *The Sea Gull* led to an offer from a prestigious company to join them for their summer season. Debbie, our first child, was five at the time, and it was decided that Hannah would go, and that I would stay with Debbie. That didn't mean spending all my time with the child. There was Mrs. Anderson, who used to be our twice-a-week housekeeper, and who volunteered to work full-time. I would be able to continue with my own work most of the day. Hannah's company customarily divided their summer seasons between two locations—one in Massachusetts, the other out on the Island. We planned for Debbie and me to join Hannah on the Island during the second half of the summer.

It had become habitual with me to begin, compulsively, on a new play while an old one was writhing in its death throes. I suppose it says something about me that I am willing to coast indefinitely on the inertia of what, for me, passes for success, but a failure creates panic. It's not the play itself that compels me, but the image of the man who wrote it. I must expunge that. So I frenziedly begin another, and frenziedly finish so that at least I have the illusion of restoration.

I was lucky this time. I found backers rather quickly—rather, *a* backer—since only one was putting up the bulk of the money, and naturally expecting the lion's share of the profits, if any. He was not a veteran in theater. He vacillated for weeks, convinced that what we needed was a "big name" in the lead role. I pointed out what he should have known: big names got big money. He offered up a percentage of his own take for the big name. I further pointed out that big names usually got a percentage of the box office as a matter of course, not as a favor. We finally settled on a name that was *well known,* if not exactly big.

To celebrate, the heavy backer invited his cobackers and me to lunch at the Plaza. There were four of us, starchy linens, ornate silver, splendid food and a general glow of optimism. It was when we were dispersing that I saw Gene Strauss for the first time in almost ten years. He was standing in the lobby.

My first impulse was to go through one of those royal revolving doors, get out of sight before I was seen, get out of range before I was spoken to. Pure, instantaneous panic. I wasn't at all sure that I could find an attitude that would hold together for the necessary time. I was too full of excitement and resentment. I wanted too much to present an ideal front ever to achieve it. I don't do too well under such circumstances. I was aware of my own disadvantage, but at the same time I was mesmerized by the sight of Eugene Strauss. Not so pale as I remembered him. Tanned, rather—or a new patina to embellish his narrow, aristocratic face. That feature was still the same: narrow. Like Leslie Howard, who, I ridiculously recalled, had been killed in an airplane accident some time at the beginning of the war. Gene was wearing one of those popular seersucker suits, a blue shirt, and—dear God!—a yellow tie.

I knew that he was older, but I didn't *see* that he was older. He hadn't put on weight. (I had, a little.) He hadn't lost hair. (I had, a little.) I noticed that he combed his hair in the same undulant way—and I also noticed that he had changed. How? I can only say this: his special destiny had settled into his form, his face, his soul —if, after all, there is one. All these observations in a matter of seconds. I was still teetering on the verge of escape. However few seconds had passed, I had waited too long. I had closed off my escape, if I ever really meant to escape. Gene saw me. I saw the look of recognition on his face, and I thought I detected an instant of hesitation, the possibility of avoidance. But he decided against it. He raised a hand, and in another instant we were standing face to face.

He put out his hand and I took it. The same iron pressure I remembered. For crying out loud, I played tennis and racquetball with ritual frenzy, yet his grip was as dominating as ever. He seemed to be having no trouble in finding the right face for the moment.

"How are you, Saul?"

"Fine, Gene. No need to ask how you are. You look great."

"Thank you. So do you."

"Lost some hair, put on some weight."

"You look the same," he insisted.

"I heard you had gone back to Hollywood," I said.

"Yes."

"So what are you doing in New York?"

"Meeting some people," he said. (Naturally not *me*!) He said, "I've been put in charge of a project. We're doing more international films. It's rather exciting. I think that's where the future of film lies. We're planning to do our next film in Italy."

Incredible! In a single line, more or less, we were once again plunged into the priority of Eugene Strauss!

"Onward and upward," I said.

"It's a big gamble," he said.

Could this really be Gene Strauss? Could we really be standing in the lobby of the Plaza talking with such casual sophistication about international films? What the hell was it about his voice? Christ, yes! He still had an accent! *It had all but vanished in the time that I knew him, and yet here it still was, a decade later! It might have been wrapped in foil and stuck in a freezer for ten years. He had* kept *it!* Cultivated *it! There must have come a point when he decided that there was more gain than loss in those interesting inflections! The world's greatest war had been fought. Millions killed. In some mysterious Straussian way, an amalgam of all that staggering history had filtered into Gene's voice!*

"Well, you have that enviable track record," I said.

"And you, Saul?" he asked at last.

I told him. I told him why I was at the Plaza, and he congratulated me. I told him of the plays I had written, and he said that he didn't know there were that many. He followed, he said, the New York theater scene closely, and he had heard about my hit play. He had meant to write to me about that, but, well, frankly, he didn't know where to write. I told him that I was on the teaching staff of the drama department of a New York university, that I gave classes in theater, playwriting. He smiled at that and said that wasn't too surprising. He had always been aware of my gift of lucidity. He guessed that I must be a very good teacher, and I made an uncontradicting grimace. I felt I must stop telling him about myself, that I was trying too hard to balance past imbalances—or present ones, for that matter. There was no need for me to do that. I had nothing to be ashamed of. I had made a satisfying career for myself. I almost remarked on the part he had played in it, but checked myself in time, fearing too blatant a call on our past association, fearing the evocation of certain particulars . . .

I broke it off by asking, "Are you married?"

"Yes," he said. "For a second time."

I couldn't help myself. I saw myself walking away from this meeting, probably never seeing Gene again, and never knowing if either of those wives . . .

"Ruth Prager figure in any of those marriages?" I asked—jocularly, you understand—a small withdrawal of interest on a shared account.

"No," he said, smiling.

The first marriage was to an actress. It didn't survive the war. The second marriage, five years ago, was to a woman who had nothing to do with the movies, the stage, anything like that. Her name was Peggy—Peggy Metcalf. This was her first marriage. He speculated that this one appeared to be permanent . . . "Are you married, Saul?" he asked.

"Yes," I said. "To someone you know."

"Really?"

"Really. Hannah. Hannah Jacoby."

I could make out a few seconds of inner exploration. Oh, I was sure he remembered the girl, but the name didn't register immediately. It was the name he was trying to place. Maybe it was the "Jacoby" that threw him. Still, it was vicariously hurtful, particularly when I recalled Hannah's sometimes infuriated, sometimes pathetic call on influence, association, *anything*!

"The girl who played Rena in your play," I said.

His face settled beatifically into penitent remembrance. "Of course," he said. "Hannah. A very talented actress. Lovely. Well, congratulations. Do you have any children?"

"A girl. Debbie. And you?"

"We have a son."

"May I ask his name?"

"Carl."

"Carl. That was the—it was Carl and Rena, wasn't it?"

"Yes."

While we talked, I saw him glance away, make a quick survey

311

of the lobby. He was waiting for his important international connections, of course. This interview would soon end. I hadn't expected to see Gene again, ever. Having done so, I was made doubly aware of how unlikely it was that it would ever happen again. He would go back to Hollywood. He would resume his special destiny in international filmmaking. I felt I must say something more about Hannah, but I couldn't. I simply couldn't use this occasion in such a favor-seeking way. There was, after all, *my* pride. But there was something I did want to ask, something that wouldn't involve my pride, something that, unasked, unsatisfied, would only add itself to the many mysteries he had taken with him down those subway steps on that cold day, with that blue vein puffy in stress, with his eyes haunted by the death of his mother.

"This is awfully childish, I know," I said, "But I'd love to see a picture of your present wife, if you happen to have one."

"I do," he said, reaching into the breast pocket of his jacket.

Gene showed me a picture of his wife. She looked nothing like Ruth Prager. She looked nothing like the movie star I had envisioned on that Klondike night, eons ago, in the matrix of time. This one had auburn hair, pale jade eyes and a smile with which I could have fallen in love—*did* fall in love, instantly!—and recovered by the time Gene had returned the wallet to his pocket.

Perhaps it was that speeding up of process that freed me to ask, "Why did you never write?"

"Ah!" he said, "there's my . . ." He raised his hand and signaled. I turned and saw a trio of very classy-looking gentlemen. "I did write," Gene said. "It was thought that my real skills lay elsewhere."

Now we were both looking at the three men who were politely waiting for Gene to be finished. I thought I recognized one. An actor?

"I meant write to *me,*" I said.

"I didn't know where to write," he said.

We both knew that was only superficially true. People find people when they want to.

"Well," I said, holding out my hand, "you have people waiting for you."

He took my hand, his grip not so cruel this time. "I couldn't write," he amended.

"Why?"

"I think you know why. . . . Listen, Saul, if you are ever in California, you and Hannah . . ."

"Yes," I said. "Of course."

I left the hotel and crossed over to the park side of the street. The sun was hot, but not sullenly hot. Exuberantly hot, rather. You could see its light dancing among the leaves of the trees. You could test its brilliance on the bright print patterns of summer dresses.

What was it that I knew?

I conjured that distant day, also sun-bright but cuttingly cold, when I had walked with Gene to the subway. I remembered how much I wanted to be done with that day. I remembered how much I wanted Gene to be gone, taking with him that whole episode of my life. All that I was feeling at that moment must have been on my face . . . *Of course he couldn't write!*

5

A PLOT DEMANDS structure, pace, resolution. Anticlimax is poison. Even a hint of it is enough to kill. Life doesn't give a damn about anticlimax. Life is shameless about cliché. It has about as much pace and decorum as the subway at rush hour. It never knows when a thing should end, and ends everything and everyone with the same dull regularity.

My own sense of the thing was that our history had ended. Meeting Gene in the lobby of the Plaza was an acceptable, even necessary, coincidence; but I didn't look for anything beyond that. Anything further would be awkward anticlimax. There would be nothing to go on. Gene Strauss had achieved his special destiny. He had inadvertently helped me to achieve mine. If there was to be a living bond beyond that, we would have sensed it even before that encounter.

As it happened, that was a wonderful summer. Hannah had a triumphant season. She was singled out again for her performance as Olga in *Three Sisters*. Debbie and I joined her out on the Island, and I found Hannah as content as I'd ever seen her. She was almost convinced of her talent and authority. She wanted to get away from the backstage rehashings and drive to the beach bungalow where Debbie and I were staying. She even insisted on doing the shopping in the morning hours, except on the day when there was a matinée. She seemed to have entered a new phase. Her dedication to her career was just as total, but she

314

seemed to want to color that totality with a better conscience. She was always the one made most miserable by her sessions of misery. There was always guilt to add to the general unhappiness. I never expected great reform—any more than I did with my parents—but I did feel there were small changes. Remorse is painful, can teach. At the very least, she would have this time to refer to. I could always remind her of the summer on the Island when she found there could be comfort in others. It might even work a little in times of defeat—although I kept a good reserve of doubt about that.

I hadn't told her about meeting Gene in our telephone conversations. I thought I would hold that until I could judge for myself her general state of being. I trusted the serenity I found enough to tell her about the meeting in the Plaza.

"And is he a big shot in Hollywood?" she asked.

"He told me he was in New York working on some kind of international film thing. It sounded big to me."

"What did he look like?"

"He looked marvelous. He looked like he had just come from his own deification."

"Oh, stop it."

"He was wearing a seersucker suit."

"That doesn't sound godlike."

"And a yellow tie."

"Yellow!"

"He was wearing a yellow tie the first time I met him. He was always a man of sartorial independence. The strangest thing was his speech. Do you remember him having an accent?"

"No."

"Well, I do. When I first met him. Just a trace of one. It got less and less. But there's an accent now. I think he's botanized the damn thing."

"Why would he do that?"

"For the cachet. Internationalism is big."

"Was he friendly?"

"I would say so. Yes, indeed. In fact, he was the one who came over and spoke to me. Had he not, I might have walked out of there without saying a word."

"Why?"

"Because the sight of him flustered me. I didn't want to appear any more affected, any less composed, than he seemed to be, but I was afraid I couldn't bring it off. I was afraid of unraveling."

"But *why*?" Hannah demanded, looking irritated.

"Because . . . I don't know . . . no, I do know. It's this: I met him at a time of my life when all the advantages were his. We only knew each other somewhat over a year. There wasn't enough time to adjust the balance. It isn't so much what he was but what *I* was. The combination of both. He changed my world. He changed *me*. One doesn't get over that so easily."

"But, Saul, don't you think you would have changed anyway, Gene or no Gene?" Hannah cleverly asked.

I smiled at that. It was, of course, true. I would have changed anyway, but . . . "But, there's really only one great change in a man's life," I said. "From child to man. Everything else is marvelously or morosely incidental. Whoever affected the change, or seemed to have affected it, becomes, rightly or wrongly, your private, all-time magus."

"Oh, crap! What's a magus?"

"Actually, I don't know."

Actually, I did know. I knew that the doctrine of the magi proposed good and evil as rival deities, both to be worshipped.

As far as I knew, Gene had gone back to glittering Hollywood, making international films with British accents and Italian beauties. Hannah and I went on living our own lives, having another child, buying a house north of the city, having fights and reconciliations and gradually settling into the rich and vexing realization that this would be our life. That is, we were doing what we wanted, but we were not doing it at a level that appeased our vanities. Which is a fancy way of saying that we went around much of the time feeling shafted.

But a shaft has two ends. We were conscious of the sharp end most of the time. Hannah was conscious of the parts she tried out for and didn't get. I was conscious of plays I wrote and were never produced. Or, if produced, produced on small budgets, Off-Broadway, a very limited run. Nevertheless, we were doing what

316

we wanted. Knowing the world better—and worse—it's a point that must be stressed.

And something else. I used the word *rich* before, and I believe I was justified in doing so. That richness was the other end of the shaft. The thrust of our lives. We lived with that as consistently as we did with headaches and bills. I never asked Hannah, but I know it accompanied her waking in the morning and her going to sleep at night, as it did me. It was with her during the day, as it was me. We *expected*. We expected each day that we might break through to a higher form, a finer perception, a final epiphany. After all, we were doing what we wanted, and as long as that obtained there was always the chance. We had that. Every day. The chance.

One had been hearing about it, but it was some time around the end of the sixties, the beginning of the seventies, that the fall of the great movie studios became a fact. Movies were being made, of course, but they were being made by conglomerates. "A New Era in Hollywood" was the way a Sunday article put it. I remember thinking of Gene when I read that article.

I didn't think of Gene very long. A play of mine—the first in eight years—was opening in a theater in the Village. It was on that opening night that I saw Gene again. He was in the lobby of the theater at the play's end. Again, I saw him first. I also saw that he was with the woman whose photograph I had seen fifteen years ago, in the lobby of the Plaza. Does that seem impossible, that recognition? It's true. She was smiling there in the heat and haze, and I recognized the smile. After all, I had fallen in love with it for five seconds. I don't forget things like that.

Eugene Strauss was by this time in his early fifties. He had to be. Perhaps the only human constant is the time-spread between you and anyone you know. Whether it's a day or a decade, the same time-spread will remain whenever you meet. Eugene Strauss was in his early fifties because I knew how old *I* was.

Now there were pouches under his eyes, and his hair had thinned, but he was still slim and elegant. He was wearing a blue blazer, the palest pink shirt, and a light-colored tie. I couldn't

317

make it out, but it wasn't yellow. It was the end of September, hot as mid-August, and I was feeling good. The play being performed had gone back to my first theme of domestic discord, but this time I had used it in a full-blown way what I had only hinted at before. The lives of the parents, not the children. The horrors of history that so many immigrants had brought with them. Hannah played the mother. She and the male lead had performed flawlessly the difficult job of two articulations—the accents of their everyday speech and the unaccented speech of memory. It could have been a grotesque babble, but it wasn't. It was perfect. And that Eugene Strauss should be standing there put a dream gloss on the perfection. I felt I was being paid back for past inequities and failings, mine and his.

Naturally, I didn't say so, but I was surprised that the woman of the photograph was still his wife. I hadn't expected that much human faithfulness in Gene's career—which was very unfair. What did I know?

I went over. Gene said, "Ah!" and he shook my hand, his grip as strong as ever. Oh, yes, his hair had definitely thinned. I could see pink scalp between the graying filaments. I shook hands with the wife of Eugene Strauss.

"You should feel very proud," she said.

"Yes, you should," said Gene. "A fine play, beautifully performed."

"Thank you."

"And the woman, of course," Gene said. "The playbill said Hannah Jacoby—"

"Hannah kept her own name for the stage," I said. "Yes, that Hannah. My wife."

"She was wonderful!" Peggy said.

She spoke with a finishing-school voice. That's probably not accurate, but let it stand. Her voice had poise is what I meant. *She* had poise—the way she stood, the way she handled what I'm sure she knew to be a situation of many, many parts. I thought to myself that only very secure people can compliment others with such wholehearted sincerity. I was not mistaken about her smile. It had a secretive, oblique charm.

"I suppose you're waiting for Hannah," Gene said.

318

"Yes."

"I'd like to say hello."

"I'm sure she'd love it," I said, almost lightheaded with the high irony taking place in this smoky, not too clean lobby. After all the years of mystery and envy to have this symbolic figure, hat in hand, as it were, paying tribute. It was a sweaty night, but I thought of ice crystals, the complex, consummate patterns of ice crystals.

Then Hannah was beside me, and I kissed her and looked at her in a way that she understood. I heard sounds of recognition from people standing about, a scattering of applause, and Hannah smiled and looked about her and said, "Thank you," and turned back to me and the people I was talking to. I could see in her eyes that she didn't recognize Gene, and I wondered what image she had retained all these years.

Gene said, "I can't tell you how much it pleases me to know that the artist who performed tonight was the girl who had played the lead in a play I had written."

Hannah's eyes widened. She looked at me. I said, "The name is Strauss—Peggy and Eugene." It was just the second or two she needed, and then she was composed, and there were handshakes and compliments and just the sort of compressed triumph one dreams about but rarely enjoys.

"Then it's not just coincidence," she said. "You knew it was Saul's play."

"Oh, yes," Gene said. "We'd read about the opening in the paper."

"Are you visiting?" I asked.

"Not any longer," Gene said. "We've moved back east . . . apropos of which, I wonder if you would be free to have cocktails with us next Sunday. I noticed that there was a matinée on Sunday, but any time after the matinée would be fine. We're having several people over, and they'll be coming at all hours."

I looked at Hannah. She said yes, of course. Well, why not? A reunion of sorts. And yet I felt oddly reluctant. Old rivalries? I didn't think so. A prescience of something I had already sensed but hadn't named.

*　*　*

The cocktail party was in one of those apartments in Manhattan that I have gazed at from street level all my life, wondering who lived there, how they acquired the vast sums of money that allowed them to live there. The windows faced the park, and looking out from one I could locate the southwest corner where Gene and I had once walked in cold, aching shock. Could that really have happened in this same lifetime? It didn't seem possible. I thought of Anna. Her ghost walked enraptured among the *distingué* guests of "Gen's" party.

There were small mountains of caviar and large bowls of cold lobster salad. There were patés, eggs in aspic, puff pastes of all kinds. Young men in white jackets carried trays of golden champagne. I remembered Leo Shulkin making a play for Hannah, his paw grasping that pristine glass of champagne. Now you didn't have to go into the kitchen to be apportioned your glass. You had only to reach out your hand.

Gene and Peggy introduced Hannah and me to their other guests. Not to everyone, that would have been clumsy and wearing, but to a special few. It didn't escape my notice that the deferential accent fell on the Kleins. All these people seemed to be connected with television or movies in one way or another. I learned that Gene had been shaken loose from Hollywood by the seismic tremor that had run through Southern California. I learned that Peggy of the enchanting smile was heiress to an enchanting fortune in proprietary drugs. I learned that this party was to mark the opening of the agency Gene was setting up in New York. It was an agency that would put together the many diverse talents and properties needed for TV or the movies. I'd heard of such agencies, and was more than a little puzzled about what it was they put together.

Naturally, I watched Gene move about, talk to people, and I was impressed by what seemed to me his untiring sociability. I suffer piecemeal collapse in such circumstances. First my back goes, then my legs, then my disposition. For the two hours that Hannah and I were there (and it had been going on an hour before we arrived), Gene had maintained the same fresh, discreet, interested manner. He was accomplished and gregarious and knowledgeable—and I didn't know him. He had clearly learned how to accept people at their own estimations—and I surely didn't know him.

"I hope we're going to stay in touch," he said, when Hannah and I left.

"Yes," I said. "Of course.

Perhaps it wasn't true at all, but it did pass through my mind that the play Gene had seen and the subsequent invitation to his cocktail party were not unconnected. He was setting up an agency. The attraction of a new play by Saul Klein mightn't have been entirely nostalgic. A man in the (new) business of putting talents and properties together mustn't overlook any bets, even old ones. On the other hand, that mayn't have been the case at all.

My play ran for three months. There was talk of Broadway again, but nothing came of it. Vietnam was reaching a crescendo. Four were killed at Kent State. The war had moved into Cambodia. The vision and the energies of the country were elsewhere. Others have said it, and I have had a lifetime of experience for confirmation: there are conditions other than those within the play itself necessary to its success. A bad play can prosper at a certain time; a good one die.

But the play would last. We were assured of that. We were told that the play would be put on again, for sure, at a more receptive time. Thirty years ago, we didn't laugh. Nor did we now.

Gene and I saw each other over the next few years, but infrequently. He would occasionally send tickets to movie previews, the kind that were held in small auditoriums, just for reviewers and other interested parties. Sometimes Gene would appear on the same night, sometimes not. When he was there, he would ask what we thought of the film. Fearing that what we had seen was something he was financially interested in, we would find something flattering to say. Most often, they were not good films.

Once he asked if we would care to go to the opera at Lincoln Center. He had an extra pair of tickets. We went and saw *Othello*. It was an immense performance, in every way. After the opera, we stopped for a drink. Gene spoke of the difficulty of finding the right kind of material for television. So much of the stuff he came across was lacking in visual appeal. At one point in the evening, Hannah and Gene had excused themselves, and Peggy and I were alone at the table.

"Were there hordes of girls in love with him a million years ago?" she asked.

"I don't think he knew hordes of girls," I said. "There was one."

"Only one?"

"That I knew of."

Peggy looked at me with that esoteric smile and with eyes I had seen before. I remembered the way Ruth looked when she asked me why Gene was the way he was.

There was a Christmas dinner—pre-Christmas, actually—at the Strauss apartment. There were about twenty people, including Hannah and myself. No scratchy *Messiah* in the background. The woman I sat next to was sure she had seen me recently at a real estate convention at the Hilton. I assured her I wasn't there. She said I had a double running around in the city. I said it was my fate to have a double running around.

After dinner, I made my way over to the window and looked down at the park. I could see street lamps delineating the pathways and vehicular roads. I looked again toward the southwest corner, but this time there were no evocations. The details could have been easily summoned up, but I gathered that the authentic ghosts were staying out of sight that night.

Gene joined me at the window. I remarked how nice it must be to have this view at all hours, in all seasons. He agreed that it was nice, but he said that one got used to it. What one did not get used to were outrages like the closing of my play. If ever a play deserved a long run! But he didn't have to tell me about plays in New York, did he? No, he didn't. Was I working on something new? I laughed and said not at the moment. I said I was too pleased with my last play to rush into something new. Besides, I didn't have the ghost of an idea. I said that time and times hadn't helped in plucking the golden apples of the sun.

"I'm sure you'll be on to something new soon," he said.

"Where are you and Hannah living now?"

"Hastings. In Westchester. We have a nice view of the Hudson. Do you remember—?"

"We were up that way this past fall," he said. "We were visiting Vince Madden. He's the fellow who's doing all the heavy investing in cable TV. You don't know him by any chance, do you?"

"No, I don't know Vince Madden," I said. I waited a few seconds, counseled myself toward a wiser course, but said anyway, "That, incidentally, was Yeats."

"What was Yeats?"

"That quote. Golden apples of the sun: 'And pluck till time and times are done/The silver apples of the moon, the golden apples of the sun.' "

"That's very nice," Gene said.

I shouldn't have done that, but I didn't want to hear any more about agencies or cable TV. I didn't give a shit about Vince Madden, and I happened to think that Yeats was as good a poet as Baudelaire. There was a corner in that nighttime park below us that contained one of the most important moments of my life. It was astonishing to me that the companion of that moment should be so unaware of it. And yet he was. I was sure that if I said, "Do you remember, Gene? Do you remember a freezing day?" he would say, "Of course I remember," but it was clear to me now that his ceremonies of significance were hopelessly different from mine.

"Aren't you going to invite the Strausses to your home?" Hannah finally asked me.

"Do you want to invite them?" I asked.

"It just seems a little peculiar," she said. "They've had us over several times. It's getting embarrassing."

"Certainly we can have them over," I said.

"It's clear he wants your friendship," Hannah said, "but I don't think you particularly care."

"It's true," I said. "I don't."

"That's a change. Why?"

"Because we just don't have that much in common."

6

IT WAS TRUE. We didn't have much in common. But I had known that even before the day we said goodbye at the subway stairs. Why would I have been so eager for him to go if there wasn't that sure sense of strangeness? Why wouldn't he have written that promised letter, or some subsequent letter, if he didn't share my feeling? On the other hand, how could I be sure that we shared anything, even estrangement, when the evidences of his life were so alien to me?

We never did invite the Strausses to our house. When Hannah took the matter into her own hands, finding me wanting in what I had never been wanting in before, common courtesy, she learned that Gene and Peggy had gone to Europe. By the time they came back, both Hannah and I were very occupied. In that way, several years slipped by. The next contact was the last one. It was Peggy who telephoned to tell me that Gene was dying, had been dying for some months, was dying very rapidly now . . .

I recalled the park, the sandwich paper, the French bread and Gene holding two fingers to his throat and saying, "Cancer."

"I'm so sorry, Peggy," I said.

"If you get the chance."

"Is he in a hospital?"

"No, he's at home."

I didn't ask what it was. I didn't want to know.

* * *

I went the next day, almost in a blind compulsion, fearing that if I delayed I would never go, and that if I never went I would be giving myself another needless bundle of remorse to juggle the rest of my life.

I had been asked to come around midafternoon, and I was sure there was a medical reason for that. I spent several nervous, morbid hours in the city, buying some things, looking at the Christmas display in Radio City, thinking of Anna Thérèse Strauss and realizing that some of the remorse I had dreaded had its source in the filigree lady.

When it was time, I took a cab to the apartment house on upper Fifth Avenue.

Peggy let me in. "Thank you for coming," she said. She wore no cosmetics, her face had thinned, making her eyes larger than I remembered them. But her smile still carried its oblique mystery. Perhaps that was one of the reasons Gene had married her: she possessed the charismatic emblem.

"How is he?" I asked, routinely, stupidly.

"The same," she said—which I took to mean worse.

"Peggy, how long has he been ill?"

"He took sick about six months ago. Listen . . . you needn't stay very long. Just a few words."

I wasn't sure whether she had said that for Gene's sake or mine. "Of course," I said.

Even while talking to Peggy, I had been secretly testing the air, I wasn't sure for what, some faint clue to the fatality within, some faint odor attempting to cover that fatality; but I was aware of nothing but a hushed neutrality. I wondered about the son, Carl. Had there been others? Did Gene's son ever wear Gene's clothes? Too late now. I followed Peggy through the two rooms I was familiar with, through a door, into another room, a study, also with windows that faced the park, with books lining the walls. For an absurd moment, I thought of going over and inspecting the titles, the binding. A weakness of bookish people . . .

"Hello, Saul."

The words were whispered. I turned and saw Gene sitting in a reclining chair, facing the window. How odd that I hadn't seen him upon entering the room. My eye had been taken immediately by the windows and the books. He was wearing a paisley robe, and an ascot. This, then, was his outfit for dying. His feet were raised on one of those automatic rests, the kind that come up when the chair is tilted back. I went to him, hesitating for a moment, waiting to see what he would do. He held out his hand, and I took it. It was weightless, pressureless, a paper construction over some thin sticks.

This was not Gene. This was something so committed to death that it could have no other identity. The features of Gene were there, but in caricature, as death would draw them. His head was turned toward the window. He said something I couldn't catch. Peggy, who stood behind the reclining chair, interpreted. She said that he had said, "Excuse my appearance."

There was nothing to say. Peggy was used to that. So was Gene. What was there to say? All the uses of language hung limp, like empty sails in a dead calm. The past was useless, worse than useless: insulting. What was it? Leukemia? Hodgkins? What difference? Whatever it was, it was triumphant.

"Thank you for coming," Gene whispered.

I nodded. Quick, quick! Something to say! I remembered a time when I thought of the needful words as a tiny school of fish that I must net out of the vast ocean of the English language.

"You changed my life," I said, not sure how I meant the words, not sure how he would take them.

Gene sat unmoving, gazing at the window. I wondered if he could see anything. All I could make out from where I sat were the buildings on the other side of the park. Slowly Gene turned to me and seemed to fix on me in a meaningful way. His words were again whispered, but distinct enough: "You mustn't feel guilty."

Then Peggy made a movement, and I knew it was time to go. I got up and touched Gene on the back of the hand. He nodded.

"How long?" I asked Peggy.

"A month. A week. Tomorrow."

"I'm sorry," I said.

"Thank you for coming," she said.

* * *

326

In the street, I asked myself what it was that I must not feel guilty about. Something that had happened between us? Something that hadn't happened? About Anna? All of these things? I would never know. Or I knew already. Perhaps the fact that I had rejected him, as he must have known. Perhaps the fact that we couldn't speak despite the rejection.

Why couldn't we speak? Because that was the inescapable truth: we couldn't speak. Not seriously, not as friends, not as one-time friends, not as acquaintances, not even as two intelligent human beings. Only trivialities. Only the balloons of speech, as in cartoons. There were so many people to whom I could speak who were not really my friends. Colleagues, students, a loud-mouthed character who owned the local deli. But since his return, every attempt Gene and I had made at conversation had vapored into nothingness. Was it because neither of us was willing to draw on the past? I don't think so. It was his world, the world he had sought, the world he had won. It didn't interest me. I had no desire to explore it. I resented that this man, Eugene Strauss, the one-time friend for whose mystical sake I had alienated friends and family, the man who changed my life, should have shaped his special destiny in this way.

But there continued to live in my mind a time when each day was an opening chrysalis, a wing unfolding. The living—or the dying—man had nothing to do with that. Nothing. I could have seen the living Gene Strauss every day and those contacts would scarcely have brushed the husk that enclosed a young man who wore his father's Savile Row suits and who had stolen a book of Baudelaire's poetry from Macy's, handing it to me and saying, "If I were a thief, I would steal it for myself, not for you."

Three days later, I was in New Jersey. The theater department of a college there had asked some weeks ago if I would be consultant to their production of—of all things!—*War and Peace in the Bronx.* I said I would. Gladly. It's the nearest thing to growing young.

I arrived at the campus about eleven, and I decided that I would have a bite before making my way to the theater. I inquired from a passing student about food and was directed to the cafeteria in the Student Union building. There, with a tuna on whole wheat and a coke, I opened the paper, looking first where I had looked for days, and there I learned of the death of Eugene Strauss.

I sat looking at the sluggish river that flowed past the windows of the lunchroom. My immediate surroundings gave me no clue to my feelings. It was rather like a tremorless earthquake, opening a large crevice in time. I realized that despite differences, disappointments, betrayals, Gene had stood in my line of mortality. Like my grandfather, my father, Gene's death moved me a notch closer to my own end.

For a reason that I cannot fathom, my mind took a strange detour, a detour that led me to the library of the school. There I made my last attempt at ferreting out information I had been seeking—well, I guess ever since that year I met Gene Strauss.

I consulted with the librarian, who looked up various encyclopedias, all of which yielded no more information than I already had. The librarian passed the problem on to another librarian, and the second librarian said, "Let's try here."

"Here" was the *Jewish Encyclopedia,* a publication I didn't know existed. We looked up Herschel Grynszpan. There was an entry. It said that when France capitulated, Grynszpan escaped to the Free Zone. However, for reasons unknown, he later returned to the Occupied Zone, where he was arrested and handed over to the Germans, who made elaborate preparations for a show trial.

In the end, the whole affair was hushed up and Grynszpan disappeared without a trace.

"I found out what happened to Herschel Grynszpan today," I said to Hannah that evening.

"Oh? What?"

"He escaped to the Free Zone in France, and then he returned to the Occupied Zone. He was handed over to the Germans. You can imagine what happened to him."

"Why do you suppose he did that?"

"God knows. . . . Do you ever look at the obits?"

"You know I don't," she said.

"Yes, I know you don't."

Hannah looked at me for several appraising seconds, then she said, "Gene is dead."

I nodded.

"Are there going to be services?"

"Yes."

"Will you go?"

"I don't know—I guess so—yes."

Another heavy pause. Hannah asked, "Why did you tell me the other first?"

"Because it was easier to tell the other first."

"Do you link them in your mind?" she asked.

I hadn't thought of it before, but I did give it serious thought then. I said yes, knowing it was right without knowing why. I'm not sure why Hannah's question should have given me access to my own feelings, but it did. I linked them in my mind, Eugene Strauss and Herschel Grynszpan. I was the one who had assigned the roles each would play in my life. Each one was, in a sense, my own creation. Herschel had by this time receded too far into history . . . but I found that I could, at last, grieve for Gene.

Epstein, Seymour,
1917-

A special destiny
